Daisy's Chain

A Story Novel
by
P.S. Lowe

Best wishes

Paulette Lowe

Published by
TrimWriting
Glendale, Arizona

This is for God; thank You for the gift.

This is for my Muse; you know who you are; you know what you did. Redeem your card at any time.

This is for my family; you are all in here somewhere.

This is for my friends; it's the only
real present I have for you.

This is a complete work of fiction, but it is all true.

Chapters

Cold Potato Morning

It was a cold potato morning when Daisy awakened. There was no heat in the little room. That was all right. The October morning reminded her of her Washington childhood. Here in the eastern Arizona mountains, the air would be clear, and there would be no city-sounds. The sun would warm her old bones later in the day. Something else would happen, too. Something unexpected.

Daisy had lived for eight decades. Her body felt it had been a long time; her mind held a different view. The last decade seemed like a camera flash; however, there were no pictures to show for the camera's activity. She had almost no memories of her seventies. Holidays and birthdays were like every other day. Her mind went to the decade before that, split evenly between the time before Douglas, her husband, had died and the years after his death requiring change and accommodation. Her fifties, that was a good time. Paulie had been with her all of those years producing a full album of memories she leafed through often. This morning she didn't care to go beyond that. It was time to get up if she was going to start. This was not the day for the luxury of peaceful, self-contentment.

She did not hear anyone in the room next to hers. They were probably still asleep. She was hungry. When Paulie and his girl-friend had brought her here for a weekend birthday trip, they had all thought the rooms would have a kitchen of some sort. She had brought along food. Unfortunately, there was only a small refrigerator and drip coffee pot. Luckily, both were in her room. She could have some cold fried potatoes, make herself coffee, and then eat in bed. She liked to have breakfast in bed.

Daisy swung her legs to the floor and found her slippers. It was only five steps to the small counter where she quickly made the coffee. While it dripped, she took the potatoes from their refrigerated space, removing a portion to a paper plate. The coffee was slow in the making so Daisy returned to the bed to eat her potatoes. They were cold, but salty the way she liked them. She picked out the fried bread and ate it with her fingers.

The coffee was made when she heard a knock at the door. "Grand, are you decent?"

"Sure I am Paulie." Her grandson walked into the room. He had pulled on jeans and T-shirt, or slept in them. Daisy couldn't tell. "Happy Birthday, Grand. I smelled the coffee. I'll pour you the first cup and let you have all the sugar packets because I know you like it sweet."

"Well, pour me a cup and yourself one also. Throw me my robe, please, then you can sit on the bed with me and use the blanket. I am pleased to have your company. There are cold potatoes if you want them, too."

Paul made a face. "I don't think I can face cold food this morning. I really wish there had been a kitchen here." He poured two cups of coffee, sugared one, and then handed Daisy her robe.

Rather than struggle to put it on in bed, Daisy stood on the cold floor and rapidly wrapped herself. She had the covers over her feet when Paul handed her the cup.

"Come and sit with me. Cover up and we'll pretend like it's old times when you used to come into the bedroom on Sundays. We haven't done this since Douglas died. It's been a long time."

"It's been a long, long time; more than 15 years. Do you still miss him, Grand?"

"I never missed him. I miss having someone, but not him in particular. We had a life together, but your grandfather was a hard-to-please-man. When he was gone, I could breathe easy again. The agitation went out of my life then, and it hasn't come back."

Paulie looked at his grandmother without knowing what to say. He knew both of his mother's parents so well. They had raised him. He was much closer to them than to their daughter, his mother, Lisa.

Daisy knew from the long silence that she had made Paulie uncomfortable, although she hadn't meant to. As the cause, she knew it was up to her to break the chain into another line of thought.

"So, why have you brought me to Trinity Peaks to celebrate? Being eighty is not such a milestone. Being here makes me think that the celebration isn't for me alone. Am I right?" Daisy was fishing for information.

"No, you're not right. I brought you here because I knew you wanted to see and feel something different than you have every other day. My gift to you - a change of scenery," said Paulie, mockingly grandiose.

Daisy had to smile. She had wanted a change of scenery. Living in Phoenix, Arizona, lacked visual variety and noticeable seasonal change. Daisy had wanted to return to her childhood home in Washington. She wanted to see the earth and sky of her youth again. Funny how as she got older, what she desired most were the things she enjoyed as a child, like the fried potatoes her mother used to make. If it was possible, what she really wanted was to see her mother again.

Daisy was now twice the age of her mother when she died. How Daisy had missed her for the first years! Then she had got on and married, had her own children and missed her mother less. There must have been years that she never remembered her at all. Lately, the feeling of loss was renewed. It was a longing.

Paulie was watching his grandmother. She seemed far away. He thought he was being kind to bring her back with a question. "What did Mom give you for your 80th anniversary of life on the planet?"

Her attention snapped to the present. Daisy immediately replied, "A usual amount of the finest that her money can buy including a trip to the day spa, new clothes, and she has promised to send someone to the house to 'do over' the bedroom! So when you see me next, I will be completely 'done over!'"

They laughed together. Daisy's only daughter and Paulie's mother made the same impression on each. They respected her success and money because she had earned both; neither wanted to live her life.

"Mom's only doing what she knows is best for you. She does the same for me. Last birthday she bought me an entire new wardrobe and then had the bedroom remodeled to accommodate a bigger closet." Paulie was still laughing. "She's still trying to make us respectable. It hasn't worked yet, has it?"

"She means so well. You just remember, if we weren't her relatives, she would probably have nothing to do with us. That would be a real pity. She would have to deal with ungrateful strangers instead of a grateful son and mother."

"She's a gratitude junkie," said Paulie.

"So what? Aren't we the better off for knowing her? I am," said Daisy.

"You would be all right without her, and so would I."

"Oh, I don't mean the material things, Paulie, I mean if she hadn't been so busy having her life, her career and social whirl, and her husbands, well, I wouldn't have had so much of you. You are the very best present that Lisa ever gave me."

Paulie was about to make a reply when his girlfriend, Erin, walked into Daisy's bedroom. "I smelled coffee and I wanted to join the party."

Daisy nodded to her grandson, pointing to the coffeemaker. "Paulie will get you some. Come up on the bed and share the blanket. It's too cold to stand there."

Erin sleepily complied. Daisy looked at her more closely. Erin was older than she had thought, possibly in her mid-thirties. She had a pleasing smile and good brown hair. Even without makeup, she had a pretty face. There was fullness, almost ripeness in her body as well. She was different from the rest of the women Paulie had brought home over the past two decades.

As Paulie brought the coffee and climbed on the bed with the two women, Erin sought to join the conversation. "This is the life of luxury: Saturday morning in bed with friends and nothing to do until dinnertime."

"You like this, do you? How come at home you're always up early doing work?" asked Paulie.

"Because I think I have to have something to show for my time away from the store. I still think that I have to do most of everything. I don't know, maybe it's just habit," replied Erin.

"What is it that you do at the store?" asked Daisy.

Erin laughed. "I call it the store, but it's really a wholesale business, not retail. I own NewMexTexCo. We provide screenprinting and embroidery services to big companies and institutions. You know, when you see baseball caps with company logos or polo shirts advertising a product, that's what my company does."

"What about the company name? It doesn't sound like the kind of shop that it is," said Daisy.

"I just made it up. It stands for New Mexico, Texas, and Colorado. I originally did business in those three states. Now, thanks to the Internet, I do work all over the United States, but I keep the name the same because I like it, and people remember it."

"And how did you get into the business? What was your interest?" Daisy was interested in a woman who owned her own business. She wanted to know if her grandson's girlfriend was really a young version of his mother.

"I liked bowling shirts. My family bowled in leagues. From the time I could push a ball down the alley, I bowled because the whole family bowled. My granddad had many of those fancy shirts that they wore in the fifties with his name in front and his sponsor's name and logo in back. When he died, I took them all to wear through college. I wanted to learn to make them, but nobody did that kind of work any more. So I got into company marketing and built a business around it. In the past five years, the business has really grown because of 'casual day' at the office. Everyone wants a company shirt to wear."

"And you work like a dog to meet your customers' quirky needs so that I never see you unless you are asleep!" said Paulie, but Daisy could see he was just teasing Erin.

"Yes, I do work hard, and my business is not very lucrative. But we have a lot of fun at work, too. My employees are the best and they work every bit as hard as I do." Erin was taking Paulie's words as criticism.

Daisy liked this new girlfriend. She had a lot of spunk. What was important to her, she fiercely defended. "How nice for you that you have nice workers. I never had much of a career and never managed anyone. I always thought that I could, I just never made any effort to do it. Lisa is the businessperson in the family. No one else seemed to want to go that direction."

"What about Uncle Jack? He always had a business," asked Paulie.

"Jack? Jack just didn't want to farm and would have done anything to get away from it. He never stuck with anything long enough to make money. He was a creative boy and man. Started I don't know how many restaurants and bars, but didn't want to run them. Always sold them and moved on to the next idea. Lots of his places became a success after he left them. He didn't seem to care. Now, he is retired in Mexico doing a little bit of nothing along with his fishing. Did I tell you that he is coming for Christmas? He's always such fun for Christmas Eve." Turning to Erin she said, "You've probably never met my son, but you're welcome to come for Christmas Eve at my condo. Even if it's only me and Jack, it will be a party."

Erin looked at Paulie as if seeking assurance that she would be welcome. Paulie provided no sign of understanding. Erin answered the invitation with "If I'm still around at Christmas, and I'm still invited, then I'll come."

Cold Potato Morning

Daisy felt that between Erin and Paulie there was some sort of tension, some sort of barrier that might have recently gone up obscuring their thoughts about the future. Whatever it was, Daisy hoped that they could overcome it. Today, however, was her birthday! She wasn't going to start the day with other people's sorrows.

"Well, you come if you can. Now, what are we going to do today? I am only going to be eighty once and I want to make some memories with the two of you. We are here and there's a whole world for us to own for the next twenty-four hours. What have you planned?"

"Horseback riding followed by white river rafting. Then we're going to go to the dump and shoot rats!" said Paulie seriously.

Daisy let out a whoop! "When was the last time you invited me to the dump? Oh, you are funny. Let's go there first then, and if we kill any big ones, I'll cook them for dinner."

Erin stared at her bed partners as they shook the bed with their laughter. Finally, Daisy said, "It's an old joke. When Paulie was a teenager, Lisa tried hard to get him to participate in the social life she planned for him. Paulie just wasn't interested. When Lisa used to ask him what he was doing with his time, he used to tell her that we went down to the dump to shoot rats. It would so exasperate her. It was only a joke. Only a joke that meant nothing."

"What did you do with your free time when you were in high school?" asked Erin.

"Much the same as now. I read, I fixed things, and I used to spend a lot of time with Granddad's electric trains. Now I read, I fix things, and I create anti-virus programs for the Internet."

"Well, I understood the trains, but not the Internet," said Daisy. "I'm old and entitled to ignore what I don't understand. Time's a-wasting, so my dear grandson, you are going to clear off the dishes from this bed and let a poor old woman out to do her morning rituals. Go on, both of you. I'll be out of the bathroom in a jiffy and you two can have it."

Paulie whisked away the remains of coffee and potatoes. He and Erin removed themselves to the other room while Daisy showered, dressed, and made up the bed. While they moved slowly into their day, Daisy went outside to see the mountain view.

There was a definite chill in the air for the sun was still low in the sky. She looked out over the canyon and up toward the jagged mountains ahead called Trinity Peaks. The view and the stillness filled her. What a nice thing for Paulie to do, bringing her here away from the city. Here she was younger than everything that surrounded her. In that sense, she felt ageless.

Daisy's mind wandered back in time to the farm. She was standing on the porch of the house and could hear her mother inside fixing breakfast. Her father was out in the fields. Her little brother was upstairs sleeping. Soon they would be together for a breakfast of eggs, potatoes, bread and jam. Daisy could see the table now, but it was set just for three. That's right, her brother, Paul, had died before he had a chance to grow up. The picture in her mind stopped at that thought.

"Grand, Grand, can you help me?" It was young Paulie calling from the door.

"Yes, I was just enjoying the view. What is it that you need?"

"It's Erin. She's not feeling well and wants to know if you have some soda crackers. She thinks that the coffee made her sick," said Paulie.

At that moment, Daisy knew what she should have known before. Erin wasn't sick. Erin was pregnant. "Here is a birthday surprise," Daisy thought.

Daisy went in to find Erin lying on the made up couch. "I know what you need," said Daisy, "you need to be back in the big bed for a little while, and you need something salty. Crackers I don't have. I'll pick the bread out of the potatoes, and you have a couple of bites. That's what I did the first time I was pregnant. It'll cheer you up too because I'll keep you company for a bit."

Erin's eyes were wide but she was mute as she dragged herself into the real bedroom. Once in bed, Daisy flipped the spread over her and went for the potatoes. She continued to talk to Erin about the past.

"It's a wondrous feeling being pregnant the first time. Scary too. It's a real shame you have the morning sickness, but that will pass. Some women are never sick, but I wasn't lucky like that. Guess you aren't either."

Daisy sat down on the bed and handed Erin the bread pieces. "Go ahead; it'll make you feel better." Erin tried one piece.

11

"This is salty, but it tastes good. I've been eating crackers in the morning, but this bread is better." Erin ate the remaining pieces.

"How did you know about me being pregnant?" asked Erin. "Did Paul tell you? He does know about the babies but he just won't talk to me about them," said Erin.

"Babies? There's more than one?" asked Daisy.

Erin nodded in reply.

"My heavenly days! Paulie didn't tell me anything. I just figured it out. Should have seen it earlier, but I pay less attention to things now. What I need to know seems to come to me when I need to know it. Well, this is reason to want to live to be eighty-one. I had been thinking that maybe I didn't care to have another year. Now I do. This is a wonderful present. I am happy for you. When are they coming?"

"Sometime in early April. I don't know how I feel about all of this. It's unexpected and I just had never thought about having a baby. I never thought I would be an unwed mother." Erin wasn't looking at Daisy.

"Oh. Are you going to be?"

"Yes, I think I am going to be. I just can't figure things out right now. I can't think clearly and that's not like me. I don't know how to run my business and keep Paul and be a mother, and...." Erin broke down.

Daisy was silent. Is it always the same? Does every pregnant woman have to suffer the hell of doubt and fear? Did her own mother? Well, Daisy did; Lisa did; and apparently, fashionable or not, Erin was going through the same blues. Like the rest of them, she was going through it without the support of a husband.

Erin did not need to hear Daisy's story. The girl would fall asleep if they stopped talking and that would be best. Erin's eyes were already closed. Daisy picked up the paper plate off the bed and walked out to find her grandson.

Paul was out on the porch. He made room for his grandmother on the double swing. The sun was fully up and warm against their faces.

After a moment, Paul was the first to speak. "So you know. I didn't want it to spoil your birthday, Grand, but I would have told you soon."

"Yes, I know. Your mother will not be pleased to be a grandmother. She thought she had escaped that. She thinks that at nearly forty, you are a confirmed bachelor. She liked you that way. It's clean. Not messy like having a family. I take it that she doesn't know yet."

"She doesn't and she may never know. Erin is talking about leaving. She tells me that I don't need to have anything to do with the babies. She's the one who is pregnant and she'll handle it herself."

"Do you believe her? Is that what she wants? Is that what you want?" asked Daisy.

"I don't know what to believe. I just don't know what to say to Erin. She is so different now than she was a few months ago. I feel that I cannot do anything right. Everything is slipping away from me and I'm just a spectator."

Daisy looked at him critically. "Bother! That's the 'only child' in you. Maybe it is my fault for raising you the way I did, but you have been around women all your life and you sure as heck know how we are. You have never been a man's man. If you don't know about women now, Paulie, then you never will. Here's your test. What are you going to do to help Erin?"

"I told you, she doesn't want me or my help," said Paul curtly.

"I don't believe her, and I don't believe that you believe her either. You're just enjoying your own misery. You did that as a kid, too, and don't I remember it! You want to be sure that everyone knows your discomfort. Well, noted. Now, what are you going to do to help Erin?" Daisy was giving her grandson no quarter.

"I don't know what to do," said Paul more in defiance than in sorrow.

"Well, are you going to marry her?"

"I've asked her, but she hasn't said yes."

"Before or after you found out she was pregnant?"

Cold Potato Morning

"After."

"Maybe that wasn't on her priority list at the time. Maybe she didn't think you were serious. Maybe she thinks that our family has a poor history in marriage. Maybe you need to ask her again. Even if she says no, what are you going to do to help her with your children? There's that to think about. Just what kind of father are you intending to be? You have to think about it before they're born or you won't get your heart into it. If you want to be a real father, put your heart in it now. Your own father didn't. Your granddad did with you, but not with Lisa or Jack."

"I think you're interfering in my life, Grand. I think it's none of your business."

"Yes, I am interfering. But it is my business because you are my family and I love you dearly. I have said my piece Paulie and I won't be raising the subject again. You know how I feel, and that's enough said. You're the one to do the doing. You've got to keep your own heart happy. I won't say anything more."

They sat without another word between them for a little while. Then Paulie got up to go inside. He wasn't gone long. "She's asleep and I don't want to wake her."

"She'll be feeling better when she wakes up. She has spoken some of her own sorrows out loud. Since she let them out of her heart, they won't hurt as much today."

"I do love her Grand. I want you to know that."

"I know that, Paulie. I know that. If you didn't love her, there wouldn't be sorrow in your heart either. Loving someone and knowing the right thing to do don't always go hand in hand."

Daisy looked down at her hands. She was lucky that she didn't have the arthritis as her remaining friends did. She reached with her right hand and took the wedding ring off her left hand. She held it up and motioned for her grandson to take it.

"I've always meant for you to have this as a memento. It's not worth a whole lot. But maybe when the time comes, you'll have a reason to share it with someone else."

"You've never had that ring off! I can't take it from you now."

"Well you can because I want you to have it. I have been a widow for a long time. I thought from time to time that I should stop wearing it, but the time was never right until today. It is my birthday and this is my gift to myself. Whatever that ring symbolized in my life is past. I came up the hill last night as one person, and I'll be going back down as a different person because I'm going to be a great grandmother!"

Just then, Erin walked out onto the porch. There was a little color in her face, a faint shine in her just-brushed brown hair and some light in her blue eyes. "I've finished off the rest of the potatoes but I'm still hungry. How about if we go down to the restaurant to eat? Is anyone else hungry?"

"I'm famished myself," said Daisy. "I intend to celebrate with pancakes and ice cream. Maybe two ice creams."

As she was speaking, she saw her grandson put his arm around the mother-to-be. Then he handed her Daisy's ring. Erin slipped it on her left hand. No one said a word. It was a picture moment when words were not necessary.

But, Daisy thought, it was corny, too. She began to laugh alone.

"What's so funny?" Paulie asked.

"Everything and nothing. When you're an octogenarian, you don't have to explain anything to anyone. Come on, let's go eat. Let's see the day so we will have a memory for the rest of the winter."

"I have to get my purse," said Erin.

"I'll get the car keys," said Paulie.

"I'll wait," said Daisy.

The couple went inside leaving Daisy a minute to rest her eyes against the past. She saw her mother and her little brother in her mind. They were so young. They never got to be old, to see the things that Daisy had seen. They hadn't seen her future any more than she could that of Paulie and Erin. Maybe that's how it was meant to be. That's what she had tried to tell her grandson. There are lots of future sorrows you can imagine, but you shouldn't. They'll come anyway. Make your own heart happy.

When Erin and Paulie came out on the porch Daisy was gazing at the Trinity Peaks. She was ready to go with them. So far, it had been a memorable birthday. She had the present she had wanted most: she had seen her mother. She had a bonus too. She had glimpsed a little of the future that would go on when she didn't. It was a fine cold potato morning.

Lisa's Christmas

Lisa Ellis had a secret. She loved Christmas. Once the calendar turned to November 1st, holiday thoughts consumed her. She loved to see the lights go up early in stores and on the outside of houses. She loved Christmas clothes and Christmas parties; Christmas presents and Christmas cards. She was high on Christmas. Always had been, always would be.

That Lisa loved Christmas was unknown to her son, her mother and her closest friends. Lisa's feelings were such a secret, in fact, no one knew how she felt. No one except her brother, Jack. Jack had so many of his own secrets, keeping another one for his sister was no burden at all.

Every year for as long as anyone could remember, Lisa planned the holiday for herself and everyone else. Even as a kid, by early autumn she was designing decorations and cards and begging for a Christmas party. As she got older and became wealthy, no aspect of the season escaped her. She arranged everything to the minute. Although it didn't seem possible, each year she surpassed the previous year in lavish parties and gifts. Each activity energized her for the next. With all the work she did, no one could imagine that Lisa enjoyed the holidays, but she actually did.

This October, Lisa felt a twinge of anticipation for the coming holidays. Mentally, she thought through the weeks ahead. Before Halloween, something happened to her that killed all thought of a wonderful season. It happened just after her mother's eightieth birthday. Her son, Paul, came to her office to take her to lunch. Since this was not a usual affair, Lisa felt some worry but dashed off with him between appointments. Before the meal even started, Paul dropped a heavy load of news. His girlfriend, Erin, was pregnant with twins. They currently had no plans to get married.

Lisa could not believe, even now in mid-November, the facts of the situation. She had no idea what to say to her son. She could scarcely remember what she said to him that day at lunch. They hadn't talked since. What was there to say?

Today at the office, Lisa thought she should call Paul. She should call his girlfriend and invite her to lunch. Without a well-thought out plan of conversation, Lisa felt lost. She had never been able to talk to Paul. They weren't all that close. Her parents had raised him when Lisa was young and alone. Later, when she married the first time, her husband saw no reason to change the arrangement. Lisa wondered what Daisy thought about the family pregnancy. Well, she wasn't about to call her mother either.

There was nothing at the office that called for her attention. It was Veterans' Day holiday and she could go shopping. She would go shopping to see if there was something she could do to prepare for Christmas. It always used to work.

Once at the mall, Lisa was uninspired. She could buy anything she wanted and wanted nothing. She thought briefly about decorating her home in a new blue and silver theme. However, little but the usual red and green and gold was being offered for sale.

Occasionally, there were 'fashion tableaus' in mauve and pink, accented with pearls, but they seemed lifeless and un-festive.

She had avoided the infant department of every store. Finally, to give her own mind a rest before leaving, she stopped by the big department in Russo's. There were lovely things in every color and children's theme. Lisa thought she could buy cribs and bedding and have the lot sent to Erin and Paul. She could give these two new babies the things her own son never had. The reality was that Lisa didn't know the mother of her grandchildren well enough to know her taste. Lisa would never give a gift that was anything less than the receiver's desire.

In the middle of the infant department at Russo's, Lisa felt tears in her eyes and her nose began to run. "This is terrible," she thought. "What if someone sees me and thinks I'm a silly, sentimental fool?" The thought of it cleared her eyes. When she looked ahead of her, she saw something she would like to buy. Hanging straight ahead were simple terrycloth one-piece sleepers in palest pastels. Neatly folded beneath were delicate blankets in the same colors. She picked out one pink and one blue with matching blankets; paid for them and went home, crying all the way to her doorstep.

At home, the message light on her phone was blinking. She listened to two business calls and then heard her brother Jack's voice. "Hey little Sis," the digitized voice said, "I'm thinking of coming for Christmas, and want to know if you'll be in Phoenix, too. I have a phone now and you can call me back if you are willing to call international. Love to you!"

Lisa played the message three times just to hear her brother's voice and write down his phone number. How Jack could always cheer her up was a wonder. He alone could make her laugh at herself. In the darkest days of her life, Jack had been her lifeline. Now, today, when she was feeling old and alone, her big brother had called her "little Sis." He made her feel young again.

She called him back immediately. "Jack," she said when he answered the phone. "I'm so glad you have a phone. I have been wondering how to reach you. How is Mexico? How's the fishing?"

"Not as good as earlier this year, but better than a day at work. How is the family millionaire? Still knocking the socks off of the real estate world?"

"Better than ever, Jack. Commercial real estate in downtown has gone up $12 a square foot and I make money on both sides."

"Good for you! How's your love life? Got another husband yet?"

"Don't tease me about that. I am fifty-six years old and not likely to remarry. Two husbands was one too many. To get rid of Harry cost me two years of commissions. I'm not changing my name for any man again. I think I will just live with the next one. Be like Paul and Erin."

"Are they still together?" asked Jack. "Mom wondered if Erin was 'the one' for Paulie. What do you think?"

"Then you don't know, do you? I thought I was the last to know, as always. Erin is pregnant with Paul's twins. They are due in April."

There was silence on the other end. Jack didn't know.

"Well, I guess that's the way this family is. I am surprised. Thought Paul was never going to be a father, end up like me. So grandma-in-waiting, how are you taking this?"

"What's there to take? I've met Erin exactly once. They aren't married and haven't made any plans to be married. So I may be the same kind of grandmother as I was a mother – absent. Oh Jack, I feel just plain depressed. I don't know what to do and feel like doing nothing. If you're coming, maybe I will make some Christmas plans."

"How about if I come, and you make no plans? For once in your life, Lisa, let Christmas do itself. I will be staying with Daisy, so you won't have to feel that you have responsibility for me. Don't get me wrong, I love the attention, but maybe this year, it's time to do something different. Maybe it's time for you to quit worrying that the holidays are perfect for everyone, and find a new way." Even more than the meaning behind the words, just the sound of Jack's voice reassured Lisa.

"Jack, what will people think? I always have the parties, buy the presents, and do Christmas dinner. What about Mom? She's eighty now. How many more will she have?"

"She'll always be around, Lisa, even when she is gone. I think that you should quit worrying about what others think and do what you would like. Go away if you want; take a cruise, but stop thinking that you have to hold up Christmas for the western world. Stores won't close if you don't buy anything. Celebrate by entertaining yourself instead of everyone else."

"I won't go away if you're coming, Jack. When do you think you can get here?" asked Lisa.

"I'll be there the Saturday before. That will give me time to help Mom do whatever she wants to do. We'll plan a Christmas Eve together. I would appreciate it if you will at least ask Erin and Paulie to celebrate with us. We'll just be family, then. Just like it was for a few times in the past."

"Thank you, Jack. I'll call Mom and Paul tomorrow. I'm so glad you're coming. It will make all the difference. Now, what do you want for Christmas? What's a good gift for a fisherman?"

"Lisa," said Jack. "There you go again. I neither want nor need anything but your happiness. Don't buy anything. Be happy for yourself. That will be quite enough for your brother who loves you very much."

"OK. I just don't know how to celebrate without presents. I want you to know I love you, too."

"I know that, my little sister. Now, you have a nice Thanksgiving and I'll see you the Saturday before Christmas Day. Call me if you are tempted to arrange a party. I'll talk you out of it."

"I will. Love you and good night." Lisa hung up the phone.

The next morning Lisa called Daisy to tell her of Jack's plans. "Oh, wonderful!" said Daisy. "I surely missed him last year. What about Paulie and Erin? I had asked them to come when we were together for my birthday. Should I invite them again, or will it just be the three of us for Christmas Eve?"

"I'm going to call them today. It's time to do something to incorporate Erin into this family. I just don't know what to do or to say. But if I call today, I will think of something."

"Lisa, are you sure that you want to do this? Erin may not want to be a part of a family gathering. She may have plans with her own family. I have been remembering how you were before Paul was born. It was a touchy time for everyone."

"But this isn't 1960 and Erin isn't eighteen. She's nearly twice that. Well, almost. I'm inviting her, not commanding her. The same with Paulie. This is just family," said Lisa.

"I'll look forward to it then. How are you doing your house this year and when are your parties? When Jack gets here he can do a little something around the house, so don't feel you have to put me on your schedule," said Daisy.

"I'm not decorating this year. I'm not having a party. I'm not going to any parties. I'm not buying a new dress. I'm just going to look around, see what I've missed, and do those things. I'll be happy to help you when you want help, Mother, but this year, I'm going to wait until someone asks me for help without rushing in first."

"Well, Lisa, what brought this on? This isn't you. Are things all right with you?"

"Yes and no. I just don't have any Christmas spirit for myself, so I don't have any to give away. I'll talk to you later, Mom. I have to call Paul. I will see you soon. I want to have lunch with you this week."

Lisa wanted to call Erin right away but didn't have her work number. "I guess I'll call Paul first," she thought. "If I don't, I'll let the day go by."

She dialed her son who worked at home. It was Erin who answered the phone. "Hello. I'm glad I got you. I was going to call you at the office," said Lisa.

"Who is this?" asked Erin.

"I'm sorry. I'm Lisa Ellis, Paul's mother."

The next five seconds of silence were like an hour. "Would you like to speak to him?" asked Erin.

"Yes, when I've talked to you a bit," Lisa said with forced brightness. "I just got off the phone with my mother. My brother, Jack, is coming for Christmas. We would like to have a family party on Christmas Eve and would like you to come."

"Who else will be there?"

"That's all the family there is. We'll be four unless you come. You can think about it if you want. But we would like you to come."

"Daisy invited me as well, about a month ago, but I wasn't sure if I was still invited." Erin sounded a little defensive.

"Well, you're invited, of course. Think about it, and then come if you can, if you don't have other plans." For some reason, Lisa's eyes were stinging even though her voice betrayed nothing.

"Thank you," said Erin formally. "Here's Paul."

"Hello, holiday Mother! To what extravaganza are you inviting me? I'll need to rent a tux, no doubt."

"You are invited nowhere but to your Grand's on Christmas Eve. I've just asked Erin, but these are separate invitations. I would like you to come together, but you can do as you wish. Jack will be there."

"I see," said Paul. "Guess you're trying to be modern since we aren't married."

"Paul, let it alone this morning. I'm not trying to be anything," said Lisa wearily. "I just found myself thinking that it would be nice to have a family holiday. I'm not up to anything else. Like it or not, Erin will be part of this family because of the babies. She should have some knowledge of it whether she wants to become a member or not. Or whether you want her to be a member or not."

For the second time in the phone call, there was a long silence broken at last by Paul. "I'm there, Mom. I wouldn't miss it. Thanks for the invitation. I really mean it. I know that this isn't what you wanted for me or for yourself, Mom. I know you're disappointed."

"I'm not sure what I am, Paul. 'Disappointed' is not a word I would choose. I'm worried about you. I'm worried about Erin and I don't even know her. I'm worried about the babies, too. So instead of spreading my worry around, I'm just going to wait and see what happens. I don't want anyone to be unhappy and for the life of me, I can't seem to control that. I need to go to work, now, so I'll go. I hope to see you before Christmas Eve. I do love you, Son."

"I love you too Mom. You'll see me. Don't worry; I'm fine, Erin's fine, and the babies are fine. Good-bye."

Lisa hung up the phone and got to work. In the days and weeks leading up to her brother's visit, she didn't shop, she didn't decorate, and she didn't send cards. She did go to free concerts, she walked in the evening, and she listened to long forgotten music. She read old stories. She changed her routine and went to breakfast every morning before work, giving up her elaborate lunches and dinners. She worked hard to keep her worries away.

Exactly one week before Christmas, on Thursday, Lisa was sitting at breakfast when a man approached her table. He was dressed casually, but nicely. He was at least sixty years old, balding, glowing with a golfer's tan. He had a relaxed manner. Lisa thought she had seen him somewhere before.

"Good morning. I've seen you eating alone every day for breakfast and thought today might be a day when you would like some company. I eat here most days, alone also. May I join you?" the stranger asked.

Lisa was startled and hesitated in reply. "My name is Bill Hadigan," the stranger continued. "I believe that you visit someone in the complex where I live. I've seen you there. I feel like I could almost know you."

Lisa regained her composure enough to ask the man to sit down, figuring that there was no harm in it. "Do you live in Sutton Place? That's where my mother lives."

"Yes I do. Your mother must be Daisy. I have joined her for many a walk. She is an interesting woman. I like her."

"You know my mother?"

"Yes. Does that make me someone you can safely have breakfast with?" asked Bill.

Lisa laughed, but it was a nervous laugh. Nevertheless, they ate together and when she said she had to get to work, Bill asked if he could take her to the movies on Friday night.

"I'm sorry," said Lisa. "I have a prior engagement."

"Can I talk you out of it?" Bill asked.

"Hardly. I'm visiting my mother. My brother Jack is coming on Saturday, and I told her that I would help her with Christmas baking. I really want to do this."

"Then can I invite myself over? I am great on clean up and I can taste test as well." Bill was clearly intent on having another meeting with Lisa.

"Well, why don't you ask her? If you're there and I am there, then we will see each other. How's that?"

"Good enough. I'll see you at your mother's," said Bill.

Friday was a long day for Lisa. She had two major deals to close and was looking forward to going home. First, however, she had to see Daisy. Maybe she could beg off baking. Daisy would understand; she always did.

Arriving at Daisy's condo at 6:00 p.m. it was already dark outside. Several porches in the complex were decorated in blinking lights. For the first time, Lisa felt festive and the stress of the day diminished. When she walked in the front door, the smell of yeast was pungent. She heard voices. Walking into the kitchen, she saw her mother, her brother and Bill Hadigan deeply involved in dough.

"Jack," Lisa cried. "You're early! When did you come?"

"Two days ago. I just thought I would surprise you a little."

"I am surprised and glad, too. Mom, why didn't you tell me that Jack was here?"

"Because I wanted him to myself for a while. Once you two are together, you're as thick as thieves," said Daisy.

Only then did Lisa turn her attention to Bill. "I see that you have met my family. You work fast."

"It wasn't hard to wrangle an invitation from your mother. I just had to promise her to get the Christmas decorations from storage."

"Yes, Lisa, why didn't you tell me that you knew Bill? He's a real help in the kitchen. I never liked to clean up, and he has been so kind to help me all afternoon. Jack has been no help at all, just entertainment, but that's been wonderful too."

For the next couple of hours, the four of them baked cookies and fruit bread, enjoying conversation as if they were old friends. Before leaving, the four of them agreed to put up the tree on Saturday afternoon.

Saturday afternoon was the same as Friday night. Festive and high-spirited, the memories, music and activity flowed naturally. Lisa found that she liked having Bill around. She told him about Paul and Erin. Bill was a good listener.

Impulsively, when Bill and Lisa were returning the empty ornament boxes to storage, she invited him to their Christmas Eve gathering.

"Well, I'm sorry, no, I can't come. I will be away starting Monday and don't know when I'll be back. I have to see to some family things." Bill offered no more explanation than that.

Lisa was disappointed but tried not to show it. In as off-hand way as she could, she said, "Have a happy holiday then, wherever you spend it." The warmth of the evening dissipated for her.

"Same to you and to your family," said Bill. "I'm off home."

The next days were busy for everyone. Lisa had year-end deals to close that couldn't wait. With Christmas on a Thursday, she really only had two days to work. Then it would be Christmas Eve. The family had agreed to meet at seven at Daisy's. It was the four of them for sure; no one knew if Erin would come. She was working on tracking down late deliveries so that her employees could go home.

The only presents that Lisa was bringing tonight were the blankets and sleepers she had brought for the not-yet-born twins. She would take the others shopping after the holidays, if that was what they wanted. She was the last to arrive. Her mother's table was set for dinner for five. The family shared a bottle of wine while Jack told his fishing stories. By eight, they were hungry and still no Erin. They sat down to dinner anyway. Erin came before desert looking hugely pregnant and very tired. Paul settled her on the couch and brought her a plate of food.

"I really wanted to be here. At first, I thought I didn't, but then I did and I couldn't. I am sorry to be late," said Erin.

"You're here, and we're glad to have you," said Daisy. "But you haven't met my son Jack."

Jack was already coming to the sofa to sit next to Erin. "How do you do? I'm the wayward uncle to Paulie here. You're here in time for presents, which is what I've been counting on. As soon as you want, you can start unwrapping. Seems as if most of what's under the tree has your name on it."

Erin ate and everyone else just talked. The few presents from Daisy, Paul and Jack to each other were unwrapped. No one said a word about Lisa's missing gifts. Finally, Erin began to unwrap her gifts. All were lovely things for the babies. Lisa's gift was last of all. When Erin saw the very soft and plain pink and blue blankets, she looked at Lisa and began to cry.

She struggled to her feet and excused herself to the bathroom. Paul followed her. Erin was weeping. "What's wrong? What did my family do? Whatever it was, they meant well. They really would like to please you."

"Please me? I can't stand it. Your family doesn't even see me. They see your children. That's what they want. Old people without a life of their own who want to snatch my babies. They didn't give me a present. Everything was for the twins. Not a thing for me! I can't stand it, Paul, I really can't. Ever since I got pregnant, it's been babies, babies, babies, even with you! Who am I in all of this?"

"I'd like you to be my wife," said Paul. "I know you have your doubts about the kind of husband I would be, but I would be fair with you. I can stay home with the kids too. I love you, Erin. It's just that I didn't do anything about it before the babies. Nothing can change that, but I would if I could. I'm just slow in doing things. Don't think so much about my family either. They don't have much experience in knowing what to do. Neither do I, but I am learning with you."

Erin stopped crying. She looked at Paul and saw the man she had loved for a long time. He was a good man. He cared about her enough to let her alone these past months. He demanded nothing, but was always there for her. He understood her as no one else did. She trusted him even if she was suspicious of his mother.

"Oh, I'm a mess now and your family is probably wondering if I am going to storm out. Paul, let's get married. Just the two of us, let's do it soon. I need you, I love you, and I want you. I'm sorry I have been so hard about this, but I had to know my own heart first. I know it now."

It was an awkward embrace in the harsh bathroom light, but they managed to find the heart of each other on Christmas Eve. They returned to a subdued living room where brother, sister, and mother anxiously searched the faces of the couple.

Jack broke the silence. "We must be ready for a little brandy to toast the holiday. Mother always has the best of something. Who's having a little with me?"

"We all are. It's a celebration. Erin and I are going to get married before you leave, Uncle Jack." Paul looked at Erin when he said this. Erin nodded.

"It will be quite a holiday then. One to remember for me. I'm off for the brandy and you can help me, Paulie."

Three generations of women sat somewhat awkwardly together when the men left the room. "I didn't mean to create such a scene," said Erin. "Thank you both for the lovely gifts for the twins."

"I didn't have an idea of what you would want for yourself," said Lisa. "Perhaps one day you would go out with me and you can pick out something to please yourself. I'd like that."

"I'm not much of a shopper, but if I don't get some new clothes, I won't be able to go to work soon," said Erin.

"I can help you with that, just name a day and we'll go. I want to be of some help to you, not just to the twins, you know. I've been where you are, and I know it's hard. I hope you don't feel that any of us is pressuring you to do what you don't want to do."

"Well, maybe just a little bit," said Erin.

"Then you should know this. I was eighteen when Paul was born. I never married his father, partly because he was not around, but partly because I didn't want to. My mother and dad raised him. I am grateful for that, but there was a loss for me. I want for you to have what you want and need to be happy and for your children to be happy. You remember that. If I interfere with your life, you remind me of that too. I don't want you to think that I'm substituting your children for the loss to me of Paul's childhood."

Daisy looked at her daughter. Was that what Lisa felt, that she had lost her son? It wasn't true. She had missed some events, that's all. Lisa was still Paul's mother and always would be. Now she would be a grandmother and that was a wonderful thing. Lisa had so much love to give, and she had the rest of her life to give it. Erin and Paul would help her. For the first time in a long time, Daisy felt that her daughter had finally broken into the circle of love that had been waiting for her.

Jack and Paul returned with five snifters on a silver tray. They passed around the time-mellowed brandy and toasted Christmas, the twins, the upcoming marriage, and each other generally. It was a fine evening.

Lisa helped her mother and her brother clean up after Erin and Paul had left. Then she left them promising to see them tomorrow. She didn't want the night to end, but it had to.

Arriving home, she changed to her nightgown and got into bed with an unfinished book. It was just after midnight when the phone rang. A voice on the other end said "Merry Christmas! I'm thinking of you." It was Bill Hadigan.

"Merry Christmas, just barely. Where are you? How did you get my number?"

"I called your mother. She said you had already gone home. I'm out in the snow in Nebraska. I won't be playing golf tomorrow here."

"So come home, and play golf in the desert. The days are warm, but the nights are cold."

"Is that an invitation? For golf, I mean? I could be there in a couple of days."

"Sure, come back and we'll play some golf. I have to warn you, however, that I may be busy. My son is getting married sometime before New Year's," said Lisa.

"Good for them! Marriage is good for young people with families. I'm visiting my daughter and her family. But, you have been on my mind. Not just for golf, either."

"And what do mean by that?"

"Everything and nothing. You're a very attractive woman, Lisa Ellis. If I were with you, I might be kissing you good night right now."

"Maybe you should stick with golf. I realized tonight that even my middle years are over. I'm going to be a grandmother."

"I don't think so. Desire doesn't have an age."

"Are you sure about that?"

"Yes, quite. If I manage to get back for New Year's Eve, will you spend it dancing with me? I will show you, perhaps, one or two steps you have missed."

Lisa was laughing. Here she was talking on the phone like some teenager, hoping that the conversation would never end. Was it really a week until New Year's Eve? Yes? Good, plenty of time to buy a new dress.

"Lisa, are you still there? Will you dance with me on New Year's Eve?" asked Bill.

"Yes. We will go dancing and look at the New Year's moon together. I'll look forward to it."

"Good night, then, and Merry Christmas to your family. Someone in Nebraska is thinking of you. Good-bye."

Before she could reply or ask him when she was going to see him again, Bill Hadigan was off the phone. Lisa closed her book and pulled herself deep into the bed and covers. Christmas was a wonderful holiday. It could still be Christmas without presents, without cards, without shopping or parties. It was Christmas because of the way you felt and because of the way other people felt, too. The best gifts were the unexpected ones like the Friday night at her mother's house. Like seeing her brother Jack. Like hugging her son and his wife-to-be. Like a phone call from Nebraska.

All those years she had worked so hard for Christmas to be perfect had not been wasted. She had needed those years the way they were, and she had no regrets. Tonight, stars covered the quiet desert, snow fell in the Midwest, and Lisa Ellis fell asleep – festive, happy, and forever high on Christmas.

Jack's Story

Jack awoke to a familiar feeling. It was nausea. The wine and the brandy, which accompanied last night's rich meal, had sent his blood sugar to astronomical heights. Diabetes was hell, but it was less hellish than any other of the known diseases he could have. Like cancer. Like crippling arthritis. Like Alzheimer's.

He got up and went to relieve himself. Then he drank several glasses of water to overcome his early morning thirst. He got out his monitoring kit to confirm what he already knew: his blood sugar was out of control. He unearthed his insulin and syringes from his suitcase. Jack calibrated a dose. Swiftly he jabbed his stomach and released the medication that would help him through the next few hours.

Because he wasn't at home and because he didn't want his mother to know about the insulin, he disposed of the spent syringe in a plastic carton he brought for just that use. He cleared away the rest of his kit and re-buried the items in his suitcase.

He went back to bed staying until he heard his mother in the kitchen. It was after nine on Christmas Day. Throwing on his old green bathrobe, he went out to join her. She was just pouring a cup of coffee. "If I can have that one," Jack said, "I'll pour a second one for you."

Daisy turned to greet her son. He looked much older than she remembered. After all, she was eighty and he, her oldest child, had turned sixty earlier this year. There was no youth left in either of them now.

"Good morning, Jack. Merry Christmas to you. Here. Take this. It is black like you like it. I have another cup all sugared for me. I thought I heard you up."

Jack took the cup from his mother and sat at the far end of her Italian-tiled kitchen table. "Merry Christmas to you, Mom. What is planned for today?"

"After last night, not a thing. Last night was the big family party. Today we can just loll around. At least that is what I intend to do. Excitement can only carry me so far now. I'm old, you know." She said this last with a twinkle in her eye, half hoping her son would deny an obvious truth.

"I intend to do a little more than that," replied Jack, ignoring Daisy's remark about age. "I have a couple of friends to visit and I would like to talk to Paul today. Would you like to go with me?"

"No. I would be a hindrance and I really just don't feel up to it. Tell you what. I would like to have my newspaper. If you would get it for me, I'll fix a breakfast tray and go back to eat in bed and read. I might even have another short nap. You can go out. Just tell me when you go. I don't always hear the door."

"Seems like we should be celebrating a little more enthusiastically."

"We had a lot of excitement last night what with Paulie finally deciding to marry Erin and her saying 'yes.' I think that's enough. Besides, we're going to have a wedding before you go back to Mexico. Probably won't be much of an affair, but it will happen in the next few days. When are you going back?" Daisy asked Jack.

"After the wedding and when I feel that you and Lisa can get along for another little while without me. I am the indispensable son and brother, aren't I?"

"That you are. Can't tell you how much I've enjoyed your visit so far. Now, please go for my paper and then you have a luxurious day ahead of you."

It didn't take long for Jack to get the paper, shower, shave and be ready for the day. Before leaving, he removed two packages from his cases to take with him. Then, he spoke to his mother again briefly and headed into the mild winter morning.

He drove to the avenue side of town in central Phoenix. There was little traffic. He was looking for an old cemetery, journeying to a spot he had only once seen. He was looking for a grave at the old Masonic cemetery. The gates were open. He drove to the far edge of the property that was now under an Interstate 17 over-pass. Parking the car, he walked to a place he had seen in his dreams a hundred times. He passed the Ellis family area, the resting place of his father and more distant family, until he came to a headstone marked with the single name: Abby. He lingered a moment there, satisfied that he had had his way. He took care to memorize the place, the sky, and take measure of the day. Jack was never coming back.

He returned to his car and drove to see his nephew, Paul. When he arrived, Erin was out visiting her family, but Paul was home working on the computer as usual. "It's a fine way to spend Christmas: two old bachelors trying to make something of Christmas Day," said Jack. "I'm glad you're here alone, though. I wanted to have a chance to talk to you before all the women come bearing down on you. Don't know about Erin's mother, but yours and mine will be stirring things up a-plenty very soon. When's the day going to be? I can't stay in Phoenix all winter."

"You won't have to. Erin and I have decided to get married on the Saturday after New Year's. You're the first to know. So, how about a beer to celebrate?"

"Congratulations. I'm sincere in that. But I think I'll be toasting you with a 'diet something.' You go ahead," said Jack.

Paul went to the kitchen and returned with a can of beer and one diet cola. For a while, they caught up on each other's lives. Jack told some true lies about Mexico; Paul talked about his latest projects. Paul had a second beer before their conversation ran out.

There was hesitancy between the two men. Chance had made them relatives. It would have been easy to keep the distance between them by simply ending the visit. Paul would have preferred it, but Jack's visit was more than perfunctory.

In every family, there is a keeper of secrets. In childhood, having one's own secrets is the beginning of autonomy, away from parents and toward worlds parents will never know. Jack had been burdened throughout his life by everyone else's secrets. His mother, his sister, his Abby, and even Paul's real father had been set free by Jack's faithful stewardship. Now it was time for Jack to take wing by giving the secrets away. Now it was safe. It was time. He was starting with Paul.

"You know, I came here today to give you something as a gift that you may or may not want. It's for you to decide," started Jack.

"You don't have to give us anything as a present. Erin and I don't need anything. Just you being here has been present enough," interrupted Paul.

"This isn't a wedding present. This isn't for Erin. This is for you. I'm going to get it from the car." Jack walked out and returned with an envelope he had put in the car this morning. He settled back into the comfortable living room chair.

"There's some words that need to be said with this letter. I know that you didn't have a dad growing up. You had my father. He loved you like a son, but it isn't the same as having your own dad. I know Lisa wasn't keen on you knowing your real father. She had her reasons. When you were about ten years old, your dad tried to get in touch with you, but Lisa wouldn't allow it and neither would Daisy. They thought you would be better off not knowing about him. He wanted to see you, so I arranged it. You came to lunch with me and met your dad, but you never knew it."

Paul was struggling to take in what his uncle was saying.

"Do you remember a lunch with me and a stranger at the Stockyard's Cafe?" asked Jack.

"No, I don't."

"It doesn't matter. Your dad saw you and that was enough for a while. A couple of times a year he would call me after that and ask about you. I even sent him a picture or two over the years."

"Did he ever see me again? Is he even alive? Where the hell was he all those years?"

"No and no. He died before Abby. He was in the state of Washington, right where he had always been. He farmed some. From about the time he first saw you, he ran a motel."

"I think I'll have another beer," said Paul.

"You can get me another can of soda since you're up," said Jack.

Jack wanted to believe that this was going well, but decided that it wasn't. He was sorry he had brought up anything. Having started, however, he was going to continue.

When Paul returned, his only question was: "What's in the letter and why did you wait until he was dead to give it to me?"

"I don't know what is in the letter. Your dad gave it to me the time he saw you. He asked me to hold it until you became a father. The way I understand it, you and Erin are having twins. Now is the time to give you the letter."

"What if I don't read it? Do I have to read it in front of you? Is that part of the deal?"

"No deal. I kept it; I delivered it. Read it or not. That's not up to me," said Jack handing his nephew the letter.

Paul took it and held it in his hands. It was unaddressed and unsealed. He opened it and unfolded a single sheet of paper. It was more of a handwritten note than a letter.

Dear Paul Waller --

I saw you at lunch today for the first time ever with your uncle. You favor your mother.

If you got this it means you're going to be a dad. I'm glad of it. I hope that your children know you. I got married and have other kids but they don't take your place.

I'm leaving well enough be. Have to believe there's enough goodness in you to carry you thru your life. All you got from me was my mother's name and a lot of thinking time. I wish I knew how to do differently. I learned slowly with the others.

It is hard for me to write this. Just want you to have something from me at an important time in your life. I hope you can be a good dad. I wasn't to you but I love you anyway.

Bob W. Johnson

Paul folded the letter and replaced it in the envelope. "Waller was my grandmother's name? I always felt it was a mistake on my birth certificate. I know that my last name should have been Johnson, but Ellis is what I am and what I will always be."

Jack nodded for lack of anything to say.

"Know what this letter is worth?" asked Paul.

Jack kept silent. He shook his head.

"Me neither. But I'm keeping it. It's the only thing I have of his, you know."

Jack shrugged. He and Paul weren't the kind of men who would ever discuss the semi-darkness that obscured their pasts. It was like being as close as possible without touching, which is the kind of love that they understood.

It was mid-afternoon on Christmas when Erin returned, providing an end to uncle and nephew's moment together and an easy escape for Jack who promised to see them both before the wedding.

Jack lost heart to make his next stop. He returned to Sutton Place to finish Christmas Day watching television specials with Daisy.

For the next few days, Jack enjoyed the spectacle of his sister, his mother, and Erin's mother putting together a family wedding. Although it was supposed to be family only, Jack thought the preparations were similar to those required for a Presidential visit. Wisely, he and Paul stayed out of the gusty activity. Then it was over and the couple went away for a few days to California.

The night before he was to leave, Jack was unable to sleep. He was thinking of Abby. He often did. In the three years since her death, his memories had become sweeter. The agony memories had been replaced with happy scenes from their life together. The first time he had seen her come into his desert bar; her painting at summer's first light; their picnics together in any kind of weather; his fiftieth birthday party; the way she smelled. God, he could still smell her. He had been so lucky.

Tomorrow he would go see her sister and give her one of Abby's paintings. It had been her favorite, a thorough break away from Abby's deeply thought-out realism. It was a painting filled with people floating through multiple horizons. The child in one part of the painting became a mother in another section and was seen again as an angel on another plane. It was a complicated painting whose color force arrested your attention. Abby had wanted her sister to have it, but Jack was reluctant to give it up. Until now. On this trip, he could see that he had so memorized every detail that he no longer needed the painting. It was etched within him. He could see it just by closing his eyes. Like now.

Waking the next morning, Jack felt rested. He told his mother he would take her to lunch after running an errand. Then he would be off to the airport and back to Mexico.

Jack didn't call ahead to see if Sarah was home that morning. If she wasn't at home, he would leave the package and believe that he had done his duty. Sarah was home when he rang the bell. She recognized him instantly.

"Hello, Jack. I suppose that you were in the neighborhood and decided to drop in," Sarah said in greeting.

"Not really. I came here for the holidays and ended up staying for my nephew's wedding. I did plan to see you before I left, however."

"Come in then. I was getting ready to leave, but my trip can wait. After three years of not hearing from you, I am wondering why you're here now." This was Sarah's comment as they walked into the spacious formal living room. "After the stink you made about Abby's funeral, you didn't even come here for it."

Jack shrank from the last remark and Sarah was sorry she had made it. She looked down to regain some sense of herself as hostess. Raising her head she said, "I'm sorry Jack, really, I am. It's just that when I am reminded that you are alive, and I am alive and worst of all, our parents are alive and Abby is dead, I want to hit something! It is so unfair that she didn't live longer."

Jack noticed that grief and sorrow quickly disfigured even women as beautiful as Sarah. It aged them instantly. He wondered if Sarah knew how much she had changed in the past few minutes. He suspected that she did, but didn't care at the moment. She would only care later, when he was gone.

"Sarah, I didn't come here to bring up the unhappy past. I came with something for you that I have kept to myself, but that you were meant to have. It's a painting by Abby. From the day it was finished, she always said that she painted it for you; she was only keeping it until you were ready to have it."

"Jack, I don't think I could stand to have any painting of Abby's now. The ones I have are put away. I should sell them or give them to a museum. She ended up with quite a loyal following, you know. I just wish she was still around to paint." Sarah said the words as if she had memorized them. They lacked any emotion.

Jack excused himself and went to the car for the painting. When he returned, he found Sarah rigid and staring at nothing. He sat the painting by her chair and took a closer seat opposite her.

Aware yet unaware of his presence, Sarah spoke again. "I don't really want her around in any form now. When she left, when she ran away, I was hurt. We were so close. And for months, even years at a time, she came back into my life when she pleased. There was never a warning that she would come and never a thought about her leaving. She was here and gone. I just plodded on from one visit to the next. I was a wife and mother, and a dutiful daughter too. I did everything I was supposed to do and Abby had a life of doing only what she wanted to do." Sarah focused her eyes directly on Jack. "I was and am jealous of her and angry at you for letting her have her way."

"There was no way to love her and not let her have her way," said Jack. "Abby knew exactly how you felt, Sarah. It hurt her because she didn't have any other way to be. Abby thought too much and felt too much and remembered too much. What you both endured as kids remained fresh to her until she died. She could only love a little at a time. You, me and anyone else."

"I guess that I always knew that, but it is a help to know it wasn't just me. It was her. Is that why you never married?" asked Sarah.

"Yes. That, and she was already married to someone else," replied Jack.

"Abby was married? I never knew it! When was she married and where is her husband?" Sarah was astounded.

"A couple of years after we started living together, Abby left. She had left before, but this time she stayed away for more than a year. I thought she was never coming back, so I sold the restaurant in Tucson and bought a bar in Prescott. She simply showed up one day and asked me if she could come back and live with me. I wasn't willing," Jack said.

"But you did get back together."

"Abby could be persistent, and she was in a financial tight. Your sister was a very private person. After about a week, she called me from Phoenix. Said her husband was threatening her and would I please come and get her. I did. I brought her to Prescott and she never left again. She began painting seriously after that. I know that she never divorced."

"Do you know who her husband is?"

"Yes, she told me. He still lives here. He has contacted me. Legally he has rights to her works. I still have several. Abby had no will. That is why I brought this painting to you. I wouldn't want him to have it when Abby meant it for you."

Jack's story had removed the edge from Sarah's emotions. Now she was curious to look at the package. It was approximately two feet square. She could feel that the canvas was unframed. Deliberately she removed the paper and string with the canvas turned away from her.

Once unwrapped, she turned the painting around. It was so vivid that the colors hurt her eyes. Holding the top of the painting with her left hand and bracing the bottom edge against her lap, she traced the movement of the figures with the fingers of her right hand. She was smiling, but her eyes were filled with tears. Without taking her eyes off the painting, she asked, "Jack, do you know what this is?"

"I only think I do."

"It's my dream," said Sarah. "When Abby and I were young, we were often sent to bed so our parents could go out drinking. Abby was afraid. I used to tell her my dreams. How it would be when I grew up. I would marry and live in a fine house with lots of children that I would love very much and never leave alone. Then when I died, I would be an angel in heaven looking down at all my children and grandchildren and great-grandchildren. Abby loved that dream and I must have told it to her a hundred times. She painted it just as I told it. I never thought she remembered those times."

"Sarah, she remembered everything. She loved you. This is just the way that she ended up showing it."

"And to you, Jack? How could you ever know if she loved you? Didn't you always wonder?"

"No. I loved her as much as I could. I had her company and her delight for nearly thirty years. She was, at her best, new every day. And her bad times never lasted for longer than I could bear them."

Sarah got up from the chair and moved the painting to the top of a desk where she leaned it against the wall. "I don't think it belongs there, but I'll find the right place for it."

She walked back to her chair. "I'm grateful, Jack, that you brought this to me. It's more than I deserved, especially after the fight I put up about the funeral and the burial."

Jack smiled at Sarah. "Well, you and your family were pretty hard on me. I was carrying out Abby's wishes. If I had my way, she would have been cremated."

"Abby wanted a service and to be buried with your family?" asked Sarah.

"Yes, she did. She told me after my father died, if I outlived her, she wanted to be buried with the Ellis family. She said she didn't have the family name, so to mark her place with only her first name."

"Do you think she is waiting for you, Jack?"

"Heaven's no! Abby is in her paintings and in the people she knew and in the people who loved her. She is out and beyond us. I think she just wanted to be covered by the earth she painted so often for a little while so she could rest before going on." Jack's own words surprised him. He felt relieved. Later he would think of this moment as the one in which his grieving stopped.

With Jack's last words, Sarah knew the visit was over. She looked at her watch. Noticing this, Jack stood up to say his good byes. He glanced a last time at Abby's dream painting.

Once he was out in the crisp January air, Jack thought about returning to Mexico. The fishing would be wonderful; the tourists less so. Tourists were interesting only if you were selling to them. He could buy a bar or a shop, but he wanted to be back in Phoenix in the spring when the twins were born. It was a next generation of Ellis family. Jack did not want to miss it. Maybe the answer was to sell to tourists in Phoenix or thereabouts for a while. He could do that. It wasn't a big deal; it wasn't a big dream. He would work on it. Life went on until your heart stopped, and Jack's good heart, set free of secrets, continued to beat strongly.

P.S. Lowe

A Nation of Two

It was dark and cold and wet the second Friday afternoon in March, unusual for Phoenix, Arizona. Erin sat at her office desk staring at the resignation letter of her office manager. The manager, Dara, was sitting across the desk. "I can't believe you're doing this, Dara. Not now. Not today. What can I do to make you stay at least until the twins are born and I can get back to work myself?"

"Erin, if I could stay, I would stay. John has accepted a promotion, which means moving to Denver. He wants me to go with him right away," said Dara, pleadingly.

"What about the kids? Are you taking them out of school?" Erin was grasping.

"Pre-school and day care aren't regular school, Erin. I won't be working for a while, so they can just stay home with me until we drive each other crazy. Actually, it will be fun to be at home for a while."

"Dara, I need you. You have been everything to me getting this business into the black. No one knows the office like you do!"

"But someone else can do this work, Erin. No one can be my children's mother. My family is what counts. John needs me to help him and I am ready to go. You'll see that after your own kids are born."

Erin felt defeated. She didn't want to be reminded that from the moment she became pregnant, she was a poster-child for motherhood. No one cared that she owned and ran a business. No one cared what happened to the business either. Well, Erin cared a lot; she just felt helpless.

"When will your last day be?" asked Erin.

"Next Friday. I know it is only a week, but payroll will be done, statements mailed, and the bills paid. I can train someone if you can hire anyone quickly. Otherwise, between you, Elena and Reid, you will just have to read the office procedures manual. It's pretty up to date."

"This is not going to be OK. I don't understand why you have to go so quickly. If you were off for a week, maybe even two, could you come back for at least a few days?"

"I don't think so. Erin, you really need to hire another manager. It's not that hard, and this is a great place to work. I'll miss it. I wasn't married when I came here and now I have a husband and two kids. This has been my second home, but I need to go. John has even hinted that I can go to school in Denver. I'd like that. My dream is still to finish my degree."

Erin looked at her manager and friend. Dara was so ready to go. She was ready for the next adventure in her life while Erin was resisting the inevitability of her own impending motherhood. In the end, Erin said all the right things, and a relieved Dara went out into the rain to her home and family.

A Nation of Two

It was after seven o'clock when Erin, alone in the building, decided to head home herself. She could come in over the weekend and make a plan for the coming week. She turned out the lights, set the alarm system and dragged her heavy body to the car for the short drive home.

Paul was at the computer when she arrived home. He was involved with a project, or a game, and didn't hear her come in. Erin walked into his office to tell him hello.

"Hey," she said. "Your pregnant wife is finally home. Did you make any dinner?"

"Nope. I thought you would like to go out for Italian."

Paul turned around to look at his wife. She looked unhappy and tired. "But we can just stay in and I'll fix soup and sandwiches. How does that sound? Come sit in the kitchen with me. Tell me about your day."

"Oh Paul, I'm too tired to even sit up. There isn't space anymore for the three of us in this skin! I'm hungry and don't have the energy to eat. On top of everything else, Dara quit today. What am I going to do? I just want to give up. Everything I worked so hard for is coming apart because I got pregnant."

Paul had no ready comfort for Erin when she was in this kind of mood. He felt helpless when confronted with the strength of her emotions. Besides, he wanted to finish a last bit of coding before leaving his computer for the night. He was close to finishing a critical piece of code for his own difficult client. If Erin had been ten minutes later, he would have been done.

He decided that the best course of action was to follow a path of least resistance. "It's Friday night. We don't have to have dinner right now. Why don't you think about a short nap? Then we'll decide about eating."

Erin looked at her husband. It was clear that he wanted to finish his work and he wanted her gone. "Well, then, I'm gone," she thought. She left the room without a word.

Paul hoped that she went into the bedroom to rest, but he wasn't sure. He turned back to his keyboard and within fifteen minutes, had his programming problem worked out. He switched off the beast and went to find Erin. His problems with Erin would not be so easily or quickly solved.

When Paul walked into the bedroom and saw Erin sprawled on her back on the bed, he was tempted to turn around. She looked tense and uncomfortable. He wondered if he could outlast the end of her pregnancy. He doubted it. That thought made him laugh. He remembered his Uncle Jack who always said, "Nothing lasts; not the bad, not the good."

Erin's voice came from the bed, "What's so funny?"

"You. Me. Us. Uncle Jack."

"What's Uncle Jack got to do with anything?" Erin asked petulantly.

Jack walked over to sit on the bed next to his wife. "Nothing. I just thought of him and I don't know why. It made me laugh."

"I'm still hungry."

"Well, I will go fix some dinner. How about tomato soup and cheese sandwiches?" asked Paul.

"Anything," said Erin.

"OK, coming up."

"Before you go, will you help me up and get me out of these clothes? Why in the world do they put zippers in the back of maternity clothes? If it weren't for you, I would have to wear this dress until I gave birth."

Paul was glad to hear Erin make fun of herself. He helped her up and out of her dress and bra and pantyhose. As she stood nearly naked, he reached out to stroke her full breasts. Her skin was warm and soft to the touch. The changes he had seen in her body over the last months had amazed him. They had given her vulnerability. Like now, Paul wanted to protect her from the emotional currents that seemed to swirl around and make her unhappy.

"Come as close as you can and I will hug you before you put on your robe," Paul said. It was an awkward embrace, but it felt good just to touch in silence.

"Now it's off to the kitchen and you can tell me about Dara while I whip up a feast for the four of us."

Over dinner, Paul mostly listened while Erin poured out her latest woes. Clearly, it wouldn't be easy to replace the office manager. He knew better than to offer to help. He never had been able to either work for or manage anyone which is why he limited his career to work he could do alone.

They had just finished dinner when the phone rang. It was Erin's mother, Ruth. Although Paul had answered the phone, he quickly handed it to his wife. It sounded like Ruth had an agenda. Although Paul liked his mother-in-law, she had moments of intensity that made him feel hostile.

"Hello, Mom. What are you doing on Friday night?" asked Erin trying to sound happier than she felt.

"I called to find out when we are going shopping tomorrow."

"Shopping? I can't, Mom. I have to go back to the shop and clean up orders that I didn't stay and finish tonight. I need to advertise for a new office manager. Dara quit today."

"Erin, you promised two weeks ago when you called off our last shopping trip that you would get out and prepare for the twins. Have you forgotten? In less than one month, you are going to have twins. Just where did you think that they would be sleeping? You have an empty room. Babies require diapers, cribs, tables, bottles, car seats, blankets and clothes. So far what have you done but empty Paul's junk out of one room?"

"Uh, I have outfits from Lisa, and Daisy made me some blankets. Maybe Paul and I can go out next week to get anything else. I really have to work tomorrow."

"Erin. I'm trying to help you but you think more of your business than you do about being a mother! You are responsible for their lives. Why won't you understand that? No one else can be their mother. That's your job!" Ruth was clearly angry that after months of prodding and then nagging, her daughter was not taking motherhood seriously.

"Thank you mother," Erin thought. "Thank you for making me feel guilty about the choices I made; for the choices I make. You just don't understand that it's not as easy for me as it was for you. All you had to do was concentrate on your children."

Erin's continued silence pushed Ruth to more rash statements. "Erin, if you won't think about making a home for the twins, then I will. No grandchildren of mine are going to be neglected by parents who are so absorbed in their own lives that they can't be bothered to make a home for their children!"

"Mom, they'll have a home and they'll have whatever they need. They're not here yet, so it doesn't matter," Erin explained weakly.

"Do you want me to take you shopping or not Erin? I'm trying to help you, you know."

"I know. I need the help and I'll call you tomorrow. If I can get everything else done, we'll go. How's that?"

Ruth softened some. "Try to think seriously about preparing for your family. I'm available all day. I'll be looking for your call."

"OK, Mom. Thanks for the reminder and the offer to help. I will call you. Good night."

Paul, who had heard only half the conversation, could tell that her mother had badgered Erin. From even his short experience as a husband, he knew better than to speak against his mother-in-law. He waited for Erin to say something first.

"What's for desert?" asked his wife, completely ignoring the phone call.

"Cookies and milk," said Paul, but he did not get up from the kitchen table.

"Paul, my mother thinks we can't make a home for the twins just because we haven't bought cribs for them to sleep in," said Erin.

"They can sleep with us until they need bunk beds! When you're no longer pregnant, there will be plenty of room," said Paul as a joke.

"Oh, please be serious. What are we going to do? And when?"

"I am serious Erin. Whenever you want to go out, we will go together or not. We don't need your mother or anyone else to tell us how to make a family." The words came out more strongly than he wanted.

"She's trying to be helpful. She just doesn't understand that the business won't run itself. I thought I would have lots of time to do things, but Christmas rush was followed by the best corporate season that I ever had. Now, Dara is leaving and I have run out of time for all the things that I thought I would do for the twins. Do you think I am making the right choices? Do you, Paul?"

"Well, you married me. That was a good choice." Paul was smiling.

"How come you always say the funniest things when I'm trying to be serious?" Erin was laughing.

Paul reached across the table to grab her hand. It was his turn to be serious. "Because that's what you need, and that's who I am. Don't forget, Erin, we are a nation of two, you and me, first and last. Having children doesn't change that. They'll need us, but only for a while. Then they'll have their own lives and we'll still be with each other."

Erin made no reply. Her husband's words had passed over her and into her like an uplifting spell. She felt lighter.

"Come on, let's go look at the empty room. Maybe we can imagine some furniture into it," said Paul.

Together they walked down the hall into the plain white room. The wood floors were clean and polished. That had been Paul's doing. The windows were uncurtained. Raindrops reflected on the panes from the overhead light. The room had a good feeling to it.

"What do you think, one half in baseball pennants and the other half in ballerinas?" asked Erin.

"Great. We will have a son who dances and a daughter who plays first base. How about something more general?

"Like what?"

"Like jungles and birds and clowns; rockets and Martians; rainbows and balloons."

"All in this little room?" asked Erin.

"All in this little room. This is a room to imagine in, to dream in. It was in this room I decided to do whatever it took to marry you," said Paul.

"Your junk room? What were you thinking?"

"About how complete you were. You are the first woman for me who had her own dreams. You didn't need to dream mine for me. I couldn't let that get away. This is a room for great thoughts and imaginings. Dreams come true here, you'll see. The twins will see, too."

"While they are sleeping on the floor," observed Erin dryly.

Paul put his arm around his wife. "Or not. Erin, if it will make you feel less guilty, bag work and go shopping tomorrow. I do not think that you'll ever be the kind of mother that yours was. You have a whole life to yourself and that is a good thing. Also you're half of a nation of two."

"Well, I don't want to be the kind of mother that yours was!" said Erin pulling away and facing her husband.

Paul was momentarily taken aback. "Peace, Erin. This isn't about them. This is about you and me and our choices."

Erin thought about a reply, but was too ashamed to say anything. Paul was a good husband and would be a good father. She was sure of that. Aloud she tried to cover her shame and close the day with pleasant words. "Tomorrow I'll think about what to do about the future. I'm going to bed. For once, I feel like I can sleep the whole night."

Erin did go to bed and fell into a deep, dreamless, restful sleep. When she awakened, she felt wonderful and clear-headed. Paul was asleep. She looked at the bright digital clock: 2:00 a.m. "Oh," Erin thought, "I want to sleep some more. Why am I awake?"

As soon as she had the thought, she knew what had awakened her: pain. She sat up. The bed beneath her was wet, but warm. This was it. The pain came again. Erin enjoyed the discomfort. In the dark, she thought to herself that this was the last time she would ever be so self-contained. This was the last night she would ever not be a mother. She began to cry. She had been so afraid to lose herself to motherhood. The fear was more distressing than the actual physical pain she was experiencing. Fear had consumed her for months. Now, there was nothing she could do. The outcome of her pregnancy was inevitable; she would be a mother soon and would have to make the best of it.

The clock said 2:20 a.m. Her tears had stopped. Paul was still asleep. Erin reached over and shook him. "Hey, if I am awake, you should be awake." Paul barely stirred. "Hey, Dad-to-be. Wake up. I don't want to sit here any longer."

"Erin," said Paul sleepily without turning over, "What's wrong?"

"Nothing that a trip to the hospital won't fix. It's time to go."

Now Paul was awake and out of bed. He looked stricken, then composed himself. He walked over to Erin's side of their common bed and kissed her hair. "Well, all right. I don't suppose you have anything ready to take with us?"

"No. This is too early to happen. I always thought there would be time, so you get to help there, too. I'm not sure that I am ready for any of this," said Erin.

"No problem. I'm ready. Follow my lead, kid. I'm here for you."

Paul helped Erin out of bed and into her dry sweats. He went to the kitchen and found a Russo's department store bag into which he stowed an assortment of Erin's personal things. Then he dressed himself.

Before they left the bedroom, Paul took Erin's hand. "Erin, I want to remember this particular moment. This is the last time we'll be like this. We're leaving as a couple, and coming back as parents. I know that has worried you a lot. I meant what I said earlier tonight. We are a nation of two and we'll go on like that. Count on me always feeling that way. You're my family of choice and I love you."

Paul loved her. Erin knew that, but it was nice to hear the words. She wished she had been better at sharing her fears with Paul over the past year. He seemed to know them without her ever saying them aloud. "I'm a lucky woman to have you, Paul," Erin said. They went into the night together under the cleared skies.

The hospital routine, although new to Erin and Paul, was just routine. Somewhere toward noon on that Saturday, the twins came. They named the girl D'Ann Marie and the boy, David Jackson.

Once Erin and the twins were safe and resting, Paul turned his attention to notifying the family. His first call was to his grandmother, Daisy. She was thrilled. His second call was to Uncle Jack, who, although reserved, was clearly pleased to be called. "Now," Paul thought, "the mothers."

By a real stroke of luck, neither was home. He left messages and requests on their machines. He was sure that both would come to the hospital as soon as they got word. Then he could go home and rest. Later, when he realized the mistake he had made, he would think that he should have rested and then made the requests.

Paul returned to see Erin after stopping at the nursery where the pediatrician was examining the twins. Paul held both of his children and spoke with the doctor who seemed genuinely pleased to be doing his work.

When he arrived in Erin's room, she looked anxious. "I have to go home tomorrow! The doctor says I have to go home tomorrow! What am I going to do? There's nothing done for the twins. I'm not ready. Why am I not ready?"

"You don't have to go home tomorrow. You can go home Monday or Tuesday or Wednesday, Erin. You can go home when you are ready."

"How do you know? The doctor says I have to leave," said Erin.

"He will have to discharge you because your insurance won't pay. That's all. We can afford for you and our wonderful Dave and D'Ann to stay a day or two more. Really, it's a matter of money."

Erin covered her mouth with her hand and Paul thought she might cry. Instead she laughed. "Money. Oh, only money. What would I do if you weren't thinking for me? But, we still have no furniture for the babies."

"Simple. I left a message for your mother to take free rein and decorate the room this weekend. I'm sure she will be totally done by Sunday. Then you and Dave and D'Ann can come home on Monday afternoon," said Paul.

"Come here," said Erin. "I want to hold you and kiss you. You've done everything. But what about the store? I need to call Dara, but I'm so tired right now."

"I've called Lisa to handle the store for a week. There's nothing about business that she cannot handle."

Paul was sitting on the edge of the hospital bed. Erin, who had been sitting up, relaxed against the pillows. They were looking at each other but turned to the door when they heard small, infant cries.

"Hello, Mom and Dad. Dr. Evans has pronounced these two fit as a fiddle. It's feeding time," said the comfortable and clearly competent nurse. She handed Dave to his mother and D'Ann to

Paul. At nearly five pounds apiece, they still seemed very, very small to the new parents.

Holding the babies was a new and awkward sensation. Sensing the stress of the moment, the nurse lowered her voice and made a suggestion. "Dad, you look tired. The new mother and I have lots to discuss with your children. Why don't you get some rest and come back around dinnertime? Your sweet ones will be right here in the room."

Paul, who had thought that he would stay a while longer, looked at Erin. The presence of the twins had brought life back to her face. "Go on," Erin said. "I need a little time. But not too much. Come back soon."

Paul handed his daughter back to the nurse, kissed Erin and left promising that he would return after he slept for a couple of hours. Sleep was already pulling on him. When he arrived home, he fell onto the couch without bothering with his own blinking answering machine.

It would be Monday before he retrieved the messages from the mothers. By then, he would realize his mistakes. By then it would be too late to change things. By then he would know that a mother's love transcends time and error. He would hope for the same for his own children.

P.S. Lowe

Pendleton VanDuyver

Even in the near summer, Pendleton VanDuyver began his day in the dark. It was the long habit of a farmer. Coffee in hand, he started his walk to the far stand of corn. He could smell the early morning wetness on the newest leaves. That smell filled him with the only peace and contentment he knew. By the time that the sun was full up, both the smell and the feeling would be long gone.

Today, Pendleton wondered if he would ever taste the corn from these fields. He hoped so, but he doubted it. The day the seed went in, he had come back to the house tired and sorry to have lived for so long. The pain in his left side had nagged all day. He knew, no matter what, this was the last season for him.

This morning, when he got to the middle of the field, he had another reminder that his time was short. He would see this crop come in, and then that was it. Well, fine. There were one or two things he had to do. Because today was Saturday, his grand-daughter would be home. There were things she needed to be told. He would talk to her today. The new plants were doing well. A couple of good days of June rain and they would be knee high by Fourth of July. Pendleton bent down and fingered the fresh leaves. He stood up and walked back to the house.

Reid Markham had lived in her grandparents' Iowa farmhouse all of her life. She had come with her mother as a toddler after her dad died in a military plane accident. Her mother, having no job skills, had left the Arizona airbase and returned to the very home she had fled with her dashing young officer. Joy Markham found no joy in Iowa. She hated the weather, the farm, and all the old-fashioned ways. She went to Des Moines every weekend to escape, leaving her child with her parents. The same day that Lyndon Johnson became President, the county sheriff found Joy dead in her overturned car. Speed and slick roads had given her a permanent ticket out of Iowa.

Reid was up fixing her grandfather's breakfast when he came back from his early morning walk. No words passed between them as he sat down to the table and Reid served him. She joined him with her first cup of coffee.

Conversation was sparse in this house. Always had been. Pendleton VanDuyver didn't set much store in what was said, only in what was done. God had put people on earth to tend it and make it orderly, productive. Didn't take much talking to do that. Just a lot of hard work. In the end, when crops were in, maybe in the winter when the earth and the farmers rested, a man could appreciate the orderliness of his work. That was enough.

Sometimes, good order was interrupted. Pendleton never questioned those interruptions. Never asked why they happened. He felt that God put them into a man's life to test his free will. Interruptions called for decisions. If you made the right decisions, orderliness was restored. If you made the wrong decisions, well then, God help you.

Pen had not needed God's help much in his seventy years. His life had run in the same orderly fashion, in the same county for all of it. People respected him in the community. He had the best land, ran a good farm, and paid his debts. He helped his neighbors and never tried to profit from their mistakes as others had, especially nowadays. He was fair, and stern and honest. That's what it took to farm now and always. That's what it took to be a man.

It appeared that this morning was no different from thousands of others. Only Pendleton knew that God was about to provide another interruption in the order of things. Because Pen had warning this time, he was going to take the opportunity to make his decisions early. When he was finished with his eggs, toast and potatoes, he took his plate to the sink and poured coffee into the large mug that sat on the counter. Coffee in hand, he returned to the table.

"Reid, how old are you now?" Big Daddy asked as if continuing a conversation already begun.

"Big Daddy, I'm twenty-one. You know how old I am."

"What are your plans?"

"I'm putting out some plants in Grammy's garden. Then do the laundry. Maybe post some of the farm accounts for you. Why? Is there help I can give you out in the field?"

Pendleton shook his head. Sometimes he couldn't understand how Reid didn't see beyond the end of her nose. "Not for today.

For your life, Reid. What are you planning for the rest of your life?"

"Help you, Big Daddy. Just like always. Help you farm. Work at the bank. Why are you asking me?"

"I'm done, Reid. I'm done with the farm. Past summer, I don't plan to be here and you need to be gone as well." Pendleton drank his coffee and looked at his granddaughter. There was nothing VanDuyver in her. She was fair and tall. If she but knew it, there was grace and intelligence in her as well. Must be from her father. But she wasn't cut out to farm. She had no sense about the land. Only thing she did well around the place was sing and do the books. She had a talent with numbers.

"You're giving the farm to Pen, Jr., then?" Reid questioned. Her uncle farmed in the next county. He was a loathsome man who had mistreated her since her mother died. Now, with her grandmother dead as well, Uncle Pen acted as if he already owned the place.

"Already did. Most of it. This was Grammy's place, Reid. She left it to him in her will. All I own is forty acres. Just forty acres. I'm selling that and giving the money to you."

"I don't understand why you are doing this, Big Daddy. You'll always farm. What are you telling me? If it's Uncle Pen, I can just leave. I can move into town. Uncle Pen would let you stay here if I wasn't around." Reid's throat was tight. She knew better than to cry. Her grandfather didn't allow that in his house. Sign of weakness, he said. Gotta take what comes your way and not be weak about it.

"I'm doing this because you don't belong here. Never have. Never will. You're not strong enough for Iowa, Reid. You're weak and dreamy. The farm is no place for dreamers. Neither is Iowa. You should have learned that at least from your mother."

"I can't be like Uncle Pen, Big Daddy. It isn't in me to be like him."

"No one's asking you to. Enough about Pen, Jr. I'm talking about you. I want you to make some plans to move. Maybe you should have gone to college. Isn't too late for that. By August. You've got until August." Pendleton had finished his conversation. He got up and took his cup to the sink. Then he went out the back door leaving Reid alone at the table at eight o'clock on a Saturday morning.

For two weeks, nothing happened. Life went along as usual. Reid went to work. She pretended that if she did nothing, she would have to do nothing. Then on the night of the first summer rain, Pen, Jr. was out at the house when she got there.

It didn't take five minutes for him to begin goading her. "So, Big Daddy's giving you forty acres. Whoeee! Maybe you can buy yourself a husband. Where are you going? To Texas to buy a dumb cowboy? Maybe you can stick cash in your blouse and stand out at an Air Force base like Joy did. Get you some kind of luckless pilot just like your mother. How about it, Reid? Or maybe you'll just spend it all on records for that stereo of yours.

You're dumb enough to do that. God knows, you're too stupid to farm." Pen, Jr. was just warming up when his father came in.

Big Daddy's appearance gave Reid the chance to go to the kitchen to start supper. Her face was flushed and her head pounding. One day, she would like to be able to say something back to her Uncle, but today wasn't the day.

Over supper, Pendleton asked again about Reid's plans. "Big Daddy, I haven't made any. I know you are disappointed in me. I know it. I just can't understand why I have to go away. Things just start and stop for me. Other people's lives seem to have flow. Mine doesn't. I had parents; then I had no Daddy. Boom, I live in Iowa. Boom, Momma dies. Boom, Grammy dies. Boom, I have to leave. I don't understand it."

"There's no understanding to have, Reid. You are going to have to hurry your plans along. That young Sterner boy, Tom, wants to buy the forty acres. Only thing holding that up is you. The money is yours only if you move."

"OK. I'm moving to town."

"Away, Reid. I want to know by Thursday where you are going. Otherwise, I'm selling the forty acres on Friday and giving the money to Pen, Jr." There was no emotion in his voice.

"I can't leave, Big Daddy. This is what I know! I just can't." Big tears splashed down Reid's face.

"Stop it Reid. Now, or I'm calling Pen, Jr. Can't! I haven't heard that since you were twelve years old. You can Reid, and you will because I don't think you can live with the alternative."

Reid shut her eyes and willed the tears away, just like she had when she was twelve and Pen had put her on the big tractor and told her to drive it. It was the day after her mother's funeral. She was alone and frightened. "Turn it on, Reid. Drive down to the far field. I'll help you hook the disks. Then you are going to plow the forty acres before supper tonight. Turn it on."

Reid had cried then, until Big Daddy said. "Reid Markham, you're weak. There's nothing to driving a tractor. Any strong girl can do it. Do you know what happens to weak people, Reid? They die. Just like your mother. Do you want to die like your mother?"

Reid had turned on the ignition and the tears had disappeared. In the weak light of January day, when the land had prematurely thawed, she plowed the forty acres alone.

"Phoenix. I'm going to Phoenix, Arizona." The words exploded out of her mouth surprising her as much as Pendleton.

"Fine. Guess Tom Sterner has a nice piece of land. We'll go to the bank tomorrow, Reid. The money will be yours." Pendleton got up from the table to get his paper and read before turning in.

"Don't you even want to know why, Big Daddy? Don't you even want to know why I'm going to Phoenix?"

"No. Why isn't important to me. You'll learn that for yourself after a while. I asked you to do something and now you've done it. It is your decision. I'm fine with that. Good night, Reid."

"Boom!" Reid thought as she sat at the table. "My life changes and nobody seems even the least concerned with why."

The next day, Pendleton and his buyer met at the lawyer's to finalize the papers. Then they went to the bank. Reid got up from her desk when she saw her grandfather enter. He had his suit on. She realized it looked big on him.

Earlier in the day, Reid had asked Mrs. Rawson, the President's secretary, if Mr. Barnes would see her grandfather when he came in. "Well, of course, honey. Big Daddy is a good customer and a bank director. I'm sure Mr. Barnes will be happy to see him."

When her grandfather showed up with Tom Sterner, Reid escorted them both to the President's office. She was going to return to her desk, but Pendleton motioned her into the office much to everyone's surprise.

"Well, Pen," said Mr. Barnes. "I thought this was just a little financial talk among men. Don't think Reid needs to be here."

"It's a work day, Robert. We're here to conduct business. It concerns Reid, too. She'll need to be here," said Pendleton directly.

"Fine, fine, Pen. Let me just get another chair." Robert Barnes brought in the extra reception chair for Reid.

Once everyone had settled, a slightly piqued Robert Barnes began affably. "How can I help you out this afternoon? Interest rates still climbing, and money is tight, but I'm here to help you all I can."

"Tom here might care about interest rates. I don't. But that's been gone over before. We just need to transfer funds from his account to Reid's account." Pendleton waited for the impact of what he had said to affect the young Mr. Barnes.

"I don't understand," said the clearly puzzled banker.

"I've bought some land from Pen, Robert. He wants the money to go to his granddaughter. We're just here to do that." These were the first words from Tom Sterner.

"Well, well, well. Didn't know you were selling land, Pendleton. You've kept it pretty quiet. Lot's of people would like to have what you have. I thought that Pen, Jr. owned the land now. Didn't Irene leave it to him?"

Pendleton thought a moment before replying to the banker. "Seems like a man can do what he wants with his own land. Only selling what I own. My own forty acres. It's still a free country, Robert. Now, we've agreed to a price, got the documents done with those damn-fool attorneys. Time for Tom to pay up and we'll be on our way."

Robert Barnes had known Pendleton VanDuyver all his life. He was a good man, but a little too direct. If the lawyers had done all their work, it was no concern of his what Pen did. If Tom Sterner was lucky enough to get Pen's forty acres, the bank would be glad to release funds until a permanent loan could be arranged.

Tom handed the papers to Robert who briefly flipped through them until he found the transaction amount. Tom had paid top dollar for about the best piece of land in several counties, but he would not own it until the corn was in.

"It'll be a couple of days before I can give you the money, Pen. Paperwork, you know."

"No it won't. It'll be today. It's not my money. It's going to Reid. Put it in her account today, Robert. Then you give her a receipt for it. I don't plan to come back. You get that paperwork done and we'll just wait here. And I could use a cup of coffee." Pendleton was beginning to enjoy himself. Reid was staring straight ahead at the window behind the banker. Tom looked at his lap.

"Certainly, Pen, I can do that, but maybe you want a couple of days to think about it. You can't give Reid money without paying taxes on it. It is an awful lot of money to give such a youngster. Why she might just pick up and move to Des Moines! Just thought you might want to get some advice about this sale."

"Phoenix, Robert. Reid is moving to Phoenix, Arizona. Taxes are my concern. None of yours. No one in this town is old enough or smart enough to give me advice. Are you going to get moving on your paperwork? I don't want Reid to stay past closing time. She and I are going to Pearl's for supper. I like my supper on time."

It was Big Daddy's last remark that surprised Reid. Supper in town. It was almost like a celebration.

Robert knew he was beaten. He excused himself. Once out of his office, he realized that he would need Reid to do the paperwork. What was going on? Why was Pendleton doing this? That question might never be answered.

To take command of the situation, he started with his secretary. "Mrs. Rawson. Seems like we have a late transaction. First, take Pen a cup of coffee. When you go back in, ask Reid to come out."

"Is something wrong, Robert?" Mrs. Rawson asked.

"No. Just need to hurry. Don't want Pen to think we're anything less than efficient."

Once Reid was at her desk, Mr. Barnes set her to work. As she typed the forms, Mr. Barnes realized that without another bank officer, the transaction could not be finalized. The head cashier was out sick, leaving only the gossipy assistant cashier to sign documents. Before Pen finished his supper at Pearl's, news of the sale would be in every farmer's ear.

Reid had finished typing. Robert Barnes took the sheaf of carbons and forms to the assistant cashier. While she studied them, Robert attempted to talk to Reid who was as tight-lipped as her grandfather.

"You need to put that money in CDs. You need to invest that money, Reid. Interest rates are pretty good right now. I can help you invest it."

"I want the money in my checking account, Mr. Barnes. Here's my deposit slip all made out. When I get to Phoenix, I'll transfer it to a bank there."

"You aren't really moving are you, Reid? I just thought it was one of Big Daddy's jokes."

"I'm going, Mr. Barnes. Now that I have the money, I guess that this is my two weeks' notice."

"Reid, are you in some kind of trouble? I mean, do you need help?"

"No trouble, Mr. Barnes."

"Could you kind of tell me why you are moving then?" asked a very puzzled Robert Barnes.

"Because Big Daddy told me to," said Reid.

The assistant cashier brought over the papers that only needed the signatures of Pen, Tom, and Mr. Barnes. It was a little after four.

Robert Barnes walked behind Reid, past Mrs. Rawson, and into the office that Pendleton VanDuyver had commandeered. It took only fifteen minutes to complete the forms. Mrs. Rawson notarized them. The big transaction was over without ceremony. Hands were shaken. Tom Sterner left first, followed by Reid and her grandfather. Only the witnesses were left. Mrs. Rawson started to say something, but thought the better of it. Somebody would tell her what this was all about tomorrow. She could easily wait. That's why she was such a good secretary.

Reid and Big Daddy made a rare appearance at Pearl's. They sat in a booth in the back. While waiting for orders of chicken fried steak, it was hard to make small talk. At home, it was easier to have a silent meal. Here, in public, it seemed like they ought to talk.

"Did you quit the bank?" asked Pendleton almost tentatively.

"Yes. Two weeks' notice today. I could have stayed on till August."

"No sense in waiting."

Their food arrived. Somewhere in the middle of dinner, Reid looked up and said "Thank you."

"Not much of a dinner to be thankful for."

"No, I mean for the money."

"It was what you were owed, Reid. Grammy made me see that. Made me see that if things went wrong for you, like they did with your mother, there wouldn't be anyplace for you to go. You wouldn't have a home. You'll have to make your own home, Reid."

"Is that why you did this? Is that the why?"

"Yes. That's enough about it," said Pendleton.

"Do you want to know why I picked Phoenix?

"No, but you're going to tell me anyway," said Big Daddy.

"Because of a song. There's a song I used to listen to about going to Phoenix."

"Oh Reid, you're such a dreamer. It doesn't make me feel proud that you plan your life by the radio."

"Well, I didn't! It's just a joke! I picked it because that's where my dad was born. Maybe I have some family there. I don't know," Reid was sorry she had said anything. She tried to soften the foolishness of what she said. "Hey, I promise you I won't waste the money. I know about money, Big Daddy."

"Reid, I said you were a dreamer, not a fool. If I thought you were a fool, I would have tried to marry you off; given your husband the money."

"Oh," said Reid.

They finished their meal and returned home. Each of them experienced relief that the future was settled. It was as if they had already parted and come together again. All the past was past. Finally.

In the few days ahead, Reid got maps and prepared for her move. The few things she owned would fit into her Dodge Duster easily. Her last day at the bank was a Friday. She planned to leave on Sunday.

On Saturday, she did her usual chores, watering her grandmother's garden one last time. When suppertime came, she wished that the corn was ready. She would miss sweet corn; it was too early for sweet corn.

Sunday, she got up, and made up her bed with fresh linen. She put the room to rights. It was time to go.

Big Daddy was in from his morning field check. They had little to say to each other. Reid was neither eager nor reluctant to go. She was content. She knew in her heart that her leaving would make Big Daddy happy. More than that she couldn't do.

He walked her out to her car. "I'll call you, Big Daddy. I'll let you know how I am."

"Write me a letter Reid. I would rather have a letter. Everyone I know has always lived right here. So you fill my mailbox if you have a mind to."

"Don't worry about me, Big Daddy. But I'll worry about you."

"No, I don't want that. I am fine and I will be fine. You go out and get settled."

"Will you write to me? Will you visit me?"

"Maybe, Reid. When the corn is in. Maybe then."

"I love you Big Daddy. I want you to know that." Reid kissed her grandfather on the cheek, stepped into her little car, and drove down the road that would take her away from Iowa.

The rest of the summer was like all the rest of the summers Pendleton VanDuyver had spent farming. The weather was a little better, the corn a little taller, or so it seemed. Pen, Jr. saw his father daily. With Reid gone, there was nothing to talk about but the weather, interest rates, and the price of corn.

Reid wrote Big Daddy regularly. He became accustomed to finding a white envelope from her in the box a couple of times a week. She had bought a house and got a job as a bookkeeper. Although he had thought she might use the money to go to college, Reid's purchase pleased him. "Can't go wrong with land. God's not making any more of it," Pendleton thought.

He did write one letter to Reid. In it, he put his wife's green-gold wedding band and her gold cross. It wasn't a letter, really. Just a few lines. The corn still was not in.

The third week in August, the corn was ready. There was a full section of field corn already sold. Then there was the forty acres of sweet corn. It would come in last. Pen would take it up himself.

Take it up he did. Bushels of sweet corn came from the field. The air was thick with the smell of it. Even though he had help, Pendleton did the work of three men in the morning sun. When they were through, Pen took two big ears of the corn up to the house. He would cook them later.

He fixed a cold meat sandwich and poured a glass of milk, read the paper for a while and dozed. It was dark when he woke up. He went to the kitchen to prepare the corn. He ate it with a little salt while he stood at the counter. "Well, I made it to enjoy my corn. I'm glad of it," Pen thought. "Did what I said I would and I guess I ought to thank God for that." The relief he felt at his accomplishment was physical. Finally, finally, he could really rest and let someone else take over the keeping up and keeping on.

When Pen, Jr. came over to the farm on the Tuesday after Labor Day, he found his father just sitting on the porch, not working. "Hey, Big Daddy, there's work to be done! No time for lazing about!"

"Yes, there's work to be done, but none of mine. Your work now. The land belongs to those who work it. Your land, your work. I see Tom's already cleared his forty." Pendleton VanDuyver looked at his son carefully. Pen, Jr. had been taken by surprise.

"Are you just going to laze about until you die on this front porch? I was counting on you to keep up this place. Me running between two counties was more than I was counting on."

"Well, you could have given this place to Reid, Pen. I'm done with farming. You got five boys of your own. Why don't you set up John or Brian over here?" asked Pen, knowing it would never happen.

"Those boys are about as worthless as Reid. They would rather do anything than get out in a field! They want to go to college or play football or anything else but work my land. Don't know what I am going to do. Don't know how I am going to keep up. I was really counting on you, Big Daddy."

"Your mistake. You wanted this place and now it is yours. Big wants come with big problems. All I ever wanted was my forty acres. I had it. The rest was a lot of responsibility I shouldered for your mother and you and your sister. Then I carried on a while longer because of Reid. Now that's done too."

"So what are you telling me? That you'll let the land waste away before you'll help me? You're just going to sit here and rock on this porch while I work myself to death?" Pen, Jr. was afraid of a future without his father's help.

"The land won't waste whether you plant it or not. You own it free and clear. Think about that. Might make your decisions easier."

"You've got a mean streak in you Big Daddy," said Pen, Jr. who had missed his father's good advice.

"No, no I don't. I'm just tired."

Pen, Jr. stomped off the porch and took off down the farm road in his truck. Pen looked at his watch. Time for the mail. Might be that there would be a letter from Reid. If there was, he wanted to read it. If there was, he was going to write her back. Corn was in. He had made it this far. He wanted to make it a little farther. Pendleton VanDuyver wanted to see Phoenix, Arizona.

Use What I Got

Having imagination and being creative are two separate physiological and psychological functions. Reid Markham knew that. She had imagination in abundance. Whole worlds ran through her head day and night, but no one would ever call her creative. At forty-four, her life had become very limited, or so she thought. The truth was, she had a full life, just one different from the one she imagined that she wanted. Reid had lived in Phoenix since her grandfather had practically ordered her out of Iowa when she was barely twenty-one.

She got a change she didn't want then. Now, Reid wanted change. She wanted to seem more like other people she saw, but did not know well, or even at all. Opportunity often follows desire. Having made up her mind to change, opportunity practically knocked Reid over.

For five years, Reid had been the chief bookkeeper for NewMexTexCo, a company that created company-logo sportswear. In her time at the company, it had grown from a small dream to top supplier. If the owner, Erin Ellis, hadn't become pregnant, Reid knew that the business would have doubled this past year. Erin had big plans to add new machines, buy a building and, of course, increase her staff.

Now, Erin was on maternity leave. The office manager, Erin's closest friend, had quit. Erin's mother was overseeing the business. Thankfully, the business ran itself in spite of Ruth Pratt. Away from work on Saturday morning, Reid thought about her job. She fixed herself a cup of coffee and searched her extensive CD library for her new copy of Mozart's "Magic Flute." Reid loved music of all types, buying more than she intended to keep. Once she found a favorite version of an opera or concerto, she got rid of the ones she considered less perfect. She was not so lucky with popular music, however. She would keep a CD even if it had only one track that she liked. That's how she managed to have well over a thousand CDs in her living room.

Reid found the CD and put it on the player. As the overture filled the early Saturday morning air, Reid hardly noticed. She was concentrating on what she needed to accomplish, as she had for two weeks. She wanted the office manager position. When Dara was office manager, staff relations were easy. Reid couldn't match that, but she understood the money side of the business. Her title of twenty years might be 'bookkeeper' but she was really a competent comptroller and financier.

Ruth Pratt was not considering Reid for the office manager position. She told Reid that the company needed a college graduate. It was said in a way that insulted both Reid and Dara, both undegreed. Interviews would be Monday with candidates who had responded to the newspaper advertisement. Ruth had arranged them without consulting her daughter Erin.

After two weeks, Reid decided to call Erin. This morning she would do it. She would ask Erin for an interview. If Erin said no, well, that was something else to think about. At nine, she called and Erin answered.

"Erin, this is Reid Markham. From work. I'm the bookkeeper."

"Reid, how nice of you to call. I know I have been away, but I haven't forgotten you. How are things?" asked Erin.

"Good. Except for one thing. I want to be considered as Dara's replacement."

Erin was no longer surprised at the directness of Reid. Reid got to the heart of business. "Sure, Reid. I will be in the office for a couple of hours this week, we can talk about it."

"No, Erin, it can't be sometime. It has to be Monday. Your mother is interviewing candidates on Monday," said Reid.

"Monday? My mother is interviewing Monday?" Erin was irritated. She had been planning to talk with her mother about the business, but found too little time in the day with the twins. Every time she spoke to her mother on the phone, tempers flared. The two avoided each other, communicating only when necessary. Ruth Pratt could not hire an office manager for Erin. No, this would not happen!

"Yes, and she won't interview me because I don't have a degree," said Reid.

Erin thought quickly. There was no way she could interview candidates on Monday. She still had not worked out any type of reliable care for the twins. She was angry at her mother for not telling her about the interviews. This, however, had nothing to do with Reid's question. Erin liked Reid and needed her for the business. "Tuesday, Reid. You can interview on Tuesday. I'll be in on Tuesday morning. We'll talk then."

"What about the people on Monday?" Reid asked.

"I guess my mother will be interviewing them, Reid. Don't worry; I'll be doing the hiring."

"Thanks, Erin. I want a chance for this. I know I can do the job."

"Reid, we'll talk on Tuesday." Erin was anxious to get off the phone so that she could call her mother. Erin hung up.

'Well, I did that," thought Reid. Before she could think about another step, the doorbell rang. It was Mrs. Gilberg, her neighbor. "I knew you were about this morning. I could hear *Isis Und Osiris* in my kitchen. A little Mozart goes a long way on Saturday morning, Reid. I wonder if anyone else in the neighborhood shares your musical taste? When the music stopped, I got dressed to see you because I thought you might be going out soon. Are you going out?"

"Yes," said Reid. "I am going out."

"When and where?" asked Mrs. Gilberg.

"This morning to someplace to buy an interview suit," said Reid all at once.

"Oh Reid, honey, are you getting the interview? I know you were worried. Did you call Erin? Let's sit a minute. Tell me everything."

They went to the kitchen where Reid provided her neighbor a cup of coffee and refilled her own mug. Reid quickly told her neighbor of her morning phone call with Erin.

"Well, good for you. I told you she would see what a valuable employee you are! Never mind about the mother. I'm betting on you!" said Hannah excitedly.

"Erin sounded mad at her mother," said Reid.

"That's OK. That's the way mothers and daughters are. I've seen lots of that in my time."

"You don't have any daughters, Mrs. Gilberg," said Reid.

"I don't have any children, Reid. But I have seen lots and I know how things are. Now, where are you going today?"

"Shopping," Reid answered. She had made up her mind to have something new. She never wore anything other than jeans or khakis and white shirts to work which were purchased from a catalog. The only other clothes she owned were dresses for the opera and two for church. Nothing suitable for an interview. "Oh," she sighed involuntarily.

"Oh?" repeated Hannah. "Reid, where are you going to shop?"

"Someplace where I can buy everything all at once," answered Reid.

"I'm sorry, honey, but you lost me. What are you shopping for?"

"Clothes. Office manager clothes! New makeup! Maybe a haircut!"

"Reid, you can't depend on clothes to make you a winner. You already are an office manager in your heart and mind. Isn't that what Big Daddy would have told you?"

"Big Daddy didn't tell me how it would be to be alone for more than twenty years and what it would be like to be a middle aged woman! Back home in Iowa, hard work was enough. It's different now. It's different for me. This is important and I am going to use everything I've got to get this job!"

The force of Reid speech took Mrs. Gilberg aback. Big Daddy had been Reid's maternal grandfather. A stern man, Reid had nevertheless idolized him. To change the subject she asked, "How much money do you want to spend? I mean, are we talking full retail here?" Mrs. Gilberg was always curious about Reid's financial situation. Reid had purchased this house when she was just a girl. They had been neighbors for two decades.

"Yes, Mrs. Gilberg. We're talking full retail." Reid was starting to find this all funny.

"Then go to the Biltmore. You go into those nice little stores with all those old skinny clerks. You have a nice figure. They'll help you spend your money. You tell them to 'accessorize' you too."

"Accessorize me?"

"You know, nice ear clips, a new purse, a nice pair of new shoes."

"Maybe you should go with me," offered Reid.

"Reid, honey, I appreciate the offer, but I got no business going. You go. Then maybe, if you have a little time later, you could take me to the market. I don't like to bother you, but there is no one to take me this week. I hate to take the Dial-A-Ride."

Although Reid would have preferred to have the whole day to herself, she didn't want to disappoint her neighbor. "How about four o'clock?" she asked.

"Fine. I'll be waiting," said Mrs. Gilberg, who showed no sign of leaving the table.

Without being rude, Reid was anxious for Mrs. Gilberg to go home. It usually took a long time, but when Reid made up her mind to do something, she wanted to do it right away, so that she didn't back out of it entirely. Like calling Erin. If she hadn't done it this morning, she would never have called. Now, she wanted to go shopping.

"Reid, honey, this is none of my business, of course, but I was wondering if you could answer me a little question?" said Mr. Gilberg.

Those words, "this is none of my business" usually meant that Reid's neighbor was about to try to involve herself deeply in Reid's business. It wasn't that Reid wanted to be secretive. Not really. She just came from a self-sufficient family. In her family, telling others your business was considered a weakness. The little practice Reid actually had with sharing was with this neighbor.

Since Reid didn't say 'no' to her question, Mrs. Gilberg plunged ahead. "Why do you want to be office manager? Now, I'm just guessing from things you have said, but you could buy and sell that little company. Couldn't you?"

"Aha," thought Reid. "This is about money." Money was a subject that Reid often avoided with Hannah. After twenty years, however, what was the point? Why would the old woman care if Reid had money?

"You know, Mrs. Gilberg. I could buy and sell NewMexTexCo. But then what would I do for a job?" teased Reid.

"I knew it. You are rich!" said Mrs. Gilberg in triumph.

"I didn't say that," countered Reid hastily.

"But you are. You are rich and you act like a church mouse. What are you saving yourself and your money for? It's not like you have family or that you're likely to have children now, Reid. Why don't you treat yourself better? Why do you care what that woman thinks of you?"

"You mean Erin?" asked Reid.

"No, the other one, her mother," said Mrs. Gilberg, nearly losing her trend of thought.

"I just care," said Reid.

"You know, you ought to stay home some afternoons and watch Oprah. Oprah would be out there having her own way, not worrying about who likes her and who doesn't."

"I'm not Oprah Winfrey, star of stage and screen. I'm Reid Markham, middle-aged bookkeeper."

"That's the point. You don't have to be! Oprah Winfrey could be just another fat, middle-aged black woman. But she isn't. She's something special. You're something special, too, Reid. Stop pretending that you aren't," said Mrs. Gilberg emphatically.

"I don't feel special, Hannah Gilberg. I don't have the kind of personality where everyone wants to like me. I never was that way. Too many years out on the farm with Big Daddy and Grammy I think," said Reid more to herself than to Hannah.

"You haven't been on the farm for twenty years, Reid. You can still be anything. You don't need everyone to like you to be special. You think about your friends and all the things you do and enjoy doing. There's many people who would like to have you as a friend, you just need to make an effort to meet more of them. You don't have to be what you've been. You can start being different today. Why don't you call your friend and have her go with you? You two have lunch, too. Spend your money on some nice things for yourself. Change the outside of you, and then see what happens," offered Mrs. Gilberg.

When Reid made no reply, Hannah Gilberg thought for sure she had hurt Reid's feelings. She didn't mean to. To Hannah, however, it made no sense for Reid to pretend to be a poor farm girl. "Somebody needs to tell her that," thought Hannah.

"I'll think about it, Mrs. Gilberg. If I'm going out, though, I've got to get going or I won't be able to take you to the store," said Reid.

"Oh, I forgot. I can't go today. My sister is going to call me, but I don't know when," said Mrs. Gilberg cagily. "Call me tomorrow after you get home from church. If it's convenient, maybe we can run up to the market then."

Reid smiled at her neighbor. Hannah Gilberg lacked subtlety, but she had a big heart and Reid was grateful for that, if not for the advice. With Mrs. Gilberg out the door, Reid could be dressed and gone in thirty minutes. She would call her friend, Carol, to meet her for lunch. Might as well make the day of it.

As Mrs. Gilberg returned home, she heard different music coming from next door. It was Reggae and probably Jimmy Cliff. When Reid was a new neighbor to Hannah, Jimmy Cliff was a regular artist on the little stereo. "Well, at least it wasn't Mozart." Thought Hannah. Reggae was Reid's choice of happy music. Maybe, just maybe, Hannah thought, maybe Reid would take her advice.

Reid started her Saturday adventure with a haircut. She walked in to the exclusive Biltmore salon without an appointment. It may have been a ritzy shop, but on a summer Saturday morning, it lacked clientele. Reid was dazzled by the attention she got. Her medium blonde hair was bobbed and fringed by a stylist named Sammy. Different girls in pink smocks shampooed her hair and then blew it dry. She was offered a manicure and products to buy. It was wonderful and she wondered momentarily why she had never tried it before. The bill was in three digits, but Reid, for once, did not allow herself to care. She paid it and over-tipped everyone. It wasn't something she wanted to do every day, but occasionally she would enjoy the pampering. She decided she would come back again.

Reid was late in meeting her friend at Tiago's Pizza/Salad Kitchen. "You know I abandoned the kids to Darrell just to be here! I told him it was an emergency and I had to take you to the hospital. When you called and said we were going shopping, I knew something was definitely wrong. When was the last time you actually bought something that didn't come from a catalog and what the hell happened to your hair?" asked Carol without drawing a pause.

"I just had it cut," said Reid.

"I can see that. I can also see that you didn't get a haircut like that at the '$1.98 Beauty College.' Sit down and get your pizza 'to go' because I am definitely taking you to the mental hospital," said Carol. "What's got into you? Are you going through 'the change' or what?"

"Do I look bad?" asked Reid as she touched her hair.

"When did you care how you looked? I have told you for years that with a little effort, your life could be much different. I haven't talked to you all week, did something happen?"

"Yes it did. I'm tired of being invisible to everyone. If you had to describe me, what would you honestly say?" asked Reid.

"That you are a terrific friend, a great cook, and a smart woman," said Carol enthusiastically.

"Did you think that when you met me? You were my neighbor for a whole year before we even spoke. How would you describe me then?"

"A church mouse. You have always been kind of quiet and you keep to yourself, Reid, but there's nothing wrong with that."

"Those are the exact words that Hannah Gilberg used to describe me!" said Reid.

"You can't take what your crotchety neighbor says seriously," admonished Carol.

"But I do. She's been telling me for years to get out and live a little. 'Spend your money on yourself,' she says. 'You'll never have a family, so spend your money on yourself.' Today, I am doing that, or at least going to try. We're shopping today and I'm going to buy things that a church mouse would shun," said Reid.

Carol pushed at her front teeth with her tongue. She always did that when she was considering what to say next. "Did that hurt your feelings, Reid? You aren't too old to have a family, you know. Don't take what people say so seriously. Don't just do something that doesn't fit you because you are hurt by an old woman."

"I've heard it before. Kenny teases me about being an old maid, you know. I don't intend to be fifty and pregnant, so don't you worry."

"Me either," said Carol, with amused relief. When the waitress arrived, Carol made a speedy order for both of them. She loved to spend money, hers or Reid's. It didn't matter. She would have a fun time of it. They ate in record time. Reid was barely able to tell her friend about the job situation before Carol was ready to shop.

Shop they did. In contrast to the hot day, the exclusive shops of the Biltmore were deliciously cool and soothing. Reid simply acquiesced to the taste of the clerks and her friend. By the time they had completed half of the stores, Reid was tired and thirsty, however, and had purchased nothing. She was ready to go home. "You are not doing any such thing!" said Carol. "We have seen some great things, but nothing right for you. I'll buy you a soda. Carry it with you. I've saved the best for last. My friend's mother owns the next shop. If she can't find what you want, then you can quit."

Reid nodded her head. Carol had too much enthusiasm to resist. Reid revived when they entered 'Paris Best.' Ellen Powers, the owner, was determined to help Reid. It was the first time all day that she had a customer who had a body worth the clothes in the shop. Ellen sent Reid and Carol to the large changing area and brought them carefully chosen outfits in size 10. In the first hour, Reid had tried on nearly everything in her size. She was standing in front of the triple mirror trying to decide if she liked the sleeveless taupe tunic with pegged off-white pants. "It needs better shoes, and perhaps a piece of jewelry?" suggested Ellen.

"Do you sell shoes or jewelry?" asked Reid.

"No. Those items are their own specialty. But I can suggest a couple of stores for you."

Reid looked at her watch. It was already 4:30. She wanted to be finished. Unaccustomed to shopping, doing more seemed like a mountain of effort. "Can you take me to them?" asked Reid.

"I'm sure you can find a pair of shoes for the outfit. Carol can help you find some nice things. I would trust her taste," said Ellen very graciously.

"I'm buying more than this. I am buying all of it except for the navy blue things. Navy is a church-mouse color," said Reid.

Carol started to laugh. Ellen Powers had no idea that Reid intended to atone for a lifetime of fashion sin in one day! "Ellen, come with us. That way we can get this done before the stores close. Let one of your other clerks package this stuff up and figure out what Reid owes. We can come back and get it on the way out."

Ellen Powers didn't think once before agreeing. She had survived in the new world of discount and Internet shopping because she catered to customers. Besides, it would be fun to be on the other side of the counter. Reid re-dressed hurriedly and the three women went out to, as Mrs. Gilberg had said, 'accessorize' Reid.

The summer light and heat were still intense when the Reid's do-over day was finished. It took the three women and the remaining clerk from Paris Best to carry the purchases to Reid's car. They were all giddy from the excitement.

Carol wanted to follow Reid home, but knew that Darrell and the kids had likely had enough of each other without her loving mediation. Reid drove home alone. Arriving, she felt a reluctance to take her purchases into the house. Once they were inside, unpacked and put into her closet and chest, it would mean that her life had changed. It seemed a little silly and emotional, too. She felt that she had finally grown up in a way that should have happened years ago. She shrugged to herself. "I can't fix that. I can only go forward now." Grammy had tried to tell her to live carefully because regret was foolish. So probably was spending thousands of dollars on clothes. "Well, I don't have any regrets about that! A church mouse doesn't live in this house any more!" she thought triumphantly.

For the rest of the evening, Reid enjoyed the pleasure of touching and arranging her new things. She listened to Jimmy Cliff sing "Many Rivers to Cross" and to the greatest hits of Joan Armatrading. She cried to "Angel from Montgomery" sung in Bonnie Riatt's throaty voice harmonized with John Prine. It was after midnight before she had showered and turned down the bed. She thought more about the day past than the days ahead. Now, it wouldn't matter so much if Erin didn't make Reid office manager. For the first time in her life, she had done something for herself without the ghosts of the past pushing her into the decision. Listening to the music tonight, the songs had been the prayers she was now too tired to pray. Before falling asleep, her last thought was of Hannah Gilberg. Sometimes it was good to have a nosy neighbor.

The Next Good Thing

Monday, Reid decided to try on her new life. She wore the new soft blue print dress and denim sandals. Normally, she wore a dress only to church, but today she was starting over. Once at the office, the dress was not enough armor to keep her tension at bay. She watched the series of candidates interview for the office manager position at NewMexTexCo. Ruth Pratt, the owner's mother, interviewed them. All wore suits, male and female. All were young. Reid kept her head down and worked on collecting receivables. Her hope was on tomorrow.

On Tuesday, Erin Ellis left the house after feeding the twins and putting them down again. Her husband Paul had agreed to care for them alone, all morning. It was a first for all of them. Erin wanted to talk to her mother before talking with Reid. It was going to take all of her nerves and tact to handle the situation.

Although she had tried to be in early, her mother was already working. In spite of the lengthy absence from her own business, Erin exchanged only minimal pleasantries with her staff. She asked her mother, Ruth, into the big office, closed the door and confronted her.

"Mom, I hear that you are interviewing candidates for an office manager to replace Dara."

"Well, someone needs to be here. I didn't know when you would be coming back and things are piling up," said Ruth somewhat defensively. "That Elena only does what she is told to do. The receptionist is on the phone with her boyfriend all day. Reid never tells me what is going on. Your salesmen just come and go, flirting with the receptionist and throwing their orders in a basket. Thank goodness the production end is better staffed! Now, I talked with some very nice, capable young men yesterday who could whip this place into shape in no time. That way you wouldn't have to spend all your time here."

"I see. Any of them have experience in clothing sales? Marketing? Bank financing?" asked Erin.

"No. But they all had college degrees, which Dara didn't, and were smarter than the lot sitting out there now!" fumed Ruth.

"Mom, did you offer the job to anyone? Were you even going to check with me before offering the job?" asked Erin.

"No, I wasn't. I'm a pretty good judge of people, missy, and I can do this."

Erin set her jaw to keep from making a regrettable nasty remark. She was grateful for her mother's help, but NewMexTexCo was Erin's pride and joy. She loved her company in a way she would never love her precious babies who were only partly hers anyway. This little company had come from nothing but Erin. It needed her and she needed it as much as she needed air! Coming in today, she realized how much she had missed it. She tried to take the edge out of her voice. Somewhat more gently, she asked, "How come you didn't interview Reid, Mom?"

"Reid? Why should I interview the bookkeeper? Besides, I figured if you had wanted her as office manager, you would have promoted her yourself," said Ruth.

Ruth's comment surprised her daughter. Why hadn't she just promoted Reid? She could have. What was it about Reid? Why wasn't she the logical choice? Erin looked out the glass window of her office. Reid was certainly more dressed up than usual. Clearly, she wanted the job. Did Erin want her?

"Erin, what's this all about anyway? I did not hire anyone. I kept notes and you can read them. They are right there on the desk in the blue folder. There are two good candidates for the job." Ruth was stung by her daughter's grilling.

Erin was about to snap at her mother, but she remembered what Paulie had said this morning. "You haven't been at work in several weeks. Not everything will have been done the way that you would do it. That's the way things are going to be from now on. Try to come home without too much anger."

Erin simply said, "Thank you. You really did a good job, but I promised Reid an interview. If it doesn't work out, I'll look at the blue folder. Now, can you go tell Elena what to do and send Reid in? Then, before I go home, we'll have lunch."

Ruth's anticipated battle with Erin hadn't happened. "Lunch is fine. Maybe you can then tell me when you'll be back at work. I've enjoyed my time here, Erin, but I want to be back at home.

Your dad misses me, too." The last statement was more truth than Ruth had wanted to share.

Erin smiled at her mother's remark. "We'll talk at lunch. Thanks, Mom."

When Reid came into the office, she carried a notebook. It contained drawings and a financial spreadsheet. She was nervous as she sat in front of Erin.

The truth was that Erin was nervous, too. Reid has obviously gone through a change that made her look slim and elegant sitting across the desk. "When," thought Erin, "will I ever be slim again? It's been nine weeks since the twins were born and I still look like Humpty Dumpty."

Somewhat awed by Reid's new "look," Erin self-consciously asked mechanical questions without interest and Reid stumbled through them. It was going badly.

"You don't want me, do you Erin?" said Reid after a time. "There's something about me that won't take the place of Dara. That's who you want. Someone like Dara."

"No, that's not it at all," said Erin who was both embarrassed and surprised. That was it. She was tired. With her mother's presence and Dara's absence, everything was different. Her mother had cleaned up the place and everything was organized; the reception area floor was clean; there was no dust anywhere. The warmth of the place was gone. Erin felt it in the dryness of her throat.

"What will you do if you don't get the position?" asked Erin.

"I don't know," answered Reid. "I've been here for a long time."

"Oh, why did I say that?" thought Reid. She was falling; she was failing. No, she had already fallen; already failed. Then she remembered what she had told Mrs. Gilberg. "I'm going to use what I've got."

"Then at least you'll be here for the rest of the day!" said Erin who had not heard what Reid was thinking.

"Does that mean I don't get the job?" asked Reid.

"No, that just means I've got to make a lot of decisions. This is my first day back; it feels like another planet. I have to take my mother to lunch. And I have to go home and take care of the twins. And I have no idea how I am going to run this business anymore," said Erin.

"Why don't you work from home like your husband does?" asked Reid.

"Because I need to be here. It's my business and I want to be here. At least I think I want to be here. Anyway what could I do from home?" asked Erin defensively.

"You could check on your orders, send your salesmen instructions on e-mail, watch your shipments on a website, and write letters. You know, the usual stuff." Reid seemed very matter of fact.

"The business isn't set up that way, although Paulie has said I should look into it. What do you know about working at home?"

"This." Reid opened her notebook, removed the drawing and handed it to Erin. It was schematic showing computers, peripherals and connections. Each work desk was marked with an employee name, function and a list of software. Erin was in two places on the diagram. One was marked "home."

"What is this, Reid?"

"It's a drawing of a new computer system. If you installed something like it, you could work at home some of the time."

"Did you do this?" Erin asked.

"I did part. My instructor did a lot of the more technical part."

"Your instructor?"

"Yes, I have been taking computer classes for a while at the County Community College. For my last class, we had to have a project that was work-related. My instructor came up with this idea for me when he found out that we didn't have a system here."

Erin looked at her watch. It was already noon. She was very surprised at Reid. Where was she going to school? How was it that no one knew it? She had no way of knowing whether Reid's idea was any good. She would have to ask her husband about it.

"Do you have any idea what it would cost to put in a system like this? I mean everything." Erin was trying to close the interview gracefully so that she could get on to her next "to do" which would, thankfully involve food!

Reid thought for a moment that Erin was just being polite, but she plowed on. "Yes, but my figures are outdated by about 90 days or so, when my class finished." She handed Erin the spread-sheet.

Erin went immediately to the bottom line. "That's a lot of money! I had no idea it could cost so much!"

"It's a lot less money than you have available for capital improve-ments, Erin. It's cheaper than additional employees or a new warehouse. You could make a lot more money by being more efficient and getting some of your volumes up instead of expand-ing your inventory. You could contract with more specialty houses, and have them ship directly to your customers. Not everything has to come in to this facility. You can track it all on a computer. From home."

Erin knew that Reid was right, but it made her angry that her bookkeeper had taken so much initiative. "This is my company! I'm gone a few weeks and my bookkeeper thinks she can run this business!" Aloud she said, "I'll think about it, Reid. Now, I really have to go."

"How long? How long will you think about it?" asked Reid.

"Until I come back to the office."

"Are you coming back tomorrow?" Reid was not backing off.

"No. Look Reid, this is just too much for me today, OK? I'll let you know." Erin just had to get away from Reid's intensity.

Reid stared at Erin for a long moment. That old feeling of being judged and left wanting started at her neck and flushed her face. "OK. I'll wait." She reached across the desk to retrieve her papers. Erin stopped her. "Hey, I said I would look at them. I can't look at them if I don't have them."

Reid stood up and left the room without further comment. Ruth Pratt came into Erin's office almost immediately.

"Lunch?" Ruth asked brightly.

Erin shook her head vigorously. "Yes, and then home. It's been a day." She looked at her mother, softened by the realization of what her mother had gone through for the past few weeks. Ruth had done a decent job, surprising her daughter. It had all been a mistake. Ruth was supposed to decorate the twin's room and Paul's mother, Lisa, was supposed to act as caretaker for the business. It had turned out all right anyway. Erin picked up the blue folder and Reid's diagram, then mother and daughter went to lunch.

Reid wasn't hungry. She was let down and bewildered. She covered the office while the rest of the staff went out to find lunch. She sat at her desk replaying the interview a hundred times. It could not be changed but it couldn't be forgotten easily either. She had been alone well over an hour, so lost in her own thoughts that she did not see a customer come in until he spoke.

"Excuse me. I'm here to pick up some baseball shirts and caps. For a boy's team. Should be ready today." The man who spoke the words reminded her of someone. She didn't remember ever seeing him before nor did she remember an order for uniforms.

"You caught me daydreaming. Could you tell me the name on the order? I'll look it up for you," said Reid.

"Could be under my name, Jack Ellis."

The name jogged Reid's memory. "Oh," she said. "You are Erin's Uncle!"

"I'm really her uncle-in-law, if there is such a thing. Her husband is my nephew."

Reid was flustered at her mistake. "Just a minute and I'll find the papers, and then you can come out back to see your shirts. I'm sorry, but I don't think that they are boxed up yet."

"Don't worry about it. I can come back tomorrow or another day. Say, why don't you just give me your name and I'll call before I come back in?" Jack thought he was being very clever in finding out her name. He was working at being casual.

"Reid. Reid Markham. If you can wait just a minute, you won't have to come back." She spoke her words hurriedly and turned to the back of the office.

Jack watched Reid stand up and go to the file cabinets. She looked out of place among the used furniture and dull walls.

Erin must be paying her help a lot of money these days to enable them to dress so nicely.

Reid found the paperwork and indicated that Jack should follow her. The back warehouse and shipping facility was cooled by swamp coolers that did little to ease the heat and humidity of the July afternoon. Reid found the shirts and caps. She unfolded one of the shirts and handed it to Jack to inspect. He gave it a cursory look. He was more interested in the pretty woman whose hand he had brushed. "The order isn't boxed and it hasn't been checked either," said Reid apologetically. "Give me a few minutes and I will do it for you. Why don't you go back to the office where it is cool? It's too hot to be out here."

Jack was amused by Reid's business efficiency. He doubted that she had ever boxed an order in her life. Certainly not dressed like this! "Since you don't look dressed to box and ship, why don't I come back tomorrow? That way we can both go back into the office," offered Jack.

Before Reid could answer, the shipping crew came noisily through the back door. All were carrying giant iced drinks for the afternoon. Seeing Reid, the girls quieted. "Mickey, can you check and box this order? It was supposed to be done by now. This customer is waiting."

"Sure, just a sec. Gotta go to my locker and put up my stuff. Maybe it will be a few minutes if you want to go back inside." Mickey didn't like Reid looking over her shoulder.

"Good. When it is done, call Elena to bring it to the front. I'm sure he'll be waiting. Tell her it's paid for so that she doesn't try to charge him again," said Reid.

"Yeah. Got it," said Mickey as she made her way to the back room that held the lockers.

Reid and Jack returned to the office. Jack was glad to have to wait. It would let him spend some time finding out about this woman called Reid. However, when they returned, the front office staff was settling in from lunch. Reid relayed the instructions to Elena, glad that the morning was over and she could at last go to lunch.

Jack, watching Reid retrieve her purse from her desk, surmised that Reid was off to lunch. He was hungry, too. He wouldn't mind some company. "Is there some place to eat around here?" he asked Reid.

"No place close unless you want burgers and fries," answered Reid.

"Not particularly," said Jack. "Where are you going?"

"I'm going up to the new hotel by the freeway. They have a salad bar in the dining room," said Reid.

"I'm partial to lettuce. If you want a little company and a ride in a truck, I'd be pleased to take you to lunch. You look too nice to eat alone," said Jack.

"What a corny thing to say," thought Reid. "Was he asking her out?"

When Reid did not reply, Jack boldly re-asked, "Would you like to have lunch with me? Then I'll come back for the shirts. Of course, if you have plans...."

"Oh, I had plans. I had big plans for today," said Reid. "So far, they haven't worked out. Sure, I'll take a ride in a truck. I haven't been in a truck since I drove Big Daddy's truck in Iowa."

Jack opened the door for Reid into the hot afternoon sun. "That's the way it is with plans. Sometimes they work, and sometimes you have to wait for the next good thing," said Jack.

Reid didn't have an answer for that. Erin might choose another office manager, but that would not be the end of all good things for Reid. The next good thing, she decided, would be lunch.

The Time Before Love

Jack opened his bar on Sunday mornings to serve coffee to the drunks of Saturday night and the other tourist shopkeepers who spent Saturday night at home. In the months he had been on Whiskey Row in Prescott, coffee at Jack's on Sunday had become a ritual. He never served food and he was gone by 10:00 a.m. You could buy, or Jack would give you, the best cup of coffee you ever had if you were early and quiet and clean.

Just into his thirties, Jack was an old soul. He had never been youthful in the ways of other men. He just missed being handsome by being agreeable. His tall lankiness and large hands gave others an impression of physical strength, yet he seldom called upon his body to do what simple words would accomplish as well. He was easy. That's what attracted people to his place.

Opening up on a winter Sunday, long before the sun had hit the mountain peaks, Jack wondered why he had spent a third of his life around alcoholics. He had never meant to tend bar much less own one. But then again he had never meant to drift from place to place either the way he had. He just wanted away from the rootedness of farming. This was as far as he could get without improving on his education. He had never had the patience for that, although when they sent a man to the moon a few years back, he wished he had been an astronaut. Yes, he wouldn't mind being a farmer even, if he could farm the moon.

In the winter, the first order of business was to turn on the ancient furnace, leaving both the back and front doors open for fresh air. Then he rewashed the already clean pots and prepared the first of the four carafes that would be ready at six. He set out disposable cups at the bar and reached under the counter for the assorted china mugs that were used by his regular customers. Most were men. Some would have been here when the bar had closed at midnight. Others had never had a drink at Jack's or anywhere else. Some owned businesses; some were bikers; some were seasonal. All were welcome. Coffee was fifty cents for all you wanted. Paying customers were expected to leave their money on the bar. At ten, Jack locked the door, counted the change and rang one sale. He had no idea if it was a money-making effort.

This month Jack was thirty-three years old. He began working in bars when he left home after high school. Since then he had owned four, two with regular restaurants. He couldn't even remember all the places he had just worked. He pretty much worked every night except Sunday. For the past decade, he served no liquor on Sunday. His bar may be open, but he didn't work it.

It was still dark when the first bikers arrived. They were seasonal and used paper coffee cups. By the time the sun was full up there were about thirty people or so there. Jack served them all and made more coffee between his rounds.

Somewhere around closing time, when Jack was making his last pass for his customers, he was surprised by a lone girl sitting at a table in the back. He hadn't seen her come in. He went to the bar, got her a cup, and walked back to her table. She looked older than the last time he had seen her. Thinner, too. Her beautiful face was the same.

"Hello, Abby. What are you doing in Prescott? I haven't seen you since Tucson. How is life in Phoenix?"

"Hello, Jack. Thanks for the coffee. Life in Phoenix is very different than life in Tucson," said Abby.

"Why are you here? Drumming up business for your paintings? Tourists are a little thin this time of year. You should visit in the spring when there's more business for your work."

"I came here to find you. I don't expect it, but I would like to talk to you."

Jack shook his head negatively and walked away. It was ten. Customers were dropping coins and bills on the bar on their way out the door. Jack poured his own cup of coffee and began cleaning up. Abby didn't move. When he began to count the bar money, she called to him. "Jack, I came to talk to you. Won't you spend fifteen minutes with me? I came a long way the hard way just to talk to you."

"I don't want to talk to you. You walked out on me a year ago without a word. I finally figured out we didn't have any unfinished conversations. I don't want to know what you have to say now, Abby."

"I want to tell you I'm sorry, Jack. I am sorry I left you Jack. I made a mistake and I'm paying for it."

Jack had expected Abby to say as much from the moment that he saw her today. Why else would she be here? Maybe it meant that she was finally growing up a little. He walked over to her table and sat down.

"It's nice to hear those words from you. I accept your apology. I missed you for a long time when you left, but it was for the best for both of us." Jack said the words that were right, but not close to what he really felt.

"Jack, I want to come back to live with you. I haven't been able to paint since Tucson. I want to be able to paint again. We had some good times together. We could have them again."

"No."

"Please. I don't have anyone else to turn to. I'm in a real bad situation that I need to get out of."

"No," said Jack no longer looking at her.

"I need you Jack. Please help me. I did a stupid thing when I left you. If I had a reason I could tell you why I did it, I would tell you now. It was a feeling I got one day. When the feeling passed, I was too far gone to come back. I wanted to and I want to now. Please, I don't have any money. If I can paint, I can make some. It's you or the end of the road for me."

Jack got up, went to the bar and scooped up the cash left there. He brought it back to the table and put it in front of Abby. "You took less than that when you left me. I'm giving you this. Take it and find your road."

Abby looked up at him. "I want to come back and live with you."

"I don't want you back Abby. My year with you taught me a few things. You are selfish and greedy. You want what you want when you want it. You have no thought to what anyone else wants. You are so afraid of someone telling you 'no' that you don't ever tell anyone anything. You just do stuff. There is something in you, Abby, that is always desperate. It drives you. You don't miss me. You don't need me. You probably don't need anyone. Painting and your desires are all you know. I used to think you were that way because of things that happened when you were younger. But I'm not sure that you told me the truth about that either. After you left, I thought it was because you're still just a kid. What are you now? Twenty one? Take the money and go back to Phoenix or anywhere else. You can't stay here."

Abby pressed the back of her hand to her lower lip. She was struggling to say something and her words were, "Can I have a cigarette?"

"You don't smoke."

"I took it up; I could use a cigarette now."

Jack retrieved a new package from his stash for sale and brought it to her along with matches. She opened the pack and started on her first of the day.

Jack watched her hands. They were graceful. For a moment he thought about touching one. He didn't.

"What if I told you I loved you? Would that make a difference?"

"You've got that backwards, Abby. I loved you. I really did. You don't know anything about love except that it is another four-letter word. Maybe that's the woman you are. Maybe it's the artist in you. It's not the kind of man I am. You took a piece out of me, but I started over. I want you to start over, too."

"I'm afraid." She stubbed out her cigarette and immediately lit another one. "When I was with you, I was afraid less. Could that have been love?"

"I don't think so."

Abby was barely holding on now. Her face had lost all its innocence. "I never lied to you Jack. You have to believe that. I didn't tell you a lot of shit. The part you heard was true. All true. It felt safe to tell you."

"I'm glad to know you felt safe for a while. I am glad you had that little bit of safety with me. But your demons are your demons."

"How come you're so smart, Jack? What about your demons? How come yours don't run your life?"

"Because Abby, I found that mine were easier to live with if I was doing something I liked to do. Mine don't bother me as long as I have a bar to open and customers to serve. I pretty much left them behind me when I got out on my own and started seeing the demons that ran other people. You seem to like to travel with yours. Now, it's time for me to close and you to get in your car and drive back down the hill."

"I don't have a car," said Abby.

"How did you get here, then?"

"I hitched."

"Well, there's a noon bus if you want to take it. Or you can catch a ride. Plenty of people are going that way."

"I'll take the bus," said Abby. She began to pick up the bills and coins from the table. This time, Jack could not resist the impulse to touch her wrist.

"It'll be OK. You'll see."

"I may see a lot of things, Jack, but OK isn't one of them."

They stood up together. "You'll find what you need down the road," said Jack. Abby didn't respond. Dejection covered her slight frame. Wordlessly she walked away from Jack and out into the winter morning.

Sometimes it is possible to lose the same thing twice. That's the way Jack felt. He had thought he was over Abby. In spite of what he had said to her, she was right about one thing. They had some great times together. When Abby was happy, she was a glorious companion. In the bar and restaurant, customers loved her. Sunday picnics after a ride in the truck with some hot sex *en route* were hard to forget. He missed her naked body beneath his hands. Those losses were real.

He had left Tucson to get over the loss. In the short hour she had spent in Jack's new town, Abby had left Jack with the same feeling of emptiness in Prescott. He dreamed of her and grieved anew.

No one saw his grief. For two weeks, his routine was unchanged until a collect call came into the bar from Phoenix on Saturday night. Jack answered the phone. It was Abby. She was crying and hard to understand. "They won't help me and I don't want to die. He'll kill me and they won't help me. Not even her. I thought she would but I can't find her." There was silence after that

"Who's trying to kill you? Who can't you find? Abby, you've got to keep talking to me." Those customers closest to the bar phone stopped talking to better overhear.

"Abby, if you are there, talk to me. Abby, talk to me." Jack was shouting. The ring of stilled bar conversations widened and there was silence on the phone line.

In a split second, it is possible for the human mind to process a thousand disparate thoughts. Uppermost in Jack's mind was that Abby had taken on a second addiction to cigarettes, probably drugs. She didn't need drugs to be crazy. She started many days that way. So if not drugs, she either was in real trouble or had permanently crossed over to the land of her personal demons. Either way, she needed help.

"Abby, say my name so I know you are still there," said Jack in his most normal voice.

The Time Before Love

"Jack."

"Great. Can you tell me where you are?"

"No. I don't know where I am. I need help because I don't know where I am." Abby's breathing was shallow. There was fear in her breath.

"Are you alone?" asked Jack.

"No. Yes. I don't know." Abby was sobbing again.

"Can you see anybody?"

No answer.

"Abby, where are you?" Jack's voice rose again.

"I'm outside. It's cold. Help me. There's no one else. It wasn't OK here and she won't help me. You were wrong, Jack. It's a bad, bad road."

Jack's heart was pounding. "I'll come get you if you will tell me where you are."

Silence.

He tried the same question again. "Can you see anybody?"

"Yes, inside."

"Then go inside and ask someone where you are. Don't hang up the phone. Ask someone inside and come back and tell me. I'll come get you. Can you do that?"

There was no answer. Seconds passed. Jack called her name. No answer. He began to watch the bar clock. One minute. Two minutes. Three minutes. There was, by now, near silence in the bar.

Jack heard static and thought the line had gone dead. Then he heard Abby say "Airport."

"You're at the airport, Abby? You're at Phoenix Sky Harbor?"

"Yes."

"Abby, go inside and sit someplace. I'm going to come. It will be a couple of hours. Can you hang on for a couple of hours?"

"No. I have to leave. I have to get down the road, Jack, just like you said."

"Yes, Abby, you have to get down the road. You don't have a car, remember? I have to come to get you. I want you to wait for me. I will find you. Just wait for me."

"I'll wait Jack. But please hurry."

Abby hung up the phone.

Quickly Jack overturned the bar tip jar searching for dimes. He dialed the number of his sister's house.

Without even a greeting Jack said, "Lisa, I need a favor. I need you to go to the airport and find Abby."

"Well, hello to you too Big Brother. I thought that you and she had split. What is she doing in town? Where are you?" asked Lisa casually.

"I'm in Prescott. It will take me a couple of hours to get there. Abby's in some kind of trouble, and I know she doesn't have money. She might do something really stupid."

"Jack, leave her be. She is like bad news on a rainy day to you. She is just a kid, too. She should go off and live in San Francisco with the rest of the hippies. You're better than she can ever understand."

"Lisa, I'm not asking for you to critique my life. I'm asking because I'm asking. Will you go find her?"

"Shit, Jack. What am I supposed to tell my husband, who by the way, still regards you as something less than an unwanted dog? Have you got any thoughts on that?"

"Nope. Yup. Tell him Daisy called. Tell him you have to go see her because she needs aspirin and nothing's open where she can go out. Now, it is a long way out to Glendale from your house. How's that?" Jack continued to feed the phone with change to cover the long distance charges.

"I would have said 'yes' anyway, brother. Can't ever seem to say 'no' to you because you hardly ever ask anything from anybody.

I need to get out. It's been a long Saturday at home. Will I recognize Abby?" asked Lisa

"Yes, you'll know her. Try the old terminal. I don't remember any pay phones in front of the new one. I'm leaving after I hang up. I'll be there by eleven or so."

"Jack this is a stupid thing for you to do. You don't know what you're in for."

"Lisa, this is a time when you're right and I'm right too. It's stupid. It's the right thing to do. Thanks for helping me."

"See you soon. Bye." Lisa hung up the phone just has her husband walked in the room. Because of her years of practice, it was easy to pass off Jack's suggested lie as the truth. She was on her way to the airport in less time than it took Jack to exit his bar.

He was lucky that Doris was working tonight. She could close for him. "Jack, I don't mind staying to close, but I've got one question."

Jack didn't want to answer any questions, but he hesitated for just a minute long enough for Doris to ask, "Do you want me to put up a sign that says 'No coffee Sunday morning'?"

Jack smiled. Doris was as good as they come. "Yeah. Do that. Thanks." He picked up a fresh box of cigarettes from under the bar, took his field jacket from the peg by the door, went out in the night to find his truck and go down the hill to Phoenix.

It had been easy for Lisa to find Abby. She was at the old terminal, which was empty. Only one skycap and a couple of airline employees were visible. They were killing time until the last plane of the night at 11:30. Abby didn't recognize Lisa even after Lisa spoke to her.

Abby looked more than disheveled; she looked dirty and hungry. Lisa noticed she had neither purse nor baggage. Abby had on jeans and a sweatshirt with nothing on under it. Lisa tried to persuade Abby to accompany her to a nearby restaurant but Abby wouldn't leave the terminal.

"Jack said he would come. I need to be here. Jack said he would come," Abby repeated herself often.

"But he won't be here for a long time yet, Abby. I promise we can come back long before he gets here from Prescott. You need to eat. Aren't you hungry?"

"No. I'm waiting for Jack." Abby was intensely focused in her wait.

"Abby, do you want to talk to me? Do you want to tell me why you are here? Why did you call Jack?" Lisa's curiosity was stronger than her desire to comfort Abby.

"I'm waiting for Jack. I'll talk to Jack," insisted Abby.

Sensing that the wait for both of them was likely to be an ordeal if it required conversation, Lisa decided to try another way. "I want to talk to Jack, too, Abby. That's why I'm waiting. Would you like to rest while we wait? I'll watch for him and you can stretch out on these seats. You can rest Abby."

"Why do you want to talk to Jack?"

"Because I am his sister. I promise you that I'll look for him while you rest."

"I have a sister, but I couldn't find her. That's why I called Jack. If I could have found Sarah, I wouldn't have to call Jack."

Abby had moved to the seat bench and seemed to calming down. Lisa said, "It's nice to have a sister to call when you're in trouble, isn't it?"

Abby didn't reply. She had shut her eyes. Lisa watched as Abby fell asleep. Lisa was relieved. She took a small crossword puzzle book from her bag and worked on words until she felt Jack's hand on her shoulder.

"Quite a scene. The women in Jack Ellis' life." He came around the bench and sat next to his sister and across from Abby who was still asleep.

"Jack, what are you going to do with her? I don't think she is well in the head. I would have fed her, but she wouldn't leave until you came," said Lisa.

"I don't know what to do. Did you talk to her? Did she say anything?"

"Well she said one thing and I observed one other. She said she couldn't find her sister, Sarah. She has a couple of visible bruises, one on her hand, and one on her neck. No comment. She has no purse."

Jack took in Lisa's words. "No comment. I'll sort it out, or I won't. Lisa, thanks. Thanks for coming. I think I owe you something for this. Now, go home and get your beauty rest. I still have the prettiest sister in all the world. Jack reached for Lisa's arm and gave it a strong brotherly squeeze.

"I live for your flattery. I don't want to see your reunion. Please call me tomorrow. I won't be comfortable until I hear from you," said Lisa as she readied herself to leave.

"I'll call. Promise." said Jack.

Lisa left and Jack awakened Abby. "You came! I wasn't sure you would. But thank you. Thank you so much." Abby was beginning to cry.

"Abby, I'm taking you back to Prescott. Are you hungry? Do you want to eat something?"

"OK. Can I have a cigarette, too? I would feel better if I could have a cigarette."

Jack fished the new pack out of his pocket. Then he realized he had no matches. "You're going to have to wait until we go up to the convenience mart on Van Buren Street. Bring your stuff. The truck is out front."

"I don't have stuff. It's just me," said Abby matter of factly.

They walked out together, but not in any sense as a couple. Jack stopped at the only all night store he knew in this part of town. He bought coffee for himself, soda and assorted snacks for Abby. He picked up the matches, too. He waited while she lit up twice and smoked in the midnight darkness. He didn't want her to smoke in his new truck. They didn't talk. Each entered the truck silently. Abby drank her canned soda and Jack drank his coffee. Then Abby took the blanket from the seat between them, pulled it over her and fell asleep. Jack turned from Van Buren Street to Black Canyon Highway. As the Phoenix streets opened to the desert darkness, Abby slept; Jack drove.

The desire for sleep was still strong in Abby when they arrived at Jack's frame Prescott house. She told Jack she just wanted to sleep on his couch. He brought her a pillow and blanket from the closet. She pulled off her shoes and socks and unceremoniously went back to sleep. Jack looked at his watch. It was after three. He took himself to bed and met up with Abby somewhere on that short road to oblivion.

There was nothing usual about the Sunday morning that began late for both of them. Abby needed everything and had nothing. She was in the shower when Jack awoke. He gave her a clean undershirt and one of his sweatshirts to wear while he threw her clothes in the washer. He fixed coffee, eggs, and sausage for breakfast. She asked for aspirin and took four.

Abby looked better and much cleaner than the night previous. She wasn't talking much. Mostly she asked Jack questions. When her clothes were dry, she changed into them and then went to the truck to retrieve the cigarettes. It was cold outside; she had no coat. "No coat, no courage, but I'm going to try to do this right," she thought.

Entering the side door, she saw Jack sitting at the kitchen table. "Jack, if I can smoke inside, I'm going to try to talk to you. Can I?"

"You can smoke in the kitchen. But Abby, you don't have to talk to me. You don't have to say anything."

"I do. I want to." Abby sat down. "First, I need to say thank you for coming to get me. You went to a lot of trouble and I didn't deserve it. When I can get some money, I'll pay you for your trouble, I hope."

Jack said nothing. He looked at her as she smoked. He had nothing to do but wait.

"This is the short version, but you'll get the highlights. Let me get through it before you ask me any questions. I got married last spring. My family doesn't know. I thought that if I could make a marriage work, then I could put away my past. I did something that I thought would finally make me less weird. He was some older than me, but not as old as you, Jack. He had money and his parents had money. It was a mistake. I think he was doing illegal stuff, but I don't know what. He never really went to work. He talked about his investments. I swear I don't know how he got his cash."

In Abby's mind a film was running. It was long and detailed. She was trying to condense it to be able to tell her story.

"You know how I can't sleep at night, Jack. You know I get up and wander. You know about the nightmares. Well, Peter didn't like them. He didn't like my painting and he didn't want me to work. He yelled at me a lot. The more he yelled, the worse I got. I had a headache all the time. Something else; he drank, lots. Last summer we had an argument once and he hit me a couple of times. I wanted to tell someone about it, but I didn't have any friends to tell. I tried to phone Sarah, but she's gone. She's not even in the directory any more. One Saturday, Peter threw out all of my painting things. I couldn't stop him. I had nothing after that. I never had any money. He wouldn't let me go anywhere without him. He paid for everything. He made sure I was never alone and checked on me. He told his family that I was crazy. They believed him."

"I believed him, too. Before Christmas, I decided to change. I would do anything he wanted. I made myself normal. I cooked and cleaned; I dressed up and put on makeup. I even went to a party of his business friends. Things were good for about a month. Then on New Year's Eve, we went to a party at a posh resort. There were lots of important people there. They were all having a good time. I tried to have a good time, but I just got drunk. When we went home, Peter screamed at me. When I tried to get away from him, he got me good. Broke my collarbone. As soon as that healed, I came here to try to get help from you. There was no one but you to call. When I left here, I stayed away from the house as long as I could, but I had to go back and try to get some money and clothes. When I did, Peter came home and said he had been worried about me. Said if I stayed, everything would be different between us. He told me I should go back to painting. He even gave me money. Not a lot, but some. Then Wednesday night, after he had been drinking, he attacked me. I thought he would kill me. He tried to. I ran and only quit when you came to get me."

"Why didn't you go to the police?" asked Jack and was immediately sorry.

"Police? Would they believe me? They didn't believe me when I was a kid. They didn't care about me when I was an eight-year-old kid. Why would they care about me now? It may be 1971, and women may be burning their bras in the street, but one thing never changes, police are men. Men stick together. It's still OK that daddies mess with their little girls. Women who get slapped around by their husbands must somehow deserve it. Shit, Jack. Just shit."

Abby was done talking. Her face was red, and she angrily lit another cigarette.

"That's it?" Jack asked. "Is that all you want to say? If you want to say more, Abby, say it now."

"Fuck him."

"Fuck him and your whole family. There's something I need to know, Abby. Does he know who I am? Does he know my name?"

Abby was puzzled by Jack's question. "No," she said.

135

"Good. Listening to you isn't easy for me. I am not sure if you ever want to tell this story again that I can listen to it. Abby, I'm not your father and I'm not your husband. Your demons are your demons. Remember that. Remember too, that you saved yourself twice in your life. That's something to hold on to until something good comes along." Jack shifted uneasily in his chair. "I have to go downtown for a while. After that, we can go to Flagstaff and come back tomorrow. You can buy yourself some clothes and go to the university art store; get some paints. How does that sound?"

"Does that mean I can stay, Jack? Can I stay?"

"The staying is up to you Abby. Always has been."

"OK. When you go downtown, will you bring me something?"

"Cigarettes?" questioned Jack.

For the first time, Abby smiled. "No. Toothbrush."

"Sure. I could use a new one, too." said Jack. "You kick around here, maybe sleep a little more. Look for a coat you can wear. I'll be back."

After Jack had left, Abby went through two closets looking for something warm. She found Jack's tan coat and a muffler. The extra-large jacket looked silly on her slender frame. She returned to the kitchen and turned on the radio. She thought about what Jack had said. She had saved herself. Maybe that was a little bit true. What was truer was that she had run to the only safe place she had ever known. Where she sat now. Jack was right about something else. Safety was not love, but there was hope in it. That would have to do.

After Jack had arranged to keep the bar closed for the day and called Doris to manage Monday, he went to the drug store on the square to buy two toothbrushes. He drove the short route home slowly. He thought about Abby. He wished she was older or he was younger, but love didn't work that way. It called your name: you answered or you didn't. While she was around, he would be mostly happy. That would have to do.

When Jack got home, Abby was waiting. He called Lisa to let her know that he would be going to Flagstaff and would be back in the bar on Tuesday. "What happened to Abby?" Lisa asked. "Did she tell you?"

"She told me about enough," answered Jack.

"Well, tell me, what happened. It's not just me, but Mother who wants to know."

"Then you will have to ask Abby sometime. I'm not going to ask for you. It's something for Abby to work out."

"Jack, she is using you. You are going to get hurt again. Why can't you see it, brother?"

"I can see it. Just like you can see that you care more about what people think about you than you care about other people. That's why you gave away Paulie. You would rather have a fashionable husband than your own son."

Lisa's cold reply to Jack's last remark was "Paulie's better off with Daisy and Dad. You know that. He's doing well. You should visit if you want to know about your family."

"And Abby is better off for a while with me. I don't have to visit to know my own family. I know you are the best sister I could ever have, Lisa. Don't take all this too seriously. No matter what happens, I'll always be your brother. The one you look up to. Tell Daisy to come visit and bring Paulie. You come, too." Jack's voice was the same no matter how Lisa reacted.

"You make me mad, Jack. But I love you. Stay in touch. Next time you call, I hope it isn't an emergency."

"It won't be. Thanks, Lisa. See you." Jack and Lisa disconnected.

When Jack went into the kitchen, Abby had his coat and muffler on. "Take off the coat. I still have to pack a few things. We need to eat before we go. Are you hungry?" asked Jack.

"Yes," said Abby as she removed the coat.

"There's soup in the refrigerator. Heat it up while I pack. There's also carrot cake. Look around for what we need to eat. Then we can go."

Jack packed. When he returned to the kitchen, Abby was eating cake with her fingers while stirring the warming soup. It was vintage Abby. No order to anything. "Well," thought Jack, "she needs to eat. She doesn't have to eat like everyone else."

Jack got out the bowls for the soup and plates for the cake. He knew Abby would eat a second helping. They ate. It wasn't long until they were on the road to Flagstaff. Instead of talking, Abby fiddled with the eight-track tape player that had come with the truck. Jack had the road and his own thoughts. "Nothing lasts, not the good, not the bad." He wanted to tell Abby that, but she wouldn't understand it any better than she could understand if he told her he loved her.

When he finally did speak, it was a question to Abby. "Are you OK?"

Abby turned off the tape for a minute when she heard his voice. "I'm safe. That's as much of OK as I can see, Jack."

"Well, you hold on to that as long as you can. You bank it until you feel OK."

They rode the rest of the way to Flagstaff with the hum of the road as the only sound.

Daisy's Chain

Some mornings when I wake up, I feel the glory of the day in the light that comes in the window," thought Daisy Ellis. For the past few months since the twins were born, she had experienced persistent well-being. For no reason at all. As she got out of bed, she looked at the clock. Only eight. "Good," she thought, "I can cook most of the day and still have a nap later."

Daisy had plans. If things worked out, tomorrow, Sunday, she would be able to finalize a part of her life that had recently resurfaced into all-consuming thoughts. She fixed her coffee and toast then retrieved her paper from the porch. At nine, she called her daughter, Lisa, to put her plan into motion.

"Hello, Mother. What are you doing today? I hope you are through with dragging things out of storage. Bill tells me that he has helped you retrieve boxes and even your big trunk. Is it all still in the front room? Why do you want to go through all of that old stuff?" Lisa's questions had a tinge of disapproval in them.

Daisy heard the disapproval. Lisa never kept anything that was not of immediate use. Her house, her clothes, well, everything she owned was stylish and up-to-date. When it came to the past, Lisa had willful amnesia. It didn't matter. This was just one more area where mother and daughter had always been miles apart. "I went through all that 'old stuff' because I was looking for things that I thought Erin might want for the twins."

"Oh mother! You're not going to burden Erin with junk are you? I just finished decorating the twin's room. The last chest will be delivered Monday. Everything is perfect. Erin won't need anything until the twins are walking." Lisa's voice sounded peevish.

"Lisa, everything I want to give Erin will go into a shoebox. She doesn't have to take any of it. I'm just offering it to her. I'm sure that nothing will clash with the ambience you have worked hard to achieve," said Daisy.

"I did work hard. Everything is perfect, and Erin is pleased. I can't imagine what you want to give her. We were poor and did not have nice things. Erin and Paul are modern people who want quality."

"If you want to know what I'm giving Erin, I would like to see her tomorrow. I thought I would take a little picnic lunch. If you will take me, we could all enjoy it together. Anyway, we weren't poor. We just didn't have what rich people had. Like what you have now, Lisa."

Lisa bit her lip. Growing up she never had any money. That was poor enough. Daisy never understood that having cash for real quality was everything! Lisa didn't want Daisy to embarrass Erin with something that would be both cheap and old. Lisa had not replied to her mother.

"Lisa, can you take me to see Erin tomorrow?" asked Daisy again.

"Do Erin and Paul know of your plans? Have you called them?" Lisa was hoping that her mother had not yet called.

Daisy's Chain

"Yes. Erin is expecting us around noon."

"Damn," thought Lisa. Aloud she said, "Mom, I'm showing a house to a very big client at noon. Then Bill Hadigan and I are going to the movies. I am sorry, but I can't change my plans. This would be a great sale for me."

"Can you show the house earlier? I'm sure Bill would change his plans if you told him where you were going." Daisy was hopeful.

"Why didn't you call me earlier? I just cannot change. Could we go on Monday? I'm free then."

"Erin wants to go into the office for a few hours on Monday," said Daisy.

"Can Paul come and pick you up?" suggested Lisa.

"I'll call and ask but it's a long trip for him. It's shorter for you and I just thought it would be a special time for us, Lisa."

"I'm sorry, Mom, really I am, but I've neglected my business for a while and I want this sale. I just can't do it tomorrow." Lisa's voice had become business-like.

Daisy knew it wasn't going to happen. "Fine," Daisy thought, "At least I asked her first, even though using Lisa was really 'Plan B'. Now on to 'Plan A.'"

"Don't worry, Lisa. I can even take a cab there. I want you to be successful and happy with Bill tomorrow. Maybe you can give me a call on Sunday night."

"Thanks for understanding, Mom. Have a good time with Erin. The twins are wonderful and have grown a lot since you saw them in the hospital. I'll call tomorrow."

As soon as Lisa and Daisy had ended their conversation, Daisy dialed her son Jack at home.

Once Jack had answered the phone, Daisy made her request without much ado. "Can you take me over to see Erin and Paulie after you close up from Sunday coffee tomorrow? I've made a picnic of sorts and you could eat there with us."

"Sure. I can be there around eleven. What's for dessert?"

"Haven't made it yet. Your choice: peach tarts or lemon pudding cake," said Daisy.

"Oh, I couldn't choose between those two. I'll be happy, very happy with either," said Daisy's son amicably.

"I'll surprise you. Thanks Jack. I just wanted to take a few things over to Erin for the twins. We won't have to be there too long. See you tomorrow."

"OK Mom. I'll see you Sunday."

'Plan A' was now in motion. Daisy was pleased. She went into the kitchen to prepare the corned beef and sauerkraut that would become tomorrow's cold picnic sandwiches. This afternoon she would make peach tarts. In her involvement in cooking, Daisy forgot the past that had so occupied her lately. By the time the day was over, all was ready for the future.

Daisy's Chain

Jack showed up Sunday right before eleven. He carried the boxed food to his truck and Daisy carried a small wooden chest and her purse. Jack helped his mother up into the high cab, waiting until she was settled and belted in before closing the heavy door. He thought she was frailer than the last time he had helped her.

Arriving at their destination, Paulie, Daisy's grandson, came out to help everyone unpack and get settled. The twins were napping when the four family members ate lunch in the sunny kitchen. They ate spicy corned beef sandwiches, homemade pickles, and cold fried potatoes with gusto. Jack had just asked, "What's for dessert?" when the twins awakened. It was their lunchtime, too.

"Thank God this is a bottle feeding," said Erin. "Paul, if you fix the bottles, I'll get them changed. Daisy, come see the babies. You'll be surprised at how they have grown!"

What surprised Daisy was the room that the twins occupied. Two cribs surrounded with drawers and shelves had been built into adjoining walls. The light wood of their construction matched the floor and the rocking chairs that sat at the foot of each crib. Fabulous scenes of woods and meadows, children and animals, space ships and trains filled the upper walls. The roman shades covering the windows were painted to match the murals.

The minute Erin approached the cribs, the babies quieted. "Well, guys, lunchtime," said Erin. "Daisy, if you will hold D'Ann while I change David and then reverse, they won't cry."

"It's been a while since I have held an infant. If you don't mind, I'll sit in the rocker and you can hand me a baby at a time," said Daisy.

"Fine. Here's the easy one, my little girl."

When Daisy held D'Ann, she instinctively started to rock the baby. It was wonderful to feel baby-warmth in her lap. When Erin switched children, Daisy could feel the difference in the two. D'Ann had been comfortable and patient. David was a mover and clearly hungry. He jammed his fist in his mouth.

While Erin changed D'Ann, she asked Daisy, "What do you think of the room? It's all a mistake, you know. But a wonderful mistake."

"A mistake? Did you want Lisa to do something different?" asked Daisy.

"Didn't Paul tell you? He left the wrong message on the answering machines. He was supposed to ask his mother to oversee the store for me and ask my mother to buy furniture for the twins so that I could bring them home. Instead, he left a message for Lisa to buy furniture and sent my mother to my store! I was furious, but it turned out all right. Well, the room turned out well. The store is another matter. My mother and I haven't settled that score yet."

It took a minute or two for Daisy to understand what had happened. Then she asked, "Does Lisa know about the mistake? She was happy to be asked to help you and Paulie. I can tell she put her heart into this room. She did all the things she never got

Daisy's Chain

to do for Paulie. Paulie didn't have much the first year, and inherited Jack's room once he came to live with us. I don't know where Lisa got her taste. Not from me, but the room is wonderful."

"That it is. I don't know if Lisa knows about the mistake. She has been a whirlwind. She rented cribs until the building was done. She designed the murals, but had two other people paint them. She would not let us pay for a thing. Said it was her gift. She is having two rugs made and the chest for the other wall comes tomorrow. She has been generous," said Erin.

Daisy said nothing. "Generous with her money, but still selfish in many ways. Oh, why can't I ever love and forgive Lisa in my heart the way I can Jack? Why even to this day am I glad that I don't have to deal with my own daughter?" thought Daisy.

It did not seem to take long to feed the twins. Jack had made some coffee to go with the peach tarts that Paulie had unpacked and sampled. Then Erin put the twins together in a playpen in the living room so the little family could have dessert.

Daisy knew it was time to get out her wooden box, but was reluctant to do so. "Maybe Lisa is right," she thought. "Maybe I am dragging in the past where it has no right to be. But I have come so far with all this, I want to go on."

Daisy retrieved her box, settled it into her lap and opened it. She removed two silver baby spoons and two silver baby cups. They were polished and newly engraved, though clearly used. "These belonged to my two children. They were gifts from my Aunt

Mary Ellen, my mother's sister. The spoons are plain, but I had the cups re-engraved. Jack's has David's name on it; Lisa's has D'Ann Ellis on it." Daisy handed the small implements to Erin. Erin looked at the cups in wonder and passed them to her husband.

The long minute of quiet was broken when Jack said, "I don't remember these."

"No reason you should. I put them away when you and Lisa no longer needed them. I saved yours for your children, Jack, but you didn't have any. Paulie, you were already beyond using such a small cup when you came to live with us. But I thought maybe they could be used again now that there are babies in the family." Daisy was looking at the empty box, not at her family.

"I don't know what to say. This is such a wonderful gift, Daisy. So thank you. As soon as I can get these kids off the bottle, I'll be using them," said Erin.

Daisy looked up and smiled at Erin. "This box is yours, too. I got it in 1934 when I graduated from high school. It's a miniature cedar hope chest. I never had a real one. I used to call it my 'history' chest because it only held the past, not the future. I had some old letters and locks of hair and baby teeth in it and a picture of my mother. I emptied out everything. I'm keeping the picture for a while longer, but the box is yours for a new set of memories if you want it."

Jack and Paul were uncomfortable. It seemed to them both individually that Daisy, their collective mother, was in an emotional

Daisy's Chain

territory that they would like to avoid. So the conversation continued with Erin alone as if the men were invisible.

"Wouldn't Lisa want this from you?" asked Erin.

"Lisa lives in the future. She dislikes the past and its memories. Erin, you may do with it as you please. I only know I have no more need of it," said Daisy.

"Well, thank you again." Lisa got up from her chair and hugged the old woman. As if on cue, the twins started to fuss. It was time for the afternoon party to break up.

While Erin tended to the twins, Paul and Jack packed up Daisy's dishes and put away the remains of the picnic. The conversation was lighthearted. When Daisy and Jack departed, everyone felt pleasantly relieved.

During the ride to Daisy's, conversation between mother and son was scant. Jack knew his mother well enough to believe that there had been something more she had wanted to say or do, but had not. Although she gave the impression that she was an open person, he knew she had an intensely private side. She had, he suspected, learned to hide her true feelings in nearly fifty years of marriage to an unemotional man.

When they arrived, Daisy went straight in and sat at the kitchen table, while Jack carried in her things. When he started to unpack, Daisy stopped him. "Jack, those dishes won't walk away if I don't get to them for a while. You go on home while there's light left."

"How about I make some coffee and stay for a bit?" asked Jack.

"No. I just want to sit and be by myself. I'm thankful that you got me to see those babies and back again. You are a good son. I do hope that Erin and Paul won't think I've intruded too much in their lives," said Daisy wearily.

"I don't think they'll ever think that. We'll be invited back; you'll see. It was nice of you to give them those things. I think that Erin was pleased, but maybe more so Paulie. He has a sentimental streak."

"He does. He does. I think he may be just a little bit like my brother, but I don't know. It was too long ago. Now, go home and leave this old woman to rest."

In spite of Daisy's encouragement, Jack was reluctant to leave. He turned his back to her and began unpacking dishes and stacking them in the sink. "You said there were letters in your memory box. Who were they from? Your mother?"

"Jack, I lived with my mother every day of my life until she died. She never wrote me a letter!" exclaimed Daisy.

"Were they from Dad?" persisted Jack.

"No. Now, I've told you twice. Go home. I'll manage for myself later. Go on." Daisy got to her feet. Jack knew he would hear no more tonight, if ever. He knew it was none of his business anyway.

Daisy's Chain

Once Jack had gone, Daisy took her purse into the living room and sat in her comfy chair, putting her feet up on the ottoman. Carefully she opened her purse and removed a handful of yellowed letters. She had recently re-read them. All in the same hand, the first from 1937 and the last from 1956, the letters were a precious burden. She did not know why she had taken them on her visit.

On the one hand, she wanted to pass them on, but who would take them? Unlike the silver cups and spoons, they had no use. Her family would be horrified to read them. Like the other boxes of useless articles she had dumped in the trash, like the usable but unwanted things a local charity had hauled off, the letters had to go. She could let them go, if only she could talk to someone about them first. If only there was someone who would just listen, who would not be hurt by what Daisy had to say.

Well, another day perhaps there would be someone. Daisy got up from her chair and went to change to her robe and slippers, carefully putting away her visiting clothes. Then she went to the kitchen, boiled water for tea, turned the radio on and cleaned up the picnic leftovers. It took a while and when she was finished, she had forgotten about the letters and the man who had sent them.

When Lisa called to ask about the visit, Daisy seemed to be disinterested in talking about anything but the room that Lisa had decorated. Daisy was full of praise for her daughter, catching Lisa off guard. "Mom, I'm glad you liked it. What did you think of the twins? I have loved seeing them almost every day. I'm sort of sorry to have missed them today."

"Oh babies are just babies. They're more special when they are all grown up. Then you know how wonderful they are. Like you, Lisa."

Changing the subject, Lisa said, "I sold the house. So it was a good day."

"Did you have a good time with Bill, too?" asked Daisy.

"We had a fine time."

"Then you didn't miss anything. I'm glad you are happy. I am very proud of all the things you do. I love you, Lisa.

"Mom, are you feeling OK? You are getting a little emotional."

"I'm fine. Come for lunch this week. But give me a couple of days to recover first."

"Sure, Mom. I will, just as soon as I make sure that the house is going to close and that the furniture gets delivered to Erin."

"Good night Lisa. Come when you can. I'm off to bed."

"Good night mother. I'll call." When the phone disconnected, Daisy went to bed.

Monday morning Daisy had one plan, to get her mother's trunk from the living room and back into storage. She would have to press Bill Hadigan, her neighbor and her daughter's current beau, into service again. Around 10:30, Daisy called him and made her request. "Sure, I'll move it for you Daisy. What about the rest of the boxes?" Bill asked.

Daisy's Chain

"There's nothing but the trunk, Bill. You can tell Lisa that the rest of the stuff she worried so about is gone on to other homes."

Bill, because of his long marriage, and long association with his mother-in-law, was smart enough not to reply to Daisy's last remark. Instead, he said he would be over before noon to move the trunk.

When he came over, Daisy was already fixing lunch and invited him to stay. "It's tuna fish on wheat toast made with lots of pickle relish, like I like it. There are leftover peach tarts, too, from yesterday."

Bill was standing in the living room. "Thanks, I will. Just let me move your locker." Although Daisy referred to the container as her "trunk," it was really a World War I issue Army footlocker. Bill called to Daisy, "I'll need the storage room key."

Daisy brought it to him. Noticing both Daisy's handbag and letters on the chair, he asked if they were going back in the footlocker. "They didn't come out so they won't go back. Trash is where they belong. Here's the key," Daisy said and went back to the kitchen.

It took only a few minutes for Bill to do his requested chore. He was sitting at Daisy's kitchen table within ten minutes, enjoying lunch. Bill's daughter and her family had recently visited him. He enjoyed talking about them with Daisy. When the tarts had been finished, Daisy told him about the trip to see the twins. Bill did not know that Daisy had asked Lisa to go. "But I'm glad she didn't go. It was not her kind of gathering. Too family. Too gushy-mushy for her. She is like her dad. Nothing like me. Maybe that's my punishment."

"Punishment?" Bill was nonplussed.

"I wanted a daughter that I could be close to, like I was with my mother. But I did something, before she was born, that I shouldn't have done. Something too emotional and risky and wrong. When Lisa came along, she was distant, like her dad, even as an infant. I felt that it was God's judgment on me to take away my last hope and dream to have the same closeness that I had with my mother," said Daisy. She sighed. "Of course, I mostly grew out of that notion, but sometimes it comes back to me. Like yesterday. Like now."

"Daisy, does this have to do with the letters in the other room?" asked Bill.

"Oh, you are a smart man. It does. It does. When I was sorting out my life, those letters were almost the first thing I ran across. I haven't read them since my husband died and I moved here."

Bill said nothing.

"I suppose you might want to know about them."

Bill said nothing, but inclined his head slightly.

"You aren't dragging this out of me. It is something I want to tell, Bill, and I guess you are the one to tell. Those letters are from the great love of my life, Herbert Covington. Are you shocked? I hope not because it is not a shocking tale. Not with what you see on the television. Back in 1934, things were different on the farm. Hebert was a town boy and I was a farm girl. He was the star of everything at school. He was the best-looking boy and so smart. His folks had a hard time making ends meet because they didn't have a farm, like we did. Nobody had anything back then, at least not cash money. We ate well and had plenty to do. Herb didn't. He was a popular boy. He used to come out to the house sometimes with his folks. My dad liked him a lot. I loved him. Young as I was, I loved him. He loved me, but he didn't want to stay in the Yakima Valley. He was tired of being poor. Wanted to have money, real money, as if that was something possible. Soon as we finished high school, he went to Chicago to live with his uncle. He wrote to me once that first year asking me to come there, but I was afraid to be poor and afraid of living in a city. I pined away for him because there was nothing for me out on the farm, not even the break of school like there had been. I know he worked many jobs. In a couple of years, he was enrolled in a business school, working nights at the stockyards. It must have been a terrible time for him."

"Time was heavy for me. I began to think I would be an old maid. I was only 20. My mother was church active. She kept me going to socials and events. The Depression had let up by 1936, but that winter it was too warm early on. When the winter came, the chill was a surprise. Lots of people fell sick including my mother. Nowadays, she probably would have recovered, but back then, there was no treatment for the pneumonia. The day she died has always been the saddest day of my life. Now there was really nothing in my life; just my broken Dad and me who couldn't comfort each other."

"Funny thing was, her death made me somehow a desirable marriage prospect. Several of the valley boys would come out to the farm to kind of court me, figuring that I would be the one who got the farm. My husband was one of those boys. He was lacking in everything that Herb Covington had: looks, grace, and an easy way. I felt sorry for him. Pleasing him gave me something to do. His company was so steady, the others dropped away. He wanted to marry me, but I didn't want to get married. I was still hoping that Herbert would come back. I wrote to him, but didn't get an answer."

Daisy stopped telling her story. The coffee on the table was cold. In spite of the spring warmth coming in the open window, Daisy herself was cold. She stood up. Bill also stood up.

"Bill you have been listening to me go on about nothing. An old woman talking. I thank you for helping me out, but you have other things to do with your afternoon," said Daisy.

"Daisy Ellis, I saw those letters, and there's a bunch of them. Are you going to finish this story or not? He must have written back," said Bill.

"If you want to hear the rest, I'll try to make it go faster, but I want to sit in my comfy chair. Let's go in the living room. Pour you some fresh coffee if you want it."

They both settled in the other room where Daisy continued her story. "I was mad not to hear from him. Somehow, that anger made Douglas Ellis seem more attractive. My few friends were married and making their lives. Some already had children. I

Daisy's Chain

wanted children. At least a boy to make up for my brother; a girl to take the place of my mother. Douglas Ellis wanted my father's farm and me, some, too. Nowadays, it is different. What we ended up with was some very unpleasant sex business. That should have stopped it, but it didn't because I became pregnant. What a time I had. I was sick from the first. My dad saw my sickness for what it was and insisted I marry Douglas. Then in the midst of all this, I did get a letter from Herbert. I was beside myself with shame. He still wanted me to wait for him."

"I hadn't waited, had I? I wrote him back and told him I was already married. Then, I had no choice but to get married. Douglas moved into the house with my Dad and me. When Jack was born, things were better for a while. I had lots to do. Herbert wrote me a couple of letters and remembered me on my birthday."

"Didn't your husband object to you getting letters from your former beau?" asked Bill.

"He didn't know. I always got the post. Always."

"That's all? That's it? Daisy, I don't get the connection with your daughter. Why should you feel that Lisa was involved in your feelings for your first love?"

"Because that's not all. After a couple of letters, I started to write him back. I used to tell him what was happening on the farm and how Jack was doing. I could write pages on nothing."

"I wrote plain every day things like what I did on first day of spring. Even wrote some about my husband. My husband had a

157

good head for business. He wasn't much of a farmer. I mean, he didn't love the dirt the way my father did, but he made better money at it. Douglas and my father rather got on each other's nerves. Daddy went to live with one of his brothers up north. That wasn't bad, just made my life a little lonelier. Douglas was fair as far as money went. Daddy got more from Douglas than he ever got out of the ground."

"I've lost my track here. I was talking about writing Jack some, wasn't I?" asked Daisy.

"No, about writing Herbert. Then you said your Dad moved out to his brother's," said Bill who was now having difficulty following Daisy's tale.

"Why did I care that Daddy moved?" asked Daisy to herself. "He came back after the war started to be with me. Well, yes. Now I remember."

Daisy continued talking aloud. "Daddy was gone when the war came and when Douglas left. See, Douglas was a very patriotic man. He wouldn't have been called up because he was too old and the sole support of his family. He volunteered and the Army took him. Daddy was going to come back and run the farm until Douglas came home. There was a time, however, when Douglas was gone and Daddy had not come back. That's when Herbert Covington showed up. Just showed up at the farm! I was surprised enough at that!"

"Herbert came back?" asked Bill.

Daisy's Chain

"He had come to see his parents. He had finished his school and was going to go to work in the shipyards at Long Beach in California. Seems like his experience in running crews at the stockyards and later on, construction crews, had got him a reputation."

"He must have been about the same age as your Douglas, Daisy. How come he wasn't in the Army?" asked Bill.

"Younger he was than Douglas. My age. He didn't get called up because of missing fingers. Or parts of. He had had an accident and lost the ring and little finger of his right hand. That kept him out of the Army. Had to learn to do a lot of things with his left hand."

Daisy had paused for a bit to remember the day she opened the front door onto the porch and saw Herbert Covington. He had taken her breath away. She could see him very clearly and for a minute, forgot that she was now old. She continued. "He had brought me store flowers that day. The first I ever had. He stayed for lunch and played some with Jack. I told him my life and he talked about his. When it was time for him to go, I grieved. All I could think was what might have been and would never be."

"I cried most of that night when he left. When I wasn't crying, I was praying for just a little more time with him. I bargained fiercely with God, something I have never been foolish enough to do again, I might add. Next morning, after he had seen his parents, he came back and never left again for a week. Then he had to leave, and I had to go on."

Jack had been following Daisy intently. He then realized what she was telling him. Lisa was the product of Daisy and Herb Covington. He wondered if Lisa knew, so he asked Daisy, "What year was this?"

"1941. Oh, Bill you have added one plus one and got three. But you are wrong. Herb Covington is not Lisa's father. If you had known Douglas, you would see the resemblance between father and daughter; it is more than physical. There is nothing of me in Lisa. I knew I was already pregnant when Herbert came around. There is no chance that he was the father. He was never anyone's father."

Although Daisy had been speaking for over an hour, she wasn't tired. She was surprised at herself. She changed position in her chair and picked up the bundle of letters. They no longer touched her.

"Trash?" asked Bill Hadigan.

"Trash," answered Daisy firmly.

"There's more to this story you aren't telling, Daisy Ellis."

"Not much more. So I'll tell it quickly. Douglas was injured in a training accident. Because of it, he wasn't fit for overseas. He came home after Lisa was born."

"And Herbert?"

"By the time the war was over, he was supervisor to a shift of one thousand men. Then he went to work for an oil company.

Traveled over the world. He was rich by the time he died. He sent me postcards from everywhere. Always a card on my birthday."

"When did he die? Was it before Douglas?"

"Oh heavens, long before. In 1956, he died of a heart attack. His sister, who was still living, brought him back home. I went to the funeral. It was all such a long time ago. Jack had left home. Lisa was going through a bad time. I thought, for the longest time, that things would never be right again. That's not ever true. Paulie was born in 1958 and came to live with us. Then I was too busy with a second family to spend much time in the past. But I miss him on my birthday."

"Do your children know this story of your life, Daisy?"

"No. Are you going to tell my daughter?" asked Daisy.

"Do you want me to?" asked Bill in reply.

"Not particularly. But you are going to do what you are going to do. With these letters gone, however, I can always deny it," said Daisy with a little mischievous grin.

"My lips are sealed. Are you sure about throwing out the letters?"

"Yes, I'm sure," said Daisy. "I no longer wish to be trapped by memories only. It's so hard to have to finish life in this body, which no longer pleases anyone, least of all me. But to have nothing except the past to comfort me is not enough!"

"Bill, you don't know this, and Lisa doesn't know it either, but I admire my daughter. I realized it when I saw the room she decorated for my great-grandchildren. It's a wonder."

"She doesn't look back! She looks straight ahead at tomorrow and never back. Not at all. Not at all." Daisy was breathing harder. "If it wasn't for Lisa, I would have gone back to the farm when Douglas died. I did go back with Lisa. Do you know what I found? In the barn, in a chest, I found a pair of my father's work gloves. I cried when I saw them. Lisa saw me try to put them into my purse. She said to me 'What do you want with those old dirty things? Granddad can't love you anymore. He's dead.'"

"That's what she said to me and I took it for a cold remark. It hurt me. I was a new widow then, and I thought I am old and I am hurt and I have no one to tell."

"But the truth is, Bill, that Lisa was right. Daddy couldn't love me after he was dead. Neither can Herb Covington. That's what I realized when I went through all my old stuff. I kept things because I wanted to shape what my children remember. I've given that up now. They know what they think they know. But I'm sure of this. They have whatever they need from the past, and so do I."

"Daisy Ellis, you're sounding more modern every day," said Bill.

"Probably not, but thanks for listening to an old woman. I feel better for the telling anyway." Daisy handed Bill the letters. "On your way out, if you don't mind...."

Daisy's Chain

"No problem. Thanks for the lunch. It's nice for a woman to fix an old retired guy some food."

"Come again, Bill. You're good company."

Bill Hadigan walked out the front door with the past of Daisy Ellis. All she had now was the future.

P.S. Lowe

Truth and Consequences

Abby looked up into the sun. Its brightness blocked out the features of the man who was studying her small canvasses spread out on a table and on the sidewalk. Although she had been painting in Prescott, Arizona, for three years, her only chances to sell were at the summer festivals, like this one in Jerome. Sales had been slow. Now late July, she was glad that today was Sunday and that she would have no more shows until Labor Day weekend. She would pack up early and drive the mountain road from Jerome to home. The weekend had been a waste. Although she had told Jack that she could support herself painting, the reality was that without Jack, Abby would be starving.

The man moved, shading Abby's vision. "What else can you show me?" he asked.

"Nothing. This is it. If you are looking for something else, there are lots of artists here. There are cowboys and Indians and land-scape watercolors. Just keep walking." Abby was irritated. If what she painted didn't please customers, it pleased her even less. She stood up and began looking for the wrappings she would need to pack up and leave. The man didn't move, and he was in her way.

"Excuse me, but if you don't like what you see, please move," said Abby tartly.

"I didn't say that," said the man politely. "I merely asked if you had anything else to show. There's a difference."

"And I told you, nothing. So, if you will move, I'll be packing up to go. I'm tired; I haven't sold anything today; it's hot."

"Do you live here?" asked the man, not moving.

"No. Prescott. I live in Prescott."

"Is that where your studio is? Do you have any new works there?" continued the man politely.

"I don't have a studio. I paint where I can. What do you want? These paintings are for sale if you want to buy one. If you want to discuss painting, go see Joe Whitehorse at the end of the street. He will talk to you endlessly. He just can't paint."

"It seems to me that if I could combine you and Joe Whitehorse, I might become rich. Then I would have a painter who could talk civilly." The man was laughing a little. "If you're leaving, may I take you somewhere out of the sun? Then maybe you would be a little freer with your conversation."

"Who are you?" Abby asked. She looked more carefully at her sidewalk shopper. He was around thirty; maybe older. His manners were mismatched with his body that was stocky like a wrestler or a Marine Corps sergeant. His cream-colored shirt was ironed and his slacks, pressed. His brown loafers were neatly shined. He was a presence on the hot sidewalk.

He reached in his pocket and pulled out a slim card case; opened it, and handed one to her. She squinted as she read the card: "Holmes DuMez, Art Dealer."

"Is that a made-up name?" Abby asked inelegantly.

"I'm not sure what you mean," answered Holmes.

"I mean, did you make up a fancy name because you thought it would get you fancy, rich clients?" Abby handed him back the card, turned her back, and continued to pack the rest of the paintings. Maybe the man would just go away. She hoped the conversation had ended.

Holmes tapped Abby on the shoulder. "When you are through packing, would you like coffee or a beer?"

Abby swung around sharply. The sun was behind Holmes and in Abby's eyes. She was frustrated. She didn't want to face Jack, having sold nothing. "OK. Sure. I would like tea or something cold. I would like to be out of the sun."

"Good. You finish. Look down the street. I'll be at that corner place on the left. I really would like to talk to you."

Abby nodded. As Holmes walked away, she noticed that he favored his right leg. It took another half hour to wrap the unsold works and carry them to the truck parked up the hill at the decaying depot. She was sure if no one would buy them, no one would steal them either. She walked back down the hill to the corner.

As she accustomed her eyes to the dimness of the bar, she hastily looked over the few occupied tables. In the late afternoon, there were some tourists, some hippies, and some bikers. Holmes was in a back booth waiting for her. He had ordered himself a beer. For her, there was a glass of iced tea and a large cola. He stood up as Abby approached the table.

"Please join me. I ordered the two cold drinks available." Abby was speechless. She sat down quickly. At least it was cool here in the back. She reached for the sugar jar, pouring the whiteness liberally into her tea. She stirred it while Holmes watched her. "If you're hungry, why don't you order something?"

"I'm not hungry. I always drink my tea this way. I like the sweet part at the bottom." Abby was beginning to feel more relaxed. Holmes DuMez was nice and Abby was hungry for niceness. She drank her tea greedily and scooped the sugary ice cubes into her mouth with the spoon.

Between gulps, she apologized for her earlier rudeness. "I'm sorry about what I said. I mean about your name. You can have any name that you want. Really."

"Holmes is my real name. My father is Tom DuMez. It's a real name, straight from the family. What about you? What do I call you?"

Abby's eyes widened, "Oh, Abby! I am sorry all over again. My name is Abby."

"Well, Abby. Do you have a last name?"

"I'm sort of between last names at this moment."

"Between last names?"

"It's a long story and I don't talk about it anymore."

"I guess that I'll just call you Abby the Painter, then. Since you don't like to talk about yourself, will you talk to me about your paintings? I'm an art dealer and I am interested in your work. It has some promise."

"You didn't buy any." Abby was direct and pointed in this remark.

"I didn't see anything I thought I could sell. That's why I asked what else you had."

"Nothing." Abby picked up her bag. "Thanks for the tea. You and nobody else are buying what I've got to sell."

"Hey, come on! This is a conversation. Just a little talk about art. There's lots more to discuss."

"Not with me. I'm down the road. Way gone." Abby stood up. She had never mastered her adolescent sense of being easily offended. Like a teenager, flight was her usual option.

"If I bought a painting from you, would you talk to me?" asked Holmes.

"Which one?"

"Doesn't matter. I'm just paying to talk to you. So let's settle on a price. You pick out a painting and then you can sit down again." Holmes seemed casual in his offer.

"One hundred dollars. No, sixty." Abby was uncertain.

"Which is it?"

"It's sixty," answered Abby.

"Seems fair. I am putting money on the table. You can sit down and we'll talk. How about some more iced tea? I think that the sugar is holding out for now." There were now three new Jacksons on the table. Holmes signaled for the waitress.

Abby grabbed the money, folded it and put it into her bag. She took out a pack of cigarettes and some matches. Nervously, she lit up. "At least I can pay Jack the trip money! I sold something, sort of," she thought.

The waitress brought another iced tea to Abby and a fresh beer to Holmes. If he was either annoyed or angered by Abby's antics, he did not show it.

"Tell me which painting I bought. Tell me how you came to paint it."

"The muddy one. This spring we had a lot of rain. Every day when I went to paint, all I could see was mud and gray skies and more mud. Everything was just drowning. After a few weeks, I began to paint pictures of the dirt. Nothing else. Then, I added little edges of other things. They were terrible except for one. You bought that one."

"Doesn't sound too interesting. Why were you interested?" asked Holmes.

"Because that's what there was. I don't make things up. I paint what's there. Do you paint?" Abby didn't wait for an answer. "If you don't, I don't think you'll understand what I'm talking about. I get up every day of my life and I want to paint. I go out every day trying to find something that comes close to my desire. For a long time, all I could see was the wet, wet earth."

"So you painted that? Then, I have my first painting of mud. What else do you do? I take it that you're not selling much right now."

"I just paint. I don't do anything else." Abby was defensive.

"What luxury that must be for you to do only what you want to do. I would like to have that luxury, but earning a living requires most of my time." Holmes was smiling and gentle. Abby wanted to trust the gentleness, but didn't.

She wasn't about to say anything about the fact that it was Jack who made painting possible for her. Without Jack, she would be lost. She didn't want to think about that wrong road. "Painting isn't a luxury, it's more like a curse. It is a rock I wake up with every morning and only put aside when I sleep. Then you wouldn't know anything about that. Besides, you don't look like you are digging ditches for a living. You look pretty rich to me."

"No, I don't dig ditches. Can't dig ditches with bad legs, can I? Can't do much of anything. I never went to college and couldn't get a job when I got out of the hospital."

Holmes DuMez had momentarily stunned Abby into silence. Like many who have suffered pain and undeserved shame, Abby had little ability to sympathize with the grief of others. Abby felt that just to know the misery of another, diminished her, for she had merely obscured and had never overcome her own grief.

She searched his face and saw now what she had only sensed earlier. It was the look she had seen on the faces of young men in Jack's place who had returned home from Vietnam with less than what they had taken.

"So, Vietnam. How long were you there?" she asked.

"Not even a whole tour," said Holmes without emotion.

"No, I mean how long were you in the hospital?"

Holmes seemed puzzled at the question. "I don't remember, but my mother tells me it was the better part of two years. Do you want the gory parts? I can tell you if you want."

Abby responded to Holmes with more passion than the conversation needed. "I don't tell my stories. I have seen enough to know I don't want to know yours. I just want to know one thing – how did you get from there to knowing fuck-all about art? Or do you know anything? You don't paint and you didn't go to college. You say you're a dealer. You're talking to me. I don't get it."

"You paint, but you cannot sell. You didn't go to college. You're talking to me. I don't get it." Holmes cleverly turned Abby's words back to her.

With her left hand, Abby rubbed her eyes. She knew nothing about this man. Yet everything he said, every motion of his head drew her to him. She looked up suddenly. "You win. I'm beat. Tell me how you know what you know. You may be as close as I ever come to knowing a dealer. There aren't any on the sidewalks of Jerome, Arizona."

"A woman, a rich one, taught me everything I will ever need to know. Everything."

"Who was she? How did you meet her?"

"Isadora St. Lawrence."

"You're making this up, right? You just happened to meet Isadora St. Lawrence?" asked Abby.

"Do you know her?" Homes returned questions while weighing his answer.

"Yes. No. I mean no. Not really. But I have been to her galleries. I know someone, sort of, that she represented. Shit, how did you meet her?" Abby was too excited to speak with precision.

"My father did custom upholstery work for her. Always did. I've known her since I was a kid. I used to help her pick out fabric. You see I can 'carry color in my eye.' It is something not many people can do. I can see a color, memorize it, and match it weeks or years later. Iso remembered that. Two years ago, I was in Dad's shop doing nothing. I couldn't do much in a wheelchair. She had closed her gallery in Scottsdale for the summer to redecorate it. Iso wanted to change her trade by picking up and representing local artists for the local market." Holmes told his story with his eyes locked on Abby's face.

"That particular day in the shop, she wanted Dad to go out and look at the pieces to be re-done. He couldn't make it that day, so she took me. She was going away for the rest of the summer and asked me to oversee some work. I couldn't get my wheelchair into the gallery. Iso said, 'Guess that means you're going to have to walk again if you're going to work for me.' I got out the crutches the next day and never have been in a chair since."

"So now that she's dead, you took over? I mean, you represent her gallery?" Abby's mind was racing ahead. Maybe Holmes could help her in some real way.

"I was her sometimes employee and always friend. What I got from Iso was an education and friendship; no more and certainly no less. I'm quite on my own. I have rented space for the season in Scottsdale. I'm looking for works to fill it."

"Oh. Will you show me? I mean, can I paint something that you will show?" asked Abby hopefully.

Holmes hesitated. He knew the answer Abby wanted to hear. He did believe, however, that to lie to her, to lead her on, would be damaging to both of them. She was so eager for recognition, even if by a dealer in his first season. He had to be honest and hope for the best. "No, on two counts, Abby. The painting that I now own of yours won't sell. I need to sell paintings. More than that, I have to sell quality if I am going to sell for a lifetime. That kind of painting is talent and a little something more – maybe more heart. When you know it is good, then I'll know it's good. Nothing less from you will do. When you paint THAT painting, I want you to call me and I'll buy it."

When Holmes stopped talking, Abby realized that she had been hanging on his every word. She wanted him to go on. She held her breath hoping he would continue. He didn't. She panicked.

"I don't know how to paint that painting! I've tried for years and it hasn't come out. Don't tell me that I have to wait until then. I can't wait for someone to tell me that I've made something good. It's not coming out!" Abby was losing even the slight control she had tried to maintain.

"Abby, I'm not asking you to wait until someone else tells you what is good. I want to know when YOU think it is good. You knew enough to sell me the best mud painting, didn't you? But you knew it wasn't good enough for me, because it wasn't good enough for you." Holmes was leaning over the table trying to get Abby to look up. He was afraid she was starting to cry.

"How old are you, Abby?" asked Holmes.

"I'm twenty-three, nearly twenty-four." Still Abby didn't look up.

"How long have you been painting?"

"Forever."

"How long have you been working hard at it?"

"Two years." Abby would not respond any more than she had to.

"How long do you think you can go on painting? How long until you have to do something else and painting will no longer be your desire?" Holmes was trying to talk to the artist that Abby had not yet become.

Abby heard the question and knew the answer: "As long as Jack lets me."

"Another year? Another ten years? In ten years you'll still be a very young woman. Is Jack your husband?"

"No. Jack is just Jack. He pays my bills and lets me paint."

"Then keep painting. You know you are a lucky girl if you have a friend like Jack. Keep painting, Abby. Call me when you have something."

"I won't call, I know. I'll never paint what I really see. I've tried." Abby gave up at that moment. Here was someone who seemed to understand her work, but he found it wanting. What did the future hold now? When would she have another chance with another dealer? Never. She knew it. Paint for another ten years? She couldn't live that long. "I can't paint anymore; there's nothing at the center."

"Yet…." Holmes said. "There's nothing at the center, yet. Do you remember you said that you were playing at interesting things around the edges of your new works? That's what I saw in your paintings. All the interest was at the edge. At least it is coming onto the canvas! I'll bet that a year ago, it wasn't there at all. Keep painting. See if the edges move to the center."

Abby was visualizing what Holmes had described. "I don't see it. I feel like I just can't see it. I keep trying, but it won't come to the canvas," said Abby miserably.

"How many paintings have you done in the past two years?" asked Holmes.

"I don't know. Probably two hundred. Maybe more. Why? I told you what I do. I paint every day."

"Abby, slow down. Paint less. Lots less. Let the images come to you. Stop forcing yourself. Spend time waiting and looking. When you have the image in your mind, when you can recall it a hundred times, then paint it. Then it will be what you really 'see'."

"How can I do that? What will I do every day? I just paint," wailed Abby.

"Find things to look at," said Holmes. "Spend time looking. Find five new things every day and really look at them."

"I've seen everything that Prescott has to offer. There aren't five things left."

"You enjoy this, don't you?" asked Holmes. "You like always having an answer to every piece of advice. It's easy not to try,

Abby. Maybe I was wrong about you. You don't want to become anything other than what you are at this moment."

"And what's that?" asked Abby petulantly.

"A painter who can't even give her stuff away."

"You don't know what I've been through! You don't know how hard it is for me to be what I want to be!" When slighted, Abby could pull words instantly from her well of self-pity.

"I don't want to know," countered Holmes. "I'm not even sure I want to deal with someone without a known last name. I just want to know if you're ever going to be as good as you want to be, because if you are, I want to sell your paintings."

"That may never happen," Abby said dejectedly.

"Sometimes, Abby, what a painter needs is a change of scenery. Why don't you try that?"

"Where would I go? I don't have a lot of options with where I am now."

"Take a little road trip. Maybe your friend, Jack, would like to go. But don't go to paint. Go to look. When what you have seen is in your memory forever, then come home and paint what you see in front of you."

"A road trip to where?" asked Abby insistently.

"Where no one else goes. Go to Phoenix and out on US 60 to Springerville. There's not much for you to see along the way.

Keep going until you reach Magdalena. Spend time there. If it is warm enough, stay out under the stars. It is better in the spring, but it is a great place anytime. Then maybe go to Socorro and down to Elephant Butte Lake. See how the water looks with the sun from both the east and west. Look at the color."

"I've never heard of those places and I've lived in the Southwest all my life. Where are they?"

"In New Mexico. They are on the map."

"Where else should I go?"

"Go down the road a bit to the south. There's a town I want you to see, a town named after a TV show. Eat Mexican food there and look at the faces of everyone in the restaurant. See how ordinary and different and how noble they are. Remember them until those faces come into your dreams."

Abby felt spent and energized; abandoned and taken in. All these feelings swirled in her as Holmes spoke. She had wanted someone to take her seriously, to talk to her about painting. Now someone had. It was different than she had imagined. There were no fireworks, no banners in the air. There was no magic. Maybe that would come later.

The summer darkness was on Jerome. Abby needed to drive home. She didn't want Jack to worry about her, especially when she wanted a favor from him. She asked Holmes for the card she had previously returned to him. "No, I need two cards." Holmes gave them to her. One went into her bag and the other went into her secret place in her wallet next to the picture of her sister.

Holmes walked her to the truck where she gave him the painting she had sold him. "Will you come if I call? Will this number be good? What if I don't call for five years?" Abby was reluctant to go on to the next part of her life where failure was more probable than success.

"You'll find me, Abby, in a year or two or ten. I'll come see what you have painted for me and I will buy it. You have my word." Holmes shook her hand and walked into the night.

Abby and Holmes met in the last year of the Vietnam War. Though it was a time of deception and broken dreams, there were still men who kept their promises. Holmes DuMez kept his.

After that July day in Jerome, Abby forgot what Holmes had told her. She struggled, painting throughout the fall. In the winter, she gave up painting completely. Desire had fled. She filled her days helping Jack at the bar and slept without dreams. She didn't miss painting.

Although an Arizona winter is neither long nor deep, the first spring day surprised Abby. She startled Jack with a request to go to New Mexico. Traditionally, Jack kept his place closed on Easter weekend. He suggested that they go then.

Jack had been pleased to see Abby lose the agitation of painting. She was a much easier companion. On Easter weekend, the two of them took the truck to Magdalena. They picnicked in a meadow of lavender wildflowers. The next day, they drove down to the Butte reservoir to watch the sun go down. It was chilly, but Abby drank in the dying light. She was still there to see the sun's resurrection on the water the next morning. Wherever she saw people, she looked hard at their faces. It was then she remembered what Holmes had said: these people were ordinary and beautiful and noble.

Once home, Abby began dreaming. Desire was strongly with her awake and asleep. Somewhere around summer, she cleaned her brushes, bought canvas in Phoenix and began to paint. It was a slow process.

Unlike the previous years, there was balance in the division of painting and her life with Jack. He looked constantly for signs of the anger and frustration that had long accompanied her creative side. He found none. Nevertheless, he kept up his guard even a year later when they moved to Las Cruces, New Mexico. He would always keep his guard up. He knew better than any art dealer did, that painting and dark emotions were in Abby's soul, not on her canvas.

Four years after Abby the Painter met Holmes DuMez, she called him. He came to Las Cruces and bought not one, but several paintings, just as he said he would.

P.S. Lowe

Lead Us into Temptation

Abby considered herself a skillful liar. The fact that she had not needed to lie to Jack or to anyone else in over four years meant nothing. Abby had learned to lie to cover up the ugly truths of her life. She had lied about her father, her husband, and countless other truths big and small.

Never, however, had she lied about something that had not yet happened, about events whose outcome was unknown. She was going to do it now. She was going to do it because there was in her a fear and a desire so at odds with each other that she was unable to paint. She was unable to do much of anything. She just existed. She believed, irrationally, that there was an answer to her emotional confusion back in Arizona. She had to get there. Soon. She had to go alone.

When Abby went out of the house in the early morning to retrieve the newspaper, it was cold, and a breezy cold at that. Though the sun was up, her heart was freezing. She thought to herself that February would be warmer in Phoenix than here in Las Cruces. She could be there, in the warm, tomorrow. She needed to go. She would tell Jack this morning that she was going. It was important that she leave right away.

Jack was up making coffee when she went back into the little house that they both rented in Las Cruces, New Mexico. Abby couldn't remember the day of the week. Did Jack work today or tonight or was he home? She should be able to remember, but she could not. She would have to ask him.

"You're up already? What time is it? Are you working today?" Abby asked her questions moving next to Jack as he stood at the counter.

"Today is Thursday, Abby. I usually don't work on Thursdays. Today is the day of the week that we, you and I, do a little something together." Jack smiled as he spoke, but he was worried. Abby hadn't painted a thing since before Christmas. When she was painting, she frequently lost track of the time. For the past few weeks, however, she seemed to be completely desensitized to time and she wasn't painting.

Abby narrowed her eyes into a frown. "Are we doing something today? Is today the day for something I have forgotten? My days are running together again. I feel like it should be spring, but it is winter."

Jack reached out and put his arm around her. "We can do anything or nothing at all. What's the lady's pleasure?"

In the moment that Jack had finished asking the question, Abby was ready to spin her tale. She smiled and said, "I want to go to Phoenix for a couple of days. I want to see my pictures again. They haven't sold or we would have some money. I could drive up today and be back on Sunday."

"I can't leave the restaurant for the weekend. State wrestling championships are this weekend. Nancy is going up to Albuquerque to see her son compete. I can't just walk away.

Maybe next weekend," offered Jack.

"You don't have to go. I want to go alone. I just want to see my paintings again. Maybe, if I see them again, I can come and paint some more. I really have to go, Jack. Can I please have the truck for a couple of days? I'll be back on Sunday."

Jack looked intently at Abby. He could always tell when she was lying. It animated her in a visible way. She was more alive in her fantasies than in reality. When Abby told the truth, when she spoke about the significant events of her life, the truth broke her. Jack had seen it. He was never again interested in seeing Abby so broken and so desolate. Not ever again. There was something else, some other reason for going to Phoenix; it wasn't to see the paintings. Jack would bet money on that.

"What am I going to use if you take the truck?" asked Jack aloud.

Abby's brightness dimmed, slightly. She was thinking hard. She was trying to find a practical answer and it was beyond her. She could think of nothing.

Jack could see that Abby was, as usual, so intent on what she wanted that she hadn't planned ahead. He thought it would be nice, for once, if Abby would put off her own desire for his convenience. What a concept! He smiled at the mere thought. It wasn't in him to deny Abby anything. If she had been selfish at times, when she was able, she was generous and kind and gay. Jack loved her most when she was like that, even knowing it never lasted. Well, since moving to New Mexico, Abby had been good. She had settled down some. They had been happy

185

together in this little town. If she took off for a while, nothing between them would change.

"I guess that I can catch a couple of rides, Abby. If you want to go, go on. But come home by Sunday. I'll miss you if you're gone too long."

Abby grinned from ear to ear. She practically threw herself at Jack in warm thanks. She was clearly relieved that she was going to be able to have her own way. She was anxious to get started on her trip.

Over a hurried breakfast, Jack asked Abby about her plans. "Are you seeing your Mother? Are you staying with your sister? Maybe you should call and see if anyone is in town and if you have a place to stay."

Momentarily, Abby had forgotten that she had family in Phoenix. They hadn't entered into her plans. "Sure, I'll call them. Maybe Mom and Sarah and I can go for lunch or something. I'm sure I can stay with my sister." Abby had no intention of seeing any of her family. She thought that she had enough money, if she was careful, to stay in a motel. It was still tourist season. She might not have enough money. No matter. She would figure that out later.

Breakfast over, Abby quickly did the dishes. She went to the bedroom to pack a few things to take. She would only be gone a few days. She did not need much. She then showered and dressed. As she was pulling the old suitcase closed, Jack came into the room. He was taking out his wallet. He handed Abby two hundred dollars in cash. "Here, you might need to buy something."

Abby wanted to refuse the money. "I have money. I haven't spent any of the advance from my paintings." The advance from Holmes DuMez had amounted to little more than Jack was offering her.

"Take it anyway. Think of it as insurance in case something happens." Jack continued to hold out the money to her.

Abby took it because she knew she would need it. Money would buy her a place to stay and nice food. She folded the bills and put them into the inside compartment of her old wallet. Jack hadn't moved away. For a moment, Abby felt sad. She wished she were the kind of woman who could have been better to Jack, who could have equaled his goodness. Abby would never be that woman. The feeling passed.

"Thanks, Jack. I'm off and I will call when I get there. I'll tell you how my paintings look hanging against a wall." Abby was acting an unfelt enthusiasm.

"It's not the phone call I'll be expecting, Abby. I expect to see you on Sunday. I'll miss you if you don't come back, but I won't wait for you if you don't show up and I won't take you back either," said Jack.

Abby smiled. "Jack, why wouldn't I come back? I'm just going to see my paintings. I NEED to see them. That's all."

Jack wondered if Abby had even heard what he meant. He suspected that she did understand and was making light of it. If she came back, and if she was happy, he guessed that was as much as he could hope for.

"Come on. Hug me and I will walk out to the truck with you. You call. Drive safely, Abby. There's plenty of time to get there today. Stay on the Interstate. It's early yet and you have time. Your paintings won't disappear before you see them again."

Abby walked into Jack's arms. He always smelled like soap and sun to her. Jack kissed the top of her head and then brought his lips to her neck and kissed the white tender skin of her throat.

Jack carried her small suitcase out to the truck, securing it on the passenger side. He helped Abby into the cab. Their small talk was unmemorable. Jack's last memory of Abby was the lightness of her hand on his as she had left the house. He wondered when and if he would see her again. Four days was a long time.

Once on the highway, Abby started to come alive in a way she hadn't been for months. She headed west on Interstate 10. In an hour, she had passed Deming and was on the west slope of the Continental Divide. Now the landscape became more desolate. Although Jack had cautioned her to stay on the Interstate, she longed to be off of it. She had no desire to see scenery or people. Outside of Lordsburg, she went north on US 70. She would drive for at least a couple of hours on the empty stretch of two-lane road with nothing but a persistent headwind for company. Abby felt free.

Lead Us into Temptation

She rolled down the windows in Jack's truck and chain-smoked her way past Duncan and into Safford where she finally stopped for gas and something to eat. It was just past two o'clock in the afternoon. She should call to find out the gallery hours so that she could see her paintings. At the little restaurant, she asked for five dollars in change and the location of a pay phone. The phone was in the back, by the public restrooms. After paying her bill, she took out the dog-eared business card of the man who had purchased her paintings, Holmes DuMez. She placed her call to the number on the card.

A man answered, but it wasn't Holmes. He wasn't at the gallery, she was told. Did she want to leave her name and number, the polite voice asked? No. Yes. Abby did not know what she wanted. What if Holmes wasn't even in town? Then what? Where would she go and what would she do? Without Holmes, she might as well go back to New Mexico.

"I'm Abby. Holmes DuMez bought some of my paintings last year, and I just wanted to see them. I thought they might be hanging in the gallery," said Abby tentatively.

"Oh, I'm so glad to talk to you," said the stranger's voice. "I admire your work. It's so different. It's really original. But I'm sorry to tell you that your paintings aren't hanging at the gallery."

Abby was crushed. For weeks, she had imagined seeing them hanging in a real gallery. She could taste the greasy food she had eaten in the back of her throat. She felt nauseous.

"Hello? Hello? Are you still there?" asked the gallery voice.

It took energy for Abby to say, "Yes."

"Are you in town? Where can Holmes reach you?"

"I'm not in town, yet," said Abby slowly. "I was coming, but if my paintings aren't hanging, I don't have a reason to come, do I?"

"Well, I'm sure they are hanging, just not here. Didn't Holmes tell you? They have all been sold. All of them. It was just crazy the way they flew out of here. I can't believe you didn't know. I know Holmes will want to see you."

"Sold? My paintings have sold? All of them? Are you sure?" asked Abby.

"Oh yes. Where are you? How can Holmes call you back?" asked the voice.

"I'm at least four more hours away. I don't know where I am staying, but I could call back when I figure it out."

"Holmes will be back for the late Thursday hours. He will be here around 5:30 or so. Will you call back then? If you can't, call me in the morning, around ten when I'm alive and at work. I'll make sure that Holmes sees you tomorrow." There was genuine enthusiasm in the voice at the Scottsdale phone end.

"OK, I'll call back either tonight or tomorrow," said Abby and then hung up the phone since she was out of coins anyway.

Lead Us into Temptation

At the DuMez Gallery, John Vickers had barely hung up the phone when it rang again. It was the owner. John told his boss of the preceding call. To John, Holmes seemed anxious to get in touch with this Abby, but that proved to be impossible. The best that Holmes could do was to wait until she called again.

When she had cradled the phone, Abby did not know what to think. She was angry that there had been buyers for her work and she had not known it. She was angry that she hadn't received any money. The anger was overlaid with a private feeling of exhilaration. She ran to the truck to get back on the road. The miles between her and Scottsdale melted quickly.

Abby at least had something to occupy her time: cigarettes and driving. Holmes DuMez had neither comfort in nor purpose to his afternoon of waiting. He felt guilty that he had not called Abby when her paintings started to sell. He should have, but he wanted to be the person who had the upper hand in the relationship. It had been his experience that when dealing with an artist, it was always better to be the one in control. With Abby tucked away in New Mexico, Holmes thought that he had at least until the end of the season to tell her that "some" of her work had sold.

What a mistake. Now Abby knew that all of her work had sold, some fifteen paintings. She was the hit of the Scottsdale art season. Her pictures sold themselves. He hadn't kept one back for his own personal collection since he knew, if he was lucky, Abby's best work was yet to come. At five to fifteen thousand apiece, there was more than two hundred thousand dollars involved. His take would be thirty-five percent.

It was dark when Abby found her way to Scottsdale. Her first thought was to go to the DuMez Gallery and then, when she had given her dealer the hell that he deserved, then she would find a place to stay for the night. It wasn't much of a plan. How little a plan it was Abby found out when she drove Jack's pickup into the downtown area. Banners were everywhere proclaiming "Parada del Sol." The restaurants in the old part of town were open and filled with tourists decked in new western clothes. Abby could not find a place to park.

She felt both frustrated and dirty circling around. Finally, she decided to drive to the rear of the Kiva movie theater. There she found a space. The smell of cigarettes flowed out of the truck cab when she opened the door. She was hardly fresh, but she was going to find Mr. Holmes DuMez to tell him how very little she thought of him.

Walking west from the theater, she crossed Stetson Drive. Abby had no idea where to find the gallery. She thought she remembered it on Wells Fargo Street, but didn't find it. She walked into Porter's Western Wear shop off Brown Street and asked for the gallery. No one there had heard of it. They suggested she try across Scottsdale Road on Fifth Avenue. She continued her westward walk. It was dark now and the warmth of the winter day had passed.

Crossing Scottsdale Road and entering the Fifth Avenue area, the only lights on were those from the three or four galleries on both sides of the street. The DuMez Gallery was the last on the left and it was brightly lit. Some cars were parked in front. When Abby pushed open the door, she recognized Holmes even though his back was turned to her. He was speaking with an older couple. Just the sight of Holmes emboldened Abby. She walked behind the couple in the open gallery not even feigning interest in the paintings for sale. She turned so Holmes could see her. Thoughts of his own words, fled. He flushed; he stammered. Abby watched maliciously.

Holmes stared at his Italian loafers. After the briefest moment, he regained his composure and called to Abby. "What a wonderful surprise. Please," he said as he turned the couple around to face Abby, "I would like for you to meet the artist that you have so admired this season."

Pushing the couple forward to a mortified Abby, he said, "Abby, please meet Avram and Glendine Tomaschov. They have purchased two of your works. They are important collectors in the Valley."

Abby was frozen. She was supremely conscious of her appearance and the smell of old travel. Her mouth was too dry to form words. Holmes was delighted to have caught her off guard. Once he recovered Abby's gracelessness with his clients, he would again have the upper hand.

"Excuse me, Glendine. It is obvious that my star artist has just this minute arrived into Scottsdale and is somewhat unready to meet her most avid collectors. Perhaps you could return tomorrow and we could all lunch together? I will call you."

Without much additional effort, Holmes had skillfully drawn the couple to his orbit and escorted them out of the gallery, all the time speaking smoothly, comfortingly, and without meaning. Once the Tomaschovs had exited, Holmes turned his attention to Abby.

"I think I am glad to see you. You look ravaged. Do you ever dress better than a sidewalk painter?" Holmes asked. His coolness would be no match for Abby's righteous fury.

"You shit," she yelled. "You sold my paintings and I didn't even get a phone call? I haven't heard from you in three months. Three months and I haven't even heard a word! I haven't been able to paint a thing because you took away everything I had!" Abby's voice was continuing to increase. "How could you treat me like that? I lost my life to canvas for you. You come, you take my paintings for nothing and then you sell them and never tell me. I want to kill you. I have a gun and I want to kill you."

Abby was panting. She raged. She had forgotten why she had come. Once she knew her paintings were gone, to see them had become the misplaced focus of the trip.

Holmes attempted to reach out to Abby, but she pulled away. She leaned forward against a fragile table. Tears came like an August thunderstorm. She wailed. Holmes merely watched in silence. The minutes went by. Holmes went to his office and brought out tissues for her. She used up a handful and then a second handful. The tears stopped. Abby was spent. Her first words were "I hate you."

Holmes laughed. "I don't believe you came all the way from New Mexico to say that. But if you did, I am glad you got it said. You look terrible and you must have been in a fire the way that you smell. Where are you staying? Why don't you go to your hotel and rest? Later, we can go over to the Grapevine for a little late supper and some wine. Tomorrow we can talk about how rich you now are."

"Rich? I am rich? How much money do I have?" Abby turned to ask the question.

"About one hundred fifty thousand, maybe more. I don't know and I haven't collected all of it, but you'll have it by summer. You're rich."

Abby closed her eyes. The room tilted, and she felt herself moving through the air. She couldn't feel her feet or her legs. She needed to hold on and grabbed at nothing. Holmes caught her arm then they both collapsed on the floor. Holmes yelped in pain as Abby feel on top of him. Energy surged through Abby. She hurriedly pushed herself off of Holmes and the floor. She jerked her dealer upright, causing him even more pain.

"God, I'm so sorry. I forgot about your legs and all, and I didn't know I was going to fall, and I'm sorry, I'm sorry." Abby stopped her rushed speech when her tears started anew.

"Abby," Holmes said, "Abby stop crying. Shape up. Come back to the office and let's sit down. I'm exhausted just watching you." Meekly she followed him back to the office.

Once in his office, Holmes sat down in his oversized chair. Abby plopped on the nearest seat. "Oh no," said Holmes, "You, being the least injured, get the drinks. There's ice in the refrigerator.

Get two cups from the file drawer. Then come over and reach the bottom drawer of my desk. There's a bottle of scotch."

Abby did as she was told. She had many hours of tending bar for Jack. She poured expertly and then sat down again. Holmes downed his scotch before the ice had cooled it. He re-poured.

"Why didn't you tell me you were coming, Abby?"

"Why didn't you tell me that you had sold my paintings?" Abby asked in reply.

"I would have as soon as the season was over. I'm not trying to cheat you, but this is my work and my risk. I have to have a way to deal with my clients without any crazy artists around. You made a real impression on the Tomaschovs. I bet they are happy to have spent about thirty-five grand on the work of a lunatic. You owe me for that and you are going to pay up. Lunch is on you at the El Chorro on Saturday."

"I'm not paying. You have all of my money. I'm not a lunatic either. You gave me a lousy three hundred dollars and made a fortune off of me!"

"And I could have lost the three hundred. Look, we have a contract. You'll get your money. I don't tell you how to paint. I waited for years for you to call me. I kept my promises to you. If you can't trust me, Abby, you won't be able to trust anyone else either. I'm the real thing. I believed in you. We are both winners."

When Holmes turned his head from her, Abby could see his neck and collarbone through his unbuttoned shirt collar. She wanted to put the fingers of her right hand lightly on that space. She remembered why she had come. She wanted just to be able to touch that skin. She had held out for years to see him again. She hadn't thought of anything but Holmes since he had taken her paintings away. Now everything was confused. Her good fortune and Holmes' success had robbed her of fulfilling her one desire.

"I'm tired. I'm dirty," Abby said as an announcement. This was no news to Holmes.

"Where are you staying? Are you staying with your sister or in a hotel?"

"I didn't make plans. I just came. I made up my mind to come today and I did," said Abby softly.

Holmes mistook Abby's tone for grief over the sold paintings. Artists often reacted badly when their works were irrevocably gone. He had experience with this. "Perhaps I can call one or two people who bought your works and you can see them. How long will you be here? Is Jack with you?"

"I didn't come for the paintings. I came alone. I don't really want to see them again. I just thought for a minute that I did. But I don't. They are gone and I can see that."

These statements worried Holmes. Abby's fury had turned to despondency. He feared for her if she was alone. "Hey, let me call Sarah. What's her number? Or, let's find you a place to stay, maybe up at the Mountain Shadows. You can clean up and we can go eat a late dinner."

"Don't call my sister." Abby wasn't looking up from her lap.

"I'll call the hotel." Holmes retrieved the phone book from his desk and found the number. In a minute, he had made the reservation.

"Well, why don't you drive on up there? Do you remember where it is? It's on Lincoln Drive. Then, I'll come get you in about an hour and we'll eat. We'll celebrate your triumph. How about it Abby? Can you do that?"

"Yes," said Abby smiling wanly. "I'll go. You will come, won't you? I just don't want to be alone in a room right now."

"Sure, I'll be there by nine-fifteen. In the lobby." Holmes was grinning. "Dinner will be on me."

Abby put her glass on the edge of the desk and stood up. She felt that the life she had come into the room with was now dancing outside of her, around her, but not in her. Holmes stood up to accompany her to the door. As he walked to her, she reached out her right hand. She locked her eyes on his and willed him to her. She touched his neck and let her fingers slide beneath his collar, stopping when she reached his smooth skin. "Oh," she exhaled. She removed her hand and said, "I'll see you in an hour. I can walk to the truck. You surprised me, that's all."

She was gone.

Abby may have thought she was surprised, but it was Holmes who was swept away. In one touch, Abby had seared him. He was struck by the pain that her soft touch had left. It was a pain that moved to his chest and then to his head. He missed her for years in the sixty seconds she had been gone.

Hurriedly, he began closing up the gallery. First, he switched off the main lights. He picked up his jacket and briefcase from the office and then set the alarm. He walked out the front door, locking it securely behind him. An hour was a very long time, he thought, as he walked the short block to his car.

When he arrived at the hotel, Abby was just checking in. She was searching for cash in her jumbled purse. He walked to the desk. The night auditor immediately turned his attention to the Scottsdale dealer. "I hope you are taking care of my number one artist. She's just come from her home in the country. We're to have a late dinner."

"Certainly," said the auditor to Holmes. To Abby he said, "You can pay when you check out. How long will your stay be?"

Abby turned to Holmes in question. "Three nights. She will be leaving on Sunday," said Holmes.

Holmes arranged to wait for Abby in the bar. It took Abby less than thirty minutes to shower and change. When she appeared in the bar, her dark hair was damp and she had no make up on. Still, she looked revived. Holmes rose from the table when she appeared. He had ordered two shrimp cocktails and a drink for himself. Abby wanted a soda. She began to eat immediately, polishing off her last shrimp before her drink arrived. Holmes pushed his untouched shrimp to her. Without stopping, she began to eat again, head down until all that remained were six tails. She drank her soda. Holmes watched in amazement.

"Are you still hungry?" asked Holmes. "Are you ready for dinner or just do another round of appetizers?"

"Yes, I'm hungry. I feel like I haven't eaten for months. I want to eat. I need to eat." She seemed oblivious to the fact that she had just eaten.

"Let's go into the dining room. No sense in being hungry."

"Can we just eat here? I don't want to move. I just want to eat."

"Sure, I'm sure that's great. Not many people here." Holmes signaled for the waiter to bring menus.

Abby couldn't decide what to eat. She wanted chicken; she wanted salad; she wanted steak. Holmes jokingly suggested that she order all three. "OK. OK. I want all three," said Abby agreeably.

For the next hour, Abby did nothing but eat. She made no effort at conversation. Holmes got no answers to any questions. He finally gave up and simply watched Abby eat.

When she was finished, Holmes asked her if she would like dessert. "Maybe later," she said. "I'd like some coffee and then maybe some chocolate cake. Is that all right?"

"Sure," said Holmes. "I don't know where you put all that food. Do you always eat like that?"

Abby blushed. "I'm a pig. A little pig. I was so empty. Do you know what that is like to be so empty? I have been empty for months and nothing fills me up. I'm hungry and hungrier and nothing fills me up."

"Are you sick? Should you see a doctor?" Holmes was a little afraid for her.

"No. I am empty. I gave everything to painting. Then you took away all of my paintings and you left me with nothing but the emptiness of me. I have been hungry ever since. I came here for you to fill me up again. You have to feed me."

"It's on to the chocolate cake," said Holmes brightly. Abby reached out and caught his hand.

"That's not enough. I need more than food. I need you to tell me what to do next. Tell me what to paint or tell me not to paint. Send me to Nebraska or Timbuktu. But help me because I can't stand being this empty anymore."

Abby's clear desperation discomfited Holmes but he knew better than to show it. "You have had some big shocks, good shocks today. You will feel differently tomorrow or the next day. Why don't you order something from room service and go get some sleep? Call me tomorrow at the gallery. Don't worry; I have seen lots of artists feel grief over a big sale. The feeling passes. You'll get some new ideas and you'll paint and forget the grief. Really. It will happen that way."

"How many artists have you found on the street on a hot summer day? How many artists have you sent to see the sunrise in Magdalena? How many have slaved for years with just one thought: to get your attention? You, the great art dealer? How many have you left with nothing? Are there more like me? Tell me that!" said Abby fiercely.

Abby let go of his hand. "No," thought Holmes, "None like you. None with your talent. None with your vision. None with your intensity." He asked Abby, "What do you want from me? I am just an art dealer. Just a crippled art dealer."

"You. I want you. I came here for you. For your attention. For your approval."

"You've got buyers. That's a whole lot better."

"Not to me it isn't. I didn't paint for them. I painted for you. There was never a day that I didn't imagine you looking at my work. Helping, criticizing, suggesting. You have been half of me. Now, I've come through for you. You have to come through for me."

"I can't do more than I am doing right now. I can sell you and represent you and make you rich. That's it. You have my approval. I believed in you and I believe in you. What else is there?"

"Let me touch you. Hold me. Tell me stories. Fill me up with you. I have wanted you for such a long time. How can I have all these feelings for you and you feel nothing for me? How can it be that way?"

"What about Jack? What about your husband?"

"I'm not married to Jack. And if I was, this is what I need. Jack will never be what you are to me. He knows it; he has always known it. I'm just asking for a little time."

"You use Jack's name."

"Only when I have to. And I do it because he lets me."

"Who are you Abby?"

"I'm your creation. I was born somebody who just existed until you found me and put the pieces into place and ideas in my head."

"I don't want that responsibility."

"I don't want to be your creation either. But Holmes DuMez, that's what happened and you are no less responsible than I am. You tempted me; you seduced me into your world of art and desire. So, here we are."

"Where's here?" thought Holmes. If there had been any seduction, it was Abby who was the temptress. He had thought of her often enough. Tonight, just a few hours ago, he had rushed to be with her. No woman had captivated him so completely since Iso had died. What would his old mentor think of this situation? She would probably say, "Boy, don't deny luck. Play your cards."

"Abby, I'm going to sit here and have another drink. I'll order you some room service. If I deliver it, then you will know something more about me. If you have to tip a stranger, then call me at the gallery tomorrow."

Abby bit her lip. She reached out and touched his cheek. Then she got up and left the table.

Room service arrived an hour later. Holmes delivered a small bottle of liquor and two glasses. Abby hadn't changed from her street clothes. When Holmes started to speak, Abby put her fingers over his lips. "I don't need to hear your voice." She led him to the chair. Bending over, she unbuttoned his shirt to his waist. She caressed his chest with her hands. She wanted to taste him. She licked him. She breathed the ripening smell of his need.

She wanted more, much more. She stood in front of him and made him look up to her. "I don't want to talk to you and I don't really want you to talk to me. I cannot undress you while you sit and I am afraid to hurt your leg. Don't make this hard for me. Just meet me on that bed."

Abby moved to the bed and threw back the spread. She pulled back the sheet and blanket, accessibly. Then she began unbuttoning her blouse. Holmes did not move from the chair. He simply watched her undress from behind. Abby shed her clothes like a snake's winter skin and left them in a heap on the floor. Then she crawled into the large bed, covered herself and stared at the unmoved Holmes.

"Are you coming?" she asked.

"Does that mean I can speak, now? This isn't exactly the most romantic encounter I have ever had," said Holmes dryly.

"This isn't about romance; it's about being hungry," replied Abby quite simply.

Lead Us into Temptation

"What am I, dinner?"

"I've had dinner."

For a moment, Holmes thought of leaving. A weaker man would have walked away. Holmes, however, knew exactly what Abby meant when she said she was hungry. He had been hungry for years until Iso came along and fed him at her great table of life. She had shown him the world and then, in the end, given it to him. For Iso he had walked again; learned the arts of dealing; become the perfect host; regained his flesh in bed. Even after his great mentor's death, Holmes had never been hungry again. Could he do the same for Abby? He doubted it. Yet he could give her something more than she knew to take from him.

Carefully he removed his shirt and folded it on the chair. Without getting up, he loosed his belt and unzipped his smooth wool slacks. He bent over and untied his shoes, placing them neatly beside the chair. He took off his socks before he stood up and removed his last two articles of clothing. If he felt self-conscious about his damaged legs, he did not show it. He walked to Abby's side of the bed and motioned her to move over. When he slid in beside her, he rolled her to her side, facing away, and pressed his full body into her back. With his left hand, he found her breast and cupped it. He brought his tongue to her neck and began to lick it moving upwards to her ear. Abby shifted and tried to turn, but he held her fast.

He rotated his thumb around her nipple until it was stiff. Holmes then pulled her beneath him swiftly pinning her wrists above her head. His mouth was on hers and his tongue had penetrated her deeply. The harder he pushed, the more Abby relaxed. He let go of her hands and she did not move them. He moved his mouth to her breasts, licking, nipping gently and sucking. Abby moved to his rhythm. His hand slipped between her legs. He teased and probed her softest flesh until his fingers were wet. Then he entered her bringing the full weight of his body on her and into her in one move. He controlled both his movement and hers, a wonderful feeling.

They stayed locked and moving until he could feel her orgasm. The tension that had held her rigid left her in waves. Good, Holmes thought. He left her and Abby made no response. It wasn't a gentle movement when he pushed her to her side so that he could enter her again from behind without putting weight on his bad leg. His rigidity made easy contact within her wet softness. It took less than a minute for him to come. He got up and made his way to the bathroom. Abby neither turned nor spoke.

After he had washed himself, he came out and put on his briefs and slacks. He went to the table, put ice in two small glasses and filled one; half-filled the other. He walked to the bed and sat down. "Have a drink." Abby sat up, pulling the sheet under her arms. She took the glass and sipped the heavy brown liquid. Then she took a gulp. It burned all the way down. Her feet tingled.

"What is it?" Abby asked.

"Tia Maria," Holmes answered. "It ought to kill the last of your hunger except for sleep."

"I didn't get to eat," fretted Abby.

"No, but you got filled up anyway," said Holmes.

"And you?" Abby asked. "And you?" she repeated.

"Me too." Holmes reached out to feel Abby's hair and then the curve of her throat. When his hand fell away, they finished the last of the drink. The alcohol hit Abby hard. When she handed her glass to Holmes, she slid down in the bed. Holmes sat the glasses on the table returning to cover her up.

"Lunch tomorrow. You're buying the Tomaschovs some lunch. I'll pick you up about 11:15. Then on Saturday, I'm going to tell a few people to come to the gallery to meet you."

"OK," was Abby's tired reply.

Holmes dressed himself and went out into the February night, pleased that he had not yet been bested by his ticket to fortune and sorry that he had no other emotion for the night.

For the next two days, Abby did whatever she was told. The days belonged to Holmes, but the nights belonged to her. Her desire for sex, like her need for food, was raw. On Saturday night, Holmes stayed until Sunday morning. He ordered room service breakfast. When it came, he decided that there was no delaying a real conversation with Abby.

"Abby, I need you to paint this spring and summer. But not a lot. I don't want a hundred of your pictures for next season.

Anything more than five would be foolish. So go back to New Mexico and paint."

"I'm not going. I've decided to stay here. I'm calling Sarah to ask if I can stay with her until I find a place to live and paint," said Abby.

"What about Jack?" asked Holmes dryly.

"What about him? He has his bar and his friends. He can go anywhere he wants. What about us?" Abby was becoming surly.

Holmes put down his coffee and concentrated energy on his words, which were accurate and exacting. "There is no 'us.' I'm your dealer and you are a painter. We inhabit different worlds. We will always inhabit different worlds. You don't have an ounce of the class or discipline needed for my world. If you had it, you couldn't paint. If you can't paint, I don't think you have a worth. I think painting is your only worth."

"What about the last three days? I came here to see you, to be with you. I don't know if I can paint without you. How can you say these things? I love you and I thought you loved me, too, even if only a little. I can't go back. There's nothing left of me there." The tears in Abby's eyes flowed down her face.

"Then, maybe it's time for a change of scenery. Get out the map and find a new place to go. When you find where you want to be, get out your paints and stay awhile."

"I love you. Doesn't that mean anything?"

"It might if it was true, but it's not true. You came here because you were hungry for someone to tell you that you are an artist. I know that look. I know many painters; lots of artists. They all get hungry. It's my job to feed them. I fed you well. I gave you everything I had to give you. Today, I'm giving you the rest. I have your money."

"I don't want it. I don't even want to live."

"I know it. That's just now. In an hour or two, when you are down the road, when you are going home to Jack, life will seem sweet because you will have the one thing, the only thing that validates your worth: money. You have lots of money. You will never be poor as long as you paint and I sell."

"How can I go back to Jack? What can I tell him? I can't tell him what I've been doing, can I? He'll never forgive me."

"Don't tell him. Give him the money. Tell him you went to dinner. Tell him you met your buyers. I know you are capable of secrets, Abby."

"I hate you!" repeated Abby with enthusiasm but without conviction.

"A minute ago you loved me."

"I do both!"

"Good. Glad to hear it. If you love me and you hate me, I must be a very great dealer. And, I am yours."

Abby was beat. She could never win verbal fights. Nothing came from her head; only from her heart. Being beaten, she was ready to leave. She had to leave. She couldn't wait to be gone. There was nothing here for her at all and never had been in this Valley.

"Give me my money," said Abby as she stood up from the table. She held out her hand as if piles of gold or precious stones would fall into it. Holmes walked over to the desk where he had placed his handsome leather case. He withdrew a single envelope, marked with her name. He handed it to her.

Abby tore it open. The cashier's check had six digits. She was thrilled. Holmes was right. This was better than sex and meant more than Holmes ever would to her. "Oh God!" Tears started all over again.

Holmes picked up his jacket and case. He was ready to leave. "Call me when you have something to show me. Let me know where you go. You have money. The world's a big place. Go see some of it."

Abby heard him but could not stop staring at the check. When he got to the door, she ran to say something, but couldn't think of what to say. She started to say "thank you," but decided she wouldn't give him that satisfaction. She simply said, "Be careful of that leg of yours. You might need to rest it for a while."

"I'll be in good enough shape the next time I see you Abby," said Holmes with a smile. He left.

It took Abby less than thirty minutes to pull herself and her things together; pay her bill, and get into the truck. Scottsdale was a distant memory. She fairly flew on the back roads to New Mexico. She couldn't wait to show Jack the check. It was Sunday. He would be waiting for her.

We Bear the Strain of Earthly Care

No matter what the sign said out front, no matter the town, no matter the year, any bar or restaurant that Jack Ellis ran was known locally as "Jack's Place." It had been that way for forty years. Today was the fourth Sunday he had opened for coffee in his new location on 7th Avenue and Thomas in Phoenix. Word had gotten around and he had more customers than he could comfortably handle alone. New faces that asked for cappuccino, latte, espresso or flavored creams were politely, but firmly, turned away. As a concession to his own changed tastes, he did serve decaf.

In the past month, Jack saw bar customers from his last stand in Phoenix a decade ago and some from much father back. They were older, just like Jack, but the patterns and needs of most people's lives never really changed. That's why Jack could always make money with ordinary people. Ordinary people needed to eat and drink; to have a place to talk with others of their kind. It had to be a clean place, an affordable place. Not much more was required. Long ago Jack had learned to keep the songs on the jukebox mellow and old; the ashtrays empty; the servers mature; the bouncer young; and never to allow any sort of gaming. No pool, no cards.

This Sunday morning, Gary Mitchell, house painter extraordinaire, was sitting with his wife. He was on his fifth cigarette and third cup of black coffee. It was barely eight in the morning. Jack had known Gary for decades. They had occasionally hunted pig and dove together. However, Gary surprised him by still being alive. Gary's sobriety had been elusive. Jack guessed that Gary's second wife had something to do with his longevity. She was a nice woman from all Jack could tell. When the crowd had thinned out, Jack took his own mug to their table to talk for a few minutes before closing.

"Gary, you're a son of a gun. You hardly drink my beer anymore, and then come in on Sunday morning and drink five dollars' worth of coffee for a buck."

Gary laughed and his wife smiled politely. "I'm sort of changing my life here. Rita has got me thinking of retiring. She wants me around the house; maybe do a little traveling before I mosey off. Problem is, I got more work than I can do. I want to do it, but just don't have enough hours."

"So, hire some help," said Jack, just making conversation.

"Tried that. Can't find anyone who wants to work regular. Can't find anyone who takes pride in doing a good job. I've got a reputation. If someone wants cheap, like these developers, they hire damn illegals. If they want a good job, they hire me. They pay me good, too." Gary shook his head.

"Well, someone will turn up. Somebody will want to work with you, Gary."

"I need someone this week. I'm starting on a doctor's house and it's just too big a job for me. I need someone quick." Gary leaned forward into Jack. "Do you know a fellow who wants work? Someone I can count on?"

"Nope. Put your card up by the door. Someone just might come in and see it," suggested Jack.

"Thanks, I will. If someone does come in looking for work, call me. I got more than one problem, too, and I might as well tell you. Anybody I get gotta be able to drive the truck. I took a fall just a month ago. Insurance doctor won't let me drive because I got a concussion. It's tough being self-employed. So I got real needs."

Rita had been watching her husband. When he had said his last bit, her face had taken on anxiety. Jack could see that she was worried probably more about Gary's health than his ability to hire help.

"If I hear, I'll call. Now, it's closing time. I must scoot. My nephew's wife just had twins. I promised my mother I would take her out to North Scottsdale to see them at the hospital. Take care and come in again soon. I'm doing chow at lunchtime. Get a sandwich when you're downtown." Jack got up and started clearing tables. After Gary and Rita walked out, Jack locked the door behind them.

Weekdays, Jack opened up around eleven. Lunch lasted until three. After that, it was just beer and booze. Every Monday so far, the Army and Air Force recruiters from just down the street came in for a cold sandwich and soda. Although he had never served time himself, Jack was respectful to the military young men. He liked them. They were different from the similar-aged men whom he had served during the Vietnam War days.

As usual, the recruiters were in on Monday. They teased Jack about serving burgers. "I'll fry them if you want to pull KP and clean out the grease traps." There was a chorus of adamant "no way" in reply.

Today's crowd was adequate, but there was no noontime rush. It was the last Monday of the month. People were making do until payday, especially the State workers. Between three and four, the laborers who had finished for the day came in for some beer. The hard liquor crowd would be in after six. Jack had noticed that he had two tiers of customers, one Anglo and one Hispanic. The Anglos were mostly older and hanging on to what they had. His Hispanic patrons were on their way up to something better. They spoke their cradle tongue among themselves, but English to everyone else. Here they met their lawyers and accountants. It was a good thing to watch. Sometimes, when he looked out from behind his bar, Jack thought he was in Mexico again.

Tuesday didn't look much different. A young Indian came in about four and sat alone. He ordered a beer but didn't drink it. Although he didn't look twenty-one, Jack was sure he was older than he looked. Jack had spent enough time close to the Navajo nation to know that most Navajos didn't much like the taste of beer. Need more than pleasure drove them to drink. He offered the boy a soda. "Got any grape?" asked the boy.

"I've got cherry cola. Close as I can come," answered Jack.

"OK," said the boy pushing away his glass of draft. Jack emptied it into the sink. "You don't pay for what you don't drink. The soda's a dollar."

Serving the boy and making a little conversation, Jack asked, "Are you new down to Phoenix?"

"I went to high school here. I've been back up in Teec Nos Pos for a couple of years. Not much happening there. Decided to come here to look for work. I got a wife and little girl up north. It would be better for them if I was working."

"What are you doing?"

"Nothing."

"What do you know how to do?"

"Run sheep. Do a little silver and bead work. Pick corn."

"Can you drive a truck?"

"Don't have a license. Don't have a car," answered the Indian solemnly.

"But do you know how to drive?"

"Yeah, sure."

Jack was thinking that he might have found someone to help Gary. Over the years, Jack had matched up people in need. He never knew much if things worked out. He guessed that sometimes they did.

"I know a house painter who needs help. Probably pays cash. Needs someone who can drive his truck, too. You want to call him?"

"Yeah. Can I use your phone? There's no phone down at the Bethel Mission."

"Is that where you are living?"

"For a while. I can stay about a week more, and then I gotta move out."

Jack walked over the wall and removed Gary's card. He took a quarter from the tip jar and handed the boy the card and coin.

The Indian walked over to the phone and called. He hung up the phone. "No answer. I have to leave if I want to eat and have a bed tonight."

"Do you want me to call later?" asked Jack.

"Yeah."

"I'll tell him you'll be here in the morning if he hasn't already found someone. What's your name?"

"Benny. Benny Lovato."

"You going to show up tomorrow, Benny Lovato? I don't like to make promises that other people don't keep."

"Yeah, I'll be here."

Several hours later, Jack rang Gary. He convinced a reluctant Gary that Benny Lovato would be of some use. "Come around noon tomorrow. I'm sure he'll be here. You can buy him some lunch. He's not much of a talker. It's their way, you know."

"I need to be working on the doctor's house tomorrow. That's way out north," said Gary.

"Go out early. Do enough to show you have been there. Then come back to town. Thought you needed help."

"I do. I don't know. Maybe I'll be there later. Thanks."

By noon on Wednesday, neither Benny nor Gary had shown up. Lunch was brisk and Jack only gave the missed appointment passing thought. Then Gary showed up asking for Benny. Jack had to admit Benny was a no-show. "But you're here, so lunch is on me. Sorry that it didn't work out. Where's Rita?"

"Home."

"Who drove you in?"

"You ask a lot of questions, Jack," answered Gary.

Gary sat at the bar, ate his lunch and drank his beer in glum silence. When he had finished, Benny walked in the door. Gary recognized him quickly. His long hair was neatly tied in a pony-tail. He had on painter whites and carried a brown sack. Gary thought "There's no sense in asking why he is late. He won't answer. Won't shake hands either. What am I thinking? He'll be more trouble than he is worth."

Jack barely noticed the two men meet. When he saw them together, they were an odd couple. However, they left together, which Jack took as a good sign.

On Friday night, Gary and Rita came into the bar after dinner. Jack made it a point to sit with them. "Where's your hired help? I know he doesn't drink, so I bought a six-pack of grape soda. It's all his."

"He went home," said Gary.

Rita rolled her eyes. "He says he's coming back."

"Yeah, he will. Went to get his wife and kid. Hitched a ride with some cousin. Bringing everyone back with him on Sunday." Gary sounded optimistic.

Though Jack had some personal doubts about the truth of that, he wanted Gary to keep believing. "So he must be working out. Can he paint?"

"Shit no. Didn't know anything. Thought we were going to paint a six thousand square foot house with brushes. Christ. I tell you this. He's good on a ladder. Doesn't blink spraying over his head from the top step of a fourteen-footer. I can't do that anymore." Gary stubbed out his cigarette. Then he lit one for Rita.

"You think he'll be back, then," said Jack.

"I hope so Jack. I gave him a couple hundred cash money. But, just in case, I had him doing all the high ceilings for two long days."

Gary showed up to Jack's on the following Monday morning. He hung around for a couple of hours, but there was no Benny. Gary left in a bad mood.

Late in the early evening, Benny walked in with an obviously pregnant wife and toddler girl.

The family clung to the door while Benny came to talk to Jack. "I need to talk to Gary. I need to use your phone."

"It's a pay phone, Benny. Go ahead. But unless you're going to tell him that you're going to work, it's a call I wouldn't make. He was here this morning, looking for you. He might have found someone else to work for him. That's free advice," said Jack.

"Had to get my family," said Benny. "Had to find a place to live."

"I can see you've got them. I guess if you did all that in three days, you've done pretty good. Give Gary a call."

Jack guessed that Benny and Gary connected, although he didn't see the family leave. It was a hot April night before Easter when he saw them again. Saturday night, Benny, his wife and the little girl entered the bar and took a table in the back. Although Jack didn't like having children in the place, he found the grape soda and sent three cans and iced glasses with Muriel to their table.

Muriel had already cleared two tables and served three more when Gary and Rita came in, pulled extra chairs, and sat down with the Lovato mini-tribe. Rita took the little girl onto her lap. Jack came from behind the bar up to their table. "I feel like there's a party going on at my own place and I don't even know why," said Jack.

Gary stood up to shake Jack's hand. "You just bring me a whiskey and Rita a beer. Bring yourself something, too. Then we've got something to show you."

Jack made the order himself and returned to the table. After setting the drinks down, Gary handed him a business card. Even if the lighting had been better, Jack was unable to read the blue script on the light blue card. He pulled his reading glasses from his pocket. It read "Mitchell Painting" in large print in the center of the card. To the left, in smaller print, was Gary's name and phone number. To the right in the same small print it said "Benny Lovato" with a cellular phone number.

Gary was clearly pleased with himself. "I got Benny to carry the phone for me. Can't stand the damn thing. They don't have a permanent address yet and no phone. It works out for us both. What do you think?"

"I think you ought to change your name to 'Lucky,'" said Jack. "I suppose that since I was the one who brought you two together, then I ought to do the toast."

Rita helped the little girl raise her grape soda can along with everyone else. "Here's to good business and a good future for the best house painters in Phoenix," said Jack. It was a funny, proud moment for all of them.

Late that night, when Jack was on his way home, he thought about Gary and Benny. They were probably good for each other. Benny would end up doing most of the work, and, no doubt, have to listen to Gary's favorite country music. But Gary would be fair. He would also overlook the fact that Benny wouldn't show up for work whenever his family needed him. "Whatever happens," thought Jack, "there was a lot of hope and innocence at the start. It's something you didn't see a lot of these days."

When Jack got home, he decided not to eat. He didn't want to do a glucose measurement. Besides, the six o'clock coffee call at the bar was less than five hours away. He went to bed. His last thoughts before sleep were of his long dead father. "I would have missed a lot if I had just stayed home and farmed. I've had the best and the worst of the world at my place. Every day is different. You never know what or who is going to walk through the door. Sometimes, if you were lucky, you could lend someone a hand."

P.S. Lowe

I Will Know Him by the Mark

J ack's hand touched Reid's naked shoulder. Her eyes opened. The light from her dream contrasted sharply with the dark of the room. She had no idea of the time. At least she knew where she was. Here in her own bed. She closed her eyes.

"Reid," Jack said softly.

"I hear you. I am just not opening my eyes," said Reid.

"I need to go. I didn't want to wake you, but I didn't want you to find me gone and feel uncomfortable."

"OK. That's nice of you. Could you look at your watch and tell me the time? There's no clock in here."

"It's nine."

"OK," said Reid again. Still she did not open her eyes.

Jack arose from the wide bed. As he dressed, he watched Reid. She was the most unusual woman he had ever known. She didn't talk much, yet he always felt that he had just had a conversation with her. They had been in bed since about three this afternoon. Very few words had passed between them, but he felt he knew Reid well.

He didn't want to leave now, but he had to go back to his bar to make sure that Saturday night ended peacefully. He wanted Reid to go, too. He wanted her company whether she was silent or not. Jack leaned over the bed. "Come with me downtown, Reid."

She opened her eyes and smiled at him. "No. I am happy just here. Call me. The phone is by the bed." She held out her hand to him and he took it in both of his.

"What about coffee tomorrow? You could come anytime before ten."

"Nope. What about breakfast after you close up? I have a mind for waffles and a little company then," said Reid.

"Will you have the Sunday paper?"

"I will have the paper, but the crossword will already be done."

"Sounds like a plan, Reid. Can I bring something over?"

"No." Reid shut her eyes again.

"I'll let myself out and lock the door." Jack kissed her hands. Reid withdrew them and smiled.

Jack left the house. August is a special kind of hot, even in Phoenix. The freshness of the shower he had taken while Reid slept dissipated as soon as he opened the door to his truck and the heat rolled out. He got in, turned over the engine and cranked up the AC. It would be cool about the time he got to the bar. He wished he had a long way to go, but he didn't. He wanted to spend time thinking about Reid. Next to being with her, it was his sole pleasure in life. At sixty, he was deeply, completely, in love with Reid Markham. How that fact surprised and exhilarated him! What a wondrous, precious little fact that nobody else in world would care about but him.

He thought briefly about the first time he had seen Reid. She was hunched over a set of books in the office of his nephew's wife. As he had waited for his order of shirts to be brought from the back, he had watched her slim hands turn the pages of a ledger. He liked the way she concentrated on her work. That was a year ago. Then in May, when he had gone to NewMexTexCo to pick up uniforms for the Little League team he sponsored, she had been alone in the office and had waited on him.

At the time, she had been upset and he had tried to cheer her up. They were talking across the high counter, one on each side, just like at the bar where he had spent his life listening to all manner of human woe and some happiness, too. Reid had wanted to become office manager for the little firm. Jack's niece-in-law, Erin Ellis, wouldn't say 'yes' and wouldn't say 'no' to the promotion. Somehow they got from that subject to lunch. At lunch, Jack had invited Reid to come to his bar on Friday night. Come she did with her widowed old neighbor, Mrs. Gilberg, in tow. What a sight they were; what a time the three of them had.

Jack was already at the bar. He lamented the fact that there wasn't enough time to have both the experience and the joy of the memory. He would call Reid as soon as he could.

Once Jack had left Reid's house, she allowed herself to waken fully. She felt deeply contented. She got up and dressed, walking into her front room to put on one or two of her CDs from her extensive collection. Tomorrow was Sunday. She would make her special batter for waffles tonight and set the table as well. That way she could go to early church and be ready for Jack by ten.

She turned on the lights, selected a CD of gospel music and a one of more modern instrumentals. She went to the kitchen and set to work. As she got out the ingredients, the rich harmony of a gospel quartet began to swim in her head. Soon she was singing along in her harmonic alto voice. "I will know my Savior by the mark where the nails have been, by the sign upon His precious skin." She loved gospel music, so different from the Lutheran music she had heard growing up.

Jack liked to hear her sing. Sometimes he asked her to sing. No one had ever done that before. Then, Jack was a first for Reid in many respects. For the twenty plus years she had lived in Phoenix, she had lived in the same house, had the same neighbors, gone to the same church. She had dated, but nothing had ever come of it. She had a few friends, worked, and spent the rest of her time gardening, cooking or listening to music. She had season tickets to nearly every music event in town.

Now there was Jack. Reid didn't know what to think about that. She liked his company. He was her boss's uncle, sort of. She had met him through work on the day she had asked for a promotion to office manager. It had been a reckless day. When Jack had asked her to come to his bar, unthinkingly she had agreed. Then she had to talk her neighbor, Mrs. Gilberg, into going with her! After that, Jack had just sort of slipped into her life. Although he worked at night, he seemed to have time to spend with her, but never pushed. He was comfortable; he was easy. Reid often found herself telling him things she had kept long years to herself.

With Jack, conversation was reciprocal. He talked about himself. That's why she knew that he had never married. He had told her about all the years with Abby, about his mother and his sister, too. He talked; all she had to do was listen. That was nice. The batter was done and Reid was beginning to clean up when the phone rang. It was Jack.

"Are you still in bed?" Jack asked.

"Nope, I'm making batter and fruit compote. If you want to eat tomorrow, I thought I would get started."

"Since you are probably dressed, why don't you come and keep me company? After I close, I'll take you for a ride."

"No. I'm going to early church and I like my sleep. I'll see you tomorrow."

"Well, I'll be thinking of you until then, Reid. I'll miss you until tomorrow."

"Good night, nice man. I enjoyed the day and I will see you tomorrow. Hope that you don't have to stay too late." When the short call was over, Reid finished up and went back to bed. Jack counted the hours until he could see her again.

Sunday morning, each of them was engaged in separate activities. Jack was serving coffee at the bar and Reid was enjoying church. She loved the little place even though it had grown both shabby and old in her twenty years of going. Once a Methodist congregation, now it was clearly non-denominational, serving a mixed neighborhood of the elderly and a new crop of struggling families.

When Reid arrived home, Jack's truck was already there. Due to the heat of the day, he was waiting in the truck with the air conditioning running. He emerged to greet Reid, handing her a lavish bouquet of summer flowers including misty pink roses. Reid stammered a difficult thank you.

Breakfast was more quiet than usual. Jack's attempts to get Reid to talk were futile. She seemed locked in a world far away from this place and time.

In most relationships, a moment like this might have been a defining one, for the worse and not the better. Jack's strength, however, was a match for Reid's quiet. He believed in himself and in his love. He concentrated on both and over the time it took to clear the table and look at the Sunday paper, his power reached Reid. She felt it calm her; moving toward the force, instead of away.

An hour's silence was broken with the words, "I never had flowers given to me before, Jack. I always grew my own. You surprised me and I didn't know what to say. I'm grateful, but I don't always react well to surprises. I'm sorry."

"Somehow, Reid, I don't think this is about a few roses. Come on, let's go sit and be comfortable in the front room. You put on music that you like and we'll just sit."

Reid found the CD that she wanted. As the quiet rhythms of Jonathan Butler filled the room, Reid sat next to Jack on the big blue couch that she loved. Jack took her hand.

"I brought the flowers, because I want you to know you are special to me. I love you, Reid," said Jack.

"What happens if I can't love you back?" asked Reid as a genuine question. She really didn't know the answer. Not being able to return love was like jumping into a fearful abyss from which she would never return. Love seemed to be something that happened to other people. Without parents or siblings, she had had no practice in what she thought love was. She had loved her grandfather, Big Daddy, but there had been no tangible exchange in that relationship. Big Daddy had been gone for nearly as long as she had lived in this house.

"You already love me, Reid. You just don't know it. But I know it."

Reid looked away from Jack and down at their hands. There was a scar that ran deep between the left thumb and index finger on Jack's hand. She had noticed it before but never asked him about it. She asked about it now.

"That's from Abby."

"Did she stab you?"

Jack laughed. "No, she left me. It was probably the second or third time. When we were living in Prescott, she wanted to go to New Mexico. She wanted to go in a hurry, so she left. I needed to sell the bar, and close up the house, thinking that we would be back. The day I was ready to leave, the truck was packed except for a couple of Abby's boxes. Abby wasn't a careful person when it came to packing. She had left some of her carving tools sticking out of a flimsy box. I ripped up my hand pretty damn good. I was mad at her for a long time afterward because it never healed well and it hurt. It was a long time ago."

Reid continued to look down at Jack's hand. She could feel Jack breathing. The music was in her mind and moving her. She felt Jack kiss her bent neck. She held her breath and raised her head. When Jack was this close, she didn't want to talk ever again.

Jack wanted to talk, however. "Let's go. We're going to see Daisy. I promised my mother a visit and a trip out for ice cream today. Come on, get up. Not a good day for self-absorption." Jack was on his feet and Reid down from her dreams in seconds.

She had no reason to go and no reason not to. She had never met Daisy, but Jack had told her about his mother. Erin mentioned her from time to time as well.

It was a short drive. His mother was not what Reid expected. She had thought that Daisy Ellis would be a duplicate of her own grandmother since both had spent their lives on farms. Daisy, however, was a small woman casually dressed in a tasteful ivory pantsuit. She looked more like a real estate agent than a great grandmother. Daisy did her best to make Reid feel welcome.

I Will Know Him by the Mark

If Daisy was a surprise to Reid, Reid, in turn, was an even bigger surprise to Daisy. She had no idea that her only son was interested in a woman again, and one so young. The three of them talked about harmless subjects until Daisy could stand it no longer.

"I think it's time for that ice cream that you promised. I want coffee-toffee and then something else, too. But, my mind tells me that it's too hot to go. Jack, why don't you get some and bring it back? I'll make some mint iced tea while you are gone."

Jack winked at his mother as he walked out the door.

Daisy wanted to know exactly who Reid was. Making small talk, however, proved impossible. Finally, Daisy stopped talking and spent her attention on crushing the fresh mint leaves. Reid absently retrieved ice from the freezer and filled the glasses. From out of the blue, as if this was part of an on-going exchange, Reid asked, "Did Abby love Jack?"

Showing no surprise, Daisy answered only, "In her fashion."

"What does that mean?"

"It means that Abby had a hard time with love. She needed Jack just to survive, just to stay on an even keel. Abby loved her painting best of all, not my son. Here, put the glasses on the tea tray. Now sprinkle the leaves on the ice while I sugar my tea. Do you take sugar? No? Neither does Jack. He's a diabetic you know. He thinks I don't know. I know. Now you can carry the tray to the table by the patio window. Jack will be back with the ice cream. We'll use the big dishes from the cabinet in there."

The two women spent the next few minutes doing familiar things. Again, out of the middle of the silence, Reid asked, "How would I know if I loved Jack?"

"If you were happier with him than without him," said Daisy without hesitation. "If you were glad to have him around even when you didn't need him, even when he made you mad or sad. Then you would know that was love."

That was the last of their tête-à-tête. For a long time, months after Jack came back with the ice cream, Daisy never heard another word about Reid or from Reid.

On the other hand, Reid thought often about what Daisy had said about love. One Saturday afternoon in late September, one lazy afternoon when Jack had come for lunch and stayed for hours, Reid wanted to talk. She forced herself away from the far off place she always went when they made love. Jack was usually the talkative one, but today was Reid's day.

"I love you, Jack. I know it. I didn't know it for a long while, but I am happier with you than without you. I think that is love."

"It's love, Reid, the kind that you can trust."

"I hope so, because mostly I'm kind of a dreamy person who wakes up confused. What goes on in my life and what goes on in my head are two different things. I've always trusted you. I never worried for a minute about trusting you. I should have, but I never did. I gave up to you the first time you kissed me because it was dreamy and real. You had a power over me because I wanted you to want me."

"I wanted you then; I still want you," said Jack as he pulled himself up to face her.

"I remember how you tasted the first time we were naked together."

"And how did I taste?" asked Jack.

"Salty and damp. I could smell you and I wanted to get inside of that smell. I gave up to the smell of you and followed it. I have told you that you have a power over me, but in giving in to you, I somehow am more myself."

"You are a beautiful woman. I'm not the first or only man to notice that."

"Stop it, Jack. I'm middle-aged and average at most. I never know why you say that to me!"

"Because it annoys you and because it is the truth. My eyes have seen every inch of you and haven't seen enough." Jack pulled the folded sheet half away from Reid. With the palm of his right hand, he rubbed her pink nipple. It became erect. He brought his mouth to hers and kissed her until she was fighting for breath.

When she turned her head away, Jack whispered into her ear, "I have to go to work."

Reid laughed and Jack laughed with her. She withdrew her desire. When Jack hugged her, the absence was replaced by the first feeling of intimacy that she could remember. Reid was as close to Jack as he was to her. When she touched his hand, she felt his scar.

Reid was asleep when the phone rang. Sensing it was Jack calling from the bar, she pulled the handset into the pillow before saying anything. The voice on the other end was not Jack. It was a voice from her past, calling her from her sleep, calling her away from her new life.

When Jack did finally call, the woman who answered seemed different from the one he left earlier in the evening. She sounded tired and sad. When she told him about her phone call, he offered to go with her.

"You can't go because you run the bar and you look after Daisy," said Reid.

"The only reason I can't go is if you don't want me to go. You can lean a little on me, Reid. I can shoulder this with you."

A reply was long in coming. "OK."

"OK what? OK you want me to go?" asked Jack.

"No. OK, I'll lean on you. Help me work on going. Help me come back."

"I'll come over in about an hour," offered Jack.

"No, just in the morning. Come in the morning."

"Reid, if you want me before then, call me. No matter the time, I can come. Otherwise, I'll be over after I close up after coffee. Are you going to church?"

"No."

"Reid, this doesn't change anything. You don't owe the past and the past doesn't own you. You don't even have to go. Just get a lawyer."

"But I want to go! I've waited a long time to go back. Now, I'm ready. I want them to see me and know that I have had a life without them." The words were flung through the wire.

Jack had some different thoughts about that. What he could picture was a motherless girl sitting atop a tractor plowing forty acres alone. For himself, Jack found that leaving the past alone was usually the best thing. Because he had rarely been able to convince others of the wisdom of his thinking, he didn't try now. About as far in the past he wanted to go was to earlier this evening when he was in Reid's bed.

"Tell you what, Reid. Why don't you make some travel arrangements and then call me? That way, if you need me early, or maybe later, I can be a little more ready."

"OK. I'll call."

It was Sunday afternoon when Jack took Reid to Sky Harbor Airport so that she could catch the plane to Des Moines. She would stay there for the night and go out to her Uncle Pen's farm on Monday morning. His funeral had been the previous week.

No one had called Reid then. They had only called when his will had been found and read. Pendleton VanDuyver, Jr., had left his entire estate to his niece, Reid Markham, daughter of Joy Markham, his long-deceased sister. He had effectively cut off his wife, and disinherited his five sons and their families.

Whatever Reid was thinking, she had shared nothing with Jack except the barest of facts. She was a changed person, captured by the beast of circumstance that turns all futures into the miserable present. The bloom of the past few months had been blighted.

"Look in on Mrs. Gilberg for me, please Jack. If I am gone a while, will you take her to the store?" asked Reid anxiously.

"I can do that. You just do what you can, what you have to do, and come back. I'm a poor substitute for you."

"I don't know what to do. I don't know if I can come back. I just have to go. Thank you for helping me and thank you for not asking me questions."

"I love you," said Jack as he hugged her.

"Daisy told me about this part. This part about love."

"Since when did my mother talk to you about love?" asked Jack, although he was rarely surprised about anything his mother did.

"Just once. She said that when you were happier with someone than without them, that was love," Reid replied.

"Daisy is a smart old lady."

Reid had to get on the waiting plane. The time had come for going on alone for a while. Reid and Jack had to part. They would be less happy, but maybe that time would be short. They hoped so.

P.S. Lowe

Learning to Live With Forgiveness

The first local person Reid Markham contacted the day after she arrived in Iowa was her old employer at the bank, Robert Barnes. A nervous, balding, overweight functionary had replaced the robust, slightly pompous man she remembered from a quarter century ago. Reid's hometown bank was just a branch of a national bank. Mr. Barnes was no longer the president, only a branch manager. Gone were his private office and his longtime secretary, Mrs. Rawson.

The one thing that hadn't changed, however, was the fact that gossip about farmers moved faster than official documents. In less than forty-eight hours after Pen, Jr.'s death, the community knew that Reid Markham was the largest private landowner in two counties.

She had told no one she was coming and arrived at the bank around lunchtime. Mr. Barnes greeted her. They went to his desk. "I thought you would at least come back for the funeral, Reid. He was your Uncle and he sure left you everything."

Reid sighed. She never had a quick reply. She felt tongue-tied, wishing she had someone, anyone to help her. She was alone and had only herself. It was no good wishing otherwise. She was still considering what to say in what was becoming a deep silence.

Robert Barnes studied Reid carefully. Phoenix must have agreed with her. Unlike most of the women around here, she looked less than her age, having both a youthful figure and haircut. She was, in fact, attractive. Still, she didn't seem to have much to say. It was a mystery why her Uncle had left his entire estate to her. "Well, she couldn't keep it," thought Robert Barnes. "The boys would see to that. That will won't make it through probate. It has probably been challenged by now!" Robert Barnes had assimilated that part of aging that assumes anyone younger is somehow a child. The VanDuyver "boys" were well into their manhood years.

Reid had decided that she had come here for one reason. She needed information. She would get it and get out, allowing Robert Barnes to think whatever he wanted.

"I came to find out if you could tell me the name of my Uncle's lawyer. Do you know who it is?" asked Reid.

"The family is all at the house, Reid. Have you been there? Have you asked them?" Robert Barnes wasn't going to cooperate without satisfying at least some of his curiosity.

"I didn't ask for this," thought Reid. "I shouldn't have come. Yet here I am, and having shown up, I'll see this through no matter how difficult it is." She knew that Mr. Barnes was probably the easiest person she would have to deal with.

"I'm staying in Des Moines at the Holiday Inn, the new one. I'll be in touch as needs crop up. Right now, I'm going to get something to eat and then head back. Thank you for your time, Mr. Barnes. I would appreciate it if you would have the lawyer call me."

"Well, no need to get huffy. I'm here to help you, but I can see that you're not interested. You're in for a rough time with the VanDuyver clan. You can't just fly in and think you own their farm. You're not strong enough to take them on and you're not strong enough to farm, Reid Markham." The veneer of local affability had completely flaked away.

Reid just stared at the aging banker and then said quietly, "I'm as strong as I have to be," then turned and left.

When she left the bank, Reid did not intend to go back to her hotel. After eating, she spent the afternoon driving down roads she had memorized years ago. The buildings had changed, but not the land. The signs had changed, but not the land. There were improvements to be seen, but the land never changed.

It was nearly dusk when she drove down the road that would take her to the house where she grew up. She stopped the car to the far east of the property and decided to walk. The fields to the south had still not been cleared. As she looked to the west, there were dark purple clouds high above the horizon that faded to a creamy yellow in the ending day. The little hills in the distance were the same purple of the clouds. Reid walked the road wondering why she couldn't see the house.

Then she saw why. It had been torn down. All that remained of the original structures was the small barn. She stood in the road and looked at the ancient building with its single window. The yellow sky was now completely hazy blue, and the remaining light gave the weathered wood a pink glow.

It was hers now, she guessed. All she could see was hers. Reid wanted to feel something, something like triumph or sadness, something like finding lost treasure. She only felt tired. She walked back to the rented car and drove the distance to her hotel.

The light on the phone was blinking rapidly when she arrived in her room. There were two messages: one from Jack and one from Gregory Johnson, her Uncle's lawyer. She called the number he had left even though it was late. He immediately answered. Reid identified herself.

"Thank you for returning my call. Robert called me this afternoon. I had no idea you were coming. But in so doing, you have saved me a lot of trouble," said the lawyer.

He seemed pleasant on the phone. Reid asked to set up an appointment the next day. "That would be fine, but it won't be until late in the day. If you wouldn't mind, perhaps we could get a cup of coffee now and that way I can give you a copy of your Uncle's will along with some other papers that I will need you to sign. There are some things as beneficiary you need to know and I would rather tell them to you."

"What kind of things? Maybe I need to get a lawyer."

"You need a lawyer, it's true, but you need to know why as well. Can you meet me?"

"I haven't had dinner yet. Where should we meet?" asked Reid, knowing that she needed to get on with this.

They agreed on an Italian restaurant not far from either one of them. Reid called Jack before leaving. There wasn't much to say, but she thanked him anyway for calling.

By the time she arrived at The Italian Garden, Greg Johnson was already waiting. He had a large portfolio with him. Reid thought him to be about her age. A nice looking man. Probably not from around here.

It took only a few minutes to order. Reid was anxious to hear what Greg had to say. His attempts at social conversation were lost on her. Knowing it had been many years since Reid had seen the VanDuyver family, the lawyer decided to give her an abbreviated family history, beginning at the end.

"Your Uncle Pen died of brain cancer. He died at home. He fought for over two years to overcome it, but lost. He had been through surgery twice and radiation. For about a year, it looked hopeful. Then around the end of June, his checkup down in Houston showed that the tumor had returned. It was inoperable and untreatable."

Reid was listening intently while eating. Without saying anything, she looked up to encourage Greg to go on. He didn't. He didn't know Reid well enough to know that she would let him talk until the story was finished.

"You are going to have to talk until you're done, Mr. Johnson. I don't know much about any of this. I haven't heard much from Iowa since Big Daddy died and that was a long time ago. You said there were things I need to know. Talk until I know them," said Reid.

"Usually, I expect the beneficiary to ask questions. That allows me not to say everything I know, and use my judgment. Since my client is dead, and none of what I am about to tell you will libel him, and since you are his beneficiary, I guess it's time to tell his story."

"I never knew anyone in my lifetime who could work as hard as your Uncle could. I only knew him for about fifteen years or so. He had one reputation as a hard working farmer and another one for his meanness. Anyone who crossed him was cut off from his business and his life. People told me he got that way after his father died."

"No," Reid thought, "He was always that way."

"I heard that when your grandfather, the one they call 'Big Daddy' died, Pen, Jr., decided to somehow replace him in the eyes of the community, but people didn't let him. Times had changed. Interest rates were tolerable, but the family farm was a dying way of life. The people who stayed in Iowa respected one thing: money. So what Pen, Jr., couldn't do with his personality, he did with money. He bought more land, more machinery and brought his own cheap labor from Mexico. He leveraged himself completely. The financial part of his operation was way beyond him, so he came to Des Moines to buy the accounting, tax, and legal help he needed. My firm gave me his account for his legal work because he was hell on earth to deal with. But as long as he made money, avoided taxes, and successfully sued folks, he paid his bills on time."

"His children, all boys, either hated him or feared him. When they could, the oldest two left. He hardly gave Brian or John the time of day again. I think they saw their mother from time to time, but that was about it. They did come for the funeral and to find out about the will."

"What about the other three? I had five cousins. What about them?" asked Reid absently as if she were counting sheep in a field.

"The next two, Benjamin and Mac, are around. They farmed some with their father, but had other jobs when they were all on the outs. For the past two years, they have done the farming that was done. Kenneth ran away when he was fifteen or sixteen. He wasn't at the funeral and no one has heard from him or seen him."

"I want to get to the last couple of years, because that's where I have the most knowledge and concern. It was about 1995 that Pen, Jr., began to get some grandiose ideas. He was well off, but he wanted to be rich. Started doing more than hedging a little corn in the market. Lost some money, but that didn't seem to sober him up. He wasn't investing, he was gambling. Then he had a car accident. He wasn't hurt badly, but he had a concussion. In the emergency room, they found he had a brain tumor."

Reid said nothing. She was finished eating and just listening.

"Yes, he had a brain tumor, a fear of dying, and no health insurance," said the lawyer as he pushed his plate away. He signaled the waitress for some coffee for them both.

"Maybe he wasn't afraid of dying as much as he feared losing control. For two years, he had extraordinary treatment. Much of the time, he was well and continued to run the farm and continued to lose money in markets. He also ran up over half a million in medical expenses. He once spent a month in intensive care in Houston."

"What that means to his beneficiary, you and you exclusively, is that you are getting a whole lot less than you think and a whole lot more problems. His family has no idea of the financial problems involved in this. The property is mortgaged heavily, the equipment payments in arrears, and there are two pending lawsuits with his brokers."

The coffee came. "OK. You said there were papers to sign. What are they?"

"Probate filings mostly. But you can get your own lawyer to review them first," said Greg.

"Can't you represent me?" asked Reid.

"I can, but I'm wondering if it is wise. If you were my client at this moment, my advice to you would be to decline his inheritance. That's my free advice."

"Are you saying that my Uncle's estate is worthless?"

"Will be if you try to inherit it. Legal fees will run an easy hundred thousand or more. You stand a good chance of losing, making it your nickel. The estate itself is probably going to settle in a couple of years to around half a million, but maybe more. Meantime there are thousands of acres to farm and no one to do it."

Greg Johnson didn't know how to evaluate this beneficiary. She didn't talk much and didn't seem to comprehend all that he had told her. She didn't look much like a VanDuyver either. He waited for some additional questions, but she seemed to be withdrawn from words. He asked the passing server for the check. It had been a long day and he was anxious to get to his family.

"What happened to Vera Ruth? Why didn't she inherit?" asked Reid suddenly.

"I'm going to have to take off my lawyer's hat here and move to pure speculation. I know you haven't seen your aunt in a long time, and maybe she was different then, maybe not. Your aunt is a long time alcoholic. I think that Pen thought the cirrhosis would get her before the cancer got him. I saw her at the funeral. I don't think she'll make it too much longer," said Greg

"Oh." Reid felt so tired now. What had she expected? Had she really thought she could come back and find the ordered world of Big Daddy and Grammy untouched by time? Yes, yes she had. She had not thought beyond the end of her nose. Not once. She shut her eyes. The Iowa world she had left so long ago came before her.

"Reid. Are you all right?" The lawyer's voice returned her to the present.

"Yes. I was trying to think of what to do. I don't know what to do. I need to see the family, though. I know I need to do that. Can you arrange it?"

"I can call them. They don't have to see you, however. I can give you a telephone number and you can call them. What did you have in mind?"

"Just call them and tell them I'm going out there tomorrow, in the morning. I'm going to think about what you told me. But I have to see them before I do more."

"I'll call them when I get home. It is early enough. You call me in the morning. Leave a message if I am out and I will call you back. Please excuse me, but I need to be off to my family. Can I walk you to your car?"

"Nice. Sure. I'll call you," said Reid as she abruptly got up from the table.

The September night was chilly to Reid. It would have been hot in Phoenix she thought as she unlocked the car and waved at the lawyer. When she returned to her room, she sought solace in a vigorous shower and then in deep sleep.

Tuesday was a perfect fall day. Reid had dressed casually and actually enjoyed her trip out to her Uncle's farm. She arrived at about ten in the morning. From the number of cars parked close to the house, she imagined that most of the family was still visiting. She parked carefully with a mind to leaving.

She walked up to the front of the house and by the time she had put her foot on the first step, the front door opened. It was recognizably her cousin John. There was a lot of gray in his beard.

Qite out of character, Reid spoke first. "Hello John. I'm truly sorry to see you at this sad time." She extended her hand. John shook it and brought her into the hallway.

"This is a terrible time, Reid. I would thank you for coming, but I'm not sure why you are here," said John.

"I'm here as family, and I'm here because your father made me his beneficiary. I'm hoping someone here can tell me why that happened. Can you?" asked Reid.

"Come into the kitchen. We can talk in there."

"OK, but first I want to say something to Aunt Vera Ruth."

"That's not a good idea just now."

"Why? I spoke to the lawyer in Des Moines. He told me that she was an alcoholic. Is she drunk?"

"No," said John, matching Reid's directness. "No, the doctor is here. We're thinking of putting her into the hospital. Her liver has failed. I don't think that anyone can care for her here."

Just then, Brian VanDuyver appeared in the small vestibule. He didn't recognize Reid and had to be introduced. The three of them moved awkwardly to the kitchen. The place looked run down to Reid. It smelled of alcohol and cigarettes and old food.

Brian looked like his father. He had the bull neck and thinning curly black hair so characteristic of the VanDuyver men. He offered Reid a beer. When she declined, he got a can for himself and lit a cigarette. They were sitting at the table when Ben and Mac appeared. It was clear that these men were the two farmers. They poured coffee for themselves and leaned against the counter. Reid was beginning to feel crowded in a silent room of strangers.

She had told Robert Barnes that she was as strong as she had to be, but doubted it now. There was a roaring in her ears. To drown it she started to talk herself.

"How is your mother?" Although she had directed the question to all of them, it was Benjamin who answered.

"Close to dead. The doctor said it's downhill now. He wants her to go to the hospital." Benjamin was answering to the floor. Then he looked up square to Reid. "You know there's no money to send her there. No insurance either. You have all the money. You have the whole mess. You want to take care of her? Why don't you go to her room? It's disgusting in there."

"Who is with her?" asked Reid.

"My old lady and John's too. Christ! I don't know how they stand it," replied Mac. The mood of the brothers was more of bewilderment than grief. Reid decided to step through the emotion.

To all of her cousins she said, "OK. First things first. Someone needs to tell the doctor to get her to a hospital. Get her there. I'm going outside. I need some air."

"Who's paying for this?" asked Ben belligerently.

"Not you. Not any of you. That's a guarantee," said Reid as she got out of her chair and headed for the kitchen door.

Fast behind her was her cousin, Mac. She couldn't remember his given name. He had been called Mac since childhood. Reid looked around for somewhere to sit down but found nothing, even though the weather was perfect outdoors. She had grown used to the Phoenix lifestyle where everyone had a patio and outdoor furniture. This was Iowa.

She turned and faced Mac, who was now very close. "What did you mean that we didn't have to pay for Mom's care? Are you paying? What gives you the right to come here anyway? Who called you and who do you think you are?" Mac's face was distorted by anger.

"I'm your cousin and I inherited what should have gone to you and your brothers. I don't know why. I came here to find out why. You tell me."

"Because the old man was a mean son of a bitch. He gave it to a real bitch, YOU!"

Reid imagined Mac as an animated tree stump. Once imagined, he lost all his power to upset her. He was comical. He wasn't a nightmare, just someone from her childhood. She had no fear of him.

Before Reid could say anything, John VanDuyver appeared at the door calling to them both to come inside. His news to them was brief. Vera Ruth was to be taken to a Des Moines hospital by her daughter-in-law. The boys and Reid were going to talk some business.

It took some commotion and a lot of work to get Vera Ruth into a car and on her way. Reid watched from the window. More and more she felt as if this scene, this distant dialogue, and even the colors of the day were some film, and not a life; not hers anyway.

When the VanDuyvers returned to the house, Reid made no effort to leave the kitchen. She heard conversation, but ignored it. Finally, the men only came into the kitchen. Except for John, they sat down rather sullenly.

John, as oldest, was first to speak. "My brothers and our families intend to challenge our father's will. They want me to make it clear to you that you are not welcome here."

"Nothing's changed, then. I wasn't welcome here as a child, and I didn't return willingly. I need some questions answered, or I will find out the information another way. By the way, before you make up your minds to 'challenge' this will, there are some facts you should know. So let's have our little exchange of information," said Reid in a voice she had never used. "I want to know your marital status and whether you have children."

"Mac, let's start with you," began Reid.

"Yes I'm married and I have two sons. What's it to you?"

"Maybe nothing and maybe everything, to you. What about you, Brian?" continued Reid.

"Divorced, no kids."

"What do you do? I take it you don't farm, least not here," followed Reid.

"I work at the electric co-op in the county. Do some line and repair work. Mostly I just do emergency work in the winter."

"And John, what about you?"

"I teach high school. I'm long time married, and I have two kids, Johanna and Pendleton."

A new sense of quiet and sadness seemed to fall over the group. The flame of hostility had blown itself to mere smoke. In answering Reid's questions, the movie of their own lives took over the thoughts of the sons.

Before Reid could ask, Benjamin spoke up. "I farm. I've always farmed; I will always farm. Right here. I live on this land with my wife. My boy is away in the Air Force."

"And where is Kenneth? Who knows what happened to Kenny?" asked Reid.

"He's dead," said Mac in answer.

"You know that? If so, how do you know that? He was just thirteen years old when I left. I heard that he ran away about 1979 or 1980. Why do you think he is dead, Mac?"

"Because if he wasn't, he would have turned up by now. He knows where his family is."

"I didn't come back for more than twenty years. Maybe he had no reason to come back," said Reid.

"You're not a VanDuyver and you're not a farmer," said Benjamin.

"I'm just as much one as you are, as any of you are! I was raised by Big Daddy and Grammy, same as your father. You have no better claim to a name or a farm than I do. What nourished you wasn't VanDuyver land, but from Grammy's family. The VanDuyver land, all forty acres, was sold for my benefit. Don't you forget that!" Reid fairly exploded with a sureness that surprised her.

"Seems only fair that we ask you what you do, Reid. Where's your husband?" asked John quietly.

"I don't have one. I have never had one. I'm a bookkeeper for a sportswear distributor. No, actually I'm the office manager," replied Reid.

"You're a bitch and an old maid," started Mac.

"I can't tell you how much you remind me of your father," replied Reid. "Now since we're done with this little show and tell, I have some information to impart to you. I wanted to know if any of you knew anything about financial management of this farm. I suspected that none of you knows the language of money. I'm not being critical, but you are all in for a shock. I have a set of papers prepared by the attorney who took care of your father's legal and financial affairs. I've read them. The bottom line to you is this: this farm is going bankrupt. Your father spent all his money saving himself. The land is mortgaged and the equipment is leased. This year's crop was sold at a loss. I'm going out to the car to get the papers."

Reid's words tasted rancid on the palate of the VanDuyver men. Ben went to the refrigerator for beer and brought three back. He and Brian lit up cigarettes. No one said a word. When Reid returned, she handed the manila envelope to John.

"Read it, today if you can. Then I think that the four of you should make a call on Greg Johnson, your father's lawyer. He's a nice guy, if you haven't met him. He's liable to give you some free advice. Take it."

"Why did he do it, Reid? Why did he leave you everything?" asked Brian.

"Big Daddy used to say that 'why' wasn't important. I think he was right about that. I came here to find out why Uncle Pen did this to me and to you, all of you. Now I know it is not important. I have my own thoughts, but they don't matter. I am going back to Des Moines now. Talk to that lawyer before you make any plans or spend any money. Can you tell me the name of the hospital where your mother went? I want to see her."

No one at the table seemed to know. John called to his wife, Priscilla, who came into the kitchen with reluctance. She told Reid that Vera Ruth was at St. Luke's. Reid asked if anyone was going there today. No one volunteered since Mac's wife had accompanied her mother-in-law.

"Well, I'll see her then," said Reid to no one in particular. "I'm sorry to be here under these circumstances. Call that lawyer. Call me if there's something, I don't know, if there's something I should know or do."

Reid started out the back door. John moved from the general numbness and walked her outside. "We should have at least had something to eat. This should have been different. Guess we're not very capable on our own. I know you won't believe it, but having Mom so sick is really the worst thing. No matter what you think, she was the center of our lives. We don't know what to do without her. She was what kept us all together. Then Kenny left and she just started drinking. He did this to her."

"No, he didn't. But you can think that if you want. He won't mind," said Reid.

"Are you coming back?" asked John.

"To the house? No, probably not or not anytime soon. I plan to get this mess, or my part of it, settled this week. I can do that if you all will figure out what is best for you. Come up to the city and I can meet you there."

John kicked the gravel in the drive. He shrugged. Reid got in the car and drove back to her temporary haven at the Holiday Inn.

It took until Friday for the VanDuyver men to meet with Greg Johnson. Reid had met with the lawyer daily; with the same constancy, she visited her dying aunt. She and Greg had worked out a plan that he was presenting to the VanDuyver men and their wives. Reid would renounce her inheritance after the death of her aunt. Reid would pay for half of her aunt's hospital bills to keep her aunt in a peaceful place. Greg would receive a set fee for straightening out the estate quickly providing that the VanDuyvers agreed to a sale of all of the family assets. The cash would be divided evenly among the five brothers. Since no one could prove that Kenneth was dead, his share would be held in trust for ten years. Reid was not present for the lawyer's meeting, but she heard about it later.

There were a few phone calls from John, one from Mac's wife and one from Brian in the days that followed. Vera Ruth died on Monday, not really surprising anyone. Her life tether had been cut loose long ago. She had just been waiting for the air to end.

Vera Ruth VanDuyver's funeral was held on Wednesday. This time Reid was both invited and attended. Real sorrow and palpable relief marked the short service. Reid went back to the house for a while and met family she had never known. It wasn't exactly a friendly gathering, yet Reid felt that she might some-day be able to return to see these families again. Maybe.

After the family wake, after she had left behind the last grief, Reid stopped to see the old barn. She wanted to have a last look. Before the sun went down, she went inside. Scattered on the floor were a few loose boards. She picked them up and put them in the car trunk. She intended to take them back to Phoenix. Of course, in the ordinary desert sun they would not have the twilight shimmer that they had now, but she would remember how the old barn had looked.

Funny how even after he died, Big Daddy was still teaching her lessons. She did not belong here in Iowa. She loved how the barn looked and smelled, the weathered wood was a sensual pleasure, but she had no desire to do the work that would have kept the barn vital. She was too dreamy. Having to be strong all the time as she had been for two weeks, was more than she had in her. Pen, Jr. had it, though. Reid was nothing like her Uncle and now she was glad of it. Big Daddy had set her down the right road and she felt again the grateful happiness she often experienced. Now, she was ready to go home.

On Thursday, she stopped by Greg Johnson's office to sign a few papers. From there she would go to the airport. Jack had said he would meet her in Phoenix at the terminal gate at Sky Harbor.

Once the papers were signed, and it appeared that everything was cleared up, Greg Johnson still had some unfinished business. Since Reid had not been totally honest with him, much less with her cousins, he decided to confront her. "I wonder if you could tell me how you knew that your Uncle died. You were here before I could notify you. If you were out of contact with the family, how did you know to come? I tried to contact you on Monday. Your office told me that you had come to Des Moines on Sunday."

"I come from a small town, Greg Johnson. Even in exile, a small town gossip reaches you."

"You are being evasive, Ms. Markham."

"I've been nothing but truthful with you and with my family, Mr. Johnson."

"I thought so, but now I don't think so. I think you know exactly why your Uncle left you his entire estate. Do you want to tell me? Attorney/client privilege, of course."

Reid was smiling. "As you reminded me, you are not my attorney. But I will give you a piece of free information. I do know. It had to do with forgiveness, in general, and specifically."

"Then why did you renounce your inheritance?" asked the puzzled lawyer.

"Because I was asked to forgive and to pass on the lesson," said Reid simply. "I have to get a plane, but I do have a favor to ask of you. Will you call Robert Barnes and tell him that I was strong enough? I didn't think I was going to make it. I did make it though! Big Daddy made sure I was strong enough. Will you?"

Sensing that no other answers were coming, Greg Johnson let it go, agreeing to the last request. Sometimes, why, if answered, would never be understood.

When Reid Markham arrived in Phoenix, Jack Ellis was waiting for her.

P.S. Lowe

An Atmosphere of Autumn

The weekend after Reid Markham returned from Iowa, she invited Kenny, her cousin, and his wife over for Sunday afternoon dinner. She invited Jack Ellis, too, to brighten the conversation. As a long time barkeeper, Jack could lighten any gathering. He had stories to tell and told them well.

It was late September, but in Phoenix, that meant that it was still too hot to eat outside at midday. Early, before going to church, Reid fixed yeast dough that would become soft bread sticks. She was serving shrimp and pasta. For her cousin's daughter, there was ambrosia salad cooling in a cut glass dish in the refrigerator. The little girl loved anything with marshmallows.

When Jack arrived, Reid was just putting the twisted sticks in the oven. The shrimp and sauce were finished. A large aluminum pot was simmering on the burner, awaiting the slender noodles that she would add when the Smyths arrived.

As always, Jack was in an affectionate mood. Reid attempted to set dishes out on her large circular table and Jack tightly grabbed her fork-filled hands. He kissed her mouth hard until she kissed him back. When he released her hands and pulled her close to him, Reid felt the wonderful warmth of his love that she had known from the first time he kissed her. She loved the way he tasted and the softness of his lips on hers. She dropped the forks on the floor. Their clatter awakened her from her reverie.

"Guess you had better wash and dry these off, my friend, or we'll be eating with our hands," Reid said as they both bent over to pick up the scattered silver.

"I've never done that before! Sounds like fun. I'm sure it would make for an interesting dinner," replied Jack.

"Oh, no. Don't try it. My little cousin thinks everything you do is wonderful. She'll copy you and that won't please her mother."

"Do you care what her mother thinks?" asked Jack.

"No and yes. I would like her to think of me as friendly family. She has, so far, but her husband hasn't been truthful with her about so many things, until recently. Now I don't know what she thinks."

"You might clue me in about what to say and what not to say this afternoon, Reid. I kind of feel like a fifth wheel today here, anyway at your family gathering."

"Well, she knows that her husband is not the orphan he pretended to be. She knows that Uncle Pen and Aunt Vera Ruth are dead. But I don't think she knows about the will or Kenny's brothers," said Reid.

"How did Kenny ever know to call you that night? How did he know about his father's death?"

"The computer."

"The computer?"

"Yeah, the computer. E-mail. Kenny stayed in touch with someone from Iowa. His one friend, the daughter of the man who bought Big Daddy's land, was Aileen Sterner. I saw her at my Aunt's funeral. Aileen sent Kenny e-mail the day Uncle Pen died, but Kenny didn't log in until that Sunday night. So he didn't know until after the funeral. Once he knew, he asked me to go to Iowa."

"Did Kenny have any idea about the will?"

"No. What he was hoping was that he had been declared legally dead."

"You have kept that from happening, haven't you?"

"Yes. Whenever the estate settles, one-fifth of it goes to Kenny. That may or may not drive the family to try to find him."

Reid looked at the clock. Her cousin should be here by now. She looked out the window and saw their car pull into the driveway. When they came to the door, only Kenny and Dianne were there. Their daughter was not with them. They did not look like a happy couple.

They both knew Jack, so introductions were unnecessary. Without the distraction of the seven-year-old, it was hard to find light conversation. Reid's meal was, as always, delightful, but everything about it seemed heavy at the time.

As soon as the table was cleared, Dianne announced that it was time to leave. Kenny looked down at the tabletop. Reid began to experience the same kind of disjointedness that she had felt whenever major changes came into her life. "Boom," said her head. "Boom," said her heart.

"No, don't leave, not just yet. Please Dianne, please sit down." Reid's words came from somewhere very unused within her.

Dianne sat back down more in surprise than in obedience.

"I don't want it to be like this. I don't want to be the holder of family secrets. I don't want you to live your lives in the same kind of silence that Kenny and I knew as children. I don't want you to have to keep on pretending that the only past you have is an imaginary one. So, I'm going to tell you what I know and then you can make of it what you both want." Reid began to rush her words.

"Kenny, I saw all of your brothers, their wives and their children when I went to Iowa. I talked to your mother before she died. I saw what changed and what would never change."

Dianne looked at her husband incredulously. Kenny's eyes never moved from the table.

"You want to know something? Your Father left me the whole farm. All of it. Did you know that? He disinherited everyone but me. What a mystery that was! What a mystery that was to me and to your brothers."

Reid felt tears coming to her hot face. Her throat was thickening. She had to stop. She could see the shiny top of her cousin's head as it bowed closer to the table. He had changed his name, but he was, in looks, still a VanDuyver. The thought of the five brothers and their thinning black hair stopped her tears.

"I spoke to your mother. She knew you were alive and well. Your Dad knew, too. I figured out that's why they left me the farm. Both of them did it. Your dad knew I would never run the farm and I didn't need the money. Big Daddy left me money. A lot of money. What Big Daddy left your father was some big shoes to fill. I finally figured that out."

"You have no right to bring this up. You have no right to talk about any of this. Not now, not ever." Kenny had raised his body erectly in his chair. His wife's face was as pale as her fair hair.

"Yes, I do have a right. You are family to me. Your brothers, too. You didn't know her, but before my mother died, there was a time when we were all young together. There were some happy times then, but her death changed that for me and Grammy, and Big Daddy, and for your father. Maybe most of all for your Dad and Mom. After that, what I remember is the silence. If we didn't talk about missing her, then we showed how strong we were. Even now, when I think of her, I have no real memories, because no one let me keep those memories alive. Not the good ones, anyway."

"When you called me up ten years ago, you wanted family or you wouldn't have called me. I'm family. Your brothers are still family to you. I believe that your mother and father loved you, missed you, even if you could not understand their kind of love."

Reid was crying. Grief was at her center. She got up from the table and went to her bedroom to find tissues. She sat down on the bed. In a couple of minutes, she saw Dianne standing at the doorway. "Come in and get something for your tears. I don't like to cry like this, but it does happen." Reid handed the blue-flowered box to Dianne.

Dianne wiped her nose. "Is all that true? Does Kenny have more family?"

"Yes, it's true."

"What happened to make him run away? Why did he lie about everything? Why did he lie to me? I feel angry and cheated. I don't understand at all," said Dianne.

"I don't know why he left. Maybe he will tell you sometime and maybe not. I just didn't want the silence to go on in my life. I am selfish and not strong enough for these kinds of secrets. I hope you understand that. I hope Kenny does, too."

"What if Kenny has done something terrible? What if he had to change his name and lie because he is in trouble?"

"Dianne, don't make this more awful than it was and is. I just didn't want one of his brothers showing up one day. If they cared at all, Kenny would be easy to find."

"Are you going to tell them about us?" asked Dianne hesitantly.

"No, not unless there is some sort of emergency. Kenny can do what he wants with the rest of the family. If he asks me about anyone, I will tell him. It's just that I am not going to pretend that they don't exist any longer. Now, let's go because I think there is enough afternoon left for all of us to recover a little bit."

When the women returned to the kitchen, Jack was making his inevitable pot of coffee. Kenny's eyes were red-rimmed, but he looked better. Jack jokingly complained to Reid that there was no desert. He poured four cups of coffee and talked a little about his latest new customers at the bar. It was hard, however, to ease the mood at the table.

When at last Kenny and Dianne left, they were leaning on each other as if emerging from a sudden storm into shelter. Reid hoped that, somehow, the couple would survive their new collective knowledge. Her only regret was that she had not yet told Kenny of his inheritance.

It took a couple of weeks for Reid to hear from Kenny. He called one Saturday morning. He asked to meet her for a late breakfast. There was no question of where they would meet. It would only be across from St. Mary's Hospital, not far from Jack's bar. Over the years, they had often met at First Shift there on Thomas Road, a place much unchanged from the time that Reid had first moved to Phoenix in the seventies.

Reid arrived first and found a booth in the back. She didn't know whether to expect her cousin alone or with his wife. He came in alone. He looked older. At least he was smiling.

"Same booth, different year," said Reid as Kenny seated himself in the smooth turquoise booth across from her. "Guess we've always had our serious conversations here, as if it were some kind of neutral ground."

"Yeah, except for the other Sunday. You really got me, Reid. My wife thinks I am some sort of serial killer. She can't understand that I have had no contact with my parents or with my brothers for so long. She doesn't understand how it was back there. She doesn't understand at all. She wants me to call them, at least."

"You don't want to call them?" asked Reid.

"No, I don't. I want to stay as far away from the past as I can get. Time didn't change anything for me, Reid. Not one thing. I feel the same about Iowa and the VanDuyvers as the day I left." There was a creeping anger building in Kenny's voice.

"That's something I always wondered about. Why did you leave? How could you take off and never come back?"

"You first, cousin of mine. You first. Since we seem to be spilling family secrets, why did you leave and never return?"

Reid looked at him quizzically. She was sure he knew the story of her simple life. Her head bowed slightly and her dark blonde hair fell into her eyes. She flipped it back. "I left because Big Daddy told me to move. It was that easy. He gave me money to move and I moved. I look back and I think he knew he had heart problems. I think he wanted me to be away when the end came. I was a misfit and he knew it. He knew I couldn't see beyond the end of my nose. I'm not much better at it now."

"I never thought of you like that, Reid. I still don't. I see someone who is smart and friendly. You have been friend, sister, and mother to me. That's why when you told Dianne about my so-called 'real' family, I got mad. I'm still mad as hell because Dianne wants me to contact them. I won't do it, and I don't want her to do it either. It's a big rock between us, Reid. You put it there."

"There was probably a better way to do it than the way I told you and Dianne. You must believe that I am sorry. I lack every kind of tact. I am also a strong believer in truth almost at all costs. Maybe at all costs. As far as you are concerned, the worst is not yet over. I have something else to tell you." Reid was trying to gauge what she was saying and what she was about to say.

"There's more? What more?" Kenny was shouting in a whisper.

"You are entitled to one-fifth of your father's estate. I didn't arrange it, but I made sure that it happened. When all is said and done, there's more than forty thousand dollars coming your way." There, thought Reid, it's over and it's out.

"But no one knows where I am. No one knows who I am. I could be dead. This doesn't mean anything to me."

"Yes, it does. You see, at least two of your brothers could use that money. In order to get your share they have either to wait ten years or somehow prove you are dead. Your dad's lawyer would do a thorough search. Then there is the problem of the people who know you are alive. Me, Aileen Sterner, and her father, Tom. I believe that sometime, you will be found. That's why I am telling you all this. It's all I thought about when Uncle Pen died. I thought of the good the money could do you, what with the new baby and all."

"What new baby?" asked Kenny.

"Oh, God," thought Reid. "I can't believe he doesn't know his own wife is pregnant!"

"What new baby?" asked Kenny again.

"Dianne is pregnant. If she hasn't told you, she will have to, soon." Reid said the last words absently. She wished herself away. Away from involvement and complication; away from hurt and frustration. She heard music and was following her mind's melody when the server came for their order.

Neither Reid nor Kenny had looked at the menu. They didn't have to. Reid ordered the same salad she had ordered since her first meal here. Kenny ordered coffee only which was quickly brought.

"Are you done? Is there anything else you know about my life that I should know? I thought you were different from everyone else in my family. But you're a VanDuyver clear through. Manipulative and money hungry. You're no different than the rest."

It was Reid's turn to be angry. "I am a VanDuyver and I'm not. I'm half something else that I will never know about! You left your past but mine left me! I didn't go looking for you. You found me. I'm not telling you what to do. I'm telling you things you should know in case something happens. If you don't want the money, don't take it."

"I won't! I don't need it!" That wasn't the truth, but it felt good to say it and maybe make it the truth later, Kenny thought. How many times had he considered what would happen to him, to his wife and children if they ever knew his secret? Now it was a reality. What could he say to them? What was his defense? He didn't have one.

The food arrived for Reid. The cheerful waitress filled Kenny's coffee and brought more fresh cream. There was between the two cousins no pretense. Dry tears of uncertainty were falling unseen.

"I've got no right to ask it, Kenny, but it's kind of the last secret left. Why did you leave home? What happened? I never asked anyone. Your mother thought it was her drinking. Your brothers said your leaving caused her drinking."

Kenny looked at Reid in pure disgust and then away to the wall. "It was nothing, nothing at all."

If Reid was surprised at his reply to her question, she did not show it. She began to eat her salad. She didn't need to know more because she believed him. So much happened in everyone's life because of a moment. She had seen it in her own life. "Boom," and her mother took a drive in the rain. "Boom," and Grammy decided to weed the garden in the hot sun. "Boom," and Big Daddy sold the farm. The little moments of others comprised Reid's early life.

"You don't know what it was like for me being youngest in the family, Reid. You left and you never came back. Do you remember even saying good-bye to me? I idolized you as a kid. Nothing ever got to you. I remember my father running you down and my brothers saying terrible things about you and your mother. You must have heard them and you were so cool. Just never said a word. You never talked back. They never got to you, Reid. Never."

"Does that mean they got to you, then?"

"Damn right. I fought being like them. I wanted to be like you and Big Daddy. I wanted to be so smart I didn't have to even talk to people because people would just respect me for being smart."

"You were always smart, Kenny. I'm surprised it worried you so."

"Don't you remember what it was like, Reid? To be a teenager? All of your experiences are like wearing a wool sweater on a hot July day. You itch. You burn. Soon you're just filled with hate and anger because no one else is wearing one. They are just laughing at you. That's how it felt. Every day is just filled with that hate and anger because no one else is like you."

Reid's eyes were wide in amazement. "No, I never felt that way. Things always bewildered me. They still do. I learned to accept what happened. Until recently, I never tried to change my life on my own. What you thought was an admirable silence was nothing more than being tongue-tied. That's all it was."

"I know that now. No disrespect, but you do lose your voice when it comes to standing up for yourself! To me, as a kid, it didn't seem that way. You seemed strong and wise, just like Big Daddy. I just kept on opening my mouth and getting beat down, so I left. From that day it was just easier to keep on going."

"Well, then, keep on going. Nothing about that has to change. All I am asking is to acknowledge who you are, my cousin. I want to acknowledge that the VanDuyvers exist so that I can go on with my life, too. Can we leave it there, Kenny?"

"I don't know. It is easier for you than for me. You haven't been lying to the people who mean the world to you. I have. I don't know if Dianne will ever forgive me. I mean, she never even told me she was pregnant! What kind of man does she think I am?"

"And what do you think she thinks of me? I have lied to her for ten years as well! I was the accomplice in your transformation. She didn't even know we were first cousins! I have no idea what she thinks, but I hope that she will come to see your point of view and mine too. I hope that she loves you enough to understand that you are first a good man. A true man. Just give her a little time. Later, maybe things will look different to you both," said Reid.

"I'm still mad at you. It isn't your life that's a mess. Mine is. Did you think about that?"

"Did you think about it when you called me when Uncle Pen died? I think you wanted to get all this out. You just thought that somehow, since you were out of the family by choice, that there would be no messiness. Families are messy, Kenny. They are always messy with difficulties and money troubles and fighting and failure. They are even messy in love and success. The VanDuyvers are no different."

"I don't feel better." Kenny signaled for the check. "But I am going home to my beautiful pregnant wife and try once again to make her understand what I don't."

The conversation between the two cousins stopped. It didn't end. Kenny picked up the check from the table without another word to Reid and paid it. Reid sat at the table alone and looked out the window. The bright sun of early morning was now midday haze. Some clouds were building in the northwest sky and the wind had come up. Reid felt a chill in her back. Someplace other than here, somewhere like Iowa, the sky and wind would tell an autumn story, she thought. Here, in Phoenix, seasons only changed in a person's heart. She was ready for the change. Maybe Kenny would be, but she could not count on it.

She thought about calling Dianne. She thought about calling Jack. What would she say to either of them? She and her cousin had done what they had done. Things just needed a rest for a while until reason and love could catch up with other emotions. Autumn was "catch-up" time. When she walked to her car, the sun was warm, but she knew the wind was blowing in another season.

When Kenny got home, his daughter, Ruby Rose Smyth was sitting at the kitchen table cutting out pumpkins that she had drawn on several sheets of orange construction paper. Although left-handed, she held the large scissors in her right hand. When he saw this, Kenny immediately said, "Put the scissors in the other hand, Rose. You're left-handed."

"Not always. Not always I'm not," said Rose. She changed the scissors to the other hand anyway. "Where's the tape? I need tape now."

"I don't know. Where is your Mom? Maybe she knows."

"She's in my room. She's still mad. Will you find the tape for me? I need it now."

"She's still mad, huh? Ruby Rose, it's me she is mad at, not you. Why don't you go ask her for the tape and then I'll help you?" asked Kenny, still ashamed to face his wife.

"I don't want to," said Ruby Rose.

Kenny didn't want to either. He just didn't. There had never been a time like this with Dianne. Anger had never been a part of their life together.

Anger had been the heart of his family. Anger and resentment. That's why he left. He just couldn't take it any more. Nothing was ever settled back then. Nothing was ever dropped. Dad was always mad at something; Mom was always mad at Dad for being mad. As for Kenny's brothers, well, anger was bred in their bones, he supposed.

That was then. He had lost nothing by leaving Iowa. He would lose everything if he lost Dianne and his precious daughter. Well, that wasn't going to happen!

"Rose," said Kenny, "I'll get the tape and then we'll get Mom to help us finish up."

Rose didn't look up from her cutting. "OK," she replied.

Kenny walked the short hall to the bedroom. Dianne was resting on the bed.

"How are you feeling?" asked Kenny.

"Tired, mostly just tired," said Dianne without any feeling.

"That's the way you were in the first months when you were pregnant with Rose."

"Did Reid tell you I was pregnant?" asked Dianne.

"Yes, she did," answered Kenny. He had not moved from the doorway.

"Your cousin can't keep a secret, can she? Are you mad?" asked Dianne.

"Mad that you're pregnant or mad that Reid told me?"

"Either."

"Surprised at both, but not mad, Dianne."

"Well, you should be because this is a mess!" Dianne sat up and was facing the wall. "Your cousin knows more family secrets! I swear I didn't mean to tell her but it came out when I went to talk to her about your real family. I feel that I don't even know who the father of this baby is! What a stinking mess."

"Daddy. Daddy," called Rose from the kitchen.

"What does Rose want?" Dianne stood up. There was weariness in her stance.

"Tape. Rose wants the tape for her Halloween decorations."

"It's above the sink. High up where she can't reach it. She wants to tape or sticker everything these days. She makes a mess if you don't watch her."

There was that word again, "mess." There was that condition, that state of being, that element to be avoided, thought Kenny. Reid was right; families were messy.

"I'll get Rose her tape, but I'm not going to watch her. I am going to let her do whatever she wants and I'm going to come back and talk to you about our new baby. The one who is going to mess up our lives and make us very happy," said Kenny.

He walked down the hall into the kitchen. Rose was concentrating on her cutting. He reached up into the high cabinet. There were two rolls of tape. He took them both and gave them to his daughter. "You be careful. Make something nice and then your Mom and I have a surprise for you."

Rose didn't look up. "Is it ice cream?"

Kenny was about to say "no," but thought the better of it. There would be time later for the real surprise. "How did you guess?"

"Because ice cream makes Mom happy," said Ruby Rose.

"Makes me happy, too, Rose. You finish up and I'll go get Mom."

When Kenny returned to the bedroom, Dianne was sitting at the edge of the bed. She motioned for him to sit with her. He went to the bed and sat without touching her.

"What other family secrets did Reid spill today?" asked Dianne.

"Just one and it was more unexpected than the rest. She says I can inherit part of the farm. I just have to show up and admit that I am alive and well."

"And will you? Will you tell your family that you are well and have a family of your own? Will you?"

"I don't know."

Dianne started to cry. She struggled to stand up. "What did I do to deserve this? What have I done that you are so ashamed of me. And Ruby Rose? What has she done? Why have you kept us hidden away from your own family?"

It was hard for Kenny to understand Dianne through her tears. "Is that what you think? That I am ashamed of either of you?"

"What am I supposed to think? From the minute we met, you have lied to me. You never told me that you had parents and brothers. Rose had grandparents she never saw! I have tried to make up for all the family I thought you never had. I feel stupid. Why is it that the wife is always the last to know?"

"Because her stupid husband didn't tell her?" offered Kenny.

Dianne glared. This wasn't working, thought Kenny.

"Dianne, I made a mistake. I left home when I was a kid. I knocked around for a long time until I decided to go to college. Then I met you. You were everything that I had missed in my life. You were perfect. There were times when I wanted to tell you the truth, but I was too trapped to go back. I was ashamed of my family. If you had met them, you would have never married me. Never. They are nothing like anyone you know. And because of you, because of Ruby Rose, I never missed them."

"How can they have been so awful? What did they do? I still don't understand. I want to understand. I don't," said Dianne.

"I can't tell you anymore than what I have already told you ten times over. I would if there was something else to tell."

"Call them. Call them and tell them about us."

Kenny knew it was going to come to this. It was the price he would have to pay. It was a door he would have to open and one that would never close easily again.

"I will call," he promised.

"When?" asked Dianne pointedly.

"Sometime soon. I don't know what I'll say. Don't get your hopes up that somehow there's going to be a reunion. I'm doing this only because you have asked me to. You and Rose are all I need. I don't need anyone I left once."

"What about the baby? How will I ever be sure that you will be here for all of us? What if you decide to just walk out like you did before?" asked Dianne.

"I won't," said Kenny solemnly.

"How can I be sure?"

"You can't anymore than I can be sure that you won't leave me. We promised each other that we would stay together 'until death us do part'. We said that in church and we meant it. There is nothing you can say that changes that for me. I'm here for you, for Ruby Rose, and for the one who isn't even born." Kenny reached out to touch his wife to make his feelings more tangible to her. They couldn't stay in this awful limbo of doubt and recrimination. Better feelings and memories would have to replace these. He said, "I promised Ruby Rose that we were going for ice cream just as soon as she used up all the tape."

"Kenny, we need to talk some more about your family."

"We do. We will. Just not today. We'll have to catch up together and move forward together."

Dianne decided that there was nothing to do but go for ice cream. The surety that had been in the center of her marriage was gone. The pain that had been its brief replacement was also gone. There was just an emptiness that needed filling. Ice cream would be a start. "I'm ready for chocolate chip," she announced to Kenny. Together they went to gather their daughter for the first family outing of their new life.

P.S. Lowe

Abby the Artist

Abby was awake, but refused to open her eyes. "Pain," she thought, "is a terrible thief. It robs you of all desire to do anything except end the pain. You don't care if it is day or night. The pain is your life."

Abby's leg hurt terribly. What had started as minor joint pain in her right ankle months ago had moved up until it now ached to her hip. Mornings were the absolute worst. Once she was involved in her day and painting, the importance of the pain diminished. This morning, however, her leg burned. She attempted to get up. The knife in her thigh made her groan loudly.

Her longtime companion, Jack Ellis, lay in the bed beside her. "Is that a comment on anything in particular?" he asked as he reached for her hand.

Abby struggled to focus on what Jack had asked. A wave of nausea kept her from replying. Her eyes were shut tightly against her leg's agony. Jack raised himself on one elbow and gripped her hand. "Abby, Abby, are you all right? Is it your leg again? Abby, you're not breathing. Breathe, Abby and stop holding in the pain."

Abby could hear Jack now. Breathe. She exhaled and a river of pain left her. She opened her eyes. Jack's face was very close to hers. "You need to keep reminding me to breathe. I think that I forget. I'm sorry to wake you up like this Jack. I didn't know arthritis could be like this," said Abby.

Jack let go of her hand and was instantly out of bed. "Dammit, Abby. Whatever you have, it is not arthritis. When are you going to stop pretending it is and go to the doctor? You are driving me crazy. Is this some kind of contest you have to win? Are you a human pain barometer?"

"Jack, don't start on this again. I'm sure it's nothing but arthritis. I stood up too long yesterday. It just did me in. I will be fine later. How about some coffee? Can you make me some coffee? Then I'll get up."

"No, I'm going back to bed just to watch you get up. I know you, Abby. You want me out of here so that you can roll out of bed without me seeing you. I heard you last night, all night. You have a fever and you moaned constantly. Abby, go to the doctor. You can't go on like this and I can't go on watching you."

"I'm not going to a Mexican doctor. I'll go the doctor the next time I'm in Phoenix." Abby smiled weakly.

"We're going to Phoenix today, then," said Jack.

"It's Saturday. There are no doctors to see on Saturday. They are all playing golf." Jack did not smile at her joke.

"Jack, next week, I'll go next week. I will call on Monday and get an appointment and I will go. Deal?"

"No deal, Abby. We're going today."

Abby bit her tongue hard and forced herself out of bed. "See, I'm up and going to make the coffee. Then I'll bring you a cup in bed and you can tell me a story."

"Abby, I'm not letting you out of this. We are going today if I have to kidnap you. This isn't some kind of deal you can make with me! For once in your life, you are going to do what is right and not what you want to do. I am affected by this, too. Think about something other than what you want to do when you want to do it." Jack's earlier concern had become pink anger.

Abby covered her face with one hand. In all the years they had been together, only one other time had Jack said these words to her. She deserved them then. She didn't deserve them now. Jack knew she was both selfish and greedy. She was self-centered in all the good and bad ways that a painter could be. He had been so good to her! She just couldn't go to Phoenix today. She had three paintings to finish. They were so important to her. How could she convince him of that? How could she have her own way for the last time?

Abby uncovered her face. "Jack, I know that you want what you think is best for me. I believe that; I have always believed it. That's why I love you Jack. I don't know what's wrong with me. I am scared to find out. Somehow, once I find out, I'll be changed. For good or ill, Jack, I won't be the woman I am today. That's why I have to finish those paintings." Abby was pleading.

"You can finish them later. You don't have a buyer. These aren't commissioned. You have no shows planned. Your agent hasn't called you since you made him rich with your show last year."

"Don't you see that's why I have to finish them? These are what I want to paint! These are me, more me than much of what I have done in a long time. These are for me, Jack. If someone else likes them in the future, great. I want to finish them before the feeling that inspired them leaves me. It will leave me, it always does. Time is a great enemy of painters. The light changes, time passes and the inspiration vanishes. Please Jack. I can finish them in two days. I can do it."

"I hate living with an artist," shouted Jack.

"I'm not an artist. I'm a painter. I may be an artist if I can just finish these. After thirty years of effort, I may be an artist if I can just finish these paintings."

"Oh, yes. I forgot your fine distinctions. You're just a painter. Forgive me. I thought you were an artist once you had sold a million in U.S. dollars. Isn't that what you've done in just the last two years? Your work hangs in every important gallery in North and South America! I can't imagine that three paintings, even if they are never finished, will make a damn bit of difference as to whether you are an artist or a painter."

"It will make a difference to me, Jack. Somehow, it will make a difference to me. I have been trying to say something in my work for years. I always feel that I just miss the mark. I have felt close in the past, but in the end, I was never happy with my work. This time I am. I just want to paint until they are done."

"Damn. Damn!" thought Jack. "I hate this mess and I hate myself for starting it. I have never understood Abby when she is painting. I love the woman she is. She hasn't changed at all in the years we've been together. She just doesn't know any other way. Selfish, lovely, artistic; my daytime sun and the moon of my nights. Shit. I don't want her to be sick."

"Jack, please. Just two days. Then we will go to Phoenix. Please."

"I'm going to make coffee," said Jack. He picked up his blue robe from the bedside table and put it on, tying the belt with a hard knot. Then he walked to the other side of the bed and hugged Abby. "I'm giving in to you, Abby. I can do it because I am older and stronger than you are. I didn't lose; I let you win."

"I know. I'm only successful because you carry me along. I know that. These paintings are about that. They're for you Jack."

"Abby, I don't believe you. You're just trying to buy me off."

"Nope. These are for you. These are about your life and my life. Together."

"And when do I get to see them? Today? I may still kidnap you and take you to the doctor."

Abby hoped Jack was kidding. She had never shown him any work until it was finished. "Sunday night. I will pack and you can go into the studio and play 'Jack Ellis, Critic.'"

"OK, then. I'm off to coffee; you're to the studio. I'm going to the restaurant to check on a few things. I'll be home around one o'clock to make sure that you eat."

"I'm ready. Thank you. I'll get coffee after I have painted a while. See you later," said Abby.

Jack went to the kitchen. Abby went to the bathroom and poured a large glass of bottled water. She took out four extra-strength aspirin and took them. She had two days to paint everything she had ever wanted to paint. She was not going to bother getting dressed.

Abby left the house through the bedroom door and entered her studio. At the far end were three easels, faced against the northeast light. The windows shed no light on her work. Abby liked to paint looking out the window. She used lamps to guide her very detailed painting. On her way to the end of the studio, she dragged an old chair. Her leg would never hold up to standing today.

She turned on the two floodlights and adjusted them to even the light on the three large canvasses. Although the two side panels were nearly complete, the larger center painting was half-done. Abby sat down to concentrate. She could see the finished paintings in front of her. There were no decisions left to make. She only had to paint what was in her mind's eye and engraved on her heart. Her subject was the past. She knew it well.

The side panels were identical in color, but not subject. The background was an earth-taupe strongly heightened with dusty orchid, sage green and creamy white. Four scenes comprised the center painting, where the subjects stood out against darkness. The colors in each of the divided areas, alarmingly bright.

In the left panel, the mountains of Washington overshadowed the picnic pictured below. A girl and a boy are chaining daisies together. The long garland loops around their necks and arms as they work to add more flowers. In the left background, a solitary farmhouse sits within a copse of apple trees. To the right, in the foreground, was a farmer in overalls looking at a pocket watch as if waiting for a train. In the left foreground, a country woman in a long dress picks white daisies. Only the boy and girl looked at each other. The remaining space is filled with criss-crossed roads and miniature towns.

The right panel was the partial facade of a house. Through the window to the dining room, a family of three is eating a formal dinner. Brilliant white emanates from the chandelier. The girl at the table gazes toward her mother. The mother is looking at the father at the end of the table. The father is looking directly out the window to a space outside of the painting. In the darker right edge of the painting, a young girl appears to be running off the edge of the canvas. There is fear in her face.

Both the left and right sections needed more definition. "That can wait," thought Abby. "I need to work on the center sections."

She reached for her paints and a fresh paper palette. She had mixed shades of purple for the upper left quadrant. Unthinkingly, she stood up to begin to paint. The pain that shot to her hip made her gag. She threw the palette toward the wall before collapsing in the chair. It took a few minutes for Abby to center herself again. "I'll do what I can do sitting down," Abby thought. Mixing the purest blues, she began on the lower right scene. She painted the view outside the window. "This is for you,

Jack," she said aloud to the canvas. "This is us together on our patio. This is how it was meant to be. This is what all else lead to."

The quadrant was finished when Jack called her for lunch. Today, the sound of his voice thrilled her. She put down her brush and limped toward his call.

More aspirin after lunch got her through the afternoon. It was dark when she gave up for the day, satisfied that she would finish tomorrow. Sunday morning was a repeat of Saturday without a morning confrontation with Jack. The painting spilled from her hands. Finished by early evening, she was very tired when she went to find Jack who was reading at the small kitchen table. "Go look. They are done."

"You look like shit. I hope that the paintings are in better shape," said Jack.

"They are. What is there to eat? Did you bring something?" Abby sat down hard in the other chair.

"There's rice, fish cakes and a glass of wine. Are you ready to eat?"

"Yes. Can you just hand it to me? Then go look. I want to know what you think."

While Abby ate, Jack went to the studio. He turned on the main lights first. He stayed away from the paintings. Looking at Abby's works was a daunting experience. She often picked subjects he disliked. He often liked works that she refused to show or sell. God only knew what he would be able to say about these three. Keeping his back to the paintings, he walked behind the canvasses and turned on Abby's painting lights. Then he turned around. It wasn't just the size of the pieces that was unusual. The colors were breathtaking. He wanted to step away from them, but the wall behind him kept him from getting any perspective.

He wouldn't take the risk of turning the easels of wet canvas. If the colors winded him, the subjects stripped his heart. Abby had unflinchingly captured his life and thrown it in his face. Every feeling of his life was in paint. He saw his mother, father and sister. The roads he had traveled with and without Abby. The places they had been together.

Minutes passed as he discovered each detail. It was hard for him to watch his life. It was agonizing to see Abby's. "How was she able to bring all that skill and discipline to pictures of her own life?" he wondered.

Jack had no idea how long it was before he was able to turn out the painting lights. He didn't need to get a better perspective. He knew that these were great paintings. There was so much to look at and so much emotion. Everyone who saw them could bring their own story to the pictures; all of the stories would be as true as the story of Jack and Abby. He turned out the main lights and walked back to the kitchen.

Abby had finished her supper and her glass of wine. Jack went to the cupboard and found a bottle of California Barberra that he had been saving. It was bottled in the year he had met Abby. He got out two fresh wine glasses and poured them full. He handed one to Abby and raised his own with this toast: "This is to Abby the artist. Painter no more."

They drank. "So, you liked the paintings. I'm glad. So very glad," said Abby. "I feel like I can finally get on with my life. The best for me is in the future."

"We're going to fly to Phoenix tomorrow, Abby. I want a future with you," said Jack.

"Let's drive. Let's close up the house and go for a couple of weeks. Get David to run the bar or close it."

"I'm not taking a two day car trip with someone who smells like you!"

"If you want me to smell like a lady, you had better do something about it! I'm just too tired," said Abby.

"That I can do. I will do you and you can do me. Drink up. This is last call until Phoenix."

They finished their wine. Jack tidied up the kitchen, carefully air corking the wine for a later occasion. Abby had stripped off her dirty nightgown and was brushing her teeth in the small bathroom when Jack came in to turn on the shower. Unlike Abby, Jack neatly folded his clothes as he removed them. They stepped into the shower together. Jack gently washed Abby's slender body and then really scrubbed her head and hair. Then he moved her away from the shower spray where he could see her naked wet body as he washed himself. In her late forties, Abby's figure had matured, but lost none of the graceful curves of her youth.

After they had dried each other with clean white towels, Abby was falling asleep on her feet. Her leg hurt, but not as much as it had earlier. She wanted a clean nightgown, but it seemed like too much effort to find one. She wanted clean sheets, too and wished she had changed them.

With her eyes shut, she started to ask Jack to do it for her. "Jack?"

"I know. Let's make it easy. We will sleep in the guest room tonight. The sheets are clean there."

She opened her eyes. "You know me too well."

"After seeing your paintings, I think you know me too well, Abby."

He grabbed her hand and they went naked to the guest bed. Jack folded Abby into the sheets and blanket, and then came in beside her, careful not to disturb her leg. He was on his side while she was on her back. He was sure she was already asleep. With his right hand, he traced the muscles of her neck. Opening his hand, he touched her breasts. How he loved her body. "You are my moon at night, Abby."

"I know Jack. I love you," said Abby as she moved into deep sleep.

Those were the words he always wanted to hear. Tonight, tomorrow and all the rest of their lives together. Tomorrow they would drive toward Phoenix. They would talk and laugh and look at all the countryside they had not seen in a while. Tomorrow night, somewhere that they were strangers, they would make love as only old lovers can, in harmony and trust.

Jack could see tomorrow as clearly as Abby could see the past. It looked very good.

Going Home

It was hopeless. Abby knew it and she wanted out of the hospital. The fire of the good fight was out. The terrors, the fears, the desires and the hopes had moved from both her mind and heart. All but one: she wished to go home and be with Jack for the last time. There were things to set straight. "Ha!" she thought. "They would both be surprised if they knew what I was thinking!"

It was true. For all of her adult life, two men had done all the thinking and doing for Abby. They had managed her money and her talent; they had met her needs and most of her wants as well. One had provided her with a real home with all the trimmings. In Jack's stability, she had had complete freedom to paint whatever visions came to her. Holmes DuMez had disciplined her craft. Holmes had provided her visions a market and the money that she had used as her security against the past. One man she made rich and the other, well, what could she say? She hoped that in some measure, she had made him happy. She wasn't sure. She would give it one last try, she thought.

She was lucky to be thinking at all. Months of intense treatment for bone cancer had left her drained and angry most of the time. Anger had become a way of life that she regretted only when she could be alone, which was infrequently. There was always the "hovering" of doctors and nurses when she was in the hospital and Jack's persistent shadowing at their rented apartment. The anger was so terrible at times, that Abby imagined that as her body wasted, the tissues and structures evaporated into ugly thoughts and words.

Abby had no idea of the time, but thought it was nearly dawn. She hoped it was. She was finished with waiting. Dr. Barkourus made his rounds early. She would tell him that she wanted to get out and she would go. The apparatus of illness and treatment would remain here. She would leave as she came, weakened, but unencumbered. She had no idea what day it was, but thought that it was Friday. If it was, she was sure to see the doctor early. Her months of treatment had given her time to memorize the routines of the movers in the world of oncology. Until today, it had been useless knowledge.

When the doctor left, she would call Jack. With his help, they would be eating lunch on the road far away from United Hospital and far away from Phoenix. She was counting on it. It would feel good to be on the road.

Dr. Barkourus came as expected. He was more than reluctant to release Abby from the hospital. She was at a critical point in her treatment and it could go either way. If successful, Abby would have another year added to her life or possibly, she could be cured. Without treatment, she might have weeks, or maybe days. All week, there had been reason to be hopeful, but yesterday, something had changed. Her red blood cell count had dropped by more than ten percent. Dr. Barkourus wanted to re-do the tests on Monday to see if there was further change. Walking away now meant that there would be no closure for him. The doctor would never know if he had helped Abby, or had subjected her pain and disfigurement to no avail.

"I don't need any more tests to know. I know. It's over and I want to leave," said Abby to her very cool oncologist.

"You don't know and I don't know. We both need a few more days. Then we'll discuss options. You'll still have options."

"My options are dying here or dying elsewhere. I am exercising my option to die elsewhere. You can sign the papers and we can do this the easy way or I can just leave. I'll yank out this damn machinery and be gone quicker than you can say 'radiation therapy'," said Abby.

"You are going to need medical help. If you insist, I'll assign you to a hospice unit."

"That won't be necessary unless they want to go to Mexico, because that's where I'm going. With Jack. Today."

Dr. Barkourus was a young man who just looked old. It was the nature of his work. This was not the first time that, in spite of his energies and his research to find the right treatment, his patient gave up. It seemed to the doctor that the giving up preceded the change in medical condition. He thought this was the case with Abby. She had probably decided to discontinue treatment, and therefore living, first. The change for the worse came after that decision. If he could, Dr. Barkourus would find a way to keep his patients from ever deciding to die. He just didn't know how to do that.

Resignation set his body. Abby's intransigence was a brick wall that he wasn't getting around. He would try one last time to appeal to her sense of concern for others. "You are going to need help if you want to leave. You cannot expect Jack to take care of you. Bone cancer is not a picnic at the end, Abby. It's likely to be very difficult. It's selfish of you to make Jack bear the weight of your illness alone."

"You think I am selfish?" asked Abby angrily. "Doctor, you have no idea how selfish I am. Dying on Jack's time would not even make the radar of selfish things I have done. I am a master of selfishness! You doctors don't know anything! Dying in Jack's bed is probably the least selfish thing I will ever get a chance to do."

"If you want to help Jack, then help Jack. I am going to need painkillers and lots of them. I would prefer morphine. I've had it enough times to know that it helps manage my head's reactions to my body," said Abby.

"You know Abby, I can't do that. I can help you if you let me get in touch with Hospice. They will make sure that you don't suffer."

"Won't do. I do not intend to stay here in Phoenix. I can get drugs in Mexico, but it will be harder on Jack than if you set me out with them to begin with. You who are so hopped up to help Jack should help me out on this."

"I can't."

"Well, can't or won't, it's the same to me and for Jack. Just do what you have to do and I'll be gone." Abby was quite finished with the doctor.

Sensing that this was the end, that there was no emotion he could tap to change the outcome, Dr. Barkourus made a few notes on Abby's chart and left the room. She was dead to him now and the fact that she could breathe and speak meant nothing at this moment. When her life was in his hands, he was tireless. Now, she would be just a statistic in the liability column of his managed care provider evaluation. He was grateful to turn her over to the administrative functionaries and return to those who might yet be a plus in his career and his life.

Being released from a hospital is at least as complicated as being admitted. Abby wasted no time in calling Jack to come to get her. She didn't have to provide him an explanation on the phone about leaving. He knew the 'why' and though it did not surprise him, he wasn't sure he was prepared to take Abby home to Mexico. It's the dying, he thought, not death. He didn't think he could stand the dying.

While Abby fretted in the hospital for the morning, Jack decided that he needed someone to talk to about the times to come. Here in Phoenix, he didn't have many choices. Even after years of absence, Jack had many friends and acquaintances, but there were none to talk to about Abby, her cancer and her impending death. There was only the family: his sister, Lisa; his mother, Daisy; his nephew, Paul. No contest, it would be Lisa if she was at home. If not, there wasn't a second choice.

Rather than call, Jack decided to go see his sister. If she wasn't at home, he would take it as some sort of omen. The rented apartment where he and Abby had stayed for months was only a couple of miles from the hospital. It was very nice and very expensive, built for executives in an old neighborhood slowly being reclaimed around 20th Street and Indian School Road. Lisa lived off Central Avenue in an ultramodern house she had purchased out of foreclosure. It was more house than a single woman needed, but Lisa was in the real estate business. To her, everything was an investment if it had land under it.

Jack arrived at Lisa's before 10 a.m. Swinging his pickup truck into the drive, he could not tell if she was at home. He would have to ring the doorbell. When he managed his way up the walkway, Lisa met him at the door. His visit was so unexpected that she imagined that he had come to tell her that Abby had died. She was prepared to be sympathetic.

Once brother and sister had settled in Lisa's comfortable peach-colored kitchen, Jack assured his sister that Abby had not died. "That's the problem. Abby wants to go back to Mexico to die. She wants me to take her there. I'm not sure I can handle it, Lisa."

The only part of Jack's revelation that surprised Lisa was Jack's reluctance to attend the dying process. That Abby would ask him to do it, alone, far into some vague Mexican province didn't surprise Lisa at all.

"That bitch!" said Lisa.

Jack covered his face. He had made a mistake in coming here. He had thought that the fact that Abby was actually dying might soften his sister. A miscalculation.

"Oh, Jack, I'm sorry. I didn't really mean that. Yeah, well I did mean it, but I didn't mean to say it and I didn't mean to hurt you," said Lisa with true remorse. "Abby's high-handed ways have always made me mad because you should have had someone who was better than that. I wanted you to have a better life than the one you had, going from place to place just to please her need to paint; her need for atmosphere. Now this. Jack, can she possibly expect you to take her to Mexico if she is that ill?"

"Oh, she expects it all right. Watching her suffer, watching her wasting away, unable to paint or to enjoy anything, it has about done me in. I don't know who is more pitiful – me or her."

"Abby is," said Lisa without hesitation. "She ought to have her head examined, but it is too late now. I don't think she is going to change. What about Hospice? Dad had great Hospice care at home. Don't you remember?"

"No, I wasn't around. Anyway, Abby wants to go to Mexico, not stay in Phoenix. I don't know that she can make the trip.

I worry that I won't be able to take care of her," said Jack, sadly.

"Then don't try."

"I've got to try."

"Jack, do you want me to go with you? I can. I don't have anything 'hot' right now. Staff can handle the office." Lisa was trying to come up with some idea that might help, although she was hoping her offer would be declined.

"With you and Abby together in my truck, I can tell you, it would be a long ride to Mexico. Thanks for offering, though." Jack smiled a little.

Lisa's mind raced ahead. She had seen Abby only a couple of times in the months she had been in Phoenix. The last time was about three weeks ago. Abby looked terrible then. "Jack, how long has she got? I mean, you've been with her every day. Are we talking months or weeks or days?"

"I don't know. She isn't eating. Can't keep anything down. She walks with a walker. She has had several transfusions. I cannot imagine her holding on for more than a week or two, but I don't know. I am guessing from what I hear at the hospital and from the folks I've seen who died there. God, I hate having this discussion."

Lisa reached across the table for her brother's hand and squeezed it. "We're going to play a little game that I play with all my salesmen when they seem to be avoiding the work that produces. I ask them, 'What is your biggest fear?' What scares you, Jack? Do you have enough money to help take care of Abby?"

"There's money and I can get more if I need it," said Jack.

"So, what's the fear? We'll figure out how to get around it if we can," said Lisa.

"Watching her suffer and not being able to help her. The more I care for her, the more I hate it. I cannot stand to touch her because she is fragile and suffering and I can't do anything but watch. I hate myself for feeling the way I do."

Lisa reflected on what Jack had said. "Daisy felt that way about our dad."

"What?" asked Jack.

"She did. After Dad died, she wouldn't do anything but sit in that old recliner of Dad's. She wouldn't cook. She would hardly eat. I went over to the house one time. It was late in the afternoon and she was just sitting in the chair. She had not changed out of her nightgown in a couple of days. I tried to coax her into getting dressed and going out. She told me that she was going to sit in that chair and do nothing until she was dead or dead tired of sitting there. She told me that she could smell the hospital waking and sleeping. The only memory she could conjure up of Dad was him curled up in a fetal position, unable to breathe. She told me she never wanted to touch another human being again. So, maybe how you feel is in the genes. You can't help what you feel, Jack. I wouldn't have made it as far as you made it."

"She said those things? Doesn't sound like Daisy."

"True story, honest. I wouldn't make it up. Not now. It is a powerful fear. You're going to need some help. It won't be me, unless you need money," said Lisa.

Brother and sister sat in complete silence. They were startled when Lisa's long-time housekeeper, Rosita, let herself into the house and walked into the kitchen. They surprised her as well. Usually, Rosita had the house to herself a couple of days a week. Seeing her housekeeper gave Lisa an idea.

"Rosie, pour yourself a cup of coffee and come sit with us for a minute. I have something I need to discuss with you." It sounded more like a command than a request, but Rosita was used to Lisa's ways.

Rosita Gonzalez put her lunch in the refrigerator and her purse in the pantry before retrieving her favorite mug from the dishwasher for her own coffee. She didn't offer any to Jack or Lisa. She was not a servant; she was a paid house-keeper for Mrs. Ellis. Rosita sat herself between Jack and Lisa at the round table.

"Good morning, Mrs. Ellis. How are you Mr. Ellis?"

"He's not so fine, Rosie," said Lisa before Jack could answer. "He needs someone to help take care of Abby. She wants to come out of the hospital and she is going to die."

Ever direct, Lisa put all her cards on the table at once. "I remember that your cousin, Lupe, used to do private duty nursing. Is she working now?"

"She works a little on and off. Mostly she helps her daughter out at the day care," answered Rosita.

"Would she be willing to go to Mexico with Jack and Abby and stay for as long as, well, for as long as it takes?" asked Lisa.

"Lupe doesn't speak any Spanish. I don't think she would go alone," answered Rosita.

"Well, what if you and Lupe went together? Would she go if you went?"

"I don't know, but I will ask her when I see her again. Mrs. Ellis, how can I go to Mexico when I work for you here? If I am gone for a week, your big house will be backwards. I need to work for you. I cannot be gone long."

Jack had been following the conversation, but hadn't agreed to anything that Lisa had so far planned. His little sister was a steamroller once started.

"Rosie, call Lupe and see if she would go. Tell her that she will be paid in addition to all her expenses, paid for twenty-four hours a day. Ask her if she can leave in a day or two." When Rosita remained unresponsive, Lisa added, "Please Rosie, as a favor to me and to Jack."

Rosita Gonzalez had performed many "extra" duties for Mrs. Ellis over the years, but nothing like this. Mrs. Ellis had been generous in the past and Rosita expected nothing less for this favor. She got up to make the call to her cousin.

Once Rosie had left, Jack spoke to his sister. "This isn't going to work. You can't just order people around and ask them an unreasonable favor. Your housekeeper doesn't owe me anything."

"She owes me Jack. If you think that I'm somehow exploiting her, think again. I pay her twice what she would make anywhere else. I donate to her church and even gave her my old car for the minister."

"You mean that the Catholic Church can't give its priests transportation?" asked Jack. He was more surprised about that than his sister's generosity.

"Rosie isn't Catholic. She is some kind of weird Protestant and so is her cousin. Don't ask me what," answered Lisa.

"We are Evangelista; Evangelists in English," said Rosita as she walked back into the kitchen.

Lisa rolled her eyes at her brother. Lisa was little concerned what splinter denomination her housekeeper embraced. She wanted someone who was trustworthy, capable and reliable. Rosie had been all of that for many years. If being an Evangelist made for good housekeepers, Lisa was all for it.

Rosita, Jack, and Lisa spent the next hour discussing the plan to take Abby to Mexico. Lupe had agreed to go and provide the care, shared with Jack. Rosie would look after the house, the meals, and act as a translator. They would leave tomorrow afternoon if Abby could travel. They discussed money. Lisa didn't blink when her housekeeper said for Lupe it would be $00 a day from the time they left Phoenix, until she returned. Lisa said she would gladly pay it. Jack would pay Rosita $00 a day and Lisa would continue to pay Rosie's weekly wages in addition. Rosita would take her own car, but Jack would pay for the expenses. It seemed cut and dried. Jack and Rosita exchanged phone numbers, agreeing to leave about noon on Saturday. Negotiations finished, Lisa sent her housekeeper home.

Jack stayed for a while longer. He wanted to say something of thanks to his sister, but he had no real words to say. He had come for help, but not the kind that Lisa had so quickly ordered. That was Lisa, however. "I'll be off. Gotta go get Abby. She will be frantic by now. You've been a help, Lisa. I want you to know that."

"You're my brother. I'm not the best sister in the world, but by God I can get things organized," said Lisa in a tone of self-deprecation.

"Yeah, you can." Jack made no move to leave.

"Well, you had better go. I guess I'll see you when this is all over."

"Sometime, I'll be back. Don't know when. I'll probably stay in Mexico for a while. You are welcome to come. I'll take you over to the coast. We'll fish a little," said Jack.

"Jack, I don't ever want to be anyplace Abby has been," said Lisa.

"Then why are you helping her out?" asked Jack.

"I'm not helping her. I'm helping you. I feel responsible for all of this mess, this mess that has taken nearly all of your life. If I had not gone to Sky Harbor airport all those years ago, Abby would have disappeared. I have had cause to remember that many times. If I hadn't gone, she would be gone," said Lisa with genuine remorse.

"I asked you to go. Same as I asked for your help now. You came through for me, whether you believe it or not. Abby was worth saving then; she is worth helping now. She made something of her life. I watched. She painted some great stuff. I was behind her because I had you behind me. We all had our moments, you know?" asked Jack.

"Oh Jack, you are worth a thousand Abbys," said Lisa.

"So are you, little sister. I'm off," said Jack as he stood. He kissed the top of his sister's head and made his way out of the morning's sanctuary and into the real day.

Getting Abby physically out of United Hospital and into his truck, then from the truck into the apartment exhausted both Jack and Abby. It was after five o'clock before Abby had settled in the bed where she fell instantly asleep. He went through the sheaf of Abby's discharge papers to see what he would need to take to Mexico. He found some prescriptions along with a diagnosis. There was no recommendation to call Dr. Barkourus.

Jack decided to take the prescriptions to the pharmacy while Abby slept. He would pick up some food for the days ahead. He left a note for Abby on the table, telling her he would be back in an hour. His errands took less time than that in spite of the Friday night rush. Abby was still asleep. Waking her seemed pointless. He made himself a ham and cheese sand-wich and grabbed a cold beer as well. Although he checked on her often, Abby didn't stir. Jack showered and found a clean pair of pajama bottoms. He put a few of his things and Abby's into an ancient suitcase.

Abby awoke at 3 a.m. The apartment was dark. She wanted to get up, but Jack had moved her walker far away from the bed. She felt rested, but not strong. She would have to wait. It was good practice for being "unselfish." She had some-thing else to practice as well: what to say to Jack to let him know that she had loved him as much as she was able. It wasn't enough, but she couldn't help that then or now.

Abby had rehearsed her speech a thousand times by the time she heard Jack in the kitchen making coffee. It seemed that as she diminished in every other way, her hearing improved. Jack looked into the bedroom. Abby saw his large frame in the doorway. "I'm awake. Come in. Where did you sleep?"

"On the couch. I didn't want to wake you. Are you hungry? I can fix you some breakfast. How do you feel?"

"Shitty and better. I want to get up and go to the bathroom. I need you to help me."

Jack stiffened at the thought of having to pick her up. He did help her, however, and they managed to prepare for the trip over the next few hours. Jack explained to her that Lupe and Rosie would be coming along. The tone of the talk was grave and Abby knew better than to even try to resist the plans that Jack had made. She wanted to be alone, but she guessed that dying was like birth; at least some strangers would surround her. She managed to eat a little to be able to take pain medication. She loathed taking it, but was fearful of the ride ahead. Just the trip home in the truck had been unbearable.

When Rosita and Lupe arrived at the apartment, it took little time to see that the small Mexican women intended to be in charge. Lupe emptied out the scant linen closet and gathered up the bed pillows. When Abby challenged her, Lupe simply said, "These are for your bed and for emergencies." Lupe then disappeared outside.

It was not clear to either Jack or Abby until they went to load up that the women intended for Jack to drive the truck alone, and they would take Abby separately in Rosita's aged, but immaculate station wagon. Lupe had converted the back seat into a bed of sorts for Abby. Rosie would drive. In the same way that the arrangement disappointed Abby, it relieved Jack. The drive was long enough, to a little beyond

Magdalena, Mexico. Nevertheless, it would be dark when they arrived, if Abby could stand the trip. The spring light would hold until about six, and then it would be very dark. Unlike the United States, there would be a paucity of road lighting once they crossed the border. If Abby was too ill, they could stay the night in Nogales.

The trip down I-10 from Phoenix to Tucson was uneventful. The desert was greener than when they had made the mid-winter trip in February, but nothing bloomed. They stopped near Tucson to let Abby reposition herself. She was fine, much to Jack's relief. Lupe and Rosie seemed almost giddy being away from their usual responsibilities.

South of Tucson, the little caravan picked up I-19 that would take them into Mexico. After four in the afternoon, the air became noticeably cooler. Eating was a priority before beginning the last leg of the trip. Lupe insisted that she wanted to eat American food before crossing the Nogales border portal. They stopped at a café Jack knew well, far away from tourists and trouble. It was a struggle to get Abby and her walker into the restaurant, but at last, they were all seated in a booth. The conversation centered on Lupe, not on the reason for the trip. It seemed odd to both Abby and Jack that Lupe, born in the Sonoran desert of Mexico and carried by hand into Arizona as an infant, had never been back. Nor could she speak Spanish other than a small vocabulary of nouns. Her parents had insistently steered her into American ways and continued to be proud that their only child had graduated from Arizona State University with a degree in nursing. Unlike her cousin, Rosita, Lupe knew more about the 4th of July than Cinco de Mayo. Their middle age trip back to their homeland was truly a road of discovery.

Abby ate fairly well. The trip to the small bathroom after supper was hard on her. When she returned to the table, she asked Jack for pain pills. She felt feverish. Lupe intercepted the exchange and looked at the bottle. She dosed out two pills to Abby. Then she put the bottle into her own purse and retrieved a bottle of aspirin. She gave two of them to Abby as well.

"Abby?" Jack asked. "Do you want to stay the night here? We can find a place and go on in the morning."

"Yes, yes I do. I am really tired. I don't think I can go on," replied Abby.

"You can go on," interjected Lupe cheerfully. "I will get you settled and you will sleep the rest of the way. No sense paying to sleep."

Abby wanted to reply, but did not have the strength. What she really wanted was to be with Jack. Her life was slipping away, and Jack wasn't with her. She would have to hold on longer.

When they had Abby settled in the station wagon, Lupe, who had been in the car, got out to talk to Jack. "She may not make it if we stop now. Tomorrow will be terrible for her regardless, so she might as well be in her home in her own bed. Do you understand?"

Jack nodded and they returned to their vehicles to make the last of the trip. They made a gas stop before reaching the crossing. Security at the crossing was tight, as it had been since the slaying late last year of Luis Donaldo Colosio, but the traffic into Mexico was far lighter than the northward crossing. The sun was setting. The waning full moon was already visible in the sky. Jack had no idea what was happening in the car that followed him. He was in his own thoughts. They were jumbled.

The past came to him. Seeing the desert ahead reminded him that he loved the sea. Abby had picked out Curcurpe, some thirty miles southeast of Magdalena, as her refuge once she had become famous. She wanted limited contact with the world of people. If Magdalena was isolated, Curcurpe was even more so. Jack had leased a run down ranch house and spent ten years restoring parts of it. On the property was a shallow tributary to the Rio Sonora. The property's elevation, some fifteen hundred feet above the desert floor, and the little river, made the area into a small oasis during the long summer.

Jack had leased a bar in Magdalena as well. Last year, when the presidential candidate, Colosio, had been assassinated and been brought back home to be buried, Jack had closed the bar for a month, fearing trouble. He had re-opened it for a while, but had finally closed it for good. He needed the place for the people, but he couldn't stay in Phoenix with Abby and keep it open, even with David's help.

Thinking of Colosio's death made him think of Abby as well. He had no idea what she wanted to happen after she died. She had never mentioned anything to him. He loathed the thought that he might have to ask her. It seemed a sad thing, possibly sadder than anything else he had ever thought of. Jack passed the exit to Magdalena and then turned off onto the little two-lane paved road that would lead them finally home. He had slowed down to make sure the station wagon was behind him. It was.

The last thirty miles quickly passed. In the moonlight ahead, Jack could see the Mission church. At night, it looked more stately, shadow hiding the decay. Because the old church was not one of Father Kino's churches like the ones in Magdalena and San Ignacio, no one was interested in maintaining it. It had no regular parish priest either. Passing the church on the left, Jack turned down the dirt road that led to the house.

He hoped that David had kept gas in the generator and not used it up or sold it. The generator powered the lights for the house. Jack got out of the truck and walked over to the car that had pulled in behind him. Lupe put down the window. "It's going to be five to ten minutes to get the generator going. Try the lights a couple of minutes after you hear it start up. Take the keys. There is a flashlight on the table by the front door and candles in the kitchen. Use those. I'll help you shortly." Lupe nodded. Jack handed her the keys and walked around to the back of the house to start the generator.

Although the moon provided a little light, Jack had brought the flashlight from his truck. He hung it on a nail in the shed to light his work. Once the generator started, Jack felt his strength ebb. The trip that he and Abby had taken together to Phoenix a few months ago had seemed positively gay in comparison with the trip home. He had felt, as did she, the uncertainty of outcome, but it had been a wonderfully happy time.

Now, he had come back alone and would leave alone sometime in the future. He would miss Abby. Whatever else she was, to him she had been everything. Taking care of Abby's needs had made Jack's life seem worthwhile. He loved her for it. Coming home for both of them would mean letting go, the difference was that Jack would have to go on to something beyond this place and this time.

It would start tonight. He would carry her in and place her in their old bed. If she would let him, he would tuck her in and hold her hand until she could rest. He would do it every day and every night that she would stay with him. He could feel tears. Well, he would have lots of time for tears. He didn't have to start now. Jack switched off the flashlight. He walked through the darkness to the front of the house. Lupe and Rosita had obviously found the lights. Abby was leaning against her walker by the side of the car. When Jack got close to her, she looked like her old self. Her dark brown hair crowned her face. She was smiling at the night sky. "I'm glad I'm here. I slept so well that I didn't wake until the church.

Do you smell the air?" Abby was not really looking for answers or comment, as Jack knew. She was just being Abby.

"Hey, my beautiful babe, shall I carry you in?" Jack had put his arm around her thin shoulders.

"No, just let me lean on you. I can make it without this," she said, indicating the walker. She slipped her arm around Jack's waist and he moved his arm under hers for support. Under the same starry sky that gave cover to Father Kino and Luis Donaldo Colosio, Abby and Jack knew, at last, they were home.

Balm of Gilead

Lupe's dire prediction that Abby would have a bad day after the trip from Phoenix, Arizona, to Curcurpe, Mexico, was unfulfilled. Once home, Abby rallied. Although she did not paint, she spent time in her studio looking at the paintings she had finished in the winter. She spent her afternoons on the patio resting and looking at the small garden beds Jack had planted for her many years ago. She especially liked the tree that was just leafing out. As each leaf bud opened, it sprayed out a sweet, sticky perfume that ringed the ground around the tree. She was never able to walk without her walker, but her appetite picked up. Best of all to Abby, Jack was spending the night in the same bed. She was so well, that her nurse, Lupe, and Lisa's housekeeper, Rosita Gonzalez, were able to travel around the Sonoran desert nearly every day. They found fresh food in markets and bought local crafts as well.

On the eighth day of their stay, Abby awoke from her afternoon outdoor nap with an agonizing pain in her back. It was difficult for her to breathe. She called out for Jack; however, Lupe came. Lupe wasn't alarmed. She brought a chair close to the chaise while Abby gasped for breath. She picked up Abby's arm and began to rub the inside of her forearm and her hand. "It's fine. I know you are in pain, but it will pass. Try and breathe a little more deeply," said Lupe.

Abby tried. Lupe continued to speak to her. "Breathe out. Wait. Breathe in. Wait. Breathe out." Over the course of a few minutes, the pain, although present, lessened. The panic that Abby felt increased. Lupe did not let go of Abby's hand. In a soft voice she said, "Abby, call to Jack again. He will want to come and help you get up. I want to get you out of this chair and inside where you can be more comfortable."

When Abby called, Jack came out. "Hi there, Jack. Abby here might just be ready to come in and have some supper. She had a bad spell, but she is better now. You stay on this side, and I'll go around to the other side of the chair. We are going to help her sit up, and then move her legs to touch the floor. She can stand up and have you as support. I'll be behind her."

"I can't," wailed Abby. "It will hurt me. Just get me some painkillers. Then I'll be okay."

"You can and you will get up," said Lupe. "We have a wonderful dinner prepared. You can get up and then we can all have a little party together."

Abby stiffened in resistance. The pain seared her again and she cried out. "Breathe, Abby. In. Wait. Out. In. Wait. Out." Lupe was speaking even as she began to move Abby and motioned for Jack's help. Abby stopped resisting.

The three of them made it awkwardly into the kitchen where Rosita was setting out the colorful dishes that comprised their meal. Abby wanted to crawl into bed, but made it to the table. The episode of severe pain reminded her to enjoy this time. There would not be many more meals at this table. She would make the best of tonight.

It was just dusk when the little group finished supper. Although Abby had said and eaten little, she had enjoyed the company. She had watched Jack. Leaving him, going on alone seemed unbearable. He had always prepared the way. She needed to tell him that, and wished she had told him in the preceding week when she had felt better. She had to find the right time to tell him.

While the cousins cleared the table and began to clean up the kitchen, Jack helped Abby into bed. He undressed her and put on her simple white gown. He had arranged the pillows so that her head would be elevated. She asked him just to move them so that she could stretch out flat. Standing next to her, Jack felt oversized and awkward. He tried to smile down at her. "How's the pain? Do you want something for it?" he asked.

"Yes. In a minute. Sit on the bed because I want to ask you something with a clear head. If you sit next to me, I'll manage," said Abby.

Jack said nothing, but maneuvered Abby to the bed and supported her while he sat down next to her. He had no idea what to expect from her.

"There's no easy way to ask you this. And when I ask you, there's no way for me to make it right, but I'm going to ask anyway." Abby's evasion puzzled Jack. He had no idea what she was talking about.

When Jack said nothing, Abby nearly gave up. This was so hard and shameful too. It reminded her of her childhood and teenage years, when shame was one of the two emotions she could manage. She plunged on. "Jack, did you ever know about Holmes and me? I thought you did, from time to time. Then when I stopped seeing him, when it was over between us, I wanted to tell you. But I just couldn't."

Not knowing what to expect before Abby asked, he would have been surprised at nearly anything. This was not a shocking, question, however and it was easy to answer. "Yes, Abby, I knew. There was a time after it started that I pretended it wasn't happening. But I did know."

"Why didn't you ever say anything? I wanted you to say something," said Abby.

"Would it have made any difference if I had been angry or put out? Did you want me to say 'Pick me or Holmes'?" asked Jack.

"No, it wouldn't have made any difference, then. It would have killed me to choose between the two of you. I don't know how to tell you this, but I needed you both, Jack. Then, a long time ago, I stopped needing Holmes. That way, anyway. He was a good dealer for me, but the rest of it was over a long time ago. I am sorry if I hurt you. I want you to know that."

"You hurt me and you didn't. There was happiness in you that lasted for months after you had spent a few days or a week with Holmes. It has always been hard for me to deny you the kindness of happiness, Abby. It made up for all the parts of your life that were painful and made you act like a wild animal. You didn't rub my nose in it, and I am grateful for that," said Jack.

Tears were in Abby's eyes. "I'm so sorry, Jack. I am sorry to have hurt you. And I'm sorry to be dying and never being able to make it up to you." Abby began to cry in earnest. Abby's tears hurt Jack more than anything did.

"Abby, don't cry. It's all in the past. I love you and I've loved you since the first time I picked you up. Every time you went away, I just wanted you to come home. You always did. That was enough, Abby. You came home to me and I loved you the more for it." Jack was crying, too. Abby slumped against him.

"I'm afraid, Jack. I am afraid to die. I don't want to leave you. You always took care of me," said Abby, miserably.

"I'll tell you something, I'm afraid, too. Somehow, babe, I know we have time to make it all right for both of us. Tonight I don't know how, but it's going to be OK. I am going to get your pills."

Abby pulled away, allowing Jack to get up. It took him only a minute to retrieve pills and a cup of water. Abby took them quickly. She had nothing else to say. The little she had said had tired her to the bone. Jack helped arrange her in the bed, covering her with both sheet and the old chenille spread. Once she was comfortable, Jack turned out the light, retrieved the corner chair, and brought it close to the bed. He sat holding Abby's hand until he was sure she was asleep. Then he got up, changed for bed, and lay down beside her, dropping off into a quick oblivion.

The next morning, Jack and Lupe were up early, both anxious to talk about the days to come. "Mr. Ellis," said Lupe, retaining her cousin's formality, "what you saw yesterday is just a little of what is going to happen. And worse. There are things that we are going to need, and among them, some kind of painkiller that is stronger than what she has now."

"What's wrong with her?" asked Jack anxiously.

"I'm guessing that the cancer is moving up her back bone. It's virulent. That's why the fever has returned. As it grows, it will produce pressure on the spinal cord and begin to fracture her bones. I think that is already happening. Sometimes, however, the cord is completely cut by the growth. Paralysis sets in. It is less painful, but awful in other ways."

Jack rubbed his face, but said nothing. It was his worst nightmare, his worst fear.

"Rosita and I talked. She thinks you can get help with some drugs if you go to a doctor in Hermosillo. There's a clinic there. A big one. Take Abby's passport and papers. Rosita can do the talking. She thinks there is a good chance you can get some morphine for cash. I will write down what you need."

"But that will take the day!" said Jack.

"There aren't many alternatives, except to go tomorrow, and that might be worse," said Lupe evenly. "This is hard for you but harder for Abby if she has to suffer. She doesn't do well with pain and there is something in her that wants to live. Something in her that is unfinished. Do you know what that is?"

"No. Not really. Abby had many secrets, most of which I don't know. If you think she is sticking around because of something unfinished between the two of us, there isn't. After last night, we have no unfinished business," said Jack.

"Maybe you do. I will try to see if I can help her today while you are away. Now, I'm going to see how she is doing and I'm going to tell her you are going away for the day."

"Let me do that," said Jack.

"No, I need her to depend on me or there is no sense at all in my being here," said Lupe.

Within the hour, Rosita and Jack were on their way to Hermosillo leaving Lupe to deal with an angry, edgy Abby. Without Jack's help, Abby refused to eat or get out of bed. Treating her like a spoiled child, Lupe ignored her, knowing that the pain would bring Abby around. By lunchtime, Abby was willing to eat if she could have something for the pain and the fever. A little broth and toast along with four pain pills and two aspirin picked up Abby's spirits. With Lupe's help, she went out to the patio garden. There was a light breeze and some clouds in the west. A shower might come up later.

Lupe sat with Abby, enjoying the afternoon. The tree in the east of the garden fascinated Lupe. She asked Abby about it. "Jack brought it from Las Cruces when we moved here. He liked the name of it and thought it had a pretty shape. It was just a little thing when he stuck it in the ground," said Abby.

"So what is its name?" asked Lupe.

"Balm of Gilead. Funny name for a tree," said Abby.

Lupe thought about the name of the tree and the amazing botanical display she had seen this afternoon. It was a fitting name. She remembered the old hymn and began to hum it. "There is a balm in Gilead to heal the sin-sick soul," ran the words in Lupe's head.

Abby closed her eyes while Lupe hummed. When the sound stopped, she opened them. The pain was back in waves. It made her cough. Lupe brought Abby a glass of cool, diluted juice. Abby had difficulty in swallowing it. Lupe brought her chair close, and picked up Abby's right hand to massage it gently.

"How are you feeling? Do you want to go inside? I can help you up."

"I want Jack. Is it time for him to be back?" asked Abby.

"Soon I think. Did you miss him today?"

"I always miss Jack. Even when I want to be alone, I miss him. I am scared to die without him," said Abby earnestly.

"Do you want Jack to die?" asked Lupe.

"Yes, yes I do," said Abby once she had thought a little about it. "It would be so easy to die if Jack was gone. It isn't going to happen that way, and it scares me."

Abby's words did not shock Lupe. She had heard them before from dying patients who clung to a spouse, a son, or a daughter. The very attachment made the death hard. Yet, Abby had chosen to die. Contradictory emotions. If living was complex, however, dying was even more so, thought Lupe. At least that had been her experience.

"Do you have Jack's picture? I can go get it and you can have it with you until Jack and Rosita return," offered Lupe.

"No. I don't have one. I wish I did. We never had a camera. I don't even know of a picture of Jack except the ones that I painted of him," said Abby.

"Do you have one of those?" asked Lupe.

"In the studio. It is too big to move, but I would like to see it again. Can you help me?" asked Abby.

With great difficulty, the two women made the short walk to the unlocked studio. Natural light came through the northeast windows behind the paintings. Even though turned away from the light source, toward the door, the paintings were highly visible. Lupe knew nothing of Abby as an artist. Her first glimpse of the large emotional paintings astounded her. They were stunning. Lupe had expected a portrait. Instead, a retablo full of bright images confronted her. Lupe helped Lisa to the only padded chair in the room.

"There are many people in the paintings. Which one is Jack?" asked Lupe.

"There on the left with his sister. They are both children. In the center, Jack and I are on the patio." Abby stopped herself. In the painting, she and Jack were sitting under the tree. Abby did not remember painting the tree. It surprised her to see how it dominated the panel.

Lupe was close to the painting. "There's your tree, your Balm of Gilead."

"I see that. Sometimes the images just come to me. That must have been the case with the tree. I could not have noticed it at the time because it was winter and the tree was leafless. I painted it from memory."

"Do you know where the name comes from?" asked Lupe.

"No, I just know what it is, if you mean the tree."

"It's a biblical reference. From the prophet Jeremiah. I think maybe you painted that tree into the painting because it meant something special to you."

"Maybe," said Abby, "but I have never read one thing in the Bible, so you can't put anything religious in it."

"No, I can't. I just thought you might want to know about the tree."

Abby resisted for a moment, but she did want to know. Maybe knowing would clear up the mystery of why it was in the painting at all.

"In the Bible story, the prophet Jeremiah laments the sins of the people of Judah for turning away from worshipping the true God. Gilead is an ancient Judean city. In the story, God is punishing all of Judah. Jeremiah laments, 'Is there no balm in Gilead, Is there no physician there?'"

"What's that got to do with the tree?" asked Abby.

"Have you watched that tree? It spurts out a perfume into the air that falls on the ground. I suspect that it only happens in the spring, when all things are re-born. Maybe you remembered that when you were painting. Maybe you remembered how the tree sweetened your life every spring," suggested Lupe.

"I think it was an accident," said Abby. "I don't pick my images, they pick me. I have no idea why it is in the picture."

"And yet it is. If you could, would you paint it out now?" asked Lupe.

"Hey, everybody's a critic, even a nurse," said Abby angrily.

"There's only one art critic in this house," said Jack as he stood in the doorway. "That's my job. Abby paints them, and I praise them. House rules." Jack had only heard part of the two women's conversation.

As usual, Abby felt that Jack had rescued her from her own thoughts, which had turned inwardly dark. She was so relieved to see him. Lupe asked Jack if he and Rosita had been successful shopping in Hermosillo. Jack said they had, so Lupe went to find what the shoppers had found.

Over Abby's protests and in spite of her pain, Jack carried Abby out of the studio and across the patio to their bedroom. As gently as possible, he laid her on the bed. She felt feverish as he held her small body against his. When he kissed her, she tasted salty. He made her as comfortable as he could. Once covered, Abby's body made only the slightest rise in the bed. Jack thought she had lost alarming dimensions in the eight hours he had been gone.

"Ice cream," Jack said. "I brought you chocolate ice cream all the way from Hermosillo. Do you want some?"

"Yes. Can I have something for the pain? I hurt all over. It hurts just to shut my eyes."

"You can have the sun, moon and stars, babe. Hang on just for a minute. I'll get us some ice cream."

Jack returned with the dishes of chocolate for both of them. Abby seemed particularly alert once she had eaten and had pills. She was, for once, interested and immersed in all that Jack had to say. They talked about the tree in the garden. Abby repeated what she had heard from Lupe. As the evening wore on, Abby's conversation became more animated. She drank a great deal of water, but refused other food. It was midnight and Abby was clearly tired, but reluctant to end the day. She had one more thing, just one more thing to say. One more favor to ask from Jack.

It was far more difficult than the conversation about Holmes on the previous night. "I want to tell you something and I want to ask something Jack. Bury me in Phoenix, not here. Promise me that you will make that happen."

"I thought you would want to be buried up in the church yard here, Abby," said Jack. Abby was crying. Jack thought he had just reached the most unbearable part of his whole life.

"No. No, I don't. I know you won't stay here after I die, and I don't want to be all alone. I am trying not to hold on too tight. I know the holding on is hurting both of us. I just can't let go, though. All of a sudden, it matters that I never had your name. It matters that we were never married. I want to be buried somewhere close to your family."

"Sure, Abby, sure. You have worn yourself out. I'm glad you told me, though. I'm glad, Abby."

"OK. There is something I want you to remember. It's something Lupe told me. Out in the studio, in that last painting, in the central panel there is a picture of you and me sitting under the tree that you planted. I didn't realize it until just today, but that tree was you, Jack. You were the tree that sheltered me and healed my life. With you, I wasn't much of person, but without you, I would have been so much less. I just wanted you to know."

Jack wanted to say something, but the talking and the tears that had exhausted Abby, had drained Jack. Gently he knelt at the side of the bed. Gently he held her feverish body. Gently he spoke words of love and comfort to her until long past the time she had fallen into a deep sleep. Every half breath that she took moved her away from him and from human love and forgiveness to the realm where he hoped she would forever know all the kindness she had missed in her life on earth.

That day, the day when Abby learned about the Balm of Gilead and talked the night away with Jack, was Abby's last good day. At first, she had a few good hours a day, but that interval became smaller and smaller until she could only manage twenty to thirty minutes without either sleep or morphine or both. Her days and nights reversed. Lupe and Jack did their best to keep her clean and comfortable. Abby died on a Friday, three weeks after coming home.

Ring of Belonging

Sometimes Bill Hadigan thought that late middle age was the best time. Gone are the terrors of adolescence, the brashness of young adulthood. Gone too are the feelings of uncertainty that plague the onset of middle age when one loathes growing older and fears death without measurable accomplishment. Oh, one is freed from all these things and sleeps well at night. There is just one little thing that cannot be overcome at any age: the desire to love. That never ends.

Bill Hadigan had been sleeping badly for several nights running. He had been dating Lisa Ellis for an entire year come New Year's Eve. She had been a revelation to him. She had energy and power and ideas. She was fascinating to talk to and a good listener, too. She had worked hard and made her own fortune. Unlike many who were self-made, Lisa was generous in everything from her money to her time. She made everything look easy. Bill wanted to marry her. His only worry was that she would say no. This was the time to ask. He did not own her; could not make her say yes, but he had hope. If he had an answer, he knew he would sleep better.

Sometimes in December, Phoenix experiences a real cold snap. When it happens, it is a surprise to have a couple of frosty nights and very cool days. This December, Lisa Ellis found out that her heat pump was not working on a very cold morning. The thermometer said it was only 58 degrees in her hallway. Her north bedroom felt much colder. She put in a call to her maintenance company while making a quick cup of coffee. Then she picked up volume two of her masterwork on Monet and went back to bed to read and stay warm.

Once warmed, concentrating on the words became difficult. Her mind wandered to the days and holidays ahead. Last year had been a turning point. It was the first year in her adult life she had not arranged a perfect Christmas. She had taken herself off the hook of responsibility and it had been the best holiday ever. She had met a wonderful man; her only son had married; her beloved brother, Jack, had moved back to Phoenix from Mexico. Now, a year later, she wondered what she should arrange or not arrange.

Last year she didn't have grandchildren and now she had two precious babies. Last year Bill Hadigan had spent Christmas Day with his daughter; this year he said he would spend the entire day with her. Surely these differences meant that she should plan something special. What could she do that would even approximate her love for the three of them? Lisa didn't know.

Jack Ellis was watching the clock on the same Sunday morning at his bar. It was the first cold day of winter. For that reason, the bar was loaded with regulars and strays who wanted hot fresh coffee. He had already served twice as much as usual and it was barely eight o'clock. He would be open until ten. In spite of his activity, the time passed slowly. Then there would be another hour to wait until he could pick up Reid from church. He was taking her to his house for a first real visit. In spite of his invitations, she had been reluctant to come. The days and nights they spent together were always at her house. Those were wonderful times. Just lately, though, Jack felt that they were incomplete. It was important to him that Reid visit his place and know how he lived. Today was the day.

In the neighborhood church attended by Reid Markham, it was the second Sunday of Advent. Today the candle of hope from the first Sunday was re-lit. Added was the candle of love. The lighting of the candle was supposed to be symbolic of God's love, but Reid was, as always, moving from the realm of the eternal to her earthly experiences. How she missed those she had loved! Her longing for Big Daddy and Grammy was a taste in her mouth. Stronger still was the throbbing, aching love that Reid felt at times like these for her Mother. When the service ended, the impatient movement of others in the pew brought Reid back to the present.

When she walked outside, Jack was waiting for her. She was ashamed that she had not once thought about him. Well, it couldn't be helped or changed. Reid had long ago given up any control of her wandering, emotional mind. No one would ever know what she was thinking. As long has her speech and behavior seemed rational, her mind could do what it wanted.

As Reid walked toward Jack, he noticed the high color in her cheeks. At first he thought it was the cold and then decided she was blushing. Imaginary thoughts showed in Reid's face. It was one of the things he found so endearing. She looked radiant.

"Hello, Jack. Is today the day for the grand tour? I worried that you would forget me and I would have to walk home," Reid said in all earnestness.

"Did you walk this morning?"

"Yes I did. It was lots colder than I had planned."

"The truck is warm. The house is warm. The sun will be warm later," said Jack as he put his arm around Reid and they walked away.

A ringing phone awakened Lisa. She had dozed off reading. As she reached for the hand piece, she realized that though the bed was warm, the room was still quite cold. She thought it was the repairman, but it was Bill.

"You sound sleepy. Did I wake you?" Bill asked.

"I dozed off. I'm still in bed because it is the warmest place in the house." Lisa looked at the clock. It was past noon.

"No heat?"

"Not today. I am expecting someone to come fix it soon. What are you doing?

"I thought you might like a late lunch someplace downtown. I'm in a mood for Eggs Benedict and maybe a little bourbon in my coffee. I don't like to eat alone. Is it warm enough for you to dress and come out?" Bill tried to sound casual.

"I should be doing something about Christmas today. Really, I haven't done a thing. No decorations, no tree, not even gift one for the twins. As a grandma, I'm a slacker." Lisa was only half-hearted in her criticism.

"Will it wait another day? Are you busy next week?"

"The way I feel, it might wait another year! Besides, if you take me out, I get out of cooking. Give me about an hour. Where are we going?"

"Up to the Dial Room. I think that the hotel has some great decorations. We can enjoy someone else's hard work."

"You make me happy. I love the view. It's what I miss about living in the condo downtown. A one story house just has no view." Lisa threw back the comforter. "I'm up and moving. See you in an hour."

When Bill hung up, he looked at his watch. He had enough time to see his neighbor, Daisy Ellis. He needed to try his idea out on her before he picked up Lisa.

When Daisy opened the door, she was surprised to see Bill. Usually he called first. She had felt the cold this morning and had dressed in a heavy purple jogging suit, now covered with a large white baker's apron. She was staying warm by staying active and doing a little Christmas baking for her grandson, Paulie.

"Come in. I need to get off my feet a bit." Daisy said to her neighbor.

"I don't want to interrupt you. Looks like you're busy."

"I'm at a stopping place. Dough can set before I roll it out. How about coffee?"

"Not today, Daisy. I just came by to tell you something."

Bill followed Daisy into the kitchen. She was curious about what Bill had to say, but he would tell her in his time. She poured a small china cup of coffee for herself and sat down.

With Daisy seated, Bill felt suddenly awkward. He felt disruptive and out of place. He wanted to change his mind. He had no idea how to proceed.

"I want to ask you something about Lisa," Bill said finally

"I thought you wanted to tell me something," said Daisy.

Bill reached in his pocket, drew out and opened a ring box. He turned it around and placed it in front of Daisy. The box contained a magnificent band in platinum with three large bezel set diamonds.

Daisy said nothing.

"I want to give this to Lisa," Bill said.

"Nice Christmas present if you're asking me. Lisa is very fond of jewelry. Don't think she has a platinum ring."

Bill couldn't tell if Daisy was just teasing him or if she didn't understand what he was trying to tell her. "It's not a Christmas present. It's a wedding ring. I want to marry Lisa."

"Is that an announcement or a question?" Daisy was having some fun at Bill's expense, but he wasn't laughing with her.

"I want to marry Lisa," Bill repeated.

"Good for you, Bill," Daisy said as she finished her coffee.

"Well, what do you think?" asked Bill impatiently.

"What do I think about your asking her? Or are you looking for my blessing?"

"I'm not asking for your permission. I want to, well, maybe, maybe know what she might say. You might know what she might say."

"I don't know. Lisa does not confide in me and she never has. She'll be pleased to be asked, though, no matter what she says. She's going to be making friends with sixty soon and it will flatter her to be asked to be married before that. If it's what you want to do, do it."

"It is what I want. But I want her to say yes."

"Have you thought of all the reasons she'll say 'no'?" asked Daisy.

"It's a long list, isn't it? I've been up nights thinking about it. I don't have her kind of money. She's been married twice. She likes having her own way. She's competitive in ways that I cannot understand. She doesn't show her emotions easy, either."

"Yes, I can see you've thought about it. Rather makes me wonder why you would want her as a wife. I love my daughter, but I never had an easy time living with her, even when she was young. But that's me, too."

Bill said nothing.

"When are you planning to ask her?" asked Daisy.

"Today. If it's ever going to be right, I think today is it."

"Then go ask. I hope somebody calls me and tells me how it turns out, though. I am too old to wait long. It was just a year ago that Paulie married. I was thinking about that this week. When Paulie got married, Jack came back to Phoenix. Then there were babies. I don't know which event was most important. I think to Lisa, it was having her brother back. Somehow, it made a difference to Lisa to have someone who just didn't care what she did. Paulie and I aren't like that. We find Lisa overwhelming and we aren't always good at hiding our feelings. Jack isn't like us. Since the day she was born, Jack just loved his little sister no matter what she did. I was thinking that if you want to marry Lisa, you might remember that."

Bill looked at the kitchen clock. He picked up the ring box and closed it. It was time to do what he had planned to do today. He left his neighbor at the table; he left with more hope.

When Reid got into Jack's truck, there were flowers waiting for her – red winter roses. That was so much like him! He was so old-fashioned in every way except in bed. He was easy but never familiar. He never took her for granted; never assumed; never presumed. After a few months of seeing him, she still felt that he was courting her.

She thanked Jack and held them in her lap for the short trip to his house. He lived in the Willo district. Neither as rich nor fashionable as the famed Phoenix Encanto District, Willo was making a strong comeback with those who had the money and inclination to fix up the small houses.

Reid had been to Jack's house only briefly in the past. Never for dinner. The house was old fashioned, a small grey structure with a porch on two sides. The neighborhood was a mixture of styles, mostly from the 1930's. There were probably no original owners left in the neighborhood. Many houses had been visibly restored. Jack, she knew, was doing a lot of carpentry on his house. It was one of the lesser homes on the street, but well kept. She could see red Christmas lights outlining the gables. She imagined what they would look like at night.

When she walked inside the house behind Jack, she immediately smelled food, something pungent and spicy. The aroma made her aware of how hungry she was.

"Jack, I'm famished. Is whatever you are cooking done?"

"Just a little chicken ranchero with rice. Do you want to eat now? I thought I might show you some of the work I've been doing first."

"I see better on a full stomach. Let's eat." Reid was already walking toward the dining room. She noticed that the oak table was set for two. Reid started toward the kitchen but Jack blocked her way. "I want a vase or something for these roses."

"No peeking, no helping, no nothing," Jack said. "I'll take care of the flowers and come back with the wine. Then, I'll serve you. This time, you're my guest."

Jack pulled out the chair for her and she sat down. He returned with both flowers and wine of the deepest burgundy. He poured only a glass for her. Lisa knew it would be good and was sorry that he would not be enjoying it with her. She sipped it while he returned to the kitchen.

From the table, Reid could see directly into the living room. Although she had seen it before, the room looked different. The furniture was as she remembered it, and placed the same, but something about the room was very different. It was darker. Reid closed her eyes to improve her memory. She opened them, once she had re-visualized the space as she had originally seen it. There had been a large painting, illuminating the room like a window. It was one of Abby's. Now it was gone. Reid felt cold.

Jack came into the dining room bearing a large salad bowl. He was happy to have Reid at the table; too happy to notice that she was not sharing his glow. In the second trip he brought in a large platter of his best dish, a Spanish chicken and rice dish he had invented and perfected in forty years of cooking. The third trip included fresh rolls and seltzer water for his own drink. All was ready. Jack sat down. He poured the water into his wine glass and then raised the glass to toast. "Thank you for being my guest, Reid Markham."

Reid lifted her glass in thank you, but only smiled instead of replying. For a moment, she wanted to ask Jack about the painting, but hunger prevented her from holding the thought. She helped herself to the platter that Jack held for her. After several mouthfuls, she said, "I only came over because you promised to feed me. This is great!"

Jack's heart was in his throat. He couldn't eat. He was filled up on Reid. He looked at her so intently that she turned away. Was it possible to feel both proud and foolish at the same time? It must be possible because that's the way he felt. He wanted to go on feeling that way forever. How Reid lit up a room and never knew it.

"I'll feed you every day if you'll marry me."

It was Reid's turn to stop eating. Jack had surprised her. She didn't do well with surprises and never had. Changes in her life had been too abrupt. She never had the time to get used to something until afterwards. She never had the time to anticipate anything. Boom! Life took another direction leaving Reid to catch up months and years later. She shut her eyes and wished Jack's words away. When she opened her eyes, they were still hanging in front of her.

They were good words, Reid thought. She didn't need to panic. This wasn't something that had to be answered or completed today. She had time to think and to consider. Jack would understand. This wasn't even a fork in the road, just another step on the journey. Reid smiled at herself. It felt so good to have a feeling of some control.

"How about if I get to finish this dinner and a few more before I answer? I mean, this is the first time you have cooked for me. Maybe you just have one recipe. I can't eat chicken every day!" Reid picked up her fork and returned to eating.

Jack let the question go unanswered. He hadn't planned to ask it anyway. It had flown from him. He knew Reid was uncomfortable with abrupt change. She tried on change until she could wear it like a comfortable sweater. He liked that about her. He had never gotten used to Abby's abrupt ways.

If it was a quiet meal, it suited the two of them. Jack and Reid were happy with companionable silence. After eating, they cleared the table together. While Jack washed the dishes, Reid made coffee, at Jack's direction, of course. While in the kitchen, Jack talked about his plans to do some remodeling in the kitchen. "Mostly it just needs work behind the scenes. Plumbing. Rewiring. A dishwasher would be nice, too. Cabinets are solid and can be restored to their original birch finish. It would be a shame to put anything too modern in this old house."

"Are you planning to stay here, then?" asked Reid.

"Hadn't thought about it. I've lived many places, wherever Abby wanted to live. I learned to work on places at first to make them livable. Later, I did it to keep busy. It seemed more like work than running the bars. I needed something to do while Abby painted and when she was gone. This time, I just wanted to make the place a little nicer than when I bought it."

"Let me see what else you have done to make it nicer."

"I thought you would never ask! Open the door at the end there," said Jack.

Abby walked to the narrow end of the kitchen and opened the door. She could smell the newness of wood and paint. Beyond the door was a room flooded with southern light. It was longer than wide and had high ceilings. Near the window was a built in desk and table. Coming away from the window to the door on both sides were floor to ceiling bookcases, some with glass fronts and narrow shelves. At the north end of the room was a small sitting area and window seat. The wooden floors of the room had been sanded and polished.

"What is this room?" asked Reid.

"A study or a lounge. Someplace to listen to music and look out the window to the street or to the back yard."

"It's wonderful, but what was it before? It doesn't seem to have been added on to the house."

"Originally it was used as a pantry and as a wash room. Most recently, it accumulated junk. The floor had pretty well rotted away from water and leaking cans of solvents, old tires and car parts. I replaced it with old flooring from a neighbor's house. The room grew up around the floor."

"Nice. What have you done lately?" asked Reid.

"That's it. I was going like crazy until I met you. That slowed me down. Seems like it is easier to spend a Saturday afternoon in your bed than at the hardware store."

"Show me the rest. I think that you've changed the front room anyway." Reid wanted to know what had happened to the painting.

"Nothing new there. If you want to see it, let's get coffee and sit. None of the electricity is working in there so you'll have to see it before dark."

They picked up cups of the fresh coffee and went to the front room. "See," said Jack. "Not much going on here. It could use some help. Maybe you could give me a hand sometime and we could get the lights working and then do some painting."

"I'm not very handy, Jack. The room looked better when the painting was in here. I thought I remembered a big one." Reid could not manage nonchalance. The missing painting disturbed her for a reason she did not know. Fear, more than curiosity, drove her to ask about the art.

"Gone as of yesterday. Another one also." Jack said.

"Why yesterday? Why would you get rid of them? I know they were Abby's. The one I saw was so wonderful in my memory. It let light in."

Jack hadn't really wanted to talk about the paintings any more than he wanted to give them up. To Reid it must look like he had hidden his former lover's artwork. He would just have to try to explain what had happened and hope that she would see that the missing paintings had nothing to do with her.

"The man who owns them came to get them, Reid. They weren't mine and I have known for a long time that I couldn't keep them. I enjoyed them while I had them. Now they are gone. I'll remember what they were like. I was the first person to see them and I've been looking at them for years. I'm going to sit and enjoy my coffee. Why don't you find a CD there on the shelf and play something that will make the afternoon nice?"

Jack went over the big easy chair and put his feet up. He watched Reid put on some music. He recognized the first few notes. She had chosen his only Christmas CD, mellow piano sounds.

"Come here and sit with me. There's room for two. I can see that there's more to making you understand the missing paintings than just telling you they're gone."

"I don't like changes like that, Jack. If those paintings were mine and were gone, I'd feel like a big piece of me just melted into the dirt. I'd feel so bad. I don't see you feeling bad and that makes me feel afraid."

Jack moved his feet and made room for Reid. Reid snuggled up next to him as if touching alone could make the fear go away. It was always so easy to fold herself next to him so that his arm was around her and their legs touched on the ottoman.

When Jack started to talk, his voice was all around her, but with her head on his chest, she could not see his face. "The paintings went to Abby's husband. He came and got them yesterday. There were legal problems after Abby died. Her dealer wanted the paintings as well, but he lost out in court. But he had had the best of Abby for years, so he couldn't complain," said Jack.

Now Reid was very glad that Jack couldn't see her face either. What was Abby doing with a husband? Why didn't she leave the paintings to Jack?

Since Reid had said nothing, Jack decided to go on. "I know what you're thinking. I can feel your wheels turning, Reid. I knew she was married, always. She never did anything to get unmarried. If she had, I am not sure that we would have married. The story of Abby and I is a long one and it's one of desire and need. Abby had a world made of sky and clouds and paint. She wasn't really grounded or practical or capable of everyday life. She needed someone to manage everyday life. That's why she needed me. I just needed to be needed. We had a life together. It wasn't a bad life, but I always felt that there should have been more to it. Maybe kids, maybe a different kind of sharing."

"But you loved her," said Reid.

"Yes I loved her."

Jack continued to speak, but Reid could not hear him. Her presence had left the room. She was a child back in Iowa watching Grammy on her hands and knees in the garden. "What happens when love dies, Grammy? What happened to mommy's love? Is it in the box with her?" the young Reid asked.

"Is that what you think, child? Are you worried about love?"

Reid nodded. "Come here, Reid. Come look at this," said Grammy.

Reid kneeled next to her grandmother. With her gloved hand, Grammy brushed dirt away from a tiny, two-leafed plant. "This is where love went. God turned it into this plant and a few others. He gave some to the birds to sing. He gave it to hungry people as food. God doesn't put love in a box and love doesn't die. It's around us all the time. You remember that, little girl. Someday before you are old as me, you'll see love again and you'll know all I say is true. Now, you're standing in my dirt and I need to finish up. You go find Big Daddy and tell him that it's time for dinner." Then Grammy and the garden and Iowa were gone.

"... sharing, but I found it with you, Reid. You are grounded," Jack said.

"Oh, you were right Grammy. Love never dies." said Reid to her dream.

Jack stopped speaking. Clearly, Reid had not been listening anyway, which was a relief. He knew she had been remembering something else.

Reid felt the earlier chill leave her body. She felt so warm that she pulled away from Jack and smiled at him. She had been afraid that Jack had not loved Abby. If he hadn't, then how could he ever understand her love for Big Daddy and Grammy and a father she had never known? They were gone, but the love didn't die with them any more than Jack's love died with Abby. Good.

"I'm sorry Jack. I think I was asleep a little bit! All that wonderful food. We've done the front room. What about the rest of the house?" asked Reid.

"What about finishing the coffee first?"

"I don't want mine. I want dessert and I want to wander through your closets and rooms."

"There's sugar free pudding in the refrigerator."

Reid made a face. "Real dessert. Real food. I am hungry all over again."

"There's spumoni ice cream in the freezer. I bought it just for you. Shall I spoon it up?"

"Nope. I am going to do it myself. I may just eat it right from the carton!" said Reid as she got up and headed toward the kitchen.

"Don't make yourself too comfortable," Jack called after her. "You don't live here."

"Yes, but I could and I might," replied Reid.

When she returned with a huge helping of her favorite ice cream, they talked about the very important nothings in their lives, work and people and loved ones present and gone. When the room began to darken and afternoon chill set in, Jack lit a fire in the fireplace. It was a nice and useless gesture since the warmth they found was in the bedroom where they made love until they were both hungry.

In the quiet and darkened bedroom, before getting up, Jack said again, "Marry me and be my one and only bride."

"In church?" Reid asked.

"In church," Jack affirmed.

"OK. I'll marry you."

"When?"

"After a while. When I'm used to the idea. When it doesn't seem so all of a sudden." As she spoke, Reid was already up and dressing herself to find food again.

If it had been up to Jack, they would be married tomorrow. He had already waited a lifetime. Even though she had said 'yes,' it wasn't enough. Just to make sure, he planned to buy a ring for her tomorrow morning. When she put it on, that would be enough.

At a little after six, it was very dark. Bill and Lisa had eaten their Sunday brunch high atop all of Phoenix at the Dial Room. They had sat on the outer revolving portion and had watched the city float below them for three hours. Afterwards they had walked across the street to the Civic Plaza to wander through the Junior League gift show. Lisa seemed to know everyone there. It was hard to make forward progress through the aisles because people stopped to wish her holiday greetings.

Bill had been pleased that Lisa introduced him around to all. In the intervals when no one was close by, Lisa would tell him how she had come to know this lawyer, or that CEO's wife. There was usually real estate or divorce or fund raising involved in every story.

"I don't think I ever realized the breadth of your friends before today," said Bill when they were out of the building.

"You mean my acquaintances, not friends," corrected Lisa. "These are people, some good and some scurrilous, who represent my business. I know them because I have seen them when theirs was the need and mine was the power to help them for money. That's not friendship. It is just good business."

"Have I met your friends, then?" Bill was nonplussed at Lisa's approach.

"Sure you have. You know Beth, my longtime friend. When I first came to Phoenix, we were neighbors. She still teaches school in Paradise Valley. She is keeper of all my secrets. She was with me in and out of two marriages. Then there is my bridge group. We are fewer now, but there used to be eight couples who played together. We stay in close touch."

"What makes them different from the other people you know?"

Lisa laughed. "I don't do any business with them! It's a rule with me. I never want a business problem or misunderstanding to hurt the friendship. So, no business."

They had reached the car. Once they were settled inside, Bill felt in his pocket for the ring box. It was still there. Before he turned on the car he asked, "Which am I, Lisa? Friend or acquaintance?"

"Do you want to sell your condo?" Lisa asked blithely.

"No," said Bill seriously. The car was cold. He turned it on but had no intention of going anywhere.

"Then," Lisa answered just as seriously, "You're neither. You're someone without category or equal in my life. You're special."

Bill reached for her and pulled her hard and close to him. "I love you Lisa. I want to marry you."

Whatever Lisa had thought about or expected for today and for the near future, a proposal from Bill Hadigan had not numbered in those thoughts. She was undone, immediately and completely. Tears of surprise suddenly flooded her eyes and spilled onto Bill's shoulder. She had no idea why.

There was a river of tears that she could not stop. She wouldn't let go of Bill's embrace and couldn't control herself. She felt the hot rush of shame and the lightness of what felt like pain as it left her body. As it left, she gasped and then the tears stopped. She let go of Bill.

"I don't know what came over me." With her left hand she tried to wipe away both her tears and makeup. She sank back into the seat and with the backside of her hand, she covered her mouth.

Bill reached across her and found tissues in the glove box. He handed the entire box to her. He turned his attention to the car, adjusting the heat and then driving away. Bill had learned to let a woman cry without interruption. She would start any necessary conversation when she felt like it.

During the drive from downtown to Lisa's home, nothing was said. When he pulled into her driveway, Lisa said, "Come in and let's have a little brandy to end the day."

Bill followed her into the house. The repairman must have come by in their absence because the house was warm. While Lisa went to the back of the house, Bill turned on a few lights and went to the liquor cabinet to find the brandy and glasses. Then he took the ring box out, opened it, and placed it next to Lisa's snifter on the low glass table in front of the sofa. He drank from his own glass.

Lisa returned. She had obviously tried to erase and cover up the evidence of her tears. Still, she looked wan, Bill thought.

It didn't take but a heartbeat for her to settle on the sofa and see the opened box. She picked it up. "It's very beautiful."

"Try it on for size, Lisa."

"I feel like you want an answer to your proposal first." Lisa put the ring back down on the table.

"You can try it on and answer me later."

"Not my style," said Lisa. "Come and sit with me. It has been a long time since I was married. A long time since anyone proposed to me. I want you to know I'm flattered."

Bill sat down, close, but not too close.

"I don't like to leave things hanging. That's not my style either," said Lisa. Whether it was the brandy, or she was just feeling better, there was a now a hint of color in her face. "But this is a big thing to do in one night. We have lives that are very separate, including children and houses and bank accounts. It would be hard, but not impossible to, well, let's say to reach accommodation on those things."

"I had two miserable marriages. I have never wanted to marry again, until tonight. I am seriously thinking about it. That's me. What I'm wondering though, is why you would want to marry again. You had a wonderful life with Alice. You grieved when she died. You have your daughters and their families. You have a good life being just who you are. Why do you want to get married again? Can I ask you that?"

"Because I want you, Lisa. Because I want to be with you."

"I'm around. I'm not going anyplace. I've already told you how special you are to me. Getting married at our age wouldn't change that."

"To me, it's different. I want to share an entire life every day with you. I want to know who you know, I want to be your always bridge partner. I want to be the one who stays after the party is over," said Bill.

"You want me to take the place of Alice," said Lisa as she picked up the ring box again.

"No. You can't take her place, Lisa. She was a good wife and a wonderful mother. The thing is, what I want with you is what I never had with her. For years I thought I had a perfect marriage. It was only when Alice died I saw that I had missed so much with her. At her funeral, I met her friends, her church buddies, and her volunteer group. I had hardly more than a nodding acquaintance with them. They knew her and loved her, better than I did. She had a whole life I did not touch. She made it easy for me to be selfish for years."

"You can't have been that selfish. You were busy running a business and making the living. Alice didn't work. That's the way it used to be, back then. That's just the way it was." Lisa was reaching for something half way comforting to say.

"That's the way it was," echoed Bill. "I believe that. I also came to believe that Alice wanted it that way. As long as she did all the things I wanted, she knew I would never ask about what she did. She had her own independence that way. I never had to worry about when the kids needed help with homework or what they wanted for Christmas. I never wrapped a gift for anyone in my life until she died! But we could have had more, could have been more to each other than that. After she had been dead for a year, I got angry. We had shut each other out and missed out. We never got a future together. That's why I retired and moved here. I thought there has to be more to life, to living, than just what I had."

"Oh Bill, you have romantic notions. Real life isn't like that. I don't think marriage is like that at all. You're just lucky in a marriage if you can stand to share a bathroom and like the same movies."

"That's not how I feel. I want to know when you sell a house and your client. I want to waste a bottle of champagne on your every triumph. I want you to ask me about my golf game and mean it. I want to have your family with us for pizza and a video. I want to know if your son is happy. I want you to go with me to buy birthday gifts for my wonderful daughters. I want to share. I want to share with you."

When Bill talked, Lisa recognized the heart in his voice. He wanted to be with her. Did Bill see the real Lisa Ellis? The one she saw in the mirror every day that no one else seemed to see? She hoped so. She picked up the box and put on the ring.

"I think it suits you, Lisa. I think it belongs there," said Bill reaching for her hand.

"I wonder what mother will think," asked Lisa aloud and quite unintentionally.

"Why don't you call her and ask her?"

"I'm sorry, Bill. I didn't really mean to say that. I mean, here I am getting a proposal and I'm thinking about what Daisy will think!"

"Good for you. I want to know that. She's a big part of your family. I don't want to exclude her, I just want to be added in. Call her. I think she is waiting to hear from you."

"She knows," Lisa acted horrified. "You talked to her first about this, didn't you? I'll have no secrets left!" Inside she was glad that there would be less explaining to do.

"It's not about secrets, it's about sharing," said Bill.

"I suppose you're right about that. But before I call, isn't there something else that comes with this ring?"

"I thought we would never get to it," said Bill as he put down his glass and stood up. He pulled Lisa to her feet as well. With all the gentle force he could manage, he kissed her strongly.

Lisa let him kiss her and then kissed him back. It felt better than closing a deal.

"Go call Daisy. It's late for her," said Bill backing out of the embrace. "I'll be here just enjoying the brandy."

When the phone rang, Daisy picked it up and said immediately, "Hello, Lisa."

The man on the other end of the call said, "I guess you weren't expecting to hear from me, Mother."

"Jack! No, I wasn't. I thought Lisa might call. She often does on Sunday nights."

"I can call tomorrow if you want to talk to Lisa."

"If you called, you must have something to say, Jack. So I'm listening to you and only you."

"I'm not sure you want to hear it."

"All the better to hear it and not stay up all night worrying."

"I'm going to get married to Reid."

"Oh, Jack. Are you sure?"

"I'm sure. She said yes, anyway. I didn't think you would be too pleased, Mother, but I am."

"Then I am pleased for you. I am only surprised for myself. But I am a very old mother. You know I am a great grandmother. I thought that was the end of it. I never thought in a million years that you would ever marry, not after Abby. She's up in the cemetery, next to Dad."

"Abby doesn't have anything to do with Reid."

"I know. I am just being a foolish old woman. Well, congratulations. Does Lisa know?"

"No, I thought I would tell you and then Lisa. She's not too keen on Reid."

Daisy didn't want to confess that she and her daughter were of one mind on this issue. Reid seemed so un-special. It was unfair to compare her to the brilliant flash that had been Abby. "Don't be so hard on Lisa. She's just protective of her brother."

"I'll look after myself. Good night," said Jack.

"Wait! When are you getting married? I didn't think to ask."

"Sometime. Haven't bought the ring yet."

"I gave mine to Paulie. If I had known, I would have saved it for you."

"It was unlikely that I would have needed it. Anyway this gives me a chance to have the pleasure of doing it myself."

"Jack, do that. Bring Reid over to the house so I can see it. I know that you're thinking I haven't been enthusiastic. You surprised me. Come by for lunch and bring Reid. I'll make it up to you."

"Sure, I'll do that." Without more, Jack hung up the receiver.

Lisa had dialed steadily, but her mother's line was busy. She would have to get her mother call waiting as a Christmas present. Why hadn't she thought of that before? But then, when had her mother's phone ever been busy on a Sunday night? Giving up she was about to leave the bedroom when the phone rang. "That will be mother," Lisa thought.

It was Jack. "Hello, little sister. How was your Sunday? When are you going to bring that friend of yours, Bill, for coffee?"

"When are you going to serve latte?" asked Lisa laughingly.

"You come, I'll make it. Things change every day. I might have to do something to make a little more money, now that I'm getting married."

Lisa stopped laughing. "What? What did you say?"

"I'm getting married, Lisa. Did you think you could have your old brother all to yourself forever?"

In all seriousness, Lisa replied softly, "Yes, yes I did. Oh, Jack. You're making me cry and I want to be happy right now."

"Then cry first so you can be happy later. You always did cry first, little sister."

"When are you getting married? Before Christmas?" Lisa was trying to speak through the day's second weeping.

"No, no I don't think so. Maybe a while later. We'll see Christmas together, you and I."

"Good! I just can't think about giving up my brother for the holidays to that crazy farm girl. I don't know what you see in her Jack. Does she ever talk? I don't think I've ever heard her say a word."

"Well, I'm not marrying her for conversation, Lisa. She's kind of quiet in bed."

"Jack," Lisa shrieked. "You can't marry for sex. I mean, you're not marrying just for sex are you?"

"There's worse reasons for a man my age to marry, Lisa." Now it was Jack's turn to laugh. "But I'm marrying her because I love her and she loves me. Seems like two good reasons."

Lisa felt ashamed by her thoughts and words. Jack had seemed happy with Reid whatever-her-name-was. She just hoped that the woman had a little more common sense than that damn painter, Abby.

"I suppose you already told Daisy. I've been trying to call her."

"Just got off the phone. Daisy is about as happy as you are. You women are a hard lot to please."

"We just want the best for you. I thought that now you're back in Phoenix, you would be giving up your Margaritaville ways. I really thought you would be a little more…."

Before Lisa could finish, Jack cut her off.

"Sophisticated? Lisa, I am just a farm boy who grew up tending bar. Besides, with a classy woman like Reid, who knows what I'll do. She has season tickets to the symphony and the opera too. Maybe she will take me. Maybe I'll go."

"She does? Reid goes to the opera? I got the impression she was kind of a church mouse."

"She's that too. Reid has interests and plans. I want you to get to know her. Do that as a present for me."

"I'm ashamed of myself, Jack. Why can't I see more good in people? Why can't I be more like you Jack? I bet if I told you I was getting married, you'd be the very first to say something nice."

"Maybe not, Lisa. I don't know that there is any man I would think quite good enough for my little sister. She should get only the best."

"What if I told you I was thinking of marrying Bill Hadigan?" asked Lisa tentatively.

"He's real close to good enough, Lisa. I like Bill. Daisy loves Bill. Has he asked you or are you just planning his future?"

"He asked."

Now it was Jack's turn to be silent. If Lisa married Bill, Jack would finally have a brother-in-law he could stand. What a funny thought. Then another thought came to him, about the past.

"Do you remember out on the farm, Lisa? Do you remember where we used to picnic with Daisy on that ridge where Dad couldn't find us? I wish we could go there now. All of us. Then we could say that now as senior citizens we found the happiness we looked for on those summer days. I am happy for you Lisa. You get married to Bill Hadigan, just as soon as you can. You start having those happy times you always looked for. Is Bill there?"

Lisa was still weeping. "Yes," she said thickly.

"You tell him he's getting a real prize in you and I'm pleased for you both. No matter what, you're still my little sister. Tell him to keep that in mind."

"I will. I will, Jack. I have to hang up now. I'm happy for you Jack. Tell Reid that. I don't always say the right thing. I love you Jack"

"Good night, Lisa."

When Jack returned to the front room, Reid was sitting in the dark eating ice cream directly from the carton. "Sex makes me hungry. I can't help it," she said apologetically.

"I'll buy you some more if you'll stay the night."

"Tomorrow's a work day for me. I need to go home."

"OK, then, I'll go warm up the truck. You finish up and come on out when you are ready. Lisa said to tell you that she's happy I'm going to get married to you."

"She did? She said that? I thought she didn't like me. That was nice of her."

"Lisa is a nice sister. You'll have to get to know her better. You have time to do that. Maybe we'll go on a picnic sometime."

Reid just smiled as Jack put on his jacket. "Lock the door when you come out. I'll be waiting."

Reid took a couple of more spoonfuls of the spumoni, then got up and returned the carton to the refrigerator. She was warm now. Jack was waiting for her. What a comforting thought. He was here today and he would be in her life tomorrow and the tomorrow after that. She picked up her roses from the dining room table along with her jacket. She took one last look at the dark front room. Maybe she would help Jack paint it. It would be something to share.

Reid was asleep in her own bed by the time Bill Hadigan arrived at his front door. It had been quite a day. Was it only this morning he had been worried about going through the rest of his retirement alone? Fat chance of that now. He was practically doubling the size of his family.

For a moment, he thought of Alice. Nothing he did now would ever make any difference to her, but maybe in her dying, he had learned how to live. She used to tell him, "You belong where you want to belong." She had meant that he belonged at his clubs, at his job, with his clients, and not at home. He had learned something from all that. He would sleep well tonight.

P.S. Lowe

Lo, How A Rose

In Phoenix, when there is an early December frost, Christmas week weather is balmy. Those who have friends and family visiting are pleased to eat lunch outside where it is comfortable to sit in the noonday sun. This year, after the month's earlier cold spell, it had turned warm indeed. The golf courses were packed with men who had escaped winter in Canada and Iowa and Michigan. Roses bloomed in yards across the Valley.

In other respects, the week was similar to that of any other large city. Malls were crowded, but commuter traffic lightened. The airport was busy; churches were well attended. Lights were on houses and decorated trees were visible in front windows. Deep in the hearts of children were Christmas wishes.

It wasn't just the warm weather that had Holmes DuMez feeling un-festive. Still smarting over the expensive lawsuit he had lost in pursuit of the last two paintings completed by Abby, Holmes found little reason to celebrate. He even lacked interest in seasonal decorating for his gallery. Normally, he kept the gallery open at least two evenings a week to attract winter visitors in Old Scottsdale. This year it remained dark. When his mother called to invite him to Christmas dinner, he declined, politely and with no explanation. He was living for the holidays to be over.

Kenny Smyth also wished the holidays were behind him. He had promised his wife he would make contact with the family he had escaped. He had given himself a time limit. He would do it by Christmas Day. As the self-imposed deadline approached, he was even more reluctant to call. It seemed hypocritical to phone at Christmas. He no longer knew his brothers and had no desire to forge new bonds with any of them. Still, a promise is a promise, especially to Dianne. School was out for the holidays. He had the time. One day he would just call. But which brother should he call?

Unlike her husband, Dianne Smyth did not have off the week before Christmas. In the fifth month of her pregnancy, everything extra she had to do for the holidays made it harder and harder to get to work on time. She always needed another hour of sleep. On the previous Sunday, Kenny had promised to get a tree and decorate it with their daughter, Ruby Rose. True to his word, he kept Rose busy all day, while Dianne baked a batch of cookies and then slept. When she awakened, the worst of the mess was gone and the lighted tree was a welcome sight.

To her, the tree signaled the end of a terrible autumn. The months past had been stressful and unhappy. The revelation that Kenny had a large and hidden family had shocked her. For a while, she thought she wouldn't recover from the knowledge, but she did recover. Kenny had made her believe that his past had nothing to do with her. It wasn't in her nature to dwell on hurt; that's why Kenny loved her. She had sufficient optimism for a city, let alone her small family.

As she drove to work on that Monday morning, she only had one wish: that Kenny would call Iowa. What could possibly happen? Either his brothers would talk to him or they wouldn't. If they did talk, it wasn't like the family would come barreling down to Phoenix expecting a reunion. After all, there was money at stake: Kenny's inheritance. Dianne hoped fervently that they would get some money. She wanted to stay at home with the new baby and money would make that possible.

The DuMez gallery was closed on Mondays. That was the day that Holmes dedicated to paperwork and thinking. He would spend time looking at the artwork he had for sale and sometimes alter displays. He made notes about artists whose works he wanted to see. He often called those artists he already represented to make sure that their relationship remained intact. Today, however, Holmes decided his home would be the best "thinking" space.

At home, he never allowed himself to be sloppy. He had shaved, showered and dressed. He thought to himself that it took longer than usual. Age was creeping up on him. He had to be more careful of his weak leg even though he always used his cane.

At mid-morning, Holmes still had not settled down to work when he heard the front door open. It was the cleaning crew. He had forgotten that they had altered their schedule due to the holiday. Well, he wasn't staying home when they were here! He would just have to go out.

Unlike Holmes, Kenny was enjoying a morning at home with Ruby Rose, both still attired in pajamas. They had pancakes for breakfast and now were playing cards in the living room. Rose loved all kinds of card games and was happy to have her Daddy to play with her. They were both on school vacation. Rose was beating Kenny soundly in a game of "Fish." When the game was at last over, it was time to clean up the kitchen and get dressed. "Are we going to the store today?" Rose asked her father.

"Yup, right after lunch. I have a list from Mom," her father replied.

"Can I buy something?" asked Rose.

"What do you want to buy?" questioned Kenny.

"Two somethings. I'm not telling you. I have Christmas secrets, too, Dad."

"Well, in that case, do you have money for your somethings?" teased Kenny.

"Yes, I have my own money."

"Then I guess you can buy whatever you have money to buy! Now, go get a bath and get dressed while I make lunch." Kenny was surprised at how his daughter had become so grown up in the past year. Like her mother, she had become thoughtful and generous. This would be the first time for her to purchase a present on her own. Kenny spun Rose around, hugged her, and pointed her out of the living room. He picked up the cards and went to make lunch. It would be a good day for a little canned soup.

Holmes DuMez drove through Scottsdale without a notion of where to go. Because of construction, he was forced to head west on Thomas Road. Here was where ritzy became Midwestern. He passed the upholstery shop. The heavy doors were locked. His dad would not reopen until well into the New Year. In the light mid-morning traffic, Holmes sailed into Phoenix in his luxury car.

He passed 24th Street. Stopping at the light he looked ahead. Everything was new except the old green sign for Beacon's Nursery. How long had it been since he had stopped there? Every week, beautiful Beacon arrangements showed up at his gallery and his home. Personally, Holmes hadn't been in the shop since Bob Beacon had died. He decided to stop in today.

He parked. The old entrance to the greenhouse was securely fenced off, forcing Homes into the main store. It hadn't changed since he was a child. In the L-shaped building, there were gardening tools, expensive bulbs and fertilizer to the left. Straight ahead were the refrigerated cases of cut flowers. In the small bend between the two areas was the window to the floral workroom. A middle-aged woman was working on a Christmas arrangement. As Holmes approached, she looked up. Before saying anything, she smiled generously. "Hello Holmes. Long time since you have been here. I hope that you are not canceling your standing orders." She walked to the counter.

Holmes recognized his oldest friend quickly. Her graying hair was pulled from her face that was without makeup. Grape cluster earrings swayed on either side of her face. The earrings matched her purple pullover sweater. That purple! Who else wore purple every day of her life except RayeLin Beacon!

"Hello RayeLin. I didn't expect to see you here. I just came in because…because I came in. I haven't been in the holiday spirit. What can you recommend to me? Something for the house?" Holmes had no idea why he had come. Aware that he had to make conversation, words sprang from him without much thought.

RayeLin looked puzzled. "That's done. Your arrangements have gone out on the truck. Had to be there before the cleaning crew left. Those were the instructions I got, anyway."

"Ah, yes, right. My assistant takes care of all that. Maybe you can do something for mother. Send her something on Christmas Eve? Do you deliver on Christmas Eve?"

"For you, Holmes, Beacon's delivers. How is your Mother?" asked RayeLin in an effort to move the conversation to something that sounded less like the meeting of strangers.

"Old. Happy. Active. The same. Are the girls around?"

There was hesitation and a sigh. RayeLin thought briefly of how much time had passed since both her brother and her husband had died. Not long, but no one ever talked about them. It was as if Bob, Jr. and Peter had never existed.

Aloud she said gently. "I'm by myself. That won't last. My daughter, Barbara, and her husband are going to move back here and run the two stores. I told them there would be more money if we just sold this land and the big acreage of flower gardens, but they want to leave the corporate world and try this. You can't tell kids anything. Even when they are old! Anne doesn't come in. She thinks that it was something in this place or in the fields that caused the cancer in her Daddy and her Uncle. It was odd both of them dying of brain cancer so close together. But look at me! I've been here longer than anyone and I'm still fine."

Holmes felt the sadness of neglected friendship. "You were and always will be fine, RayeLin. Don't be too hard on Anne. I know what it is like to lose the ones you love and admire. If you can find one thing or one person to blame, then somehow you can live with the anger instead of the pain. I am still that way about Abby. Why didn't she go to a doctor for God's sake! She could have been alive and painting today." He leaned heavily on his cane.

RayeLin had stopped all pretense of work and was resting her hands on the counter. "Anne will do what she has to do. For me, most of the awfulness has passed. I'm lucky to have the girls and their families. I have this place that keeps me busy if not rich. How is the richest art dealer in the world doing? I haven't seen anything about you in the papers lately. Seems like you dropped out of the social column. Are things good with you?"

"If you read the paper, then you know that I lost my court case over Abby's last works. I am only sorry that it was such a sordid mess. Seems like all the goodness that came from knowing Abby turned ugly in the end. Abby told me that she was married. I had no idea how 'forever' a marriage could be when it came to community property," said Holmes with a little heat.

"I only know what was in the paper," said RayeLin.

"That was bad; the rest of the story, was much, much worse. At the time, I thought that having those paintings would bring Abby back to life for me. I would have never sold them because I don't own a single work of hers. Not one. For me, not having a painting turned out to be the biggest regret of my life."

"But surely you could buy one back at some time in the future," said RayeLin in hopeful suggestion.

"It wouldn't be the same." Holmes paused to regain his famous sense of presence. "But business is good. I don't do much and I make money, even though much of the thrill is gone. Used to be that painters didn't have agents and copyrights and lawyers. I made deals on handshakes. I took chances. Some worked, some didn't. Now I have my people work with some artist's people. We get a deal on paper. The magic isn't there."

"Is that because Abby isn't around anymore?"

"Oh, Abby was definitely part of the magic! It's more than that. I just don't see the kind of work that I like. One painting looks pretty much like the next. They say when that happens, when you lose your third eye, it's time to quit."

"What else would you do?" asked a surprised RayeLin.

"Maybe work in Dad's upholstery shop. Do a little interior decorating. I could make a living."

RayeLin laughed at the thought of Holmes covered in the dust and odor of his father's shop. That definitely wasn't going to happen. To Holmes she said, "I've been thinking of calling you for a couple of months. There was something I wanted you to see."

"You're not going to show me one of those ridiculously expensive orchid twigs that are all the rage now, are you?" asked Holmes in mock horror.

"We don't carry any. Beacon's customers continue to believe that more is more and less is less. We give people good value for their money. No, I want you to look in the greenhouse. Go stand by the koi pool. There's something interesting there."

"A new fish?" asked Holmes.

"Yes," laughed RayeLin, "a new 'fish'. Go look. It may not be visible for long." RayeLin turned back to her worktable without further explanation.

Dismissed, Holmes did as he was told. He entered the aged greenhouse. The dampness and the pungent earth odor welcomed him. The shallow pool was in the very back of the building, invisible from where he stood. He made his way there slowly. As the pool came into sight, he immediately saw RayeLin's "fish."

A young girl sat on the corner of the pool, her legs balanced on the two edges as she faced forward. Because he was standing behind her, Holmes could only see that she had a large board in her lap. To her side was a simple box of watercolors. She was painting the pool and the koi.

Holmes did not want to disturb her but he wanted to get a better view of her work. In attempting to move one step closer, his cane hit a clay pot with a clatter.

"Hello," said the girl without turning around.

"Hello to you. I am sorry to disturb you. I didn't know anyone would be here. My friend told me to walk through the greenhouse. I used to come here when I was young." Holmes walked to a spot beyond where the girl was seated. He sat down on the pool ledge, facing the girl, but not too close. The ledge was very cold.

The girl looked up. She was older than Holmes had thought. The slightness of her figure had deceived him. She brushed her long dark hair away from her face and pushed her glasses to the bridge of her nose. "Do you know RayeLin?" she asked.

"Yes, yes I do. For a long time. She and I used to come out here together and plan our lives. She taught me all about koi. I can see you're interested in the fish as well." Holmes was hoping to find a way to get a better look at the painting in progress.

"I don't know about the fish. I'd rather paint flowers, but nothing is blooming right now except ugly poinsettias and mums. Not worth painting."

"What is worth painting then?"

"Roses. Cactus flowers. Anything orange or purple. RayeLin lets me spend time here when I can get away. Sometimes she makes up something for me to copy."

"Well, RayeLin is a good kind of friend to have when you need to get away." Holmes wondered what the girl was escaping. She had stood up and placed the finished painting on the ledge to her left, far away from Holmes. If he was going to get a good look at it, he would have to ask. "Would you mind showing me your work?"

"Sure you can look, but it's still a little wet and not quite right. I don't think my sister will like it." She handed her board to Holmes. The first thing he noticed was the careful way she had taped the paper to the board. The paper seemed to be of high quality as well. "She knows her craft," thought Holmes.

There were three fish in the painting at asymmetrical angles. Their bodies seemed to undulate in the pale aqua water she had washed over them. Although watercolors had never been his specialty, he thought this idea was fresh, yet had strong elements of the purity of Japanese painting. He held the painting out at arms' length and compared it with the greenhouse pool. He liked the rendering better than the reality.

"Your sister should love it," Holmes sad as he handed the board back. "But you didn't sign it."

"It won't make any difference to her. She'll know that I did it," said the girl with resignation.

"Is your sister an art critic?" asked Holmes.

"No, just a critic in general. A little hard to please."

"Would it make any difference if I said that I liked it?"

"Not to my sister." The girl closed her eyes and sighed. "It's not fair for me to talk about her like that and not tell you the whole truth. My sister Jacqueline is autistic. She likes fish and has a big saltwater tank in her room. She watches it day and night like television. She doesn't talk, so we never know what she likes, just what she doesn't like. Thanks anyway." The girl had packed up everything and was holding out her hand to Holmes.

He shook it. "You didn't tell me your name. I want to tell RayeLin that we at least met."

"Carmen Luk. People call me Luki. My mother hates it, but what can I do? She's from Costa Rica and my father is Chinese. I just tell her that I am lucky to have a mother like her."

"Do you live with your family, then?"

"Oh yes. The old maid still lives at home and teaches school."

"You don't look old enough to be out of college," said a surprised Holmes.

"Way old. I'm twenty-six." Carmen looked at her watch. "I've got to go. My parents are going out to lunch and I am sister-watching. It was nice meeting you. Did you tell me your name? I'm bad at remembering names."

"Holmes DuMez."

Carmen's eyes widened. Here was a name that she knew. "Oh no. I didn't know. I've never seen you. RayeLin said she was going to call you. Oh! She didn't call you, did she? I'm so embarrassed."

Holmes was humbled by Carmen's reaction to his name. How he wished at this moment to have no reputation to live up to or possibly to live down. "RayeLin didn't call me. I just dropped by to see her in the spirit of Christmas. She told me to visit the greenhouse. She didn't tell me anyone was here – so why be embarrassed? I liked your painting. I was truthful and would like to see more of your work. My expertise is not watercolors, however."

Carmen was thinking of a reply that didn't sound stupid. Her heart raced. She felt hot. She felt childish. She would have to say something soon or Holmes DuMez would think that she was the autistic sister. She decided on formality. "Mr. DuMez, I'm honored by what you said." She couldn't think of anything else to say. What had he asked her anyway?

Holmes waited a long string of seconds to make sure that there was nothing more Carmen wanted to say. "I would like to see more of your work. Do you have a portfolio?"

"Uh, no. I don't think you understand that I just paint because I like to paint. I sell my stuff at the swap meets sometimes and sometimes at a local show. The really bad stuff I just throw away."

"Well, my suggestion is that you don't throw anything away for a while." Holmes smiled at Carmen. He searched for his card case in his pocket. He withdrew an elegantly engraved gold case, selected a card and handed it to Carmen. "This is my card. I want to hear from you. Keep painting. Bring your work to me."

Carmen took the card. "I guess you mean that?"

"I'm as good as my word. You know, we might have some business to do together. Would you like that?"

Carmen nodded her head. She tucked the card into her backpack. She was silent as she gathered up the rest of her things and walked out of the greenhouse. "Now," she thought, "maybe my mother will think I am lucky after all."

Holmes lingered. Here in the greenhouse, all was like it had always been. Through three generations of Beacons, the place was barely changed. Maybe that's why he had been drawn here: to re-find a comfort that would neutralize the more recent bitter past.

When he returned to the main building, there were several customers for Christmas cut flowers. Holmes waited to talk to RayeLin. When she was available, he said, "That was some 'fish' out in the greenhouse. Where did you find her?"

"She teaches school with Anne. She likes to paint flowers and she comes here to paint them. I don't know much about art, Holmes, but it seemed to me that she had a special talent. She could use encouragement, which is why I kept meaning to call you. Did I waste your time?"

"I don't have time to waste. I would have liked to talk a little longer with her. She has talent. Don't know if she has what it takes to be a great talent. There was a time when I could wait a long time to develop a new artist. I can't imagine waiting five or ten years to have something salable."

"So nudge her along," said RayeLin.

"I can't very well demand to see what she hasn't got," replied Holmes.

"Send her seven roses in a silver vase," suggested RayeLin. "Carmen has two weeks off for school vacation."

"Nudge? That's a shove." Nevertheless, he thought it was a useful idea.

"Times are changed." RayeLin moved the two steps to the counter and picked up a plain white card. "Here," she said, handing the card and a pen to Holmes. "Say something inspiring."

Holmes made a face. He inhaled and didn't exhale until these words were on the card. "Your first commission. I'll pick up and pay for my painting on New Year's Eve." Then he signed his name. He showed the card to RayeLin. "Does this meet with your approval?"

She rolled her eyes. "What color roses?"

"Assorted on the color except no red. Have you got a silver vase?" asked Holmes.

"Sure, for a price. But then, I didn't think you wanted anything less than the best."

"I don't," agreed Holmes. "You're my oldest and best friend. I think that I still owe you."

RayeLin came around through the doorway at the end of the counter. She hugged Holmes, but was mindful of his cane. "Visit more often. Come over to the house and we'll have a good run down memory lane. Come over during the holidays. I mean that!" said RayeLin.

Holmes held her tighter. "I will do that. Merry Christmas," he whispered in her ear. He left the nursery feeling he couldn't wait for New Year's Eve.

Ruby Rose Smyth was eating her soup alone while her father showered and dressed. She liked to put a bit of peanut butter on a plain cracker and float it in the soup. She didn't really like the soup at all, just the soggy crackers.

She was planning what she wanted to buy. She needed two presents. One for the baby and one for Reid. At school, she had decorated and kiln-fired two coffee mugs for her parents. She had brought them home, already wrapped, on the last day of school.

The phone rang. Rose ran from the table to pick it up, hoping it was her mother. "Hello. This is the Smyth residence, Rose speaking," she answered.

The young, polite voice surprised the male caller. He guessed it was his niece. "Hello Rose. My name is John. I would like to speak with your Dad. Can he come to the phone?" John VanDuyver asked.

"I have to go check. Does he know you?"

"He used to know me."

Ruby couldn't decide if this was a salesman or not. She wasn't supposed to answer the phone. She was supposed to let the machine answer and just listen until she knew who it was. If this was a salesman, she was in real trouble.

"Are you selling something?" Rose asked the unknown caller. "I need to know, first."

John VanDuyver laughed. He knew better than to make a comment that would confuse the child. "No, I'm not a salesman, but it is very smart of you to ask first. I'm in Iowa and I'm calling long-distance."

"OK. I have to go get him." Ruby put the phone down on the counter and raced to the bedroom door where she knocked loudly.

"I'm getting dressed. Is that your Mom on the phone?" asked Kenny?

"No. It's a man named John. He said he wants to talk to you in Iowa." The message was a little mistaken by the eight-year old.

The door flew open and there stood Kenny, without shoes or shirt, only wearing socks and jeans. "What?" He grabbed Rose by the shoulder, but instantly let go. He had scared her.

Faking calm his heart did not feel, Kenny told Rose he would take the call in the upstairs bedroom. "You go and hang up the phone, OK?"

Ruby did as she was told. Her Dad had acted mad even though it wasn't a salesman on the phone. She was sure it was someone important. Now, sitting at the table, her soup was cold and she didn't want it anymore. It seemed to be taking a long time for her Dad to talk to the man.

The time agony experienced by Ruby Rose was nothing compared with that of her father. From the minute he heard his oldest brother's voice, time vanished. The room vanished. The earth disappeared. Two voices, hesitating, faltering, failing; only these remained.

"This is your brother, John VanDuyver," the conversation started. "I decided to call today because I could do it alone. I found out you were a teacher and figured you would be home on the first day of winter break, like me. Rest of the family is out doing shopping. I promised my wife I would call you. If I called today and I didn't get you, I'm off the hook to my wife." John wasn't going any farther than that until he heard something back from the other end.

"I'm not alone," Kenny said in a very strained voice. He couldn't think of anything else to say.

"Was that your little girl on the phone? She has nice manners." John tried to make a conversation.

"Yes, that was Ruby Rose. My daughter. She is out of school, too." As an afterthought, he added, "My wife is at work."

"Is this a good time to call, then? I wouldn't want to call at a bad time," said John.

"Yes. Rose is having her lunch. Then we're going out."

"I don't want to keep you. I just wanted to call, but I don't know what I wanted to say. Guess you know that Reid Markham fixed it so that you could have money from the farm. She never let on for a minute that she knew you were alive. Found it out from the lawyer, but it didn't surprise me. I always thought you were somewhere."

"I'm alive. I've been alive right here in Phoenix for a long time," said Kenny without any hint of conciliation.

John thought that Kenny's anger was untouched by time's healing ways. Still the anger even though Kenny had left all the work and sorrow behind. He had run from it while John had stayed to the bitterest of ends. "I must have learned something from the staying and Kenny must have learned something from the leaving," John thought kindly.

Aloud he said, "I've thought about you since you left, Kenny. I always hoped you were fine and seems like you are. Aileen Sterner told me you are a teacher. I never figured you for that. I've been teaching in the same high school in the same town for nineteen years."

Kenny tried to think of something to say in reply. It had been so long since he had imagined his family. Over time, he had lost what he thought he remembered about the past. While the anger remained, the facts had melted away like pieces of chipped ice. He couldn't even remember what had interested his brother in school. He said, "I teach computers. Do you have computers in your high school?"

"Sure we do. Internet, too. Not fancy computers, but enough to help the kids find out about the world. In the winter, on weekends, we have lab time so that there is something for the older kids to do. Write e-mail to people, you know. Do research. Look into colleges. I know there wasn't anything like that for you, Kenny."

"How was it possible to have the emotions, the negative, destructive emotions, when clear memories of what created the feelings were gone?" thought Kenny. He seethed. To his brother he said, "Computers wouldn't have made a difference to me. I just had to get away."

"I know that," said John hurriedly. "I'm calling you to tell you that I know that. I'm only speaking for myself, not for the others. Every year I see kids who must have been like you. Kids who need to go. They won't survive if they have to stay. I have tried from time to time to help them, but it's no good, because deep down, I don't understand what drives them away. I didn't understand what drove you. I was different. I didn't like the farm any better than you; I just didn't think I had to leave everything to leave the farm."

Kenny had listened to his brother. In the now silence, his anger spilled into words. "I didn't just leave the farm! I left the meanness and nothing that was living on the farm. You and Brian were always gone. You never noticed how Dad and Mac were to me. How Dad was with Mom. I couldn't stop it, so I ran from it. Never once, not one time have I had any regrets about leaving."

"I did notice, Kenny, I just couldn't stop it. That is why I never looked for you. I knew you were better off gone or even dead than caught with Dad and without help," said John.

The most feared words had now been said, John thought, and the brothers were still alive. Into the silent receiver he said, "I guess that I am the only one with regrets."

It was impossible for Kenny to reply to John's last remark. The phone stayed in his hand, however.

"Well, I guess we have cleaned the barn on that one," said John. "My plan was just to call and tell you that you are welcome to any money coming from the farm. That's all. You have a good holiday with your family. I liked talking with my niece. I was thinking about her name, Ruby Rose. I have a couple of kids. Girl came first. She was named after me, Johanna. Then a boy. I wanted to name him David James. He ended up with the name of our Dad, Pendleton." John hurried to the next sentence. "But he was named for Granddad. I hope that someday, my son might be something like our grandfather. That's a piece of the past I don't want to lose."

"I wanted to lose it all, John. I barely remember Old Pen. Reid remembers him. Talks about him and Grammy. I think the memories I have came from Reid. They don't feel much like my life," said Kenny.

"I don't believe that. Do you remember Miss Ruby Diamond?" asked John.

A hot flush began to creep from Kenny's neck to his face. Quetly, he replied, "No, just stories about her."

"Maybe you remember this story from Grammy or maybe you heard it from Reid. Miss Ruby was a change-of-life baby born to a long-time childless couple. When she was born to the Diamonds, her daddy named her Ruby so that she would always have names as precious as she was to him. I thought you might have remembered that story," said John. "I mean your daughter has an ordinary last name, but two first names: a gem and a flower."

"You have no right to talk about my daughter," said Kenny hotly.

"I wasn't. Not really. I was talking about the past, a little piece that we both have in common. I guess I was hoping that there were one or two things in your past that were worth bringing into the future. Even if one of them was only a name."

Kenny felt trapped. He felt the need to justify himself all over again to family. His name for his daughter was a dear, dear secret and yet, someone who really knew him, had guessed it so easily! "I don't know what I'm supposed to say." This was both Kenny's question and confession.

John had something, now, that he wanted very much to say to his brother. It was the reason for the phone call. "You and I cannot fix the past, Kenny. Dad and Mom are dead. We are still living. I thought you and I could go on from now. Can we try?"

Eternity if about five minutes long if you are eight years old and have nothing to do but wait. Ruby Rose Smyth had tired of waiting for her father's conversation to finish. She had lost patience with being polite. She came to the upstairs bedroom, loudly whispering to her Dad from the doorway, "Are you done yet?"

Forgetting that he needed to answer his brother, Kenny answered his daughter's question first: "No."

The answer to Ruby came to John as well. John felt the finality of his brother's word. He wondered how to end this last phone call. Then Kenny started to speak again. "I'm sorry, John. Ruby Rose is getting a little impatient to go out."

Kenny had motioned for Rose to come sit with him on the edge of the bed. He put his arm around her, holding her tightly. It was the way that her small self pressed against him that made him feel warm. She gave him safety, loving as she did without conditions. She was his family, his blood and his life. He hoped that she would never have any reason to abandon her family.

John was unaware of the activity at the other end of the line. "Did your 'no' mean not now or not ever?"

"What? What are you saying?" Kenny was also confused. His daughter's appearance had removed his attention from the phone call.

"I was asking if maybe we could find a way to go on from here," John said. "I thought you said 'no.' Does that mean not ever, or just not right now?"

"I don't know what it means. I was so sure that I never wanted to see any VanDuyver again. I can't imagine why you want to see me. The money from the farm makes things worse. I've changed. I'm different than I was. I can't go back to being a VanDuyver."

"I don't want you to do that," interjected John, defensively and hastily. "It's only a name. We all changed, Kenny. It just seemed that the worst is over. Maybe we can start over at being brothers, at least." John was as far out on a limb as he could go.

Maybe it was a longing and maybe it was the sincerity of his brother's voice that softened Kenny's hard edge. Dianne had said that all of the brothers had been damaged equally by the harshness of un-loving. She maintained that Kenny had no right to believe that he suffered alone. The brothers had only revealed the damage differently. Kenny had to admit that his brother had made the leap across the past, something Kenny did not do on his own. John spoke neither of forgiving or forgetting but of going on. That was a thought that Kenny hadn't come to, but an idea he liked.

"What about the others?" asked Kenny. Once more Kenny bristled at the idea that they might "forgive" him. How could he live with the intimacy of assumed wrong-doing? Kenny was no "Prodigal Son," returning for the needed shelter that follows squander.

"I don't know. I didn't ask them before I called you. I had the interest. I called. They have to do what they want. You have to do what you want," said John.

Kenny was again silent. It was both what John had said and the way he had said it that reminded Kenny of Old Pen. Your past found you even when you changed your name and lived in Arizona.

"I appreciate the call, John. I need to think about it more," said Kenny wearily.

"More than I hoped for. I'm going to go. It's good to hear your voice. I'll expect to hear from you after a while." John VanDuyver hung up the phone before Kenny could change his mind, believing that there would be a second call and that Kenny would make it.

Kenny hung up the bedroom phone. His normally bouncy daughter was quiet beside him. "Who was on the phone?" Ruby asked more out of habit than true interest.

Kenny thought about telling his daughter an easy lie. That lie would doubtlessly lead to a second. Might as well start with the truth. "That was your Uncle John VanDuyver."

"Do I know him?" asked Rose.

"Not yet, but you may meet him sometime." Kenny's reply seemed sufficient to Rose who bounded off the bed, announcing that she was "Ready. Ready. READY!"

As she left the room, Kenny thought of what had brought him to this moment with his daughter. How could all that anger and rejection have produced this wonderful child, this Ruby Rose? The answer seemed just beyond his understanding unless it was as simple as John had said. Some of the good past we bring, however unwittingly, into the future. If he could remember that thought, he would tell Dianne when she came home from work.

Families Are Messy

The dawn of the new millennium didn't much interest Daisy Ellis. Her children, Lisa and Jack, had stopped by in the afternoon for a visit before their evenings of planned festivities. It was the first time she had seen her children together and alone since they had announced their marriages before Christmas. No one came to see Daisy without staying for a bit of something to eat. Suspecting that she might have company, although she didn't know who it might be, Daisy had spent her morning preparing consommé chicken salad, and chocolate icebox pie. When Jack and Lisa showed up, they were expecting to take Daisy out to eat and were surprised to be the guests of their mother.

"Oh, Daisy," Lisa said when she realized that her surprise visit seemed no surprise at all to her mother. "Jack and I wanted to take you out and you have spent all morning working! Why don't you just put that food away, change your clothes and we will still go out? We can all have some champagne to celebrate the New Year!"

"Lisa, I prepared this food to be eaten. You and Jack are here and we can eat the food. There isn't a restaurant in town with better food than what I make for myself," said Daisy. After nearly sixty years with her headstrong daughter, Lisa still could be irritating. Whatever Lisa planned, she wanted to carry out, and she could be insensitive to the hopes of others.

"Jack?" Lisa said imploringly to her brother. Jack looked sheepishly at the floor, rubbed his chin and smiled.

"Seems to me that I would like to have my mother's cooking and my sister's company this afternoon," Jack said in conciliation. He had been the go-between between mother and daughter for as long as he could remember. He had an ability to de-fuse situations.

"Good, it's settled then," said Daisy. How she loved her son's ways. How much easier he was to please than her daughter. She regretted that thought, but it didn't make much sense to regret the truth. It was what it was. "Jack, if you will set the table and Lisa if you will make tea, we'll have a nice celebration right here." Daisy was already moving toward the kitchen.

The real reason, of course, that Daisy wanted to stay home was that over the past months, she realized that she was losing her hearing. In public places, where there was the usual din of other diners and background music, Daisy could not follow a conversation. Today was a day when she wanted to talk to her children. She had been feeling uneasy about their proposed marriages. Maybe not about the marriages, but about their futures. It was a nagging feeling, not a worry she could name. In spite of her life-long desire to stay out of her children's decisions, she wanted to talk to them to assure herself that all was well.

In Daisy's bright kitchen, she was the undisputed queen. She directed Jack to the good china and Lisa to the silver tea service. "Don't bother with the tray, but do put out the pot and the sugar and creamer as well. I'd rather have tea from silver than champagne any day."

Conversation was spare during the preparation, but when they were ready to eat, all were in happy good spirits. For the three of them, sitting at the table together was a familiar experience, although they had not been together like this in months.

Jack first brought up the subject of marriage. "Baby sister, you have a big ring, but I haven't heard of the wedding date yet. I may have to close down the bar to attend. My loyal patrons will need a place to go, and I'll have to give them lots of notice."

"If I leave it up to Bill," said Lisa, "it's tomorrow. He just wants to get married. I was thinking about sometime in October. Too late to do a spring wedding and summer is just atrocious. Too hot; everyone leaves town. Besides, we haven't settled on a place to live yet. We've only begun talking to the lawyers about combining and protecting assets."

Jack put down his fork and Daisy set down her teacup loudly. They looked at each other and then at Lisa. Their silence was like a bright, white light in an already bright room. Lisa felt their heat. "What? What did I say? You asked me a question, Jack, and I am trying to answer it. Why do I feel like I'm doing something wrong?" asked Lisa.

"Lisa, are you getting married or forming a corporation?" asked Jack.

"What the hell do you think? You think it is easy at my age to get married? Did you forget husbands number one and two? I'm not going to let everything I worked for, all that I built, slip away from me through a marriage that may or may not work out. I tell you something else, Big Brother, you would be wise to do the same thing! You have nothing but your bar to support you for your golden years and Reid could get half of that if something went wrong," snapped Lisa.

The words that flew angrily out of Lisa were like the ones Daisy had heard so many times before. Even as a girl, anything that threatened Lisa's security made her angry and suspicious. By being defensive, she tried to ensnare others into seeing the world and people in the same suspicious way. Maybe this was why Daisy worried about this next marriage. Lisa had few experiences of warm, sharing relationships of trust. Without such experiences, how could she hope to build a marriage with Bill Hadigan? These thoughts swirled in Daisy, but she didn't say anything to Lisa. Instead, she looked at her son. She loved him more than any living thing on earth, and hoped that his feelings were not hurt by his sister's outburst. After decades, Daisy worried about her son's feelings.

"You haven't said when you are getting married, Jack. You question me as if I was on trial, but I notice you haven't said anything about your own date. I may have been married before and gloriously unsuccessfully, too. You, dear brother, haven't tested those waters," said Lisa edgily.

"Until Reid, I never found a woman who wanted to marry me. We picked out a ring, two rings really. When I collect them, we're going to set a date. We were thinking of April, or early May. Reid has a funny feeling about getting married during Lent. So, probably after Easter," said Jack easily.

"It's already practically January!" exclaimed Lisa. "You cannot get a wedding together in four months. Where are you going to live? You have a house, unfinished. She has a house, God knows where. This is a community property state, in case you have forgotten. If you both sell your houses before you get married, you can put the proceeds into separate accounts, protected from community property by a pre-nuptial agreement," said Lisa breathlessly.

"Lisa, I think you are determined to rope Jack into your own problems," said Daisy, cautiously.

"I am not. I am just sick of this whole business of marriage! You tell people you are getting married and suddenly, everybody is giving you advice or going mushy about love. It's been about two weeks, and I am already sick of this," said Lisa. Tears quickly dropped on to her face.

"Of course you are. Frankly, I'm surprised that you are still engaged," said Daisy. She had meant the comment in a kind way, but Lisa fumed.

"What's that supposed to mean? I guess I have always disappointed you. I have made many mistakes, but at least I have made something of my life and I did it without anyone else's support. You and Jack just rolled along with whatever came along. You never held a job and Jack has done nothing but hang out in bars his entire life. If either one of you ever had a crisis, I mean a real crisis, who would have to bail you out? Me, that's who. I do a lot for you mother, and you never seem in the least grateful. You love Jack the most. I have always known it. I married the wrong men, but why is that worse than Jack hanging out for decades with that painter and never bothering to marry her? Why is what I do any worse than you staying in a marriage for years without any love or respect?" Lisa was, as her brother said, "on a roll." She was just beginning on a tirade that could suck the life out of a large continent.

"Stop it," said Daisy and Jack in unison. Hearing their voices at the same time in the same tone made Daisy and Jack start laughing. Lisa thought they were laughing at her. Abruptly she left the table, went to the counter, and cried noisily. Daisy poured herself another cup of tea while waiting for Lisa to compose herself. These outbursts were sudden, but generally short.

In less than a minute, Lisa was wiping her face on a snatched paper towel. "Well?" she asked as she returned to the table. It was a single word and a broad question addressed to both her mother and brother. Jack was going to say something, but no thoughts came together.

In a way, Daisy was grateful for Lisa's outburst. All of the fears and sad feelings that had surrounded Daisy's heart for days were quieted. In less than a minute, Lisa had put out all of her anger and hardness for all to hear. It was heartbreaking, but cleansing.

"Lisa, I love you. I have always loved you, but it's harder than loving Jack. Jack is like me and you are like Douglas. The things that I disliked in your father are the things I dislike in you. You disappointed me. Not for the reasons that you think. My disappointment comes from never being able to be close to you in the way that I was close to my mother. You never needed me and you don't need me now. I needed my mother and loved her even years after she was dead. I wanted to give you the security of a mother's love that I had. You didn't need a mother any more than you needed a husband. You were about money and ambition and having things. Jack and I were about being needed in little ways, not in big ways. What I disliked so in Douglas was that once I had done what he needed me to do, which was marry him so that he could get my father's farm, he never needed me again until he got sick. Jack needed me and later Paulie needed me. That's what I did for a life. It often seemed like a real job, even though no one paid me for it." Daisy was silent just for a minute to take a sip of her tea to soothe the dryness of her mouth.

"I'm an old woman. I won't be around long enough to burden you. If I seem ungrateful for all that you have done, it is because I never wanted you to feel that you had to help me out. Believe it or not, I will probably not outlive my money, Lisa. If you fear that you will have to take care of me, I want to relieve you of that fear. The only thing I want of you or for you is to be happy with someone. I want you to know the difference between cash money and your heart. I just wanted you to have the security of love instead of money. But I know that you have to find that out for yourself."

"I don't need your permission, Mother," said Lisa.

"You never needed it or wanted it. You have to do what you are going to do. As old as I am, as old as you are, you are still my daughter. You will always be my only daughter. The biggest failure of my life is you. I failed to give you the security you wanted and needed. When I hear you talking about your marriage as if it was a house sale, I see the scared little girl who practiced speeches in front of a mirror for hours to make sure everybody thought you were wonderful. I just see your fear and I am sorry for myself and for you. You are a success nevertheless. You have made a good life for yourself and you are generous. You did it without help. You started from the absolute bottom." Daisy stopped speaking. She had no idea how her words would be understood. Lisa would be just fine and would find her happiness with or without Bill Hadigan.

Jack listened to his mother with the same love and admiration he had always had for her. Daisy rarely spoke her feelings, but when she did, there was a directness in them that relieved him. Yes, he needed to be needed. Abby had needed him. That's why he stayed with her. Did Reid need him? He was unsure. Could he love someone completely who didn't need him? It was a question for Daisy.

"Why did you stay with Dad?" asked Jack. "I've never asked, but I am asking you now. You said he didn't need you. Did you love him? Did you love him all those years?"

Jack's questions startled Daisy. She felt like Pandora after unleashing the spirits from the box. She had over spoken, and now the question that she never answered for herself was being asked aloud by her son. Even if she knew the answer, she would have lied, but she didn't know the answer. She stayed because it was the times; divorce was not an option. She stayed to protect her children from the coldness of their father, and failed to protect them. She stayed because she loved Herbert Covington with all her heart. Once she couldn't have him, being married to Douglas Ellis didn't seem to matter. She had a house, children and friends, and things to do. All of those things were more important than her husband, who hardly mattered at all. All of those reasons were true, but one reason alone did not dominate.

"Oh Jack, I can hardly remember. I wake up every day, and your father is as vague to me as some character in a book I read long ago. Here I am trying to tell both of you to go ahead, follow your hearts and get married. I shouldn't say anything at all. I was watching the TV a few years back, though, and I heard something that rather applies to my life with Douglas. Some woman was talking about marriage and why you should stay married. She said 'When you are young, you want each other; when you are old, you need each other; only the years in-between are hard.' I married young and was married for over forty years. Do you think you will be married for forty years?"

Daisy hoped that she had sidestepped Jack's question. Thankfully, Lisa seemed to be so self-absorbed that she was not paying attention to the answer.

Daisy was wrong on her assessment of Lisa. "That's no answer, Mother. I want to know, too. Why did you stay with Dad?"

Daisy was not about to be further bullied by her daughter at her own kitchen table. "Because I did. Because it was a habit. Because maybe he didn't need me, but I needed him. That's all I am going to say about it, Lisa, now or ever. I guess I started this in a way, so now I am finishing it. I got married; I stayed married. It's got nothing to do with what you two propose to do."

"You and Dad weren't exactly a wonderful couple together. No wonder Jack and I have a bad marriage track record," said Lisa to her mother.

"We were what we were, Lisa, and I repeat that it has nothing to do with the choices you both are now making. I want both of you to know something else. I miss being married. I miss being even a little something to someone I live with. I was just about five years older than you both are now when Douglas died. It's not him I miss as much as having someone in my life. I didn't get the second chance that both of you have now. I think that you both might be happy, even this late in your lives. I would like to be around to see that happiness, especially for you, Lisa."

"I don't believe you," said Lisa.

"I think you won't believe me. You've had years and years of being locked out of love. Do you think I don't know that? Do you think I don't know what a hard man Douglas was? I remember it all. Lisa, you were just sixteen when you left home. Jack was already gone, but I never got over your leaving. Never once did Douglas ever mention your name, not for two years. I had no one then and I thought I would lose my mind living with a man who never said a word about his own children. I stayed to be there when you came back. You came back with Paulie not even born. Then I stayed for Paulie. I thought it would mean something to him to have me there every day of his life to do the things you couldn't do for him. I thought it would mean something to you, too. Yes, I could have done differently. Back in 1963, I applied to go to college just to think my life might still be something. That never worked out either. I was accepted, though. It was a proud moment for me."

Jack stared at this mother. Nothing she did would ever surprise him although she had many secrets. He had accepted her as a part of his life, present and absent, for all of his life. He had long ago separated his feeling for her from his feelings about his father. Daisy was right; Douglas had become vague while Daisy had become a sharper image that he carried with him. He never analyzed the feeling and did not intend to start. He was a bystander, an interested bystander but no longer engaged in the past of his family. He and Daisy were like two trees in a forest that had endured and stood with each other without much real communication for many years. They were nourished in the same soil; rained on by a common rain; warmed by the same sunlight. She knew him without conversation and without justification. He knew her in the same way. He was sorry he had asked about Douglas. It had brought up too much of the past for the two women in his life. Well, at least it was too much for Lisa.

Lisa was clearly flummoxed. Daisy had said the words aloud that Lisa had lived with forever. "Love locked out." She had seldom been a part of what really felt like love. She had loved Jack her whole life, but the time they had been together was overwhelmingly overshadowed by the many years apart. Her years away from her son were in the same category. What Lisa could never get over, was that it was her choice to be apart from them. Life with her brother and life with her son came with messy impediments. Being with Jack meant dealing with Abby; life with Paulie would have meant maternal responsibility that she neither wanted nor felt. In exchange for avoiding the mess, she was locked out of the love. As long as she was on the other side of the door of love, she was in control. She had opened the door with Bill and now wished she could close it. Tears came again into her eyes.

"I never intended to have my little party make you cry, Lisa. You go on and fix your make up. I'll have Jack do some coffee and we can have a little desert. I think we need a little sweetness before the New Year comes," said Daisy as she stood up from the table.

Lisa was all too happy to escape, picking up her large handbag off the counter as she moved hastily to the bathroom. Jack and Daisy said nothing in Lisa's absence. They didn't need to.

The table had been re-set with fresh dishes, cups, silver and napkins that proclaimed "Happy New Year!" in garish colors. Perfect triangles of chocolate pie were on each plate. Jack and Daisy were drinking coffee when Lisa returned to the kitchen. Her plan was to leave instantly. However, she had come with her brother, and he was going to have pie before leaving. Hesitantly, Lisa sat at the table. She looked simultaneously composed and sad. Makeup could not repair her emotional damage.

Jack enjoyed one bite of pie and sat down his fork, pushing the pie away. "Seems like I forgot I'm not supposed to have pie. Had to have one taste. Sometimes that's all we get, just one taste in life."

"What's that supposed to mean?" demanded Lisa.

"It means that I am a diabetic, little sister. Even Daisy's pie is not worth an extra shot to me at my age. I am going to be a bride-groom. I want to live long enough to enjoy it."

Lisa looked at her mother. "Did you know this? Did you know that Jack was a diabetic?"

"Yes and no. This is the first he's said. But I guess he hasn't been any too careful about hiding it so I suspected."

"Love locked out," thought Lisa. "I never know a damn thing even about my own brother." She remembered how for the past couple of years, Jack had avoided alcohol and sweets. It made no impact on her at the time, but it did now.

"Jack, I'm so sorry. When did this happen? I'm so very sorry, but why didn't you tell me?" she asked struggling to stay calm.

"Because you can't do anything about it. It isn't cancer, Lisa. I'm fine, just limited. Forever limited. I think it hurts Reid more than me because Reid is such a good cook. It's a big part of her life and I can't eat half of what she fixes. We'll get along. Nothing to be sorry about."

Lisa's mind was racing along to the future. She had heard what happened to diabetics, losing feet and legs and kidneys or spending years on dialysis. This was terrible! Jack didn't seem in the least concerned.

"Jack, do you have health insurance?"

"Sure, of a sort. I think in the old days that it was called 'major medical.' I've always had health and life insurance from the business. It was a good thing, too. When Abby got cancer, she had insurance. Why the interest?"

"How could Abby have health insurance when you weren't married?"

"Because she was always my employee, at least on paper. I set it up like that years ago. If you work for me, you get health insurance for the big things. Abby's cancer cost a lot, but not as much as it could have cost."

"What about Reid, now? Does she have health insurance? Life insurance?" asked Lisa rapidly.

"I guess so. Why are you so concerned about insurance?" asked Jack.

"I just want to know that no matter what happens, you have insurance. You're sick and anything could happen. I want to know that you will be taken care of."

It was on Jack's tongue to question his sister's motives for this turn in the conversation, but he had long years of practice in not asking the obvious and in ducking painful truths so that he could just go on. Lisa was also in for another surprise. He had something to tell both his mother and his sister that he had been saving for the right occasion. Now seemed like the right occasion.

"Not to worry. I am hooking up with a rich woman. She's going to promise to take care of me and I'll do the same for her." Jack chuckled at the surprised looks he was receiving from Lisa and Daisy.

"Reid's rich? Or are you talking about someone else?" asked Lisa.

"Yes indeed, Reid is one rich woman. Didn't know it until we agreed to get married. She thought I needed to know and wanted to know if that would change my mind. I told her I was more interested in her in the bedroom than in the bank."

"You're disgusting," said Lisa.

"You're surprising," said Daisy. "Reid seems like the least likely person to be rich. I thought she was just a bookkeeper for Paulie's wife. She's a mouse. Where did the money come from?" To Daisy, the conversation was suddenly very interesting.

"I don't know the whole story but what I can tell you that a long time ago, Reid's grandfather gave her the proceeds of the sale of forty acres in Iowa. Reid came here to Arizona and invested it. Lisa, she bought real estate. Thought that might interest you since that is how you made your money. Guess she hung on to it for a good bit and then sold half. Invested it in the stock market. She made millions. About two years, she sold half of that and bought some building companies. Now she is getting ready to sell them. She has a real talent for money, just not spending it."

"Holy shit," said Lisa.

"Yeah, well, now you know. Kind of takes the edge off the future, doesn't it? Reid is a remarkable woman in many respects. But I would marry her if neither one of us had a dime, Lisa. I love her that much. She's not like you and God knows she's not like Abby, but she's the love of my life and I'd like you to at least like her and be happy for me."

"I am happy for you. I'm very happy. I'm just not happy for me right now, said Lisa.

"Mother, I have to run over and see Bill about tonight. Jack, I'll be back in just a few minutes then you can take me home. I think I need a nap before we all go out tonight!" Lisa was up and out the door before Daisy had said a word.

"Well, you have surprised me today, son. I haven't seen enough of Reid to know if I like her or not, but I'm happy for her, too. She's getting a prize in you and one that I'm sorry to give up, but I'm ready to. You think Lisa is going to get married?" asked Daisy.

"Could be she is over telling poor Bill Hadigan to get lost. Maybe she's not. Hard to tell with her. Her lifestyle is all she has had for a long time. She's not likely to give it up for a real life."

"Well, that apple didn't fall too far from the tree."

"Are you talking about Dad?"

"Yes, Douglas. He wanted a lifestyle; I wanted a life. He wanted what he was born without and married me to get it. I wanted what I had been born with, a loving family and mother and I had you two to get it. But it wasn't like what I had, not for a minute."

While son and mother cleared up the detritus of the luncheon, Lisa literally ran to see her fiancéwho lived in the same condominium complex as Daisy. Bill Hadigan answered the door in his bathrobe, towel in hand.

When Lisa saw him, without his usual well-coordinated clothes, without his well-shined shoes and freshly shaved face, her heart almost broke. Here was the man she would see in this way for the rest of her life. Worse, he would see her that way!

Casually, he invited her in. "I'm on my way to the shower. Just kicked around and slept in getting ready for tonight. I wasn't expecting company, especially not you! If I had known you were coming, I would have….well, I would have started my day earlier. Sit down, I'll just freshen up and I'm ready to start the New Year."

"I just came by to ask you something. Something quick. Jack and I were visiting Daisy and were roped into one of her lunches. We were talking and it reminded me that I wanted to ask you something." Lisa lost her breath as she spoke.

Bill and Lisa were standing about three feet apart. The front door remained open. "I'm not staying. I just want to ask you something. I hope you understand."

"Great, ask me," said Bill never expecting the question that Lisa urgently wanted answered.

"Bill, if I was poor, I mean, if I had never had a job, or made money and was just a plain old woman, would you still want to marry me? I mean, how much difference does money make to you?"

Bill didn't answer. What was Lisa asking and why now? This felt like a test and one he could easily fail. It was one he had failed with his first wife. He stared at Lisa, first at the ring he had given her which was still safely on her left hand. Then he looked at her face. That's when he could see she had been crying. Her flattering clothes, matching shoes and expensive thick, gold necklace made his ring seem small; almost insignificant. Seconds must have ticked by. In spite of Lisa's will to stop them, tears dripped from her face to the floor.

"Money means everything to me," said Bill slowly, "because it means everything to you. Lisa, you are the woman you are because money gave you the ability to have what you want when you want it. There's nothing wrong with that. If you didn't have money, you wouldn't be you! I can't imagine you as a poor housewife under any circumstances. Neither one of us is young enough to think that life is going to be greatly changed in the future. You will always have your money. Me loving you is a product of that. It's a fact. It's not a negotiation. Come here."

Lisa did not move. So Bill moved closer to her and hugged her until she hugged him back. He felt comfortable to her. He felt right. She brought her hands away from his embrace and placed them on his chest, her well-manicured hands gently rubbing his chest through the open gap in his robe. Her head was resting on his shoulder.

They were standing in the doorway when Jack appeared. He looked stricken. Then came those words, those terrible words that everyone dreads hearing. Four words that change lives, turn destinies, and break strong families. The words came from Jack, but they were not about Jack. They were about someone else. The theoretical terrors that Lisa and Jack and Daisy had imagined and discussed on the last day of the old year were gone. They were replaced with a new reality.

"There's been an accident," said Jack. He turned and walked to his truck before Lisa and Bill could release each other from their own intimate happiness.

Strong Enough

Officer Nick Calmelat and his partner, Mark Boyd, were nearly to the Northeast Phoenix police substation on Union Hills Road when they were called to yet another accident on the last day of the old year. They thought they had escaped overtime. The accident was on SR 51, south of Northern in the southbound lane. From the radio traffic, it was apparent that it was bad. Normally, the Department of Public Safety would handle a freeway accident such as this. However, major events requiring freeway closure and fatalities involved the Phoenix Police and the Fire Department as well. Besides, during the holidays, there was more than enough work for all public service personnel. A quick turn on Bell Road from 32nd Street and the officers were practically on the freeway southbound.

Traffic was light, even for a Friday afternoon. Nevertheless, the officers had to do some on-shoulder driving once the traffic stopped. Theirs was the third car on the scene arriving shortly before Lt. Antonio Alvarez of the DPS who had made his way northbound. "Tony" Alvarez and Nick had been classmates at South Mountain High School and later attended the same community college studying law enforcement. Tony's ambition, good looks, and his people skills had moved him promotionally ahead in the DPS, faster than his friend, Nick. The first officers to arrive had covered a body in the wide median. Nick, Tony and Mark took a quick look around.

A semi was in the median about 400 yards or more from the crash site. It looked like a shiny new pickup truck had been rolled and then struck by a southbound vehicle. Nick heard the sound of many sirens. Tony became the Officer-in-Charge, directing Nick and Mark to assist the other four officers in checking the victims. Tony grabbed the semi's driver as a potential witness. Within the next 15 minutes, there were at least 30 additional personnel on the scene. Nick was working with the Fire Department paramedics to remove the driver of the southbound vehicle who was unconscious. A medical helicopter was already visible. Unable to assist further in the removal of the man, Nick took over the direction of the helicopter landing. His partner was fully engaged with the victims of the pickup truck.

Tony yelled at Nick to find out where they were taking the victim. When he found out, Tony directed him to handle emergency notifications and accompany the victim to United Hospital. Nick arrived at the car as the helicopter staff was moving the victim away. That was when he saw that there had been another person in the car. The two medical techs were peeling off their gloves, relieved to turnover their charge when Nick asked about the second victim. The youngest of the medical techs, a woman, shook her head.

"Man or woman?" he asked.

"Woman. She is dead. There isn't any reason to hurry now. We're waiting for some equipment and then she goes to County," said the other EMT.

"Who fished the ID? Do you have anything?" Nick asked them both.

He was handed a wallet, new from the looks of it. "What about the lady? Anything on her?"

"Not yet."

Kenny Smyth was the name on the driver's license inside. There was some cash and one credit card. Tucked in with the cash was a folded card, labeled "Emergency Contacts." The card was also new. Nick surmised that the wallet had been a recent Christmas present. The card listed two names: Dianne Smyth and Reid Markham. Maybe the wife and the mother, Nick thought. Assuming the victim was with his wife on New Year's Eve, Nick decided to contact the presumed mother. He made calls from his cell phone. The first number was a no answer. On the second ring of the second call, Nick reached Reid. It was never easy doing these notifications, but Nick conveyed the facts quickly, before emotion could ruin the call. He agreed to meet Reid at the Emergency Room of United. She was probably closer to the hospital than he was. Once the medical helicopter had taken off, Nick needed to be going. He briefed Tony and headed to the car.

Mark would likely be one of the last officers on the scene. Nick worried about stranding his partner, but didn't say anything to him as he took off in the squad car they shared. He guessed that Mark could catch a ride back to the station sometime when the investigation was over and the freeway reopened for normal traffic.

The Emergency facility at United Hospital was well-designed to keep staff and anxious relatives separated. Nick parked around back to enter through the side door made for the exclusive use of emergency service personnel like paramedics and police officers. He grabbed a quick cigarette on the patio before going through the automated double doors. He figured he had five or ten minutes free before meeting Reid Markham. When Nick did walk through the door, the waiting room was packed.

The area looked like every family in town was awaiting the outcome of a holiday tragedy. There were no seats. Anxious parents, brothers, wives and uncles hung on, near the walls and against the windows, whispering loudly. Every phone was in use.

Looking around, Nick saw a woman he knew would be Reid Markham. She stood out. She was an attractive woman, dressed in blue jeans and a stretchy white shirt. She held a red sweatshirt and black purse in one hand; with the other, she pulled her hair away from her anxious face. She had cornered an EMT who was involved in a different incident. Nick heard her ask about Kenny Smyth. "Bingo," thought Nick. "If she is the guy's mother, she was a child bride."

He walked up to the two and introduced himself. The EMT was relieved to get away. Reid's eyes locked on Nick's face. As he told her the bare facts about the accident, she never blinked. Her frozen pose gave Nick the creeps. She provided neither visual nor oral confirmation that she had heard or understood what he had told her.

One of the Emergency Aides that Nick knew interrupted him. They were looking for identification for the victim. Nick had stupidly left it in the car. "We're taking him up to surgery. We can't get him stable down here. He's lost a lot of blood," said the aide.

"His name is Smyth with a 'y'. Kenny Smyth," said Nick as he headed out to the car. To Reid he said, "Stay here, I'll be back in a couple of minutes. I need to talk to you."

When Nick returned with Kenny's wallet, Reid was gone. "Damn," thought Nick. Looking over the ocean of waiting faces, he did not see her. He doubted she had left. Maybe she had gone out the front entrance. Maybe she smoked and wanted a cigarette. He knew he did. There was nothing to do but hoof it on out there to find her.

Reid, who had never smoked, had found her way to the third floor surgical wing by following a nurse into the rear elevator that was reserved for staff and patients. Although the nurse looked at her critically, Reid remained firm in her focus to find her cousin. She had called Jack from Mrs. Gilberg's house. Reid had taken Ruby Rose over there to help the old woman make "New Year's Cakes" for dinner tomorrow. She had provided Mrs. Gilberg with the little information about Kenny and the accident that she had, promising to call as soon as she got to the hospital. When the elevator opened and she stepped out onto the third floor, the corridor and off-hall waiting room were empty. There was no one she could ask about Kenny. Convinced that if she waited, someone would come out of the surgery doors, Reid decided to wait. Later she would look for Jack and call Mrs. Gilberg.

The clock above the surgery doors read 3:33. Standing there, Reid felt as if she had been flayed alive. Everything hurt. She was aware of every cell in her body and its particular activity. Things that should have occurred without effort, like her heartbeat, her breathing, and the blinking of her eyes, became nearly conscious activities. She could feel herself hear sound. Every thirty seconds measured on the large wall clock in front of her, she reminded herself that she was alive.

Half-minute intervals ticked by. She didn't add them together. It was too much activity for her brain. The sensation of pain was replaced with cold. In the first half minute, the cold moved from her hands to her shoulders. Two half minutes more and cold moved down her spine and into her legs. The clock became invisible, and Reid Markham finally felt nothing.

The first time that Jack Ellis saw Reid on New Year's Eve, a paramedic was kneeling over her crumpled body. She had collapsed in the hallway outside of surgery, hitting the uncarpeted floor headfirst. The Phoenix Fire Department paramedic had found her on his way out of surgery where he had accompanied her badly injured cousin. At three in the afternoon, the young man was technically off duty. However, the last day of the last day of the century had already been a nightmare. In one shift, he had completed six calls, the last one involving yet another drunk driver and multiple fatalities.

Swiftly moving from the elevator, Jack knelt on the other side of the unmoving form. He had just spoken with her. How could this have happened? Jack's first words were "Don't leave." The paramedic pulled a stethoscope to his ears to listen to Reid's heart. He rechecked her pulse before looking up.

"What happened?" asked Jack.

"Do you know this woman?" asked the paramedic.

"Yes. Her name is Reid Markham, my fiancéShe called me about twenty minutes ago. She said to come right away. Her cousin had been in a car accident."

"Talk to her, see if you can bring her around. She has vitals, not strong, but she has them. I need help. Emergency is a mess. I need to go there to get help. They may help me, but they won't help you. Talk to her, touch her. Try to get her to wake up. I'll be back."

In five steps, the paramedic was out the door and down the stairs. Jack gripped Reid on the shoulder. "Reid, Reid, wake up. Wake up. It's me, Jack. Open your eyes. Please Reid, wake up." There was no response. In a crouching position, Jack was cutting off all circulation to his lower legs. He had to move. He sat flat, his back sending signals of complaint. With this left hand, he could hold Reid's right hand. Jack continued talking to her for what seemed eternity. He watched the stairway entrance, but the door remained closed. Then the elevator doors opened and the young paramedic came out alone carrying a blanket and pillow. "Help is on the way," he said.

He tucked the pillow under Reid's feet and covered her up. Under the blanket, he rubbed her hands. "Keep talking, fella. We got to get her to come around."

After two more minutes of persistent stimulation, Reid's unfocussed eyes opened. She started to struggle to sit up. The paramedic grabbed her upper arm and began to pull her over. "Roll her to her side," he barked to Jack. Jack pushed. The remains of Reid's lunch came up. Because she was facing the paramedic, he got the worst of it. Nevertheless, he calmly wiped her face with the blanket, folding it away from her face. "Hey lady, good for you. Take some deep breaths; you're going to feel better." Reid stared back at the stranger blankly. Her face had color, but her dilated pupils obscured the blue iris of her eyes. She couldn't see Jack who was behind her.

The elevator door opened and an aide and a doctor rushed out. The paramedic moved out of the way. Jack stayed in place. While the aide lowered the gurney, the doctor took the paramedic's place and rechecked Reid, all the while talking to her. Reid made no attempt to answer. She had no idea where she was. The three men in front of her reminded her of something, but she could not imagine what it was. It was important. She shut her eyes.

She heard Jack's voice. He was calling her. Why couldn't he help her? Why couldn't she see him? She imagined she felt him. She was moving involuntarily. Opening her eyes, she saw Jack. Her head hurt. Jack was holding her hand while unseen hands lifted her up. She wanted to throw up again. She shut her eyes and the feeling passed. She heard Jack's voice, "Breathe, Reid, breathe slowly. Keep your eyes shut, just breathe."

She inhaled and exhaled. She felt better except that her head hurt terribly and the light seemed to burn through her eyelids. She was being strapped down. Then she could feel herself rising. Voices. "...down to Emergency. ...what's she doing here? Identification? ...head wound, but doesn't look serious. ...Pregnant? Is she pregnant?"

Reid tried to make sense of what she heard. "Pregnant? No, Dianne was pregnant. Where was Dianne? Where was Kenny? She had come to the hospital. She must be in the hospital. Kenny was in the hospital. Where was Dianne? Why couldn't she remember where Dianne was? Dianne was with Kenny, but that wasn't right."

The three somber men maneuvered the gurney into the elevator and accompanied Reid down to Emergency. The doctor bypassed the charge nurse who was, in any case, too busy to handle less than life or death at the moment. He found a space for the gurney and pulled the scanty curtain around both Reid and Jack. "Stay here," he said.

Jack caught the doctor's jacket sleeve. "Is she OK? Is she going to be OK?"

The surprised doctor was about to jerk away, when he realized that the poor man had a right to know something. It would not matter if the paperwork wasn't done for five minutes or five hours on a day like today. "I think she's through the worst of it. She has a bump on her head. Talk to her and try to keep her from going to sleep. Right now, I'm setting out a diagnosis of concussion. The problem is, she fell in the hospital, which means more questions and more paperwork. If it had happened at home, you probably wouldn't even bring her here. She needs to be monitored, and she has to be signed in to be monitored. Can you answer questions for her?"

"Sure, I mean, I guess," said Jack. He realized he was still holding onto the doctor.

"What was she doing up there? How did she fall?"

"I don't know. When I got here, she was already down," said Jack.

"How did you know she was here?"

"She called me at my mother's house. Said her cousin had been in a car accident and he was here. I came into Emergency and couldn't find either of them. Then I heard that a man was taken to surgery on third floor so I went up, too. She was there with the paramedic. Right outside the surgery doors."

"Well, she's going to be OK. She'll get some help. Then I'll be back. Stick around with her, to help her remember where she is. If you can let me go, I can get her help. I need to track down the paramedic for his side of this. If you see him, see if you can flag him down."

Jack nodded, and then released the doctor's jacket. The doctor was off and running.

It didn't take long for help to come. A veteran nurse swooshed back the curtain to find a patient and civilian in the area normally curtained off for wheelchair storage. Fast on her heels came a harried young man from Emergency Admitting. Everyone was talking at once for a few seconds until a Phoenix police officer stuck his head into the apparent squabble. Then everyone stopped mid-question and answer.

The officer could see Reid well enough to know that he had found the person he had sought for the past half-hour. She was his only contact with at least two of the accident victims and now she looked down for the count. Like the paramedic before him, the officer was technically off-shift and therefore on holiday overtime. "Good," thought Officer Calmelat, "that new sofa for Marie is going to get paid for tonight."

"Who's in charge?" asked Nick Calmelat amiably.

No one said a word. He motioned to the nurse. He had worked with her before and she was a tough old battle-axe. "What have we got here?"

"I have no idea! Dr. Lutz sent me to find a woman with a concussion. Said she had fallen in the hospital. Have you any idea what the paperwork will be on this? It has been a bloodbath in here, which I have to clean up and put back together. I came in at three and this is what I found – a hospital liability. Great way to end the century. That's what I know."

Officer Calmelat nodded. "And you are, sir?" directing his attention to Jack.

"Jack Ellis."

"Your reason for being here?"

"Reid called me. She said to come to United Emergency. Her cousin has been in a car accident. I came and couldn't find her so I went up to third floor surgery. There was a paramedic with her where she had fallen."

"What's going to happen with her? Is she conscious?" asked Nick.

The three at Reid's makeshift bed turned as one to look at Reid. No one had paid attention to her during the past confusion and conversation. She was either unconscious or asleep. Jack called her name and moved her gently. Her eyes fluttered.

"I need to talk to her," said the officer.

"Well you can cool your heels on that one!" exclaimed the nurse. "If anything else happens to her, mine is the head to roll. I have no intention of doing anything but what I am directed to do by staff. You march on outside and have one of those nasty cigarettes I smell on you. Go use your fancy phone for an hour or maybe two hours. This kid has things to do before Dr. Lutz is free. Out of here." She turned on Jack. "You, out as well. Sit at a desk at the counter. Junior, here, will be with you in a minute."

With the officer and Jack dismissed, the nurse busied herself with removing the dirty blanket away from Reid and yelled impatiently for additional help. Jack and Nick made their way out of the cramped space.

"You smoke?" Nick asked Jack as the moved into the waiting room. "Nope," Jack answered. "You need to call someone?" offered the officer. "What am I going to say?" asked Jack.

"Do you have any idea why your wife is here?"

"Reid isn't my wife, yet. I know her cousin was in an accident. What I don't understand is why his wife isn't here. I thought I would find Dianne with Reid."

"Who is the closest relative, the next-of-kin?" asked Nick.

Jack stared at the officer without answering. "Whose next-of-kin? Dianne's? Kenny's? Reid's?" He couldn't comprehend the question. He didn't have to at that moment. The young man from Admitting was motioning him to the desk. Gratefully, Jack eased himself into the stiff chair.

Officer Nick Calmelat walked beyond the desk and out into the fresh air where he could get a quick puff and call Marie. It was going to be a long night. Might even be a double shift. He'd be in the hospital and not on the streets. For an officer on New Year's Eve, this was as good as it gets. It would be an hour or more before he could talk to the presumed next of kin. He made one call to his partner, Mark, who had been lucky enough to leave the scene to accompany the second body to County Hospital. Since the victim was pronounced dead at the scene, Mark would be out of County and at home soon.

It was two hours, not one before Nick saw Reid Markham again. In the interval he had made contact with Tony Alvarez, who gave him more information and a harder task as well. Nick wrote some names down as well as a few cryptic notes. He checked with the charge nurse before walking to the back of Emergency where Reid and Jack remained tucked away.

"How's that guy I came in with?" he asked. "Accident victim. Bad off."

"Is that the guy the lady who fell wants? Her cousin or something?" The nurse answered Nick's question with two more.

"That's him. Did he make it?"

"He's still up there on third floor," she answered.

"What about the lady? Can I talk to her? Is she going anywhere?"

"Yes, you can talk to her briefly. She's supposed to be admitted because she fell here, but she doesn't want to stay. Says she'll stay until her cousin is out of surgery." The nurse returned to her paperwork and picked up a waiting phone line.

Reid had been moved to a hospital bed, dressed in a worn hospital gown, and examined by Dr. Lutz. A precautionary IV of Lactated Ringers dripped at 100 into her left arm. Automated devices monitored her pulse and blood pressure. Nick looked at the displays. Pulse was around 100 and blood pressure at 100⁄5. She was doing well.

"Hey," he said. "You're looking better. Feel like talking to me?"

Reid opened her eyes. "My head hurts. Who are you?" Reid thought the officer looked familiar.

"Officer Nick Calmelat. I am here to talk to you about your cousin. Kenny Smyth, is it?"

The officer was standing at the foot of the bed. Reid was flat on her back. Just trying to look at him made her head pound. She started to push herself up on one elbow, but couldn't manage it. "Can you come closer?" she asked.

The officer stepped around the end of the bed, gingerly moving the IV stand back a couple of feet. "How's that?"

"Ok. What about Kenny? How is he?"

"Still in surgery. I just asked. Are you his closest relative? I need to ask some questions for my report and the hospital needs a next-of-kin, just in case."

"He's married, but his wife was in the accident with him. I don't know where she is. I don't think that she is here. He has a daughter."

"Do you know how to get in touch with the daughter?"

"Yes, but she is only eight years old. Why do you need her? What are you going to tell her?" Reid's mind was racing to find a thought that was just beyond her. She was trying to catch that thought.

"Can you give me a telephone number and an address?" continued Nick.

The elusive thought that Reid had been chasing stopped abruptly. She had caught it. She shut her eyes against the light and the moving room. "Boom," she said softly. "Boom, Boom. Poor little girl."

Officer Calmelat thought Reid was slipping into an unconscious state. Jack, trapped against the wall and encumbered by machines, nevertheless threaded his hand to Reid's shoulder. When he touched her, Reid turned to him. "Dianne is dead, isn't she?" Jack looked questioningly at the officer.

"Do you remember me telling you that? I told you that and then you disappeared."

"I remember," said Reid continuing to look at Jack. "I just couldn't stand it. I couldn't stand it. One minute you have a mother and then, Boom, you have none."

A new anxious thought came to Reid. "The baby. Dianne was pregnant. What about the baby? Could they save the baby?"

"No." To Nick, it didn't make sense to go into detail. Leave that to someone else. It wasn't his part of the case.

"I need to know how to contact the daughter. Do you have any idea where she is? Apparently her grandparents are frantic trying to find her," asked Nick.

"Her grandparents?" asked Reid thinking of her aunt and uncle. "You've made a mistake. They are dead." To Jack she said, "You've got to help me get out of here. Ruby Rose is with Mrs. Gilberg. I need to go get her."

"Whoa, just a minute there," said Nick. "I take it that Ruby Rose is the daughter? Dianne Smyth's parents are trying to find her. They are very much alive and wondering where she is."

"Oh," said Reid. "Yes, of course, but they are in Denver. Kenny's parents are dead. Ruby Rose is here. She's with my neighbor. I left her there when I came to the hospital. She doesn't know there has been an accident. You can't go tell her! I have to be there. She can't hear that her mother is dead from a stranger."

"We'll send someone from Child Protective Services to put her in touch with her grandparents. They can tell her. Just let me know where she is."

"No they can't. Do you know what it is like to hear your mother is dead over the phone? I was twelve when my mother died in a car accident. My grandfather called me on the phone to tell me. I was alone in the house when I heard. You are not going to do that to a little girl. Do you understand? You are not going to do that." Too many feelings and thoughts were converging in Reid's aching head.

An aide appeared from behind the curtain maneuvering a wheel-chair into the right shin of the officer. "Excuse me. I've got to get this lady up to XRay for a head CT."

When Nick involuntarily stepped back, the aide grabbed Reid's hand to check her hospital wristband against his order sheet. Reid pulled her hand away and said irritably, "I'm not going anywhere except home. I have to get home. Jack, tell them I have to get home."

"Are you refusing treatment, then?" implored the aide. "If you are refusing treatment, then I have to get a nurse or doctor to write that down. It's not a bad test. It doesn't hurt or anything. I'll just help you into the wheelchair and we'll be back in a jiffy."

"I'm not going! Are you deaf? I'm going home and I'm going home right now." Reid's voice carried through the curtain and out into the floor catching the attention of the nurse. The nurse brought her bulk into the crowded space. Nick was insisting that he needed to talk to Reid; Reid was trying to get out of the bed and asking Jack for her clothes; the aide whined to the nurse; the nurse attempted to bark orders to everyone. All were unaware that for the present, the Emergency Room was experiencing an unexpected lull in customers. Theirs were the only voices.

Dr. Lutz heard them. He went over to the curtain and pulled it completely back exposing all to the emptiness of the place. His sole concern was his patient. From the looks of her animated state, he guessed that she was better and out of danger. If the last day of the year was a preview of the last night of the millennium, he wanted to free up the space and possibly finish paperwork before the next round of sound and tragedy.

To the aide, Dr. Lutz said, "I've changed my mind about the scan. See what you can do to round up equipment that has ended up on other floors during the day. We'll need it tonight." To the nurse he said, "Call surgery. Find out the status of this lady's relative." Both the nurse and aid were glad to leave.

To Officer Calmelat, Dr. Lutz was less authoritarian. "That leaves the four of us. It is in Unity's interest to admit this patient. She is refusing to be admitted. It might be in everyone's interest, while we have her in observation if you go over what you know about the accident. Then maybe some of us can go home."

Nick had to admire this doctor. He seemed cool and constant. "You do a lot of Emergency work, Doc?"

"That's all I do. I understand trauma. It is something I can walk away from when it is over. Now, what do you know?" Dr. Lutz directed the conversation and the emergency activity once again.

Nick pulled out his small notebook and began to verbalize his notes. "At about 2:30 p.m. today, an accident occurred on SR 51 in the open stretch south of Northern Avenue. Three boys in a pickup truck, a new one, were headed north at about 70 m.p.h. The driver had been drinking at a girlfriend's house before he picked up his friends to go out to the desert to do some shoot-em-up celebrating. According to witnesses, they were paying little attention to the road when a semi advanced on them. The boys drifted in front of the truck. The truck clipped them and the pickup driver lost control. He flipped into the median and then into the incoming traffic."

Nick had stopped speaking; three pair of eyes and ears remained tuned to him. He flipped the pages. "Kenny Smyth and his wife were traveling at about 55 m.p.h. in the left-most southbound lane. There was no other immediate traffic. The teenager's truck landed within 10 feet of the southbound car. One of the truck's passengers was ejected when the truck rolled. The middle passenger was dislodged at impact and killed instantly. The driver of the truck is in good condition with a few broken bones. He is at St. Joseph's. The other passenger died at the scene."

Nick stopped again because he wanted to make sure he spoke clearly and directly to Reid, without error and with less emotion than he felt. "The DPS arrived within four minutes of receiving the report and called in Phoenix PD and Fire Department help. I was probably the third car there. At the time I arrived, no one was aware that your cousin's wife was in the car, it was too badly crushed for her to be visible. Once we got her husband out, he was airlifted here. Then we found the wife. She was dead. I didn't know until I spoke to you that she was pregnant. Her husband was unconscious and losing blood visibly."

Reid had closed her eyes as the officer spoke. In the silence of a few seconds that followed, she asked, "How did you know to call me?"

"Your name and several phone numbers were on a card in your cousin's wallet. They were also in the wife's purse along with her parent's name and address. It clearly said to notify you in case of an emergency. I called the numbers until I found you."

"Oh," said Reid softly. She wished there was something else she could think about, something she could say.

"So, are you the next-of-kin of Kenny Smyth? You see, when we ran him, there are some irregularities. He seems to have been born fifteen years ago, but his ID says that he is 41 or 42. He never lived anywhere before Phoenix, yet his social security number was issued in Texas. It is a little irregularity we would like to know about."

From the corner of her eye, Reid could see the tough, short nurse hovering. Reid avoided the officer and looked at the nurse. "How is he?"

The nurse crooked her finger at Dr. Lutz. Together they stepped out of earshot of Nick and Reid and Jack. Dr. Lutz came back alone. "Ordinarily, I don't do this. I don't get this involved. Your cousin isn't going to make it without extraordinary measures. Even with those, there is no guarantee. He isn't breathing on his own. He has had seventeen units and they are having trouble raising his blood pressure. They have removed his spleen and dealt with some of the internal damage, but now they are asking to amputate his leg. The surgeon wants to do it. The word from staff is it won't make any difference."

It is possible to have a million thoughts in a few seconds. Pictures, images, words all came to Reid. The officer was right. There was no Kenny Smyth before he met Dianne. He was born in her love. Without her, he would be just another VanDuyver pretending not to be needy. Aloud she said, "I don't want that."

"Are you the next of kin?" repeated Officer Calmelat.

"Yes I am," said Reid emphatically as if emphasis could turn the lie into an acceptable truth. "Can I see him?" Reid asked the doctor.

"No." said Dr. Lutz. "I'm sorry, but you cannot go into surgery.

"Then, let him go. Let him go to God and to Dianne. Can I see him before I leave?" Tears began streaming down Reid's face. Dr.

Lutz said nothing. He was getting involved in something that he could not control and he didn't like it.

Nick Calmelat turned his full attention to Reid. "I don't believe you for one minute, Ms. Markham, anymore than I believe that Kenny Smyth is the real name of the fellow upstairs. I want some answers and I want them before anything else changes. Who is Kenny Smyth?" The Officer was standing his ground.

Jack, silent for most of the afternoon and into what was now the darkness, answered the police officer. "Kenny Smyth is Reid's son. You don't get any closer than that for next-of-kin."

With that outrageous comment out, Dr. Lutz left. He went to the first available phone to make the call to surgery. He didn't believe for one moment that Reid Markham was the mother of the man upstairs. He had examined her. She was in terrific shape for a woman of her age, but he doubted she had ever been pregnant. He was sure she had never brought a baby to term. He thought to himself, "That's why I work trauma. No long term relationships, no messy cases requiring follow-up." The thought made him very happy as he called upstairs.

"Can you find my clothes and take me home now, Jack?" implored Reid.

"I need to ask you some more questions," continued Nick as if the previous conversations had never taken place.

"I don't need to answer any. Kenny is as good as dead. Dianne is dead. Neither of them ever hurt anyone in their lives. They were just another married couple that you wouldn't ever notice if you saw them twice on the street. They are a statistic to you. They were family to me. Jack, please, I have to go to Ruby Rose. Mrs. Gilberg will be frantic." Reid was now completely sitting up, her bare legs dangling over the side of the bedside.

Nick realized the futility of any further action on his part. His natural curiosity would never be satisfied. He wasn't sure if he believed that the man and woman he had seen today were mother and son. Nevertheless, he could let it go. He would have the man's fingerprints to check against the national database soon enough. Lot's of people aren't who they say they are, but that didn't always make them criminals.

"Can you answer a question for me, Officer? There's something I don't understand," said Reid. Nick didn't say anything so Reid continued. "I thought that they had put up rope wire barriers in the median to keep accidents like this from happening. I thought I heard it or read it. I'm sure I did. How did that truck cross those barriers?"

It was time for Nick to quibble with the truth. The truth was that most of SR 51 had been delineated with barrier. Governor's orders. One stretch had not been completed before the holiday. It was just too dangerous to do without closing the freeway. The main arterial to the airport couldn't be closed, so the four-mile stretch would be done after the end of the holidays, in mid-January. To Reid, Nick just said, "There's a little strip that isn't done yet. That's where the accident occurred."

It took a while. There were lots of forms to sign before Jack and Reid could leave United. Before they actually did leave, Dr. Lutz, against his better thoughts, took Reid to see her cousin who had been moved to a clean bed in a private room for her visit. She saw Kenny's cut face and held his bruised hand that was only cool, not yet cold. She couldn't help crying. "Fly away, cousin. Fly away to God," said Reid as she replaced his hand on his chest and turned away from Kenny for the very last time.

"He really was your cousin, then?" asked Dr. Lutz.

"Yes, he was. I don't know why Jack said anything different than that. Maybe he wanted to protect me or protect Kenny. Kenny has brothers. They are the real next of kin. Kenny ran away from home when he was a kid. No one lifted a finger to find him when he was living. That's a sorrier, sadder story than Kenny and Dianne dying."

Jack had waited for Reid outside of the room. He had seen enough of dying to know that last memories should be the ones of last good times. He was worried about Reid; worried about the living. She looked as broken as Abby when he had first met her. Somehow, some way, Abby had survived all those years. Reid was made of stronger stuff than Abby.

Reid had stopped crying when she found Jack. They made plans to leave her car and go to Mrs. Gilberg's in Jack's truck. On the way there, they stopped and picked up sodas and burgers that they ate hungrily on the way home, finishing in the driveway of the little house where only the front room light was on. It was going on eleven o'clock.

Reid made no move to leave the truck. The porch light came on and the front door opened revealing Mrs. Gilberg. "I don't want to go in," said Reid flatly.

"Do you want me to go with you?" asked Jack.

"Yes, of course I do. I can't do this alone. I was thinking all the way home that I could never be a doctor or a policeman," said Reid.

"That's a funny thing to be thinking about," said Jack who was truly confused by Reid's comment.

"Oh, what I mean is that I can't stand having to tell people bad news. It is worse than receiving bad news. I thought about Big Daddy calling to tell me that Mommy was dead. I thought about how he and Grammy could never talk about her. I was so hurt all my life by their silence. Now I understand it. As much as they were hurt, they just didn't want to have the hurt of telling someone else, me, about it, or even talking about it. The telling is the awful part. Not the knowing, the telling. I cannot do the telling without you and Mrs. Gilberg there, too. That way it will be like we all told her and none of us has to be alone in it."

"It's pretty late. Do you think Ruby Rose will be awake?"

"I don't know. If not, we'll have to do it in the morning. Probably best in the morning. I need to call Iowa and Denver. That's the easiest thing I have to do." The porch light blinked several times.

"We have to go in." Reid opened her door and Jack did the same. They met on the path to Mrs. Gilberg's door. "Stay with me tonight, Jack. I need you. Without you, I'm more alone than I have ever been."

Earlier today, Jack had been troubled by a thought. Did Reid need him or was he just around in her life. Now he had his answer. "I'm with you Reid, tonight and tomorrow. You are the love of my life and I knew it long before this night happened. I'm around for the next century, too." Jack smiled a little at that. Together they went in to talk to a very anxious neighbor.

Ruby Rose slept through to the dawn of the New Year. It was morning before she had to know, that like her cousin Reid, life could change without your consent, leaving you a powerless child. The difference was that Ruby Rose would be protected and helped, loved and cared for, in ways that made healing possible. Ruby Rose would never fear tomorrow, or dread an imagined future. The interior sound of booming thunder would never trouble her as long as she lived.

Saving Grace

She came out of the bathroom, already wearing the bra slip that had lain on the floor for most of the afternoon. He was standing by the window, looking outward to the dark clouds that hung low in the early evening southwest sky. "The monsoons are here, maybe early," he said. She did not reply.

Earlier, while he had slept, she had looked out the window for an hour. When she bought this house, Reid had chosen this as her bedroom because of the window. Only at the winter solstice did light directly enter the room, at the darkest point of the year. She had planted a tree whose branches now moved in the hot, late afternoon breeze. Originally the family room, she had, over the years, remodeled the house to improve the location of all the living spaces. Still, this was the best room in the house.

Reid sat down on the comfortable reading chair. She watched Jack as he stared out the window. Although they had made love and napped in the long, July afternoon, there was a distance between them. They had been quarreling for some time. Sex could not heal it. Reid wasn't sure if love would either.

"I'm going away for a little bit," said Jack as he turned from the window. He had been aware of Reid's presence for some time before he spoke.

"When are you going?" asked Reid.

"Tomorrow. I'm going to Mexico tomorrow. I have a chance to go fishing and I haven't been out on the sea for a long time."

"For how long? I thought maybe you would drive with me to pick up Ruby Rose from her grandparent's in Colorado," said Reid without much hope.

"I don't know. Depends on how good the fishing is. I've closed the bar for the month. I may be gone for a month," said Jack.

"OK. I hope you have a nice time. Is there anything you need? Anything I can get for you?" asked Reid.

"No. I'm set. What are you going to do?"

"I don't know. Maybe I'll go out and get a job. With Ruby Rose gone and you gone, I don't have much to do. Seems like I was busy for a long time, and now there isn't a lot going on."

"We could get married in Mexico. That would be something to do," said Jack.

"Jack," pleaded Reid softly.

"I know, I know. What we have is what we have had all year, Reid. A Mexican standoff. I wish you would change your mind."

"I wish you would change yours, Jack."

"When I asked you to marry me, all you asked was to marry in church. I agreed to that. Now, you've made conditions and I can't say yes to them, Reid."

"I can't say no to what I need to do for Ruby Rose." Reid was looking at her hand where there should have been an engagement ring. There was nothing there.

"You're not the only relative that Rose has," continued Jack. "She has a lot of family. She can go live with someone else. Just because Kenny and Dianne asked you to take her, you don't have to take her. John would be thrilled to have another little girl to raise with his own daughter, Johanna. He seems like a good man. Her grandparents want her, too. They were willing to fight you for her, but your money killed that. I don't understand you. You were raised by your grandparents."

Reid sighed. Wanting to raise Ruby Rose was irrational. She didn't need Jack to remind her of that. She had been through whole sets of counselors and doctors to discuss it. When Kenny and Dianne had been killed in the car accident, Reid became obsessed with raising their living child. Ruby Rose was eight at the time, now she was nine. Reid had quit her job to provide a level of continuing care for the little girl. She had shepherded her through the school year and sent her to counseling. She had fought Dianne's parents for temporary custody in both Arizona and in Colorado. She had threatened her own cousins in Iowa if they so much as thought about taking control of the little girl's life. Now Jack.

"Is it my money or is it that you aren't willing to marry me if I adopt Ruby Rose?" asked Reid.

"It's both. But I'm not in a mood to discuss it. I love you Reid, but I didn't sign up to raise a daughter at my age. I have everything that I want in you. That's all I want or need."

"You might be a good father for her. She adores you, Jack. What will I ever tell her if you leave our lives?" asked Reid.

"Whatever you think is best. I'm off Reid. I have to go see Daisy before I go. I promised to have supper with her."

"Do I have a way to get in touch with you? Where are you staying? I don't even know who is going with you." Reid felt that her own life was walking out the door with Jack.

"Lisa and Bill are going with me. Bill rented a place. I have no idea if there is phone there or not. If I can, I will call you. If not, I'll be in touch later on," said Jack without real commitment.

Reid knew that more discussion was fruitless. Probably this was the "good-bye" she had never thought about. It didn't hurt. It felt like absolute nothingness. "OK. Check in when you get back, maybe. Tell Daisy hello from me." Reid got up out of the chair and left the room, leaving Jack standing and alone.

She was in the kitchen when he left. He had given her a perfunctory hug. To speak would have seemed too significant and too painful. Jack thought when he got in the truck that leaving Reid that way was like watching the tide change. The tide doesn't make an announcement. It comes in and then after it has already changed, after it has begun to wash out, then you notice. Then it's too late to know when the change happened.

Once Jack was out of the house, Reid thought of making her own supper, but she wasn't hungry. In the last few months she had lost so much weight that she had aged. Her previous interest in cooking had vanished. Was it only six months ago that all of this had started? "Boom!" thought Reid. "Boom! You have a life and a future and then you have nothing all over again." She went to her bedroom. The sky was beginning to darken with clouds. Soon it would rain. She stretched out on the bed to watch the monsoon come in. Jack was wrong. The monsoon wasn't early. It was right on time.

Jack wasn't in much of mood when he arrived at Daisy's. It was storming and had begun to rain hard just as he pulled into her short driveway. The darkness of the late afternoon matched his mood. Letting himself in, he was aware that his elderly mother had made an effort to fix a meal for the two of them. The house smelled like good food. Jack found Daisy in the kitchen stirring gravy on the stove.

"Hello, Daisy. What's for dinner?" asked Jack as cheerfully as possible.

"Chicken, potatoes, sweet corn. Fruit and coffee later. Suit your diet these days?" asked Daisy.

"Great. No one makes chicken like my Mother." Jack, seeing that everything was ready, sat at the table.

"Reid's a fair cook from what I've seen and I hear," said Daisy.

"She is, although I haven't seen much of her cooking lately."

Daisy let the comment drop and set out food on the table. The reward of fixing a big meal in this weather was going to be the pleasure of eating it, not talking about something unpleasant. Throughout the dinner, Jack talked about the impending trip.

"I thought this was supposed to be Lisa's and Bill's belated honeymoon," said Daisy. "I don't know why they are taking you along."

"Because what else do three semi-retired folks have to do in the summer but go to Mexico and fish a little?" said Jack. "Besides, I speak enough Spanish to keep us out of trouble."

"Is Reid coming down for a bit?" asked Daisy.

"I don't think so. No, I'm sure that she isn't. She has to go up to Colorado to pick up Ruby Rose later in the month. I guess school starts early in August."

"Too early for you to get married before it starts? I haven't heard anything for months about you two getting married."

"And you won't," said Jack.

It was the sharpness in Jack's voice that surprised Daisy. She was aware that her son's relationship had been under recent strain. If he wanted to tell her about it, he would. She wasn't asking, though. She changed the subject back to the trip.

The storm had blown its way through by seven. Jack had helped Daisy clean up the kitchen and was on his way out the door when his sister arrived, carrying sacks of food. She breezed into the kitchen and sat down her load heavily. "Lisa, whatever in the world have you got there?" asked Daisy.

"Well, I don't want you to run out of things while we're gone. So I thought I would bring over some essentials to stock you up," said Lisa breathlessly.

Daisy started to say something to her daughter, but thought the better of it. Daisy was quite capable of getting done whatever needed doing. She had friends who drove and her grandson, Paulie, would come by if she asked him. While Lisa made a show of her exhaustion, Daisy and Jack put away frozen food and an odd assortment of canned and bottled goods that seemed more like exotic party fare than daily provisions. Jack once more announced his intention to leave.

"Oh, can you drop me off at home?" asked Lisa. "Bill brought me by but he had to call his daughter, so he went on to the house. When we saw your truck, I thought you could run me back."

"Sure, if you want to go now. I've got a few things to do myself," said Jack.

"Like see Reid? Have you two kissed and made up?" asked Lisa.

Jack didn't answer. His sister lacked any sort of tact when it came to family relationships. She could finesse a multi-million dollar real estate deal, but she walked all over her family. Always had and always would. That was just Lisa. Finally, he said, "We've kissed, just haven't made up."

Lisa realized that she had spoken way out of turn. She was sorry, but curious, too. She had not seen much of her brother. She had been too busy with her own marriage and new life. That's why she had invited both Reid and Jack to Mexico. It was clear from the first, however, that Reid wasn't coming. Just as well. Lisa would enjoy her brother's company. He and Bill got on so well together, that they would be content to let her stay out on the beach while they fished. Saying she was sorry was not part of who Lisa was. She glossed over her gaffe.

"Mother? Anything else you need? I think you will be good. I will call when we arrive and tell you where we can be reached. Paulie said he'll be checking on you." Lisa reached her mother with a quick peck on the cheek and a hug.

"Oh, Lisa, you've done enough. I'll be fine. You have a wonderful time. You too, Jack." Daisy ushered both her son and daughter out the door.

In planning the trip to Mexico, Jack made it a point to avoid the roads, beaches, cities and towns that he had visited with Abby. It was his way of keeping memories, just memories. Confronting the changes that had happened in the past five or six years, even in a slower moving country like Mexico had a way of stirring up the pain of the way things had been. At least the door of Abby's memory could stay closed, unlike the memories of Reid.

It was a long day's drive to the small coastal village between Cabo Lobos and Cabo Tepoca. Once in Mexico, the caravan of Jack's truck and Lisa's elegant sedan turned west at Santa Ana to Mexico's Interstate 2. At Caborca they went south on a barely improved road that they followed until they reached the beach of Cabo Lobos. From there, it was only a short trip to El Desemboque where they would stay. There was about an hour of sunlight left when they arrived, plenty of time to unload at the renovated house that was one of a dozen in the compound reserved and maintained for wealthy American tourists by a local consortium of officials and businessmen.

The house had both reliable electricity and unreliable phone service. The furniture was sparse, but new. From the screened-in porch, the view was toward the west, to the water. The exorbitant rent that the group paid included a housekeeper who came in the morning and left after the mid-day meal was cleared away. The beds were changed regularly and made daily; dishes were washed, and the tile floor was swept.

By their second day, the threesome had settled into a routine. Lisa had brought clothes, cosmetics and shoes from Paris. Qlckly, however, she found that she lived in her swimsuit and the only cosmetic she required was sun block. She had piles of paperback books and magazines to read. She found herself sleeping long hours including a few hours after lunch. As she had suspected, Jack and Bill fished and boated for the better part of every day, coming home to eat. In the evenings, the group played cards, walked the beach or drove to a nearby cantina or hotel for coffee or a drink.

The hurriedness of life in America was forgotten. They found themselves thinking of nothing but the moment, or the sunset, or the fish retrieved from the gulf. In the second week of their communal vacation, Jack decided to call Reid, although he wasn't clear why or what he would say. It didn't matter since there was no answer at the house. He tried again in the evening, but there was still no answer. He left no message.

The next day, out on the hired fishing boat, Bill Hadigan noticed that Jack sat on the deck without ever dropping a line. Attempts at conversation by the captain and by Bill were politely but firmly, rebuffed. Bill, who always had more interest than luck in catching anything, put away his gear and suggested that they call it a day. The wind had come up, hot and relentless. It surrounded the small craft with the smell of sea decay dredged up from somewhere far away. They were an hour or more away from the small marina.

Jack had a need to talk as he sat in silence, but it was Bill who started the talking. "Had enough of the beach bum life?" asked Bill.

"Not particularly. Today didn't seem a day for fishing. I think you wasted your efforts," said Jack.

"Nothing tugged the line, but the day wasn't wasted. I'm doing what I always wanted to do and said I would do: fish in Mexico. That little vision carried me through many a contract negotiation. It took me a lifetime, but I finally made it," said Bill

Jack said nothing, continuing to look out to the seemingly endless water. Shore was not visible.

"When are you going to close up the bar and retire for good, Jack? We could come down here every month."

"I pretty much come and go as I like now. The place is closed for a month. I don't work every day. If I don't have the bar, I don't have enough to stay busy."

"Believe me, being married to your sister has become my full time job," said Bill, laughing a little.

"Lisa has had that effect on many people, including a couple of other husbands," said Jack.

"Not complaining. Being with Lisa is exciting and unpredictable. This is the first time I have ever seen her really relax. It is a blessing that her cell phone doesn't work or she wouldn't ever calm down. But I love the excitement and I love her."

"I would have bet money that she wouldn't marry you. She surprised me and Daisy," said Jack.

"In real estate terms, I was a 'motivated buyer!'" said Bill. "How about you? Are you and Reid going to get married? If it's an off limits subject, you just say the word."

"Are you asking for yourself or my sister or my mother or for Reid?"

"Just myself. You seem done in today, Jack. I heard you try to call Reid."

"Didn't reach her. Don't know what I want to say to her. I just found myself missing her. Thought I might tell her that. But what's the point?"

"What's the point of missing her or the point of telling her that you miss her?" asked Bill.

"Both. Neither. There was a time there that I thought we would marry. Reid is a special woman. She hung a star in my sky. I forgot for a while that most of my life is passed. The future looked good. I was pretty much the only thing in her life and she was the only thing in mine."

"That's what you thought, huh? Then this thing with the little orphan girl happened. I hear that Reid wants to adopt her. You don't want a kid?" asked Bill

"I can collect my social security this year. I don't think I'll be around long enough to raise a nine-year-old little girl. Reid has been taken over by Ruby Rose. The things we used to do, the plans we were going to make, they got tossed," said Jack.

"Well, I for one, am glad to hear this. I spent a few years thinking I was the only old fool there was. Now I have an old fool for a brother-in-law. I've got to find me a beer." Bill walked to the cool chest sitting outside the small boat's cabin. He retrieved a cold bottle and the rusty opener, popped the cap and downed half the bottle. He plunged his hand in the cooler again to find the last can of diet soda. It was grape, not cola. "Jack will just have to make do," thought Bill.

Bill returned to his chair and sat heavily, tipping over his bottle in the process. He handed the unopened can to Jack. Holding the dripping empty bottle, Bill raised a toast. "Here's to two old fools."

"I don't think I'm drinking to that," said Jack in protest.

"You've got to. You are saying the same things I used to say both before and after my first wife died. I used to think that without me, she didn't have much of a life. Truth was, she had a great life that I just didn't know anything about. She had to die before I found out. That first year after she was gone, I didn't grieve. I sat around and felt sorry for myself. My life was over. I had hit the ceiling at the plant and had no real friends or hobbies for retirement. Golf in the Midwest is a three month sport."

"You got over it, or my sister wouldn't have a husband," said Jack dryly.

"Nope. I didn't get over it. I was forced out of it. After Alice died, my girls used to alternate having me over for Sunday dinner. One Sunday, my youngest called to say that she and the family were doing something else and she disinvited me for dinner. It was the longest Sunday of my life in the middle of the winter. There wasn't even a football game to watch on the TV. It was pretty depressing. Later that night she called to see what I had done for the day. I was pretty put out at her and told her so. She said to me, 'Dad, get a life' and hung up the phone. Oh, I'm not saying that I didn't have some hard feelings, I did. But the girls ganged up on me. They stopped being my life. I had mostly forced them into being what their mother was to me. They arranged things, did things, and I showed up."

Jack had just listened to Bill without looking at him. Now, land was coming into view. The thought of coming ashore didn't please Jack. The problems he had throughout his life were on the land, not on the water. Leaving the water meant having to deal with the problems on shore. If not today, then some day soon.

"So you are just calling me an old fucking fool, then?" asked Jack

"Pretty much. I never thought Alice would die before I could retire. You never thought I would marry Lisa. Both things happened though. Living is risky business. Good things do happen. My daughters redeemed me by pushing me away. I hardly recognized it at the time. A nice woman like Reid and a little daughter might be yours. Might not, but they might be." Bill went to get a full beer that he was determined to enjoy. He had said what he wanted to say. Just another old person, saying his piece and pleased with himself for doing so.

The harsh wind that had brought in storm clouds in the west had also swept away the fetid gulf odor. Jack looked back over his shoulder to the banked thunderheads. He had been on these waters many times. He could read the summer clouds better than the fishermen could. The air would be still for a while. The storm would break before late in the afternoon with a hard rain ending before dusk. The clouds would provide for a magnificent sunset display. "Reading the clouds was a lot easier than reading a woman," thought Jack. There is a rhythm and predictability to clouds. Anyone can read them if they take the time, but women are all different." Jack had lived with the unpredictability of an artist without ever really caring about the future. He guessed it wasn't fair to demand more from Reid. Unlike Abby, Reid gave. She wanted to share Ruby Rose with him.

More women in his life. He had been surrounded by women and loved by them. Except for Bill Hadigan, the men in Jack's life had been transient. Mostly they had stopped in the bar for a season or ten and then passed on. A strong image of his father, Douglas Ellis, came to Jack. Douglas hated the sea and the idleness of fishing. He had been a hard man. Late in his father's life, a grandson, Paulie, had been thrust on him to bring up. Douglas had changed after that. He found the heart to spend time with the boy. He learned to bend, teaching the youngster about model trains and carburetors. Paulie got the attention that Jack had missed. Jack remembered what Bill had said; something about kids being a "saving grace."

That thought erased the darkness of the morning. Jack looked at his brother-in-law who was getting tipsy from the potent combination of beer and the sun. "Senior citizens, hell!" thought Jack. "We're just two old guys who got lucky."

Jack would call Reid tonight. If he reached her, he would tell her that he would try to work things out. There was one thing he wasn't going to compromise on: he wasn't wearing a tuxedo to the wedding, no matter what. He would tell Reid that, too.

P.S. Lowe

Saving the Best for Last

Reid looked around at the sparse congregation at the late-July Sunday service. At 9:30 in the morning, it was sweltering outside and not much better inside. The swamp cooler was of little value during the humid days that characterized the Phoenix monsoon season. The church's air conditioning had gone out and there was no money to replace the unit. It had worked thirty years, as Reverend Tim noted, and repair was out of the question. He asked for forbearance and announced that the sermon would be uncharacteristically short.

"Repair was out of the question." Reid didn't listen to much beyond those words. She felt that way about her life at this minute. Jack was gone and had not called. Ruby Rose seemed happily ensconced at her grandparents' home in Denver. She wanted another week with them.

For the second time in her life, Reid was unhappily alone. Her aloneness felt like her fault, as if she had willed the wrong things to fruition. She wanted to change it all to the way she had envisioned it instead of how it had come to be. Months ago, she had seen a future with Jack Ellis as her husband and Ruby Rose as her near-child. Reid wanted to make up for the loss of Ruby Rose's parents, but it could not be done. She wanted Jack to help create the family that Ruby Rose lost, but he didn't share that dream.

How could Reid repair all that separateness that her will had caused? She had come to church to pray about it, to seek an answer. No answer had come. People were standing for the hymn of dedication and Reid was still lost in her own prayers.

On her way out, Reverend Tim stopped Reid. "I need to talk to you, Reid. Can you come by the office this week?"

"Yes, or maybe. I was going to be out of town, but now I don't know if I am going." Reid liked the minister of this small Methodist congregation. He brought heart and soul to his work. She wondered for a moment why he would want to speak with her and then she knowingly smiled. Tim Curry was good at all of his duties except for one: the financial one.

"What's the matter, Tim? Has the church secretary cooked the books or is that what you want me to do?

"Something of the latter, I'm afraid. We're in a financial crisis Reid, and you are the only church member I know who can help. Will you stop by?"

"Yes, sure. Tuesday morning I'll be by about nine. How's that sound?"

"Thank you, Reid. Maybe with your talent, the show will continue."

Reid had no desire to go home after services, but she really had no place else to go. Putting her car into the garage, she walked to her neighbor's house instead of into her own. She rang the bell to Mrs. Gilberg's.

Hannah Gilberg came to the door dressed in full makeup but her oldest cotton housecoat. "Reid, honey, I just knew you would come by today. It's too terrible a day for you to be alone. I've made us some lime tea. Come sit in the peacock chair and I'll bring you some. Seems like the only time we use the front room is when it is so hot!"

Reid settled herself into the darkened living room using the rattan peacock chair that dominated the small room. Mrs. Gilberg brought tea and set it out on the none-too-steady rattan table. The fan turned noisily overhead reminding Reid, as always, of some seedy oriental tearoom. Mrs. Gilberg padded around noisily in her oversized slippers until she plopped on the couch. She drank her iced tea with gusto and poured herself a second glass before asking Reid, "What's making you unhappy but the heat?"

There was nothing subtle about Hannah Gilberg. "Church air conditioning is out. I think Tim Curry wants me to buy a new one," said Reid.

"Ha! Are you going to oblige that nincompoop? Seems to me that you have been tapped for a few other items these past few years. What is the matter with that man? Can't he raise money himself? You need to get him motivated in that direction. You're too easy."

"I can well afford to give the church the money," said Reid defensively.

"Why should you? Why is it no one's responsibility but yours if the bills are paid?"

"I don't know. I just feel that way."

"Stop feeling that way. You always do, you know when things aren't so happy for you. Some women go buy a new outfit, but you lay another gold dish on the altar. You still won't feel the better for it."

Reid said nothing and sipped her tea.

"What happened to your get up and go? What happened to that fabulous woman that used to live next door to me?"

"She got lost on the way to arranging the perfect life – husband and child."

"Reid, honey, now don't take this wrong, but if you were my daughter, I'd paddle you right this minute. There's times, and this is one of them, when you have that kind of selfishness that comes of being an only child. You got an idea about how things should be and you just carried it all out all by yourself without ever thinking of everybody else involved. There were lots of people affected by what you have done for the past months, but you haven't listened to any of them. You made up your mind, and then did things."

Reid was incredulous. Then she was hurt. She felt tears coming on. "I wasn't an only child, Mrs. Gilberg, I was an orphan." Barely were the words out when the tears came.

"Oh, Reid. That's the real truth, but there is kind of an emotional truth there too. You were either alone or in the company of your grandparents. You never had to share with other people.

Everything is either yours or not yours. You are generous but you don't really share. I can't explain it, Reid. There's just a lot of distance in you." Mrs. Gilberg pushed herself out of the chair and went to the bedroom for a box of tissues.

Returning, she shoved a handful of paper into Reid's hand. "You need to stop crying. It's too hot for a day for tears and there's too many years since you were a kid to cry like that."

"I feel like crying. I feel abandoned."

"Blow your nose and dry your eyes. This isn't the first time this has happened and it won't be the last time. Did you ever think that Jack and Ruby Rose fled because you were holding on just too tight? You were trying too hard to make a perfect little family out of pieces of other families."

"All I wanted was for Ruby Rose feel special and part of a family," said Reid. "I didn't want her to go through life like I did where things just happened and there was no support for her and for her dreams. I want her to have dreams. Dreams that come true."

"You want to be her mother, Reid. You aren't. You will never take her mother's place just as no one will ever take your mother's place. The difference between Ruby Rose and you is this: she has many people who will love her for the rest of her life. She has a family to get to know. You've been trying to rob her of that because there was no one else but your grandparents for you. When they died, you had no one left until luck brought you and Kenny together."

"So, what are you saying?" asked Reid. "I should let my cousin John raise her or Mr. and Mrs. Madden?"

"No, not unless that becomes a mutual agreement. What I'm saying is stop pushing! You are her legal guardian. That should be enough for now. Look after yourself a little bit."

"What about Jack, since you are giving advice so freely," asked Reid.

"You are on your own with Jack. I suppose he will call you."

"What if he doesn't call?"

"He'll call," assured Hannah.

Reid looked closely at her neighbor. "I've known Hannah Gilberg all of my adult life. She has been the only person really close to me all these years," thought Reid. "Yet, when I think of the people who meant the most to me, I think of dead people as if they were still living. And it took a broken air conditioner to figure it out."

"I'll be waiting for Jack to call. Anyway, how did you get so smart without having any kids?" asked Reid jokingly.

"I'm an old woman and I've seen lots of things in my life. I know how things are, just ask me. Now, since it is a hot day, I was thinking that I want a banana split instead of lunch. You could take me."

"Hannah, I'm tired. I'm going home for a nap. Then I think that on such a hot day we should have ice cream and a movie. If you want to go, we could go out around two." That said and Mrs. Gilberg satisfied that she would have an outing, Reid returned home to the coolness of her own home and her nap.

Reid was deeply asleep when the phone began ringing. The answering machine had already picked up. Jack was leaving a message by the time Reid picked up the phone. "Jack, I'm here. I was just asleep."

Jack was glad that Reid was home. He had no idea of what kind of message he would leave. Hearing Reid's voice moved him more than he had imagined anything could. "I thought you only had a Sunday nap when I was around," he joked.

"Oh, Jack, when are you going to be around again? Are you coming home soon? I am so sad that you aren't here. I was crying this afternoon because Mrs. Gilberg told me I was selfish about you and Rose. I'm sorry I was selfish, Jack. I'm sorry."

"Reid, what's this about? I just called to tell you that I miss you." Jack was truly perplexed at Reid's first words. It was like walking into the middle of conversation, but then again, with Reid, that wasn't the most unusual occurrence, either.

Reid paused then said, "I miss you too and I want to see you again soon. Very soon. Can you tell me when you are coming back?"

It was Jack's turn to pause. Should he ask now and risk ending the conversation at the point he left it weeks ago? He needed to know. "Is Ruby Rose there? Have you picked her up yet?"

"No, she isn't and no I haven't. I need to talk to some more people about her. Maybe the best thing isn't for her to be with me. I hope it is best, but I want to talk to her grandparents and to you. Maybe I have been trying to live my life over through her, only changing it. I thought I was sure, but now, I don't know."

The sun on the porch where Jack had taken the phone was hot. Jack was sweating. Maybe it wasn't just the sun. "Are you changing your mind about adopting Ruby Rose, then?" Jack didn't know if he was hopeful or not.

"I haven't made up my mind about anything. I don't have it figured out. I finally woke up to what everyone has been trying to tell me for months. You. Carol. Dr. Baliss. Hannah told me, just told me not to pretend that my life and Ruby Rose's are the same. There was something inside me that made me want to make them the same. You and I, and the Maddens, and maybe even John VanDuyver, we need to figure out something that works for her."

"What changed your mind, Reid? You aren't just saying this to get me back to Phoenix, are you?" Jack's experience with both Abby and his sister, Lisa, had made him sometimes suspicious of women's motives.

"A broken air conditioner in church. I thought today that all the love we had had was broken, Jack. That is couldn't be repaired.

Daisy's Chain
—————
Saving the Best for Last

But we are people, not machines. We can adjust to things that happen. I am slow to adjust. I've been like that always. I hear sounds in my head, crashing sounds telling me that everything has changed."

For the hundredth time, Jack felt as if he had come into the middle of a conversation that Reid was having with either herself or some remote person. Yet, he understood her, sort of. He had seen the sound that she heard on a couple of occasions. There was that time when her Uncle died. There was the time he had proposed to her. "Do you hear the sounds now, Reid? Is that what changed your mind?"

"No, I didn't hear the sound of anything but Hannah reminding me to come back to the land of the living and sharing. I heard Tim Curry at church, too. The booms have gone. They are gone."

"I'm not sure what you are trying to tell me, Reid. I'm not sure at all." Sweat poured over Jack. If Reid had been with him, if he could have reached out and touched her, it wouldn't matter if the words were lost. He would know what she meant if he could touch her. With only the phone to touch, the truth was lost to him.

"I kept losing people, important people to me, Jack. Everyone loses people like that, but I never replaced them, not really. I'm nearly 50 and I kept thinking about Grammy and Big Daddy and what they thought about me. I missed my Mother and wondered what she thought about me. I never knew. When Kenny died, well, I thought I had to raise Ruby Rose to be true to what I said I would do, at a time when I never thought I would have to do it. I have been living with the dead for so long. They've left, Jack. They left to give me space for the living. For you. For Rose. For Hannah and for people I don't even know yet."

"That sounds hopeful, maybe the most hopeful thing I've heard in a long time, Reid. I've been wondering if there was room for me yet."

"There's room for everybody, but mostly you. Will you come back?" asked Reid.

"I'll be back."

"Soon? Soon will you come back?"

"It depends, Reid. It depends on whether you still want to get married. I have thought about that a lot while I was out on the water. I am finally tired of the sea. I'm tired of many things I've done and tired of waiting to do things I've never done. Marriage is one of those things."

"Do you believe in coincidence, Jack? Do you believe that some-times coincidence is like a little message from God telling you to do something and making it possible for you to do it? I believe that happens."

Jack was looking for a straight up answer but he knew when Reid didn't provide it, he would have to hear how she got to her answer. In that, she wasn't a whole lot different from Lisa, but she was very different from Abby. "I hadn't thought much about coincidence, not much at all."

"Well, I do. I got a little message from Tim Curry today. He was preaching on the Marriage at Cana. Most people remember that story as where Jesus turned water into wine. The part I never understood was when one of the Apostles says, 'You have saved the best until last.' That's you. I want to marry you."

"Well, it's yes, then. I had my heart set on it. I won't deny that. You disappointed me when you wouldn't say yes and mean it. But I guess you mean it now."

"I mean it. Whenever you want, I'll be ready," said Reid with a soft voice and a great deal of conviction.

"I'll be back within the week. Did you mean that soon?"

"If you want. It doesn't matter. All the rest that comes will be easy. The hard part is over."

"What about Ruby Rose? Aren't you worried about her school? What will she think if we get married?" asked Jack.

"I don't know. It's important, but I was more concerned with what she would think if we didn't get married. She's just a child. All you can do with a child is show them love and point them to good things. I guess try to make sure that she has lots of loving people around her. Hope for the best."

"Do you? Do you just hope for the best?"

"I do, Jack. Before, the best was an idea and a vague idea at that. Only now, the best has a name. Yours."

"I think you are trying to flatter an old man," said Jack with all the lightness he could manage.

"Did it work?" asked Reid, hoping that she had been clear on that. She loved him. Did he finally understand that?

"It worked. Sometimes, Reid, I don't know what to think or say around you. I love you and I love your confusing ways. I believe that we belong together."

"We do. I love you Jack."

"I love you, Reid. I'll be back as soon as I can make arrangements."

"I'll be waiting," said Reid as she hung up the phone. "I've waited a whole lifetime," she said to the room. She looked at the clock. She had only fifteen minutes to get ready to take Mrs. Gilberg to the movies. No, ice cream first. Then she could tell Mrs. Gilberg, no Hannah, tell Hannah that she had been right. Jack had called. Today she would practice sharing good news. She could let go of the silence. There was no one to protect and the dead could no longer judge her. "I'm leaving, Big Daddy. I'm going on to places you never knew. Places of the heart."

At two on the dot, Reid was knocking on Hannah Gilberg's door. Together, over outrageous sundaes they would speak of all the possibilities for a marriage and a life for Ruby Rose. Some of those plans would actually come about.

The Tie That Binds

A Marc Cohen CD was playing as Reid wiped the kitchen counter. There was a line of lyric she enjoyed about the ghost of Elvis. Memories of the dead could be powerful even when you had never met the deceased. The ghost memories of Big Daddy and Grammy had become less frequent in the past year. However, for the last two days, the ghost of Abby, a woman she had never known, had haunted Reid.

The clock said it was 9:30. Reid had been up for hours. She had showered, eaten breakfast, laid out her new dress. At one o'clock this afternoon, she was meeting Jack and his family in church to be married. The Maddens would be there, too, bringing along Ruby Rose. They would stay with Rose for the week that Reid and Jack honeymooned in New England experiencing the kind of autumn that they had only seen on calendar pages.

In a while, Carol would come by. Carol would be Reid's matron of honor. Carol, the best girlfriend in the world. They would be laughing and carrying on like it was not a wedding day at all. Carol's husband, Darrell, would walk Reid down the aisle.

Today, Reid didn't have to worry about Ruby Rose. The Maddens would dress her and escort the young girl to the church. Ruby didn't want to be in the wedding and Reid hadn't pushed her to join the wedding party. Together they had decided that Ruby could take pictures and Reid had purchased three disposable cameras with wedding logos on the box for Ruby to use as she pleased during the day. Before Carol came, Reid called Ruby and the Maddens at the hotel where they were staying. All seemed well.

The past year, following the deaths of Kenny and his wife, Dianne, the Madden's only daughter, had been a series of small triumphs and many sad plateaus. The breakout from grief accelerated only when Jack and Reid had decided to marry and then go on with their lives. The Maddens had seemed relieved that the guardianship of their granddaughter would have permanence. They could continue to be the adoring, but not custodial, grandparents.

Jack spent the morning with his mother, Daisy. It was the last time Daisy would know her son as a bachelor. Tomorrow and for ever after, he would be a husband. That thought was something to ponder. For all the years that Jack and Abby lived together, Daisy never thought of her son as anything but a single man. The decades had gone by without Daisy ever thinking of Abby as family. In fact, there wasn't a single time that Daisy could even remember having a loving thought about Abby. Today, on the day of her son's marriage, Daisy felt the accusing presence of Abby. Even on this happiest of days, Daisy felt deeply ashamed.

Jack had come to his mother's for a late breakfast. It was like many other Saturday mornings he had spent with her. As usual, his mother had fixed ham and eggs with fresh biscuits. They had eaten in her small kitchen. The conversation had been a monologue by Jack, describing the trip he had planned with Reid. Around eleven, Lisa and Bill came by. Lisa made a Loretta Young entrance, sweeping into the kitchen, bedecked in a rich russet silk dress and coat; bejeweled in Mexican Fire Opals set in brilliant gold. Bill slipped up to the coffee pot to pour himself a cup and to watch the drama his wife would introduce into Daisy's quiet kitchen.

"Jack," she cried in horror, "why are you still here? You need to get dressed! The ceremony starts in just 2 hours."

Before Bill could join the table group, Lisa was on to her next topic. "Daisy, your hair is a mess and you aren't dressed either. Now off with you. I'll just shoo Jack home and then help you get dressed."

Without moving, Daisy said "Lisa, there's time. I'm going to clean up the kitchen and then shake on that dress. There's no need to fuss with my hair, and don't think you can do it either. I'm wearing a hat."

"Mother, you don't own a decent hat. Besides, no one else will have one on. What are you thinking?"

"I'm thinking that I want to wear a hat and I am going to do it. Now, unless you intend to clear the table and do dishes, I'll be finishing my work. I'm not the bride and I am old enough to have my own way."

"Mother you'll ruin the pictures if you wear a hat. Even Reid will be bareheaded." Lisa's voice was moving up rapidly in pitch.

Jack looked at his mother and then his sister. Some things never changed. His bossy sister was one of them. His stubborn mother was a second. "I'll be running along," Jack said addressing his mother. To his sister he said, "See you later. If I'm not there by ten past, I'll just let you handle that."

Lisa's eyes widened and she was about to give a serious answer to Jack when she realized that he was just joking. Her lungs deflated. "Oh Jack, you just love to get my goat, don't you?"

Jack moved to give his mother a dry kiss on her cheek. "Yes I do. I'll be there. Wouldn't miss it for the world. I don't get married every day."

What Jack had meant as light banter alluding to his late-aged single status stopped the conversation. The three of them had one collective, silent thought: "Abby," the woman all had known and not known. The ghost passed from the room into the space of their hearts that the living Abby had never occupied.

Once Jack was gone, Bill volunteered to do the dishes so that the women could fuss with themselves and each other. In the bedroom, Daisy sat at her ancient cherry dressing table to brush her hair and gently cream and powder her face. It was the one piece of furniture that Lisa had not been allowed to touch when she had designed and then paid for the renovation of the room for her mother's eightieth birthday a couple of years back. The furniture was all modern light maple. The walls were the palest of blues, done to a faux marble smooth surface, while the carpet, drapes and bedclothes were in varying hues of rose. Daisy would have preferred dark furniture and accents of green and yellow.

Lisa looked in the customized closet for the dress she had purchased for her mother to wear.

"Get out the navy dress. That's the one I'm wearing, Lisa. Get down that box, too. There's a hat in it."

"You can't wear that dress, mother. You wouldn't. You can't do that to Jack and Reid."

"I'm not doing anything to them. And, Missy, you don't have to act so horrified. I thought about it. I always liked that dress and wore it only once. It is perfect for today. It pleases me to wear it."

"You wore that dress to Abby's funeral. How can you wear it to Jack's wedding? Wear the dress that we bought for the wedding."

"I'll wear it sometime, but not today. She's been on my mind for days. I'm ashamed I didn't treat her better," said Daisy as she looked at her daughter as a reflection in the mirror.

"Abby," said Lisa resignedly.

"Abby," replied Daisy.

"You didn't say anything to Jack about her, did you?"

"No. No, I did not! My thoughts have been my thoughts."

"Wear the new dress, please, don't wear that navy dress. It makes me sad and it will make Jack sad, too."

"Jack wasn't at Abby's funeral. Jack won't care a whit what I wear. I am wearing it to remind me that maybe Jack would have married Abby if I could have loved her in some way. I am reminding myself to put myself out to love Reid and her little cousin, too. Maybe then I can feel that Abby forgives me."

"Abby was already married, thank you very much! Anyway, she's dead," said Lisa vehemently.

"All the same, Lisa, it might have been different if I could have loved her. She could have been family in love. I think that Abby always knew that we, and I mean me, you, Douglas and Paulie, I think she knew that we didn't love her."

"She wasn't worth loving. She was a selfish, selfish person. She didn't know anything about love. How can you condemn all of us for not loving her? She never wanted to be a part of our family. Never. All she ever wanted was Jack and then she cheated on him! She never wanted us." Lisa's face was red with the anger that filled her head.

"I've thought about that. She was so afraid of people. None of us ever visited her and I never went to see any of her paintings, even when she invited me. How did I ever think that I was the one being rejected? What did any of us know about Abby? I hardly knew her at all. What I see now is that she took Jack away from me and from the family. In twenty-five years, I don't think I knew her for twenty-five days. It might have been different and it isn't. Therefore, I'm wearing the navy dress for Abby. I'm wearing the hat, too."

"Mother you are morbid."

Daisy's Chain
The Tie That Binds

"And old, Lisa, morbid and old. It happens when you get on past eighty. I have had a lot of time to think about my son getting married and not really anyone to talk to about it. Abby's memory has been my only companion for the last few days. I feel that I owe her something and this is the only thing I can think of to do."

"It's a wedding, not a wake. There's no use in you pretending that dress is a hair shirt."

"Lisa, it's a dress, just a dress that I like. It suits the day and my frame of mind. Look at you. You're dressed to outshine the bride and I know why that is, too."

"I'm dressed for a wedding," said Lisa, defensively.

"No, you're dressed to make sure that everyone will know that you are a woman of reckoning. You are dressed to impress, to attract attention to yourself, just like always, and it is only family. Just a little family wedding at church. A farm boy is marrying a farm girl."

"I would hardly call Reid Markham a farm girl," snapped Lisa. "She's worth millions. And Jack hated the farm. Just hated it."

"Still and all, Lisa, they are very simple people who have struggled in love and without love. Now they have each other. I want them to know that we are behind them, too. They have family. We didn't do that for Jack and Abby."

While Daisy had spoken, Lisa had plunked herself ungracefully on the bed. Now she could feel tears coming up. She sniffed loudly and went to the closet, searching wildly for the dress and hat. The hat was easy. She took the box down and brought it to the bed, opened it and removed the tissue wrapped object. It was a small cloth hat with a veil. Daisy went to the closet and easily found the dress. She stepped out of her housedress, hanging it up carefully. She brought the dress out and asked Lisa to help slip it over her head.

Lisa did so and zipped it up. The dress was nice if a little dull.

"OK, Daisy. Sit at the table and I'll fix your hair and hat." Expertly she pinned her mother's hair away from her face and set the hat on her head. Daisy smiled at her reflection and reached for some lipstick to finish her makeup.

Lisa was not happy. She never was when she lost a battle with Daisy, especially when her mother had been right about the dress and the hat and about Abby, too. She did not know which rankled her the most. Lisa didn't want to tell Daisy that she had dreamed about Abby. In the dream, Abby was drowning in a shallow river like Rosetti's depiction of the drowned Ophelia. Lisa couldn't bring herself to pull Abby from the river. It had disturbed her greatly. There was no interpretation of the dream that she could bear. The memory of the dream would not leave.

Lisa looked at her mother in the mirror. Impulsively she squeezed Daisy's shoulders and felt their frailty. "Don't leave me mother, I need you." The words escaped Lisa suddenly.

Daisy seemed not at all surprised by the remark. "Now who is being morbid, Lisa?" asked Daisy brightly. "I could use another cup of coffee."

Lisa glanced at her watch, an accoutrement she would not forego for any occasion. They had more than an hour before they needed to leave. "Yes, but I think I'll have mine iced."

Bill was just finishing the dishes when mother and daughter came into the kitchen. Whatever had happened in the bedroom had been good for Lisa. She looked calmer. "Well, this might be a good day for a wedding after all," he thought.

When Jack left his mother's house, a part of Abby had come with him. He imagined her in the truck sitting next to him. They rode in silence. When he got to the house, she walked in with him. The spaces that her pictures had once occupied remained empty. He walked through the house. He and Reid had agreed that the house would be too small for a family of three. They were looking for a larger house in the same old neighborhood. After the wedding, Jack would move temporarily into Reid's house. Or maybe they would build a house together. They weren't sure. It didn't seem that important right now.

"I have my heart set on her," Jack said to the empty bedroom. "I haven't set my heart to anything before. Not a job, not a place, not a person, not even Abby." He went to the small nightstand and took out a box containing the matched wedding rings he needed to put into his suit pocket. He and Reid had picked them out together, gold bands set with three diamonds: one for Jack, one for Reid, one for Ruby Rose.

For just a minute, while he was looking at the rings and before putting on his new suit, he thought of Abby. If Jack was capable of feeling guilty, he only felt guilty that he could remember so very little of Abby. She had always been in the present. Abby had a past when she came to stay with Jack and they had never planned the future. It always arrived as the present. With Reid, it was different. With Reid there was today and yesterday and tomorrow. There was always a future with Reid because she thought about it. She made plans for the opera, plans for Ruby Rose, plans for a new house. That's what he loved about Reid; there was a future with her.

Jack got dressed. He finished packing the new suitcase that was opened on the bed. Tonight he would spend the night in Reid's bed and they would fly to Vermont in the morning. It was a nice step into the future. When he was finished, he carried the suitcase to the truck and returned to lock the house. He looked once more at the empty living room wall, closed and locked the door. Abby had already left.

The little Methodist church on Campbell had been opened early by the Minister, Tim Curry. He had awakened at 5:00 a.m. from a troubled sleep, a rare occurrence. He felt haunted by a feeling that there was so much in his life undone. He had dreamed of unfinished lives silenced by death, his own and others. They were dismal thoughts that he had hoped to shake before official-ing at a 1 o'clock wedding of his favorite parishioner. It was to be a small affair, but an important event for Reid and in the life of his personal ministry.

Tim had come to the well-worn sanctuary to pray for the couple, Jack and Reid, whom he would marry. He often came here to pray rather than attempting the spiritual task in his busy house-hold. Tim held prayer sacred and envied his Catholic colleagues who had the daily duties of mass to help them focus on the spirit needs of each day. Prayer wouldn't come. He waited an hour, and nothing came to him that seemed worthy of God's attention.

Reid's wedding flowers arrived, just as Tim had decided to leave the sanctuary. Although the church's wedding volunteer was there to handle the delivery, Tim stayed until the abundant stands of white roses were placed. "Well the roses will have to suffice as my prayer-offering today," Tim thought. He locked the sanctuary for the coordinator and went to his small office to work on his stack of administrative duties in the couple of hours he had left before the wedding.

Before anyone else arrived for the ceremony, Abby entered the sanctuary. She wanted to see everyone come through the doors. The roses, fresh and pungent, vibrated in the otherwise unadorned space. Abby wondered why she had never painted roses when she was alive, especially ones like these. So enchanted was she by the cut flowers that real time slipped away from her. When she turned from the bouquets, Jack was in place at the altar with his hand outstretched to Reid who walked to him on the arm of a stranger.

Tim Curry had hoped that Reid and Jack would write vows to exchange with each other, but the couple insisted on a traditional service. Traditional services seemed flawed to Tim. They expressed the commonness and the ritual of the experience, but the uniqueness of a particular celebration was always lost. As he began the short service, Tim's voice sounded joyless and even nervous.

P.S. Lowe

Gratefully, Tim stopped speaking for an interlude of music by a tenor soloist. He had no idea what words, what special words he might say to this group next. He looked over his shoulder and shuddered as he felt an invisible passerby. A rose fell from the far arrangement as if dropped by a single hand.

Tim faced the congregation thinking about the relationships of all assembled. First the oldest: Daisy. Jack was her son; Lisa, her daughter; Bill Hadigan her son-in-law. Then there was Paulie, Daisy's grandson, his wife Erin and their twin children. Erin's parents were there as well. Reid's cousin and the grandparents of the cousin were there. There was Carol, Reid's best friend, and her family. Hannah Gilberg was with Carol. Then there were the three others who sat together but apart from everyone else: a distinguished man escorting a young Asian girl and a middle-aged woman dressed in purple.

It seemed to Tim that he was like those three, out of the tight little circle. Yet he was here and they were here at that moment to celebrate a new beginning. Perhaps they were here for a different reason. Before the thought fully formed to his mind, Tim knew what he had to say and knew what he would do. Though his heart felt compelled and urgent, his voice was calm. Taking Reid's hand in his right and Jack's in his left, he turned the couple to face the congregation.

"We are a small group today, yet precious and happy. We have come to wish well to Reid and Jack and we have come to wish ourselves well, too. I'd like each of you to come forward and make a circle holding hands with one another."

Clearly surprised to be asked to participate in the wedding ceremony, the little congregation moved slowly to the front. The
three non-family guests were more reluctant to come forward.
The unknown man maneuvered himself and the two women
next to Jack, and separating Jack from his sister, Lisa let go of her
brother's hand reluctantly.

Once the circle formed, Tim continued a minute of silence before
beginning again.

"As believers, as Christians, we affirm that the greatest gift of all
is the gift of God's love. A marriage is but one symbol, one affirmation of that love. This circle is yet another affirmation of the
ties of love. In the twelfth chapter of Romans, St. Paul has
wonderful words of love, which I repeat, in part, as a reminder
to our group and each of us individually, to keep love alive. St.
Paul says 'Let love be genuine; hold fast to what is good; love one
another.'"

"He goes on to exhort us to never flag in zeal; to rejoice in hope,
be patient in tribulation, practice hospitality and also to live in
harmony with one another.'"

"There is a thread of experience and association between and
among all assembled here. The name of that thread is love, the tie
that binds. It has withstood all that has happened before this
moment. More than loss, more than sorrow, it is love that has
made each of us strong in ourselves and with each other. It is
love that removes the darkening scales from our eyes that have
held fast enmity and fear. Love has wings to carry away the past
and make the day new. What we have is that new day for every-

one assembled, but especially for Jack and Reid. So I ask that Jack and Reid step forward and exchange the rings that will mirror this circle in their memories."

Jack pulled out the rings from his pocket handing his first to Reid, which she then placed on his left hand. He then did the same for her. Tim motioned for them to rejoin the circle.

"You are married in the sight of man and God. Let us rejoice together with a brief prayer. Please bow your heads."

When Tim's prayer had ended, the wedding guests lined themselves up on either side of the aisle so that Reid and Jack could walk together into the Narthex. Tim watched as the little group followed the couple out the door. It had turned out better than he had anticipated, better than he had hoped. He remembered the fallen rose and went to rescue it, but when he looked, it was gone. Well, he thought, maybe someone had picked it up.

Someone had. This was how it ended for Abby. It was a new day for her as well.

Daisy had changed into her robe and slippers by six p.m. She was sitting in her comfy chair holding both her corsage from the wedding and a circular of this week's TV programs. She thought she had an interest in watching television, but she really just wanted to rest in her contentment. It wasn't often she had had the privilege of enjoying real peace of heart. It was a luxury, as any old woman knows. Most of life is about the disturbances others bring to our lives and the ones we create for ourselves.

Daisy's Chain
_____
The Tie That Binds

Most of life, Daisy thought, is about activity and real, physical things. Even talking out loud is physical.

Sometimes, however, there are moments when you just know, in an un-named, un-physical way, that all is right with you and with the world of your loved ones. These are the times without a future; times without a past. These are the times when love shines through as its naked self directly to the heart, independent of memories and uncaring of hope. Love that wanted nothing and asked nothing, but just to be. Daisy felt that.

But, then again, she was only human. The feeling settled to a large corner of her heart. She got up to fix a bit of supper before turning in for the night.